The Heroic Slave

A Cultural and Critical Edition

FREDERICK DOUGLASS

Edited by Robert S. Levine, John Stauffer, and John R. McKivigan

THE HEROIC SLAVE

FREDERICK DOUGLASS

The Heroic Slave

A CULTURAL AND CRITICAL EDITION

Edited by

ROBERT S. LEVINE,
JOHN STAUFFER, AND
JOHN R. McKIVIGAN

Yale UNIVERSITY PRESS

New Haven & London

Published with assistance from the National Historical Publications and Records Commission.
Published with assistance from the Louis Stern Memorial Fund.

Yale University Press books may be purchased in quantity for educational, business, or promotional use. For information, please e-mail sales.press@yale.edu (U.S. office) or sales@yaleup.co.uk (U.K. office).

Printed in the United States of America.

Library of Congress Cataloging-in-Publication Data
Douglass, Frederick, 1818–1895.
The heroic slave / Frederick Douglass ; a cultural and critical edition ; edited by Robert S. Levine, John Stauffer, and John R. McKivigan.
pages cm
Includes bibliographical references.
ISBN 978-0-300-18462-4 (pbk. : alk. paper) 1. Washington, Madison—Fiction. 2. Slaves—United States—Fiction. 3. Creole (Brig)—Fiction. 4. Slave insurrections—United States—History—19th century—Fiction. 5. Mutiny—United States—History—19th century—Fiction 6. Douglass, Frederick, 1818–1895 Heroic slave. I. Levine, Robert S. (Robert Steven), 1953– editor. II. Stauffer, John, 1965– editor. III. McKivigan, John R., 1949– editor. IV. Title.
PS1549.D66H47 2015
813'.3—dc23 2014029869

A catalogue record for this book is available from the British Library.

This paper meets the requirements of ANSI/NISO Z39.48–1992 (Permanence of Paper).

10 9 8 7 6 5 4 3 2 1

NATIONAL ARCHIVES
NATIONAL HISTORICAL PUBLICATIONS & RECORDS COMMISSION

Contents

Acknowledgments

For their assistance with documents and images, we would like to thank the Harvard University librarians Emily Bell (in Government Documents), Gregory Eow (Widener Library), and Peter Accardo (Houghton Library); the University of Maryland librarian Patricia Herron; and the knowledgeable staff at the Library of Congress. For their helpful suggestions along the way, we are grateful to Celeste-Marie Bernier, Deborah Cunningham, David Brion Davis, Henry Louis Gates, Jr., Howard Jones, Jim Oakes, Robert Paquette, Manisha Sinha, Robert Stepto, and Zoe Trodd. Offering crucial assistance with the text of *The Heroic Slave*, which was developed at the Frederick Douglass Papers at Indiana University–Purdue University Indianapolis, were Eamonn Brandon, Kate Burzlaff, James A. Hanna, and Rebecca Pattillo. Their work was supported by the National Historical Publications and Records Commission and the Indiana University School of Liberal Arts at Indianapolis. Robert S. Levine did much of his work on the edition while a Guggenheim Fellow, and he is grateful for the support of the Guggenheim Foundation. For their encouragement and advice, we are pleased to thank Sarah Miller, Heather Gold, and Margaret Otzel, our editors at Yale University Press. Our thanks as well to the Press's anonymous readers and to our skillful copy editor, Kip Keller.

Introduction

On 25 October 1841, the slave ship *Creole* left Richmond, Virginia, for New Orleans, the largest slave-trading market in North America. The brig carried 13 sailors and crew, 6 white passengers, numerous boxes of tobacco, and 135 slaves, worth about $100,000 (around $3 million in 2014 currency). Eight days later, as the *Creole* sailed through the northern Bahamas, 19 slaves rose up in revolt. Within a few hours they had taken control of the ship and forced a crewman to sail the brig to the Bahamas. They put into port on New Providence at Nassau, the largest settlement in the Bahamas, populated chiefly by blacks who had been freed by Great Britain's 1833 Emancipation Act. The *Creole* reached Nassau on 9 November. The mutineers appealed to the British authorities, who within a week had freed the 116 slaves not participating in the rebellion, but detained the mutineers; in March 1842, they, too, were freed. The rebellion was comparatively civil: 1 crewman and 2 slaves were killed. Taking into account the numbers liberated versus those killed, it was one of the most successful slave revolts in North America.[1]

Twelve years after the rebellion, Frederick Douglass published

1. For good historical overviews of the *Creole* rebellion, see Howard Jones, "The Peculiar Institution and National Honor: The Case of the *Creole* Slave Revolt," *Civil*

The Heroic Slave, a historical novella about the *Creole* mutiny, in the 1853 *Autographs for Freedom*, a fund-raising volume edited by Julia Griffiths, a British friend and the managing editor of his newspaper.[2] Douglass then serialized the novella in March 1853 in his newspaper, *Frederick Douglass' Paper*. His only work of fiction, *The Heroic Slave* is one of the earliest examples of African American fiction, and it is part of an American canon that was profoundly shaped by the historical fiction of Sir Walter Scott, James Fenimore Cooper, Catharine Maria Sedgwick, Nathaniel Hawthorne, and many others. The *Creole* rebellion not only was important in American history and politics, but also had an impact on Douglass's career, moving him toward a more radical position on the uses of violence to achieve black freedom. In *The Heroic Slave*, Douglass addressed the abolitionist movement, the trans-Atlantic history of slavery, interracial friendship, black leadership, and the relationship between journalism, fiction, and history. With his skillful use of setting, point of view, and stylized theatrical dialogue, Douglass also offered a rousing good read, making one almost lament that this was his only work of fiction. It is not surprising that over the past thirty years, *The Heroic Slave* has emerged as an essential text in the nineteenth-century American literary canon. This cultural and critical edition provides, for the first time, an authoritative text of *The Heroic Slave*, along with primary and secondary materials that will help readers explore the novella's historical, biographical, and literary contexts.

The *Creole* mutiny electrified the nation and helped escalate sectional tensions over slavery. Southerners (and some northerners) were outraged that British authorities chose to free U.S. slaves, espe-

---

War History 21, no. 1 (1975), 28–50; George Hendrick and Willene Hendrick, *The Creole Mutiny: A Tale of Revolt aboard a Slave Ship* (Chicago: Dee, 2003). An important recent reassessment is Walter Johnson, "White Lies: Human Property and Domestic Slavery aboard the Slave Ship *Creole*," *Atlantic Studies* 5, no. 2 (2008): 237–63.

2. Copies of the 1853 *Autographs for Freedom* were distributed at antislavery meetings as early as December 1852.

cially those who had taken violent action against their masters. They viewed the British as endorsing slave insurrections—their worst nightmare—while also denying Americans their legal right to the domestic slave trade. In response, many southerners demanded war with England and threatened to start it themselves. The abolitionist newspaper the *Liberator*, reprinting an article from the Portsmouth, New Hampshire *Journal*, summed up their position by imagining a particularly boisterous southerner who announces to the nation: "'If you will not go to war to defend us in this right of slave-trading, we will begin the fight ourselves, and plunge you into a war, whether you will or no.'"[3]

Additionally fueling southern fury was the decision by the U.S. Supreme Court just a few months before the *Creole* rebellion to liberate 54 African slaves who, having been illegally imported to Cuba, mutinied on the Spanish slaver *Amistad* before drifting into Long Island Sound. The leaders of the rebellion were jailed in Connecticut, and between 1839 and 1841 became celebrities of sorts as they were interviewed in their cells and then involved in court trials that made them sympathetic to many northerners. The charismatic leader of the rebellion, Cinqué, a Mendi village leader from West Africa, helped make the *Amistad* a cause célèbre in the United States and abroad. The black abolitionist Robert Purvis argued that Cinqué helped inspire the leader of the *Creole* rebellion (see the Purvis selection in part 4 of this volume). In both the *Amistad* decision and the *Creole* case, many southerners, along with proslavery northerners, concluded that judges in England and the United States endorsed slaves' rights to rebel against their masters.[4]

The *Creole* mutiny underscored for southern planters that their peculiar institution was under siege. Although they produced two-thirds of the world's cotton and were the wealthiest Americans, they

3. "Case of the *Creole*," *Liberator*, 7 January 1842, 2.

4. Don E. Fehrenbacher, *The Slaveholding Republic: An Account of the United States Government's Relations to Slavery* (New York: Oxford University Press, 2001), 195.

nevertheless felt deeply threatened by the swift rise of antislavery sentiment throughout the New World. For millennia, slavery had been an almost unquestioned institution, recognized as a byproduct of civilization. When the United States was founded, slavery was legal everywhere in the New World. But in little more than two generations, the northern states and most of Central and South America had emancipated their slaves. Southern slave owners increasingly saw themselves as living on an island of slavery in a growing sea of freedom, and it horrified them.

Southern leaders sought to reverse this trend. Envisioning a future slave empire that would extend into the Caribbean, they succeeded in annexing the slave republic of Texas in 1845, which helped spark a war with Mexico that brought millions more acres of slave territory into the United States. Additionally, many leaders wanted to annex the slave colony of Cuba. To support their dreams of expansion, southern writers articulated a powerful proslavery ideology, drawing heavily on the Bible and other canonical texts, from Aristotle and St. Augustine to John Locke and Thomas Carlyle, to support their claim that slavery was socially and ethically beneficial to the expanding nation.[5]

Because they recognized how powerful antislavery testimony could be, southern politicians did everything they could to censor antislavery writings and speeches. Their efforts to suppress civil liberties in the northern free states largely failed. But throughout the slave states, where there already was a de facto understanding that antislavery thought was anathema, they banned the circulation of antislavery literature and criminalized antislavery utterances. In the U.S. Congress, southern politicians during the 1830s worked with their northern allies to implement the "gag rule," a procedure that automatically tabled thousands of antislavery petitions in an effort to prevent debates over slavery in the House and Senate. This effort to

5. See Matthew Pratt Guterl, *American Mediterranean: Southern Slaveholders in the Age of Emancipation* (Cambridge, Mass.: Harvard University Press, 2008).

cut off debate, which was strongly opposed by the former president and now congressman John Quincy Adams, further heightened sectional tensions and produced exactly what southerners didn't want, which was more debate about slavery in Congress.[6]

Ironically, southerners' outrage over the *Creole* rebellion helped repeal the gag rule, which had been implemented in 1836. Joshua Giddings, an antislavery congressman from Ohio, joined with John Quincy Adams to protest the suppression of antislavery debate. In the wake of the *Creole* uprising, Giddings proposed resolutions supporting the black rebels. In response, southern congressman censured Giddings, who immediately chose to resign in protest. Two months later, his constituents expressed their outrage over the suppression of free speech by reelecting Giddings in a landslide. When he reissued his resolutions, southerners no longer tried to silence him, having recognized that "gagging" politicians greatly antagonized northern voters. Although the gag rule remained on the books until 1844, it "morally ceased to operate" after the controversy over Giddings's resolutions.[7]

Southerners' belligerent responses to the *Creole* mutiny highlighted to antislavery northerners the degree to which the "Slave Power," an oligarchy of the South's most powerful leaders, sought to *nationalize* slavery. Southerners expected the federal government (and foreign powers) to support their peculiar institution. But antislavery northerners viewed such support as an affront to democratic and Christian values. William Ellery Channing, among the nation's most prominent ministers and intellectuals, was especially troubled by northern "doughface" politicians, who placated southerners as an expression of their loyalty to the Union. Southerners expected

6. See William Lee Miller, *Arguing about Slavery: The Great Battle in the United States Congress* (New York: Knopf, 1996).

7. Joshua Giddings, *History of the Rebellion: Its Authors and Causes* (New York: Follet, Foster, 1864), 197; James Brewer Stewart, *Joshua R. Giddings and the Tactics of Radical Politics* (Cleveland: Press of Case Western Reserve University, 1970), ch. 4; Miller, *Arguing about Slavery*, 444–54. A selection from Giddings is included in part 2 of this volume.

the federal government "to spread a shield over American slavery abroad as well as at home," he noted in *The Duty of the Free States, or Remarks Suggested by the Case of the Creole* (1842). Such a perspective contradicted American jurisprudence and morality, Channing emphasized. Slavery was neither a national institution, nor could it be "recognized by the law of nations."[8]

Borrowing from William Blackstone, the British legal theorist who profoundly shaped American jurisprudence, Channing and other antislavery leaders argued that the natural law of freedom trumped positive law, except in local municipalities and states. The *Somerset* case of 1772, which freed all slaves who set foot in England, did not recognize property in human beings. And the Slavery Abolition Act of 1833, which freed all slaves in the British West Indies (and nearly all the rest of the empire), including non-British slaves who arrived there, operated according to a similar legal understanding. The articulation of "freedom national," which was emphasized by Channing and others in the wake of the *Creole* rebellion, would become a foundational platform of the Republican Party when it formed during the 1850s.[9]

Antislavery northerners, who were dismayed by southerners' attacks on the British for harboring the *Creole* rebels, were equally dismayed by Daniel Webster's insistence that the British either return the slaves to their legal owners or else pay some form of restitution. Webster, the secretary of state under President John Tyler and a former Whig senator from Massachusetts, had long been regarded in New England as a great "champion of liberty."[10] But in

8. William Ellery Channing, *The Duty of the Free States, or Remarks Suggested by the Case of the Creole*, 2 vols. (Boston: William Crosby, 1842), 1:8, 29; Charles Sumner, quoted in Edward L. Pierce, *Memoir and Letters of Charles Sumner*, vol. 2 (Boston: Roberts Brothers, 1893), 200. After reading a draft of *The Duty of the Free States*, Sumner, Channing's friend and protégé, suggested revisions on several legal points, which Channing adopted; see Pierce, *Memoir*, 2:194. A selection from Channing's *Duty of the Free States* is included in part 2 of this volume.

9. See James Oakes, *Freedom National: The Destruction of Slavery in the United States, 1861–1865* (New York: Norton, 2013), 22–25.

10. William A. Stearns, *Sermon in Commemoration of Daniel Webster* (Boston: James Munroe, 1852), 26.

his official letter to Edward Everett, the U.S. minister to England, he argued that the British had illegally freed the *Creole* slaves, whom he regarded as murderers, and that it was therefore incumbent upon Britain to make amends to the slaves' owners. Whatever Webster may have thought of slavery itself, he believed that the Constitution and other U.S. legal documents protected southern slave owners and that U.S. law should be honored on the high seas. Webster quickly softened his attack on the British while negotiating a treaty with Lord Ashburton over boundary disputes. As a result, the Webster-Ashburton Treaty of 1842 did not prevent Britain from declaring future slave rebels free upon reaching British soil. Nevertheless, many antislavery northerners concluded, well before the Compromise of 1850, that Webster valued the Union more than freedom and could no longer be trusted on the slavery issue.[11]

When it came to freedom, antislavery northerners saw in the black leaders of the *Creole* parallels with the nation's revolutionary heroes, especially given the resonant American Revolutionary name of the principal leader of the rebellion, Madison Washington. As reported in numerous antislavery newspapers, Washington was a Virginia slave who had escaped to Canada and then returned to the plantation in an attempt to free his wife, only to be captured and reenslaved. He was subsequently sold as a "dangerous slave" to the trader Thomas McCargo, who put him aboard the *Creole* with other slaves to sell in New Orleans. To antislavery northerners, Washington's heroic and essentially nonviolent attempt to rescue his wife resembled his leadership during the rebellion, in which he coupled his desire for freedom with clemency toward his former captors. Even the *Creole*'s crew acknowledged that Washington had spared the lives of the ship's captain, a French sailor, McCargo, another trader, and McCargo's son. A newspaper article headlined "The Hero Mutineers," published in the 7 January 1842 issue of the *Liberator*, can be taken as representative of abolitionists' sentiment toward Washington; the anonymous author called him "the master

11. Jones, "The Peculiar Institution and National Honor," 45.

spirit" of the rebellion and likened him to the American Revolutionary founders whose names he bore. Such journalistic portrayals encouraged slaves to strike for their freedom and suggested that rebel slaves were as worthy of citizenship as whites. No wonder that, in the wake of the *Creole* mutiny, two lines from Lord Byron's *Childe Harold's Pilgrimage* (canto 2; 1812) became a common refrain for many black and some white radicals, including Frederick Douglass: "Hereditary bondsmen! know ye not / Who would be free, themselves must strike the blow?" Douglass used the line as an epigraph in *The Heroic Slave*, omitting the restrictive "hereditary": *all* bondsmen seeking freedom must strike the blow.[12]

Frederick Douglass and Madison Washington became public heroes at almost precisely the same time. Washington was front-page news beginning in December 1841, after the crew of the *Creole* returned to New Orleans. He was immediately cast as a hero by antislavery northerners; and when stories of his attempt to liberate his wife became known in the spring of 1842, he was further celebrated. Douglass, after escaping from slavery in Maryland in 1838, settled in New Bedford, Massachusetts, with his wife, Anna Murray, a free black woman. Already literate and skilled as an orator, he preached in the city's AME Zion church while earning money as a day laborer. He subscribed to the *Liberator*, the Boston organ of the American Anti-Slavery Society, edited by the great abolitionist leader William Lloyd Garrison. He read the *Liberator* as devoutly as his Bible, "mastering" its contents each week. As he later remarked: "The paper became my meat and my drink."[13] In August 1841 he attended

12. "Madison Washington: Another Chapter in His History," *Liberator*, 10 June 1842, reprinted in part 2 of this volume; "The Hero Mutineers," *Liberator*, 7 January 1842, reprinted in part 2 of this volume. See John Stauffer, *The Black Hearts of Men: Radical Abolitionists and the Transformation of Race* (Cambridge, Mass.: Harvard University Press, 2002), 113, 150–51, 187, 226.

13. Frederick Douglass, *My Bondage and My Freedom*, ed. John Stauffer (1855; New York: Modern Library, 2003), 212; Douglass, *Narrative of the Life of Frederick Douglass, an American Slave*, ed. David W. Blight (Boston: Bedford/St. Martin's, 2003), 119.

a national abolitionist convention in Nantucket, where he spoke to a mostly white audience of five hundred people. On the strength of his speech, he was hired as a full-time paid lecturer for the Massachusetts Anti-Slavery Society, an auxiliary of the Garrisonian-controlled American Anti-Slavery Society. In December 1841, the same month that the *Liberator* featured news of the *Creole* mutiny, a journalist termed Douglass "a hero" when describing his performance as a speaker: "This is an extraordinary man. He was cut out for a hero. . . . He has the 'heart to conceive, the head to contrive, and the hand to execute.'" The assessment echoed descriptions of Madison Washington from antislavery journalists. In fact, Douglass would portray Washington in *The Heroic Slave* in almost identical terms: "He had the head to conceive, and the hand to execute."[14]

Douglass resembled Madison Washington in other ways as well. Both were given names "unfit for a slave, but finely expressive for a hero," as the newspaper article "The Hero Mutineers" said of the latter. Douglass had been born Frederick Augustus Washington Bailey, his two middle names reflecting great republican leaders. Like most fugitives, he had discarded his surname after reaching free soil, taking on the new surname "Douglass"—the Scottish lord in Sir Walter Scott's poem *The Lady of the Lake* (1810)—as a way of marking his social ascent.[15]

Then, too, they were both large, strong men who had fought their way to freedom while displaying leniency toward their oppressors. Madison Washington commenced the mutiny by throwing off two men who had seized him. The turning point in Douglass's life as a slave, as he often noted, was his famous fight with Edward Covey, a "slave breaker" from Maryland's Eastern Shore, to whom he had

14. N. P. Rogers, *Concord (N.H.) Herald of Freedom*, 10 December 1841, quoted in Philip S. Foner, ed., *The Life and Writings of Frederick Douglass*, 5 vols. (New York: International Publishers, 1950–75), 1:48; Douglass, *The Heroic Slave*, in this volume, 14. The quotation draws on similar ones in the Earl of Clarendon's *History of the Rebellion and Civil Wars in England* (1703) and Edward Gibbon's *Decline and Fall of the Roman Empire* (1788).

15. "Hero Mutineers," *Liberator*, 7 January 1842.

been hired out. During their epic, two-hour battle, Douglass could probably have killed Covey. But he went "strictly on the defensive," as he later wrote, and after two hours Covey gave up, having been "mastered by a boy of sixteen." The effect was extraordinary; as Douglass noted in his *Narrative of the Life of Frederick Douglass, an American Slave* (1845) and *My Bondage and My Freedom* (1855): "I now resolved that, however long I might remain a slave in form, the day had passed forever when I could be a slave in fact." Covey never whipped him again. A slave who refused to be flogged was already more than "half free."[16]

Douglass, who would have read accounts of the *Creole* rebellion in the abolitionist press, greatly admired Washington's heroism. This was no doubt partly owing to their similarities. But it was also an age of hero worship. Having read Thomas Carlyle's hugely influential book on heroes, Douglass acknowledged that he, too, was a hero-worshipper, and Washington would emerge as one of his heroes.[17] In the first few years after the rebellion, however, Douglass felt constrained against publicly lionizing Washington. His first public mention of Washington in a speech was in 1845, more than three years after the uprising.[18] This silence stemmed partly from Douglass's commitment during this time to the American Anti-Slavery Society's emphasis on moral suasion as the sole means of ending slavery. Pacifism was the defining doctrine of the society, and Garrison and his associates did not hesitate to criticize abolitionists—notably, blacks and Liberty Party members—who condoned or sanctioned militancy. For example, when the black abolitionist Henry Highland Garnet, a minister and Liberty Party member, celebrated

16. Douglass, *My Bondage and My Freedom*, 137, 138, 140, 141.

17. Ibid., 211.

18. Douglass's first mention of the *Creole* mutiny was in 1843 or 1844. During a speech in Pittsburgh, he burlesqued Webster's, Clay's, and Calhoun's demands for restitution in the *Creole* case, but apparently without mentioning Madison Washington or violent means. See "Colored Orators," *National Era*, 28 July 1853, in which the journalist describes hearing Douglass on the *Creole* "at Pittsburgh, nine years ago [or] more."

Madison Washington as a revolutionary hero in an address at an 1843 black convention, the American Anti-Slavery Society rebuked him: "Trust not the counsels that lead you to the shedding of blood." Douglass, who was at the convention, also dissented from Garnet's militancy. There was "too much physical force" in his address, he said. He wanted "to try the moral means a little longer," adding that Garnet's address would lead to "insurrection," which would be a "catastrophe."[19]

Two years later, Douglass offered a dramatically different perspective on the *Creole* rebellion. During an October 1845 speech in Cork, Ireland, he transformed Washington from a violent insurrectionary into a revolutionary hero, echoing Garnet's praise for the man. "Madison Washington had in imitation of George Washington gained liberty," he proclaimed, but white Americans "branded him as being a thief, robber and murderer."[20] Developing the parallels between American Revolutionary heroes and Washington, he claimed that the condemnation of Washington, which was rife among southerners (and among many northerners, too) stemmed largely from racism, which kept them from seeing how Madison Washington acted in the tradition of such celebrated Virginia patriots as Thomas Jefferson, Patrick Henry, and George Washington.

Why this profound shift? Much had changed for Douglass between 1843 and 1845. In May 1845 he published his *Narrative of the Life of Frederick Douglass*, which made him nationally famous, virtually a household name; but it also greatly jeopardized his freedom. Fearing fugitive slave hunters, he fled to the British Isles for protection. No longer under the watchful eye of the American

19. "The Buffalo Convention of Men of Color," *Liberator*, 22 September 1843; *Minutes of the National Convention of Colored Citizens, held in Buffalo, on the 15th, 16th, 17th, 18th and 19th of August, 1843* (New York: Piercy and Reed, 1843), 13. Henry Highland Garnet delivered his "Address to the Slaves of the United States of America" at the 1843 convention in Buffalo, New York; a selection from the speech is in part 2 of this volume. See also Garnet, "A Letter to Mrs. Maria W. Chapman, November 17th, 1843," *Liberator*, 8 December 1843.

20. Douglass, "American Prejudice against Color," in this volume, 113.

Anti-Slavery Society's leaders, he could now speak his mind more openly. He had already been reprimanded by the society, as he later remarked in *My Bondage and My Freedom*, "for insubordination to my superiors," and he had discovered that most white abolitionists were not immune to the racial prejudice that pervaded the country. Many white colleagues patronized him: just "give us the facts," said one, and "we will take care of the philosophy." But in the British Isles, Douglass experienced "a perfect absence of everything like that disgusting hate with which we are pursued in America." Similarly, while many white Americans treated the *Creole* rebels as murderers, most Britons viewed them as heroes. As one British editorial writer proclaimed, they were as "justified in their actions as prisoners of war."[21]

After spending nearly two years touring the Britain Isles as an antislavery lecturer, Douglass was tempted to remain there permanently. He was so popular in Britain that he regularly filled auditoriums, some of which held over seven thousand people. Often in his speeches he invoked the heroism of Madison Washington and his fellow rebels. British sympathizers purchased Douglass's freedom, much as they had given Washington his liberty; and they raised an additional $2,000 as a cushion for Douglass against financial worries. After returning to the United States, Douglass used that money to purchase a printing press so that he could start up his own newspaper, the *North Star*, a decision that frayed his relationship with Garrison, the editor of the *Liberator*. Reunited with his family, Douglass moved to Rochester, New York, which lacked an abolitionist newspaper and yet was a Liberty Party stronghold and a hub on the Underground Railroad.

In Rochester, Douglass befriended people who had personally

21. Douglass, *My Bondage and My Freedom*, 215; *The Frederick Douglass Papers*, ser. 1, ed. John W. Blassingame et al. (New Haven, Conn.: Yale University Press, 1982), 2:59; "The Case of the *Creole*," *Times* (London), 21 January 1842; see also "The *Creole*," *Times* (London), 3 February 1842; "The *Creole*," *Times* (London), 16 February 1842; "The Affair of the *Creole*," *Times* (London), 25 March 1842.

known Madison Washington. As a result of these friendships, he no doubt heard more stories about Washington. Hiram Wilson, a Quaker abolitionist living in Canada, had opened his home to Washington; and Douglass got to know him through their involvement in the Western New York Anti-Slavery Society. Lindley Murray Moore, a Rochester abolitionist, had harbored Washington as well, and had also raised money to help him on his journey back to Virginia to free his wife. Douglass and Moore lectured at many of the same events, including Rochester's 1852 Independence Day celebration, where Douglass gave his famous speech "What to the Slave Is the Fourth of July?" And Moore contributed an essay to *Autographs for Freedom*, the collection of antislavery writings in which *The Heroic Slave* was first published.[22]

Douglass's remarks on Washington between 1843 and the publication of *The Heroic Slave* in 1853 (which can be traced in part 3 of this volume) reveal his growing fascination with the *Creole* rebellion. That interest paralleled his loss of faith in peaceful means for ending slavery. Events in the late 1840s, and then the passage of the Fugitive Slave Act of 1850, radicalized countless abolitionists, such as John Brown, who became a friend of Douglass's. In moving to Rochester, Douglass effectively abandoned the paternalistic influences of the American Anti-Slavery Society, which advocated nonresistance and considered politics, government, and violence equally corrupt. Initially, his newspaper sought to bridge the divide between nonresistance and the Liberty Party, which justified the use of force by calling on every loyal American to interfere with slavery wherever it existed. But in 1851, Douglass officially turned his paper into an organ of the Liberty Party, changing its name from the *North*

22. "Madison Washington: Another Chapter in His History," *Liberator*, 10 June 1842; "Seventh Annual Meeting of the Western N.Y. Anti-Slavery Society," *North Star*, 23 January 1851; Lindley Murray Moore, "Religious, Moral, and Political Duties," *Autographs for Freedom* (Boston: John P. Jewett, 1853), 114–15; "Mass Anti-Slavery Convention in Rochester," *North Star*, 20 March 1851; "Celebration of the National Anniversary," *Frederick Douglass' Paper*, 1 July 1852; "Editorial," *Frederick Douglass' Paper*, 27 May 1852.

Star to *Frederick Douglass' Paper* and switching his loyalties from Garrison to Gerrit Smith, a founder of the Liberty Party and its three-time presidential candidate (he was also a wealthy benefactor who helped Douglass with some of the funding for his newspaper). Significantly, Gerrit Smith, William Lloyd Garrison, and Madison Washington are the only three historical figures in *The Heroic Slave*. Smith is described as "a devoted friend" of blacks, who would receive Washington "gladly."[23]

Inspired by the *Creole* rebels, Douglass planned a trip to Nassau in February 1852, no doubt hoping to meet with Madison Washington. According to articles in his newspaper and in the *New York Tribune*, the purpose of the trip was to obtain "antislavery impressions" that would give him "ample materials" for writing an account of the rebellion. Included among these materials would have been the words of Madison Washington, for the article in *Frederick Douglass' Paper* noted: "Nassau is the home of the heroes of the *Creole*. Madison Washington himself is there." Although Douglass ended up not visiting Nassau, his plans suggest his continuing deep fascination with Washington—a fascination that eventually inspired him to write *The Heroic Slave*.[24]

The publication of *The Heroic Slave* in *Autographs for Freedom* (January 1853; see figure 1) coincided with the legal settlement of the *Creole* mutiny. Britain refused to pay restitution for the liberated slaves, but agreed to establish an Anglo-American claims commission to assess the case. The umpire, Joshua Bates, was a Boston partner in the House of Baring, a British financial firm that had financed the Louisiana Purchase. On 8 February 1853, Bates ruled that the authorities at Nassau had violated "the established law of nations" and that southern claimants were entitled to compensation for the loss of their property. Two years later, Britain paid the former owners a fair market value of $110,000 for their slaves. At the

23. Douglass, *Heroic Slave*, in this volume, 18–19.

24. "Letter from Wm. C. Nell," *Frederick Douglass' Paper*, 18 March 1852; "Brooklyn Items," *New York Tribune*, 25 February 1852.

AUTOGRAPHS

FOR

FREEDOM.

BOSTON:
JOHN P. JEWETT AND COMPANY.
CLEVELAND, OHIO:
JEWETT, PROCTOR, AND WORTHINGTON.
LONDON: LOW AND COMPANY.
1853.

1. *Autographs for Freedom* (1853), title page. Collection of John Stauffer.

very moment when the legal system declared a victory for southerners, Douglass offered a literary brief declaring victory for the rebel slaves. From this perspective, he emphasized that fiction was more effective than law in representing the truth of the *Creole* affair.

What are the truths that Douglass explores in *The Heroic Slave*? One is that fiction has the potential to be more honest, or authentic, than nonfiction narratives of the *Creole* rebellion, a number of which are included in this edition. The journalistic accounts of Madison Washington, both proslavery and antislavery, based their assessments of him on scant evidence—primarily, depositions taken by whites aboard the *Creole*. And this evidence was conflicting: Washington could reasonably be construed as either a temperate revolutionary hero fighting for his and his compatriots' freedom, or a tyrant. According to some accounts of the rebellion, at its outset he shouted to his fellow rebels, "We have begun, and must go through," followed by a threat to the other 116 slaves: "Come up, every one of you! If you don't lend a hand, I will kill you all, and throw you overboard." In describing Washington as a hero, antislavery journalists ignored evidence of such coercive threats. Douglass avoids the conundrum of parsing the scant historical record by acknowledging at the very beginning of *The Heroic Slave* that "glimpses" of Washington "are all that can now be presented": "We peer into the dark, and wish even for the blinding flash, or the light of northern skies to reveal him. But alas! he is still enveloped in darkness." Having made this concession, Douglass goes on to portray Washington as a sublimely fascinating fictional character based on the historical record.[25]

Douglass had long recognized that truth telling was, along with rhetoric (the art of persuasion), one of the abolitionists' most potent weapons against slavery. Historical fiction enabled him to couple honesty with his rhetorical gifts. His planned trip to Nassau in Feb-

25. "Protest of the Officers and Crew of the American Brig *Creole*," *Liberator*, 31 December 1841, in this volume, 66; Douglass, *The Heroic Slave*, in this volume, 4.

ruary 1852 hints that he may have hoped to write a nonfiction account of the *Creole* rebellion, based on interviews with Washington and other participants, before recognizing, right around the time of the 20 March 1852 publication of *Uncle Tom's Cabin*, that he could do even more through the power of fiction. Stowe's novel, which Douglass greatly admired, sold an unprecedented 10,000 copies in its first week of publication, in large part because serialization of the novel in the antislavery weekly the *National Era* from June 1851 to April 1852 had sparked interest in the book. *Uncle Tom's Cabin* sold 300,000 copies in its first year and became the publishing phenomenon of the nineteenth century. As Douglass would do in *The Heroic Slave*, Stowe characterizes her narrative as one based on historical facts: the narrator declares in the final chapter that the "separate incidents that compose the narrative are, to a very great extent, authentic, occurring, many of them, either under her own observation, or that of her personal friends." Stowe further authenticated her novel by publishing *A Key to Uncle Tom's Cabin* (1853), which presented the "facts and documents upon which the story was founded."[26]

Douglass was one of the first newspaper editors to recognize the degree to which Stowe's novel was converting millions of northerners into antislavery advocates who would resist the Fugitive Slave Law and heed the "higher law" of God. In April 1852, his newspaper included an in-house review of *Uncle Tom's Cabin* (probably by the managing editor, Julia Griffiths), which concluded: "We doubt if abler arguments have ever been presented in favor of the 'Higher Law' theory, than may be found here." Over the next two years, Douglass publicized and promoted Stowe's novel, hoping that Stowe would donate money earned from her novel and antislav-

26. Harriet Beecher Stowe, *Uncle Tom's Cabin*, ed. Elizabeth Ammons (1852; New York: Norton, 2010), 400; Stowe, *A Key to "Uncle Tom's Cabin"* (Boston: John P. Jewett, 1853), title page; Joan D. Hedrick, *Harriet Beecher Stowe: A Life* (New York: Oxford University Press, 1994), 223; David S. Reynolds, *Mightier Than the Sword: "Uncle Tom's Cabin" and the Battle for America* (New York: Norton, 2011), 126–67. See also Thomas F. Gossett, *"Uncle Tom's Cabin" and American Culture* (Dallas: Southern Methodist University Press, 1985).

ery tours to help him create a black mechanics institute in Rochester. Flattered by Douglass's attention, Stowe not only contributed a poem to the volume of antislavery writings in which *The Heroic Slave* appeared but also gave the volume its title, as reported in the 13 August 1852 issue of *Frederick Douglass' Paper*: "The gifted authoress of '*Uncle Tom's Cabin*' has christened it '*Autographs for Freedom*.'" In essence, the success of *Uncle Tom's Cabin* paved the way for *The Heroic Slave*, the first historical fiction by an African American.[27] And though Stowe never gave Douglass the funds he was hoping for, they had a genuinely productive literary relationship. In *The Heroic Slave*, Douglass departs from Stowe's idealization of the nonviolent, Christlike Uncle Tom by depicting a black-skinned hero who is more than willing to use violence to gain his freedom from slavery. And in Stowe's second antislavery novel, *Dred* (1856), she responds to Douglass's conception of a more activist black heroism by creating her own black-skinned revolutionary hero, Dred, who, like Madison Washington, adopts violence in his war against white enslavers.[28]

A second large truth, or insight, that Douglass emphasizes in *The Heroic Slave*, going against the grain of his 1840s commitment to Garrisonian moral suasion, is the productive confluence between

27. "Literary Notices," *Frederick Douglass' Paper*, 8 April 1852; "Second Anti-Slavery Festival," *Frederick Douglass' Paper*, 13 August 1852; see also Robert S. Levine, *Martin Delany, Frederick Douglass, and the Politics of Representative Identity* (Chapel Hill: University of North Carolina Press, 1997), 71–75. William Wells Brown's *Clotel*, first published in England in November 1853, similarly defines itself as a historical novel. Much like Stowe, the narrator asserts the historical authenticity at the opening of the last chapter: "Are the various incidents and scenes related founded in truth? I answer, Yes. I have personally participated in many of those scenes. Some of the narratives I have derived from other sources; many from the lips of those who, like myself, have run away from the land of bondage." See Brown, *Clotel; or, The President's Daughter: A Narrative of Slave Life in the United States*, ed. Robert S. Levine (2000; Boston: Bedford/St. Martins, 2011), 226.

28. Robert B. Stepto, "Storytelling in Early Afro-American Fiction: Frederick Douglass' 'The Heroic Slave,'" *Georgia Review* 36, no. 2 (Summer 1982): 355–68; Levine, *Martin Delany, Frederick Douglass*, 144–76.

slave resistance and abolitionism. By the late 1840s and early 1850s, Douglass had come to recognize that slave resistance could play a crucial role in the antislavery movement. Slave resistance had inspired the formation of the first abolition societies by calling attention to the barbarities of the slave system that gave rise to such violence. As an ex-slave who often still defined himself as a fugitive, Douglass understood that slavery was what he called "a *state of war*" between master and slave. There could thus be no peace in the nation until slavery was abolished. The *Creole* rebellion had highlighted for him the problem of insisting upon pacifism as the sole means of ending slavery.[29]

Douglass's Madison Washington seems to embody the essential abolitionist doctrine of slave resistance, summarized in Romans 13: "Resistance to tyrants is obedience to God."[30] But he isn't simply physical in his resistance; he is eloquent as well. The only hint in the historical record of Washington's oratorical skills is his brief, arresting address to his fellow mutineers to commence the rebellion, followed by his threat to the slaves. From the historical silences, Douglass uses fiction to give Washington the voice that dominates

29. Douglass, "Slavery, the Slumbering Volcano" (1849), in *Frederick Douglass Papers*, ser. 1, 2:153. On slave resistance as central to abolitionism, see Douglas R. Egerton, *Death or Liberty: African Americans and Revolutionary America* (New York: Oxford University Press, 2009); Gary B. Nash, *The Unknown American Revolution: The Unruly Birth of Democracy and the Struggle to Create America* (New York: Viking, 2005); Peter Linebaugh and Marcus Rediker, *The Many-Headed Hydra: Sailors, Slaves, Commoners and the Hidden History of the Revolutionary Atlantic* (Boston: Beacon, 2000); David Brion Davis, *The Problem of Slavery in the Age of Revolution, 1770–1823* (Ithaca, N.Y.: Cornell University Press, 1975); Seymour Drescher, *Abolition: A History of Slavery and Antislavery* (New York: Cambridge University Press, 2009); Manisha Sinha, *The Slave's Cause: Abolition and the Origins of American Democracy* (New Haven, Conn.: Yale University Press, 2014).

30. Douglass captures Romans 13 in his address to Tom Grant in *The Heroic Slave:* "You call me a black murderer. I am not a murderer. God is my witness that LIBERTY, not malice, is the motive for this night's work [the rebellion]." A few months after publishing *The Heroic Slave*, he employed the exact quote, common among abolitionists, in a lecture; see Douglass, "The Claims of Our Common Cause" (1853), in *Life and Writings*, 2:255; Douglass, *The Heroic Slave*, in this volume, 48.

the novella. Washington's eloquent defense of his rebelliousness enables Mr. Listwell, the white hero, to empathize with him. Mr. Listwell is aptly named; he can "listen well" to what this black leader has to say. In part 1 of the novella, Listwell is politically transformed after eavesdropping on Washington's eloquent words. Washington's "soliloquy" rang "through the chambers of his soul, and vibrated through his entire frame." "From this hour," Listwell vows, "I am an abolitionist." Washington even comes close to converting Tom Grant, the overseer on the *Creole*, who was modeled on the historical William Merritt (see Merritt's deposition in part 2 of this volume). "The fellow loomed up before me," Grant says of Washington. "I forgot his blackness in the dignity of his manner, and the eloquence of his speech. It seemed as if the souls of both the great dead (whose names he bore) had entered him."[31] Douglass suggests that rebellion alone will not convert whites into viewing blacks as equals and citizens. Effective abolitionism required rebellion plus truth-telling eloquence. His hero unites both rebelliousness and eloquence in order to undermine slavery and racism, much as Douglass was trying to do.

With his emphasis on the interracial dynamic of Washington's eloquence, Douglass approaches black rebellion very differently from Herman Melville, whose *Benito Cereno* (1855) is the other great novella of black rebellion at sea published during the 1850s. Whereas Washington gains the allegiance of the main white character in *The Heroic Slave*, in ways that Douglass hoped would gain the allegiance of his white readers, Melville chose to create a black rebel, Babo, who speaks ironically and archly and then, when captured, chooses not to speak at all. Melville works through irony and indirection; Douglass, consistent with his commitment to abolitionism, works more directly in articulating his themes. But different as the novellas may seem, they are similarly committed to the use of

31. Douglass, *Heroic Slave*, in this volume, 8–9, 49.

theatrical form, in the sense that both works present blacks as performers in white slave culture. Melville philosophically explores the psychological interdependence of masters and slaves; Douglass more directly challenges white mastery.[32]

There is a third large truth or insight in *The Heroic Slave*: slave rebels and abolitionists were willing to embrace any society in which they could live as free and equal citizens. In his historical accounts and novella, Douglass presents Madison Washington as "protected" by the British lion's "mighty paw from the talons and the beak of the American eagle." Though Douglass invokes American Revolutionary ideals, his novella displays no overarching or unconditional loyalty to the United States; instead, it is an uncompromising critique of American society and liberal (that is, white male) democracy. The state of Virginia, in part 3 of the novella, is presented as having descended from the glory days of the American Revolution to the point of being identified with spittoons and heavy drinking, a place where intemperate racist whites delude themselves into a sense of self-worth by thinking of themselves as superior to blacks. By emphasizing the fallenness of American culture and ideals, *The Heroic Slave* offers a powerful vision of black nationalism when the blacks of Nassau embrace the African Americans of the *Creole*. Douglass and his fictional hero would ideally prefer to remain in the United States, for it is their birthplace and the home of their families and friends. But the novella suggests that if this were not the case, that if the nation continued to fail to live up to its

32. See Maggie Montesinos Sale, *The Slumbering Volcano: American Slave Ship Revolts and the Production of Rebellious Masculinity* (Durham: Duke University Press, 1996), a selection from which is in part 5 of this volume; Eric J. Sundquist, *To Wake the Nations: Race in the Making of American Literature* (Cambridge, Mass.: Harvard University Press, 1998), ch. 2; Maurice S. Lee, "Melville's Subversive Political Philosophy: 'Benito Cereno' and the Fate of Speech," *American Literature* 72, no. 3 (2000): 495–520; John Stauffer, "Interracial Friendship and the Aesthetics of Freedom," *Frederick Douglass and Herman Melville: Essays in Relation*, ed. Robert S. Levine and Samuel Otter (Chapel Hill: University of North Carolina Press, 2008), 134–43; Stauffer, *Black Hearts of Men*, 190–94.

democratic ideals, then new nationalist realignments would be in order.[33]

The black nationalism that emerges at the end of *The Heroic Slave* may seem at odds with the conventional understanding of Frederick Douglass, who is often cast as a "representative American," an integrationist, a non-emigrationist, and (after the Civil War) a Republican party hack. But Douglass had a long-standing fascination with black history and black nations; he considered the possibility of immigrating to Haiti in the late 1850s, when he was especially disillusioned about the prospects for blacks in the United States; and near the end of his life, he held a consulship in Haiti and then represented Haiti at the 1893 World's Columbian Exposition in Chicago.[34] With its emphasis on violence and black community, *The Heroic Slave* speaks to values that Douglass had long embraced but had tempered while working for the American Anti-Slavery Society. Moreover, the novella offers insights that are at odds with the traditional historiography of abolitionism, which conceives of the movement as primarily white and nonviolent. Douglass recognized that abolitionists were radical critics rather than boosters of American society, and that blacks had absolutely crucial roles in the movement. Even Listwell, the white abolitionist, who can seem relatively passive, becomes implicated in black violence and transnationalist dissent when he decides, at the very last minute, to give Washington "three strong *files*."[35] In the version of events presented in *The*

33. Douglass, *The Heroic Slave*, in this volume, 26. On black nationalism in the novella, see Krista Walter, "Trappings of Nationalism in Frederick Douglass's *The Heroic Slave*," *African American Review* 34, no. 2 (2000): 233–47; and Ivy G. Wilson, "On Native Ground: Transnationalism, Frederick Douglass, and 'The Heroic Slave,'" *PMLA* 121, no. 2 (2006): 453–68; a selection from Wilson's essay is reprinted in part 5 of this volume.

34. See Robert S. Levine, *Dislocating Race and Nation: Episodes in Nineteenth-Century American Literary Nationalism* (Chapel Hill: University of North Carolina Press, 2008), ch. 4.

35. Douglass, *The Heroic Slave*, in this volume, 40. Convinced that the journey to New Orleans would be peaceful, the officers of the *Creole generally* allowed the slaves to move around the ship without constraints, though at night they were put

Heroic Slave, without those files Washington would have found it difficult to act; but without having listened to Washington in the first place, Listwell would not have offered those files. In this way, Douglass points to the crucial role played by black oppositional voices in the abolitionist movement. Through the friendship between Listwell and Washington, he also points to the multiracial possibilities of the novella's transnationalist vision.

Appearing in the 1853 *Autographs for Freedom*, which had American and British editions, and then serialized in *Frederick Douglass's Paper*, *The Heroic Slave* had a considerable readership at the time of its publication. As an indication of its popularity, there was even a pirated edition, probably published in 1853.[36] After that printing, there are just a few references to the novella before 1975, when Philip S. Foner included it in the *Supplement* to his five-volume *The Life and Writings of Frederick Douglass* (1950–75). In *Frederick Douglass: The Colored Orator* (1891), Frederick May Holland commented briefly on *The Heroic Slave*: "Early in 1853 he [Douglass] published in his own paper a highly wrought story, which had already appeared in 'Autographs for Freedom,' entitled 'The Heroic Slave.' It is based on actual adventures of Madison Washington, who set himself free by his own courage some ten years earlier." Presumably, these remarks would have inspired some admirers of Douglass's writing to seek out his novella. Three decades later, *The Heroic Slave* made an odd appearance in Alain Locke's *The New Negro: An*

---

into separate male and female slave quarters. Douglass invented the detail about the chains for his novella.

36. See Celeste-Marie Bernier, "A Comparative Exploration of Narrative Ambiguities in Frederick Douglass's Two Versions of *The Heroic Slave* (1853, 1863?)," *Slavery and Abolition* 22, no. 2 (2001): 69–86. The second version of *The Heroic Slave*, published in either 1853 or 1863, is almost certainly a pirated version, as Bernier suggests, despite the title of her essay. In this likely pirated edition, the decade in the publication year on the title page is obscured, so this second version was published in either 1853 or 1863. In our judgment, the likely pirating would have been in 1853, when the novella was before the public eye; Bernier hypothesizes a Civil War reprinting in 1863.

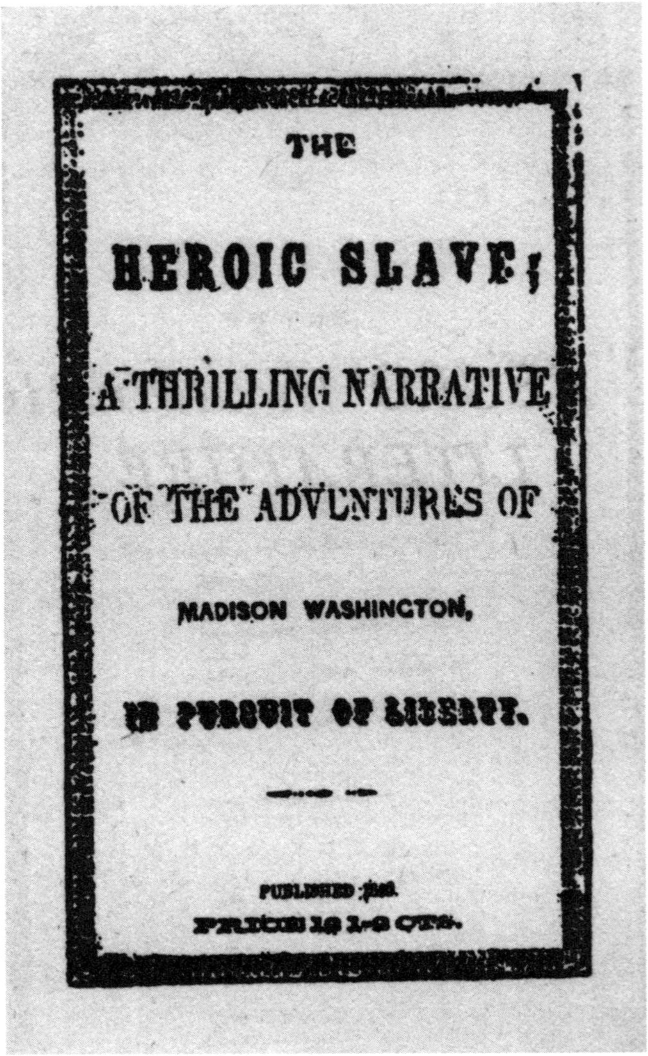

THE

HEROIC SLAVE;

A THRILLING NARRATIVE

OF THE ADVENTURES OF

MADISON WASHINGTON,

IN PURSUIT OF LIBERTY.

PUBLISHED [illegible]

PRICE 12 1-2 CTS.

2. Pirated edition of *The Heroic Slave*, from Alain Locke, *The New Negro* (1925). Widener Library, Harvard University.

Interpretation (1925), an influential collection of essays on black art and culture published at the height of the Harlem Renaissance. The illustration accompanying William Stanley Braithwaite's chapter, titled "The Negro in American Literature," depicts the cover page of the pirated edition of *The Heroic Slave* (see figure 2). Over the course of his essay, Braithwaite refers to Douglass's autobiographies but not *The Heroic Slave*, so the illustration offered just a tantalizing glimpse of a Douglass text that probably most readers of *The New Negro* knew nothing about. It wasn't until Foner's 1975 reprinting of the novella that *The Heroic Slave*, over 120 years after its initial publication, was again widely disseminated.[37]

This cultural and critical edition of *The Heroic Slave* brings the novella to a new generation of readers. We begin with an authoritative text of *The Heroic Slave*, which corrects the errors in the first printing in *Autographs for Freedom* and draws on Douglass's newspaper printing and the British edition of *Autographs* as well. In part 2, we offer a representative selection of contemporary responses to the *Creole* rebellion, including newspaper reportage, depositions, and political writings. Many of these texts served as important sources for Douglass, who spoke or wrote about Madison Washington a number of times from 1845 to 1861. Part 3 collects virtually everything Douglass had to say about the rebellion during that sixteen-year period. Douglass wasn't the only writer with an interest in the *Creole* rebellion. Part 4 presents six narratives of the uprising, including several that have not been republished since their first appearance in the nineteenth century. These narratives help us better understand what Douglass chose to emphasize and leave out in

37. Frederick May Holland, *Frederick Douglass: The Colored Orator* (1891; New York: Funk and Wagnalls, 1895), 220; Alain Locke, ed., *The New Negro: An Interpretation* (New York: Albert and Charles Boni, 1925), 28. Prior to Foner, Abraham Chapman reprinted *The Heroic Slave* in *Steal Away: Stories of the Runaway Slaves* (New York: Praeger, 1971). Important subsequent reprintings of *The Heroic Slave* can be found in Michael Meyer, *Frederick Douglass: The "Narrative" and Selected Writings* (New York: Modern Library, 1984); Ronald T. Takaki, *Violence in the Black Imagination: Essays and Documents* (New York: Oxford University Press, 1993); and William L. Andrews, *The Oxford Frederick Douglass Reader* (New York: Oxford University Press, 1996).

his own telling of the story. Storytelling is key to Robert B. Stepto's 1982 discussion of *The Heroic Slave*, and that essay, which initiated modern scholarship on Douglass's novella, heads the cluster of criticism in part 5 of the volume. Here critics address gender, black nationalism, violence, and other important topics, including matters of literary form and artistry. As the selected bibliography at the end of the volume indicates, *The Heroic Slave* has emerged as a major text in Douglass's canon, a novella that continues to engage readers with its compelling vision of reform, black revolution, and the quest for human freedom.

PART 1

The Text of Frederick Douglass's *The Heroic Slave*

The Heroic Slave.

Part I.

Oh! child of grief, why weepest thou?
   Why droops thy sad and mournful brow?
Why is thy look so like despair?
   What deep, sad sorrow lingers there?[1]

THE State of Virginia is famous in American annals for the multitudinous array of her statesmen and heroes. She has been dignified by some the mother of statesmen. History has not been sparing in recording their names, or in blazoning their deeds. Her high position in this respect, has given her an enviable distinction among her sister States. With Virginia for his birth-place, even a man of ordinary parts, on account of the general partiality for her sons, easily rises to eminent stations. Men, not great enough to attract special attention in their native States, have, like a certain distinguished citizen in the State of New York, sighed and repined that they were not born

1. From the hymn "God Is Love," in George N. Allen, *Oberlin Social and Sabbath School Hymn Book* (Oberlin, Ohio, 1846).

in Virginia.[2] Yet not all the great ones of the Old Dominion have, by the fact of their birth-place, escaped undeserved obscurity.[3] By some strange neglect, *one* of the truest, manliest, and bravest of her children,—one who, in after years, will, I think, command the pen of genius to set his merits forth, holds now no higher place in the records of that grand old Commonwealth than is held by a horse or an ox. Let those account for it who can, but there stands the fact, that a man who loved liberty as well as did Patrick Henry,—who deserved it as much as Thomas Jefferson,—and who fought for it with a valor as high, an arm as strong, and against odds as great, as he who led all the armies of the American colonies through the great war for freedom and independence, lives now only in the chattel records of his native State.[4]

Glimpses of this great character are all that can now be presented. He is brought to view only by a few transient incidents, and these afford but partial satisfaction. Like a guiding star on a stormy night, he is seen through the parted clouds and the howling tempests; or, like the gray peak of a menacing rock on a perilous coast, he is seen by the quivering flash of angry lightning, and he again disappears covered with mystery.

Curiously, earnestly, anxiously we peer into the dark, and wish even for the blinding flash, or the light of northern skies to reveal him. But alas! he is still enveloped in darkness, and we return from the pursuit like a wearied and disheartened mother, (after a tedious

2. Probably a reference to the New Yorker Martin Van Buren (1782–1862), eighth president of the United States (1837–41). Douglass was angered by Van Buren's support of the Compromise of 1850, which included the notorious Fugitive Slave Law requiring northerners to assist in the capture of runaway slaves.

3. Virginia's nickname and official slogan at the time when it became one of the original thirteen states of the United States.

4. Douglass refers to three Revolutionary leaders from Virginia: Patrick Henry (1736–1799) became famous for his revolutionary declaration, "Give me liberty or give me death!"; Thomas Jefferson (1743–1826) was the third president of the United States (1801–1809) and the author of the Declaration of Independence; George Washington (1732–1799), unnamed here, commanded the principal American field army in the Revolution and became the first president of the United States (1789–1797). "Chattel": slave.

and unsuccessful search for a lost child,) who returns weighed down with disappointment and sorrow. Speaking of marks, traces, possibles, and probabilities, we come before our readers.

In the spring of 1835, on a Sabbath morning, within hearing of the solemn peals of the church bells at a distant village, a Northern traveller through the State of Virginia drew up his horse to drink at a sparkling brook, near the edge of a dark pine forest. While his weary and thirsty steed drew in the grateful water, the rider caught the sound of a human voice, apparently engaged in earnest conversation.

Following the direction of the sound, he descried, among the tall pines, the man whose voice had arrested his attention. "To whom can he be speaking?" thought the traveller. "He seems to be alone." The circumstance interested him much, and he became intensely curious to know what thoughts and feelings, or, it might be, high aspirations, guided those rich and mellow accents. Tieing his horse at a short distance from the brook, he stealthily drew near the solitary speaker; and, concealing himself by the side of a huge fallen tree, he distinctly heard the following soliloquy:—

"What, then, is life to me? it is aimless and worthless, and worse than worthless. Those birds, perched on yon swinging boughs, in friendly conclave, sounding forth their merry notes in seeming worship of the rising sun, though liable to the sportsman's fowling-piece, are still my superiors. They *live free*, though they may die slaves. They fly where they list by day, and retire in freedom at night. But what is freedom to me, or I to it? I am a *slave*,—born a slave, an abject slave,—even before I made part of this breathing world, the scourge was platted for my back; the fetters were forged for my limbs. How mean a thing am I. That accursed and crawling snake, that miserable reptile, that has just glided into its slimy home, is freer and better off than I. He escaped my blow, and is safe. But here am I, a man,—yes, *a man*!—with thoughts and wishes, with powers and faculties as far as angel's flight above that hated reptile, —yet he is my superior, and scorns to own me as his master, or to stop to take my blows. When he saw my uplifted arm, he darted beyond my reach, and turned to give me battle. I dare not do as much as that. I neither run nor fight, but do meanly stand, answering each heavy blow of a cruel master with doleful wails and piteous cries. I am galled with irons; but even these are more tolerable than the consciousness, the *galling* consciousness of cowardice and indecision. Can it be that I *dare* not run away? *Perish the thought*, I *dare* do any thing which may be done by another. When that young man struggled with the waves *for life*, and others stood back appalled in helpless horror, did I not plunge in, forgetful of life, to save his? The raging bull from whom all others fled, pale with fright, did I not keep at bay with a single pitchfork? Could a coward do that? *No*,—*no*,—I wrong myself,—I am no coward. *Liberty* I will have, or die in the attempt to gain it. This working that others may live in idleness! This cringing submission to insolence and curses! This living under the constant dread and apprehension of being sold and transferred, like a mere brute, is *too* much for me. I will stand it no longer. What others have done, I will do. These trusty legs, or these sinewy arms shall place me among the free. Tom escaped; so can I. The North Star will not be less kind to me than to him.[5] I will follow it. I will at least make the trial. I have nothing to lose. If I am caught, I shall only be a slave. If I am shot, I shall only lose a life which is a burden and a curse. If I get clear, (as something tells me I shall,) liberty, the inalienable birth-right of every man, precious and priceless, will be mine. My resolution is fixed. *I shall be free*."

At these words the traveller raised his head cautiously and noiselessly, and caught, from his hiding-place, a full view of the unsuspecting speaker. Madison (for that was the name of our hero) was standing erect, a smile of satisfaction rippled upon his expressive countenance, like that which plays upon the face of one who has but just solved a difficult problem, or vanquished a malignant foe; for

5. Escaping slaves fled northward, hiding by day and moving furtively at night. Often their only guide was Polaris, the North Star, which they found by tracing the handle of the Big Dipper, or Drinking Gourd, constellation.

at that moment he was free, at least in spirit. The future gleamed brightly before him, and his fetters lay broken at his feet. His air was triumphant.

Madison was of manly form. Tall, symmetrical, round, and strong. In his movements he seemed to combine, with the strength of the lion, the lion's elasticity. His torn sleeves disclosed arms like polished iron. His face was "black, but comely."[6] His eye, lit with emotion, kept guard under a brow as dark and as glossy as the raven's wing. His whole appearance betokened Herculean strength; yet there was nothing savage or forbidding in his aspect.[7] A child might play in his arms, or dance on his shoulders. A giant's strength, but not a giant's heart was in him. His broad mouth and nose spoke only of good nature and kindness. But his voice, that unfailing index of the soul, though full and melodious, had that in it which could terrify as well as charm. He was just the man you would choose when hardships were to be endured, or danger to be encountered,—intelligent and brave. He had the head to conceive, and the hand to execute. In a word, he was one to be sought as a friend, but to be dreaded as an enemy.

As our traveller gazed upon him, he almost trembled at the thought of his dangerous intrusion. Still he could not quit the place. He had long desired to sound the mysterious depths of the thoughts and feelings of a slave. He was not, therefore, disposed to allow so providential an opportunity to pass unimproved. He resolved to hear more; so he listened again for those mellow and mournful accents which, he says, made such an impression upon him as can never be erased. He did not have to wait long. There came another gush from the same full fountain; now bitter, and now sweet. Scathing denunciations of the cruelty and injustice of slavery; heart-touching narrations of his own personal suffering, intermingled with prayers to the God of the oppressed for help and deliverance, were followed by

6. Song of Solomon 1:5.

7. The Greek mythological hero Heracles, known to the Romans as Hercules, was a mortal son of the chief god Zeus and famed for his strength.

presentations of the dangers and difficulties of escape, and formed the burden of his eloquent utterances; but his high resolution clung to him,—for he ended each speech by an emphatic declaration of his purpose to be free. It seemed that the very repetition of this, imparted a glow to his countenance. The hope of freedom seemed to sweeten, for a season, the bitter cup of slavery, and to make it, for a time, tolerable; for when in the very whirlwind of anguish,—when his heart's cord seemed screwed up to snapping tension, hope sprung up and soothed his troubled spirit. Fitfully he would exclaim, "How can I leave her? Poor thing! What can she do when I am gone? Oh! oh! 'tis impossible that I can leave poor Susan!"[8]

A brief pause intervened. Our traveller raised his head, and saw again the sorrow-smitten slave. His eye was fixed upon the ground. The strong man staggered under a heavy load. Recovering himself, he argued thus aloud: "All is uncertain here. To-morrow's sun may not rise before I am sold, and separated from her I love. What, then, could I do for her? I should be in more hopeless slavery, and she no nearer to liberty,—whereas if I were free,—my arms my own,—I might devise the means to rescue her."

This said, Madison cast around a searching glance, as if the thought of being overheard had flashed across his mind. He said no more, but, with measured steps, walked away, and was lost to the eye of our traveller amidst the wildering woods.

Long after Madison had left the ground, Mr. Listwell (our traveller) remained in motionless silence, meditating on the extraordinary revelations to which he had listened. He seemed fastened to the spot, and stood half hoping, half fearing the return of the sable preacher to his solitary temple. The speech of Madison rung through the chambers of his soul, and vibrated through his entire

8. The name of Madison Washington's wife is not recorded in surviving historical records. Douglass knew several of the people whom Washington had met in Canada and in the United States after his first escape from slavery; see the Robert Purvis selection in part 4 of this volume. Douglass either learned her first name from these people or invented a fictional one.

frame. "Here is indeed a man," thought he, "of rare endowments,—a child of God,—guilty of no crime but the color of his skin,—hiding away from the face of humanity, and pouring out his thoughts and feelings, his hopes and resolutions to the lonely woods; to him those distant church bells have no grateful music. He shuns the church, the altar, and the great congregation of christian worshippers, and wanders away to the gloomy forest, to utter in the vacant air complaints and griefs, which the religion of his times and his country can neither console nor relieve. Goaded almost to madness by the sense of the injustice done him, he resorts hither to give vent to his pent up feelings, and to debate with himself the feasibility of plans, plans of his own invention, for his own deliverance. From this hour I am an abolitionist. I have seen enough and heard enough, and I shall go to my home in Ohio resolved to atone for my past indifference to this ill-starred race, by making such exertions as I shall be able to do, for the speedy emancipation of every slave in the land."

Part II.

"The gaudy, blabbling and remorseful day
Is crept into the bosom of the sea;
And now loud-howling wolves arouse the jades
That drag the tragic melancholy night;
Who with their drowsy, slow, and flagging wings
Clip dead men's graves, and from their misty jaws
Breathe foul contagions, darkness in the air."

Shakspeare.[9]

FIVE years after the foregoing singular occurrence, in the winter of 1840, Mr. and Mrs. Listwell sat together by the fireside of their own happy home, in the State of Ohio. The children were all gone

9. *The Second Part of King Henry the Sixth*, 4.1.1–7. Douglass uses a common nineteenth-century spelling of Shakespeare.

to bed. A single lamp burnt brightly on the centre-table. All was still and comfortable within; but the night was cold and dark; a heavy wind sighed and moaned sorrowfully around the house and barn, occasionally bringing against the clattering windows a stray leaf from the large oak trees that embowered their dwelling. It was a night for strange noises and for strange fancies. A whole wilderness of thought might pass through one's mind during such an evening. The smouldering embers, partaking of the spirit of the restless night, became fruitful of varied and fantastic pictures, and revived many bygone scenes and old impressions. The happy pair seemed to sit in silent fascination, gazing on the fire. Suddenly this *reverie* was interrupted by a heavy growl. Ordinarily such an occurrence would have scarcely provoked a single word, or excited the least apprehension. But there are certain seasons when the slightest sound sends a jar through all the subtle chambers of the mind; and such a season was this. The happy pair started up, as if some sudden danger had come upon them. The growl was from their trusty watch-dog.

"What can it mean? certainly no one can be out on such a night as this," said Mrs. Listwell.

"The wind has deceived the dog, my dear; he has mistaken the noise of falling branches, brought down by the wind, for that of the footsteps of persons coming to the house. I have several times to-night thought that I heard the sound of footsteps. I am sure, however, that it was but the wind. Friends would not be likely to come out at such an hour, or such a night; and thieves are too lazy and self-indulgent to expose themselves to this biting frost; but should there be any one about, our brave old Monte, who is on the lookout, will not be slow in sounding the alarm."

Saying this they quietly left the window, whither they had gone to learn the cause of the menacing growl, and re-seated themselves by the fire, as if reluctant to leave the slowly expiring embers, although the hour was late. A few minutes only intervened after resuming their seats, when again their sober meditations were disturbed. Their faithful dog now growled and barked furiously, as if assailed by an advancing foe. Simultaneously the good couple arose, and stood in mute expectation. The contest without seemed fierce and violent. It was, however, soon over,—the barking ceased, for, with true canine instinct, Monte quickly discovered that a friend, not an enemy of the family, was coming to the house, and instead of rushing to repel the supposed intruder, he was now at the door, whimpering and dancing for the admission of himself and his newly made friend.

Mr. Listwell knew by this movement that all was well; he advanced and opened the door, and saw by the light that streamed out into the darkness, a tall man advancing slowly towards the house, with a stick in one hand, and a small bundle in the other. "It is a traveller," thought he, "who has missed his way, and is coming to inquire the road. I am glad we did not go to bed earlier,—I have felt all the evening as if somebody would be here to-night."

The man had now halted a short distance from the door, and looked prepared alike for flight or battle. "Come in, sir, don't be alarmed, you have probably lost your way."

Slightly hesitating, the traveller walked in; not, however, without regarding his host with a scrutinizing glance. "No, sir," said he, "I have come to ask you a greater favor."

Instantly Mr. Listwell exclaimed, (as the recollection of the Virginia forest scene flashed upon him,) "Oh, sir, I know not your name, but I have seen your face, and heard your voice before. I am glad to see you. *I know all*. You are flying for your liberty,—be seated,—be seated,—banish all fear. You are safe under my roof."

This recognition, so unexpected, rather disconcerted and disquieted the noble fugitive. The timidity and suspicion of persons escaping from slavery are easily awakened, and often what is intended to dispel the one, and to allay the other, has precisely the opposite effect. It was so in this case. Quickly observing the unhappy impression made by his words and action, Mr. Listwell assumed a more quiet and inquiring aspect, and finally succeeded in removing the apprehensions which his very natural and generous salutation had aroused.

Thus assured, the stranger said, "Sir, you have rightly guessed, I am, indeed, a fugitive from slavery. My name is Madison,—Madison Washington my mother used to call me. I am on my way to Canada, where I learn that persons of my color are protected in all the rights of men;[10] and my object in calling upon you was, to beg the privilege of resting my weary limbs for the night in your barn. It was my purpose to have continued my journey till morning; but the piercing cold, and the frowning darkness compelled me to seek shelter; and, seeing a light through the lattice of your window, I was encouraged to come here to beg the privilege named. You will do me a great favor by affording me shelter for the night."

"A resting-place, indeed, sir, you shall have; not, however, in my barn, but in the best room of my house. Consider yourself, if you please, under the roof of a friend; for such I am to you, and to all your deeply injured race."

While this introductory conversation was going on, the kind lady had revived the fire, and was diligently preparing supper; for she, not less than her husband, felt for the sorrows of the oppressed and hunted ones of the earth, and was always glad of an opportunity to do them a service. A bountiful repast was quickly prepared, and the hungry and toil-worn bondman was cordially invited to partake thereof. Gratefully he acknowledged the favor of his benevolent benefactress; but appeared scarcely to understand what such hospitality could mean. It was the first time in his life that he had met so humane and friendly a greeting at the hands of persons whose color was unlike his own; yet it was impossible for him to doubt the charitableness of his new friends, or the genuineness of the welcome so

10. Beginning in the early 1820s, fugitive slaves from the United States began to settle in Upper Canada (also known as Canada West), where they formed their own communities. Although not restricted legally, the fugitives were not welcomed by many white Canadians.

freely given; and he therefore, with many thanks, took his seat at the table with Mr. and Mrs. Listwell, who, desirous to make him feel at home, took a cup of tea themselves, while urging upon Madison the best that the house could afford.

Supper over, all doubts and apprehensions banished, the three drew around the blazing fire, and a conversation commenced which lasted till long after midnight.

"Now," said Madison to Mr. Listwell, "I was a little surprised and alarmed when I came in, by what you said; do tell me, sir, *why* you thought you had seen my face before, and by what you knew me to be a fugitive from slavery; for I am sure that I never was before in this neighborhood, and I certainly sought to conceal what I supposed to be the manner of a fugitive slave."

Mr. Listwell at once frankly disclosed the secret; describing the place where he first saw him; rehearsing the language which he (Madison) had used; referring to the effect which his manner and speech had made upon him; declaring the resolution he there formed to be an abolitionist; telling how often he had spoken of the circumstance, and the deep concern he had ever since felt to know what had become of him; and whether he had carried out the purpose to make his escape, as in the woods he declared he would do.

"Ever since that morning," said Mr. Listwell, "you have seldom been absent from my mind, and though now I did not dare to hope that I should ever see you again, I have often wished that such might be my fortune; for, from that hour, your face seemed to be daguerreotyped on my memory."[11]

Madison looked quite astonished, and felt amazed at the narration to which he had listened. After recovering himself he said, "I well remember that morning, and the bitter anguish that wrung my

11. The daguerreotype was the first commercially successful photographic process. The image was made in the camera on a silvered copper plate. The French inventor Louis J. M. Daguerre (1787–1851) perfected the process after a decade of experimentation. Douglass himself was fascinated by photography; see, for example, his lecture "Pictures and Progress" (1861).

heart; I will state the occasion of it. I had, on the previous Saturday, suffered a cruel lashing; had been tied up to the limb of a tree, with my feet chained together, and a heavy iron bar placed between my ankles. Thus suspended, I received on my naked back forty stripes, and was kept in this distressing position three or four hours, and was then let down, only to have my torture increased; for my bleeding back, gashed by the cow-skin, was washed by the overseer with old brine, partly to augment my suffering, and partly, as he said, to prevent inflammation. My crime was that I had stayed longer at the mill, the day previous, than it was thought I ought to have done, which, I assured my master and the overseer, was no fault of mine; but no excuses were allowed. 'Hold your tongue, you impudent rascal,' met my every explanation. Slave-holders are so imperious when their passions are excited, as to construe every word of the slave into insolence. I could do nothing but submit to the agonizing infliction. Smarting still from the wounds, as well as from the consciousness of being whipt for no cause, I took advantage of the absence of my master, who had gone to church, to spend the time in the woods, and brood over my wretched lot. Oh, sir, I remember it well,—and can never forget it."

"But this was five years ago; where have you been since?"

"I will try to tell you," said Madison. "Just four weeks after that Sabbath morning, I gathered up the few rags of clothing I had, and started, as I supposed, for the North and for freedom. I must not stop to describe my feelings on taking this step. It seemed like taking a leap into the dark. The thought of leaving my poor wife and two little children caused me indescribable anguish; but consoling myself with the reflection that once free, I could, possibly, devise ways and means to gain their freedom also, I nerved myself up to make the attempt.[12] I started, but ill-luck attended me; for after being out a whole week, strange to say, I still found myself on my

12. As with Washington's wife's name, Douglass either learned about the existence of the slave rebel's children from abolitionist friends or invented them for literary purposes.

master's grounds; the third night after being out, a season of clouds and rain set in, wholly preventing me from seeing the North Star, which I had trusted as my guide, not dreaming that clouds might intervene between us.

"This circumstance was fatal to my project, for in losing my star, I lost my way; so when I supposed I was far towards the North, and had almost gained my freedom, I discovered myself at the very point from which I had started. It was a severe trial, for I arrived at home in great destitution; my feet were sore, and in travelling in the dark, I had dashed my foot against a stump, and started a nail, and lamed myself. I was wet and cold; one week had exhausted all my stores; and when I landed on my master's plantation, with all my work to do over again,—hungry, tired, lame, and bewildered,—I almost cursed the day that I was born. In this extremity I approached the quarters. I did so stealthily, although in my desperation I hardly cared whether I was discovered or not. Peeping through the rents of the quarters, I saw my fellow-slaves seated by a warm fire, merrily passing away the time, as though their hearts knew no sorrow. Although I envied their seeming contentment, all wretched as I was, I despised the cowardly acquiescence in their own degradation which it implied, and felt a kind of pride and glory in my own desperate lot. I dared not enter the quarters,—for where there is seeming contentment with slavery, there is certain treachery to freedom. I proceeded towards the great house, in the hope of catching a glimpse of my poor wife, whom I knew might be trusted with my secrets even on the scaffold. Just as I reached the fence which divided the field from the garden, I saw a woman in the yard, who in the darkness I took to be my wife; but a nearer approach told me it was not she. I was about to speak; had I done so, I would not have been here this night; for an alarm would have been sounded, and the hunters been put on my track. Here were hunger, cold, thirst, disappointment, and chagrin, confronted only by the dim hope of liberty. I tremble to think of that dreadful hour. To face the deadly cannon's mouth in warm blood unterrified, is, I think, a small achievement, compared with a conflict like this with gaunt starvation. The gnawings of hunger conquers by degrees, till all that a man has he would give in exchange for a single crust of bread. Thank God, I was not quite reduced to this extremity.

"Happily for me, before the fatal moment of utter despair, my good wife made her appearance in the yard. It was she; I knew her step. All was well now. I was, however, afraid to speak lest I should frighten her. Yet speak I did; and, to my great joy, my voice was known. Our meeting can be more easily imagined than described. For a time hunger, thirst, weariness, and lameness were forgotten. But it was soon necessary for her to return to the house. She being a house-servant, her absence from the kitchen, if discovered, might have excited suspicion. Our parting was like tearing the flesh from my bones; yet it was the part of wisdom for her to go. She left me with the purpose of meeting me at midnight in the very forest where you last saw me. She knew the place well, as one of my melancholy resorts, and could easily find it, though the night was dark.

"I hastened away, therefore, and concealed myself, to await the arrival of my good angel. As I lay there among the leaves, I was strongly tempted to return again to the house of my master and give myself up; but remembering my solemn pledge on that memorable Sunday morning, I was able to linger out the two long hours between ten and midnight. I may well call them long hours. I have endured much hardship; I have encountered many perils; but the anxiety of those two hours, was the bitterest I ever experienced. True to her word, my wife came laden with provisions, and we sat down on the side of a log, at that dark and lonesome hour of the night. I cannot say we talked; our feelings were too great for that; yet we came to an understanding that I should make the woods my home, for if I gave myself up, I should be whipped and sold away; and if I started for the North, I should leave a wife doubly dear to me. We mutually determined, therefore, that I should remain in the vicinity. In the dismal swamps I lived, sir, five long years,—a cave for my home during the day.[13] I wandered about at night with the wolf and the bear,—sustained by the promise that my good Susan would meet me in the pine woods at least once a week. This promise was redeemed, I assure you, to the letter, greatly to my relief. I had partly become contented with my mode of life, and had made up my mind to spend my days there; but the wilderness that sheltered me thus long took fire, and refused longer to be my hiding-place.

"I will not harrow up your feelings by portraying the terrific scene of this awful conflagration. There is nothing to which I can liken it. It was horribly and indescribably grand. The whole world seemed on fire, and it appeared to me that the day of judgment had come; that the burning bowels of the earth had burst forth, and that the end of all things was at hand. Bears and wolves, scorched from their mysterious hiding-places in the earth, and all the wild inhabitants of the untrodden forest, filled with a common dismay, ran forth, yelling, howling, bewildered amidst the smoke and flame. The very heavens seemed to rain down fire through the towering trees; it was by the merest chance that I escaped the devouring element. Running before it, and stopping occasionally to take breath, I looked back to behold its frightful ravages, and to drink in its savage magnificence. It was awful, thrilling, solemn, beyond compare. When aided by the fitful wind, the merciless tempest of fire swept on, sparkling, creaking, cracking, curling, roaring, out-doing in its dreadful splendor a thousand thunderstorms at once. From tree to tree it leaped, swallowing them up in its lurid, baleful glare; and leaving them leafless, limbless, charred, and lifeless behind. The scene was overwhelming, stunning,—nothing was spared,—cattle, tame and wild, herds of swine and of deer, wild beasts of every name and kind,—huge night-birds, bats, and owls, that had retired to their homes in lofty tree-tops to rest, perished in that fiery storm. The

13. Probably a reference to the Great Dismal Swamp, located along the coastal plain of southeastern Virginia and northeastern North Carolina. The region had been a site for runaway slave maroon colonies since colonial times.

long-winged buzzard and croaking raven mingled their dismal cries with those of the countless myriads of small birds that rose up to the skies, and were lost to the sight in clouds of smoke and flame. Oh, I shudder when I think of it! Many a poor wandering fugitive, who, like myself, had sought among wild beasts the mercy denied by our fellow men, saw, in helpless consternation, his dwelling-place and city of refuge reduced to ashes forever.[14] It was this grand conflagration that drove me hither; I ran alike from fire and from slavery."

After a slight pause, (for both speaker and hearers were deeply moved by the above recital,) Mr. Listwell, addressing Madison, said, "If it does not weary you too much, do tell us something of your journeyings since this disastrous burning,—we are deeply interested in everything which can throw light on the hardships of persons escaping from slavery; we could hear you talk all night; are there no incidents that you could relate of your travels hither? or are they such that you do not like to mention them?"

"For the most part, sir, my course has been uninterrupted; and, considering the circumstances, at times even pleasant. I have suffered little for want of food; but I need not tell you how I got it. Your moral code may differ from mine, as your customs and usages are different. The fact is, sir, during my flight, I felt myself robbed by society of all my just rights; that I was in an enemy's land, who sought both my life and my liberty. They had transformed me into a brute; made merchandise of my body, and, for all the purposes of my flight, turned day into night,—and guided by my own necessities, and in contempt of their conventionalities, I did not scruple to take bread where I could get it."

"And just there you were right," said Mr. Listwell; "I once had doubts on this point myself, but a conversation with Gerrit Smith, (a man, by the way, that I wish you could see, for he is a devoted friend

14. In the Old Testament, the cities of refuge were towns in the kingdoms of Israel and Judah that offered the possibility of trial by law for those accused of manslaughter (Numbers 35:11–34; Deuteronomy 19:3–13).

of your race, and I know he would receive you gladly,) put an end to all my doubts on this point. But do not let me interrupt you."[15]

"I had but one narrow escape during my whole journey," said Madison.

"Do let us hear of it," said Mr. Listwell.

"Two weeks ago," continued Madison, "after travelling all night, I was overtaken by daybreak, in what seemed to me an almost interminable wood. I deemed it unsafe to go farther, and, as usual, I looked around for a suitable tree in which to spend the day. I liked one with a bushy top, and found one just to my mind. Up I climbed, and hiding myself as well as I could, I, with this strap, (pulling one out of his old coat-pocket,) lashed myself to a bough, and flattered myself that I should get a *good night's* sleep that day; but in this I was soon disappointed. I had scarcely got fastened to my natural hammock, when I heard the voices of a number of persons, apparently approaching the part of the woods where I was. Upon my word, sir, I dreaded more these human voices than I should have done those of wild beasts. I was at a loss to know what to do. If I descended, I should probably be discovered by the men; and if they had dogs I should, doubtless, be *'treed.'* It was an anxious moment, but hardships and dangers have been the accompaniments of my life; and have, perhaps, imparted to me a certain hardness of character, which, to some extent, adapts me to them. In my present predicament, I decided to hold my place in the tree-top, and abide the consequences. But here I must disappoint you; for the men, who were all colored, halted at least a hundred yards from me, and began with their axes, in right good earnest, to attack the trees. The sound of their laughing axes was like the report of as many well-charged pistols. By and by there came down at least a dozen trees with a terrible crash. They leaped

15. Gerrit Smith, a New York antislavery reformer (1797–1874), helped organize the Liberty Party and was elected to Congress in 1852. A philanthropist, Smith gave approximately 140,000 acres of land in upstate New York to three thousand black settlers; beginning in the early 1850s, he also helped finance *Frederick Douglass' Paper*.

upon the fallen trees with an air of victory. I could see no dog with them, and felt myself comparatively safe, though I could not forget the possibility that some freak or fancy might bring the axe a little nearer my dwelling than comported with my safety.

"There was no sleep for me that day, and I wished for night. You may imagine that the thought of having the tree attacked under me was far from agreeable, and that it very easily kept me on the look-out. The day was not without diversion. The men at work seemed to be a gay set; and they would often make the woods resound with that uncontrolled laughter for which we, as a race, are remarkable. I held my place in the tree till sunset,—saw the men put on their jackets to be off. I observed that all left the ground except one, whom I saw sitting on the side of a stump, with his head bowed, and his eyes apparently fixed on the ground. I became interested in him. After sitting in the position to which I have alluded ten or fifteen minutes, he left the stump, walked directly towards the tree in which I was secreted, and halted almost under the same. He stood for a moment and looked around, deliberately and reverently took off his hat, by which I saw that he was a man in the evening of life, slightly bald and quite gray. After laying down his hat carefully, he knelt and prayed aloud, and such a prayer, the most fervent, earnest, and solemn, to which I think I ever listened. After reverently addressing the Almighty, as the all-wise, all-good, and the common Father of all mankind, he besought God for grace, for strength, to bear up under, and to endure, as a good soldier, all the hardships and trials which beset the journey of life, and to enable him to live in a manner which accorded with the gospel of Christ. His soul now broke out in humble supplication for deliverance from bondage. 'O thou,' said he, 'that hearest the raven's cry,[16] take pity on poor me! O de-

16. An allusion to Psalms 147:9, the phrase, often in the form "the young raven's cry," is found in a number of hymns from the nineteenth century; Douglass's source may have been Charles Wesley's "Son of Thy Sire's Eternal Love" (in *A Collection of Hymns: For the Use of the Methodist Episcopal Church, Principally from the Collection of Rev. John Wesley* [New York, 1845]).

liver me! O deliver me! in mercy, O God, deliver me from the chains and manifold hardships of slavery! With thee, O Father, all things are possible.[17] Thou canst stand and measure the earth. Thou hast beheld and drove asunder the nations,—all power is in thy hand,—thou didst say of old, "I have seen the affliction of my people, and am come to deliver them,"[18]—'Oh look down upon our afflictions, and have mercy upon us.' But I cannot repeat his prayer, nor can I give you an idea of its deep pathos. I had given but little attention to religion, and had but little faith in it; yet, as the old man prayed, I felt almost like coming down and kneel by his side, and mingle my broken complaint with his.

"He had already gained my confidence; as how could it be otherwise? I knew enough of religion to know that the man who prays in secret is far more likely to be sincere than he who loves to pray standing in the street, or in the great congregation. When he arose from his knees, like another Zacheus,[19] I came down from the tree. He seemed a little alarmed at first, but I told him my story, and the good man embraced me in his arms, and assured me of his sympathy.

"I was now about out of provisions, and thought I might safely ask him to help me replenish my store. He said he had no money; but if he had, he would freely give it me. I told him I had *one dollar*; it was all the money I had in the world. I gave it to him, and asked him to purchase some crackers and cheese, and to kindly bring me the balance; that I would remain in or near that place, and would come to him on his return, if he would whistle. He was gone only about an hour. Meanwhile, from some cause or other, I know not what, (but as you shall see very wisely,) I changed my place. On his return I started to meet him; but it seemed as if the shadow of approaching danger fell upon my spirit, and checked my progress. In

17. Matthew 19:26.

18. Acts 7:34.

19. A corrupt tax collector, Zacchaeus climbed a tree to view Jesus and then publicly repented for his sins after receiving Jesus' love (Luke 19:1–10).

a very few minutes, closely on the heels of the old man, I distinctly saw *fourteen men*, with something like guns in their hands."

"Oh! the old wretch!" exclaimed Mrs. Listwell, "he had betrayed you, had he?"

"I think not," said Madison, "I cannot believe that the old man was to blame. He probably went into a store, asked for the articles for which I sent, and presented the bill I gave him; and it is so unusual for slaves in the country to have money, that fact, doubtless, excited suspicion, and gave rise to inquiry. I can easily believe that the truthfulness of the old man's character compelled him to disclose the facts; and thus were these blood-thirsty men put on my track. Of course I did not present myself; but hugged my hiding-place securely. If discovered and attacked, I resolved to sell my life as dearly as possible.

"After searching about the woods silently for a time, the whole company gathered around the old man; one charged him with lying, and called him an old villain; said he was a thief; charged him with stealing money; said if he did not instantly tell where he got it, they would take the shirt from his old back, and give him thirty-nine lashes.

"'I did *not* steal the money,' said the old man, 'it was given me, as I told you at the store; and if the man who gave it me is not here, it is not my fault.'

"'Hush! you lying old rascal; we'll make you smart for it. You shall not leave this spot until you have told where you got that money.'

"They now took hold of him, and began to strip him; while others went to get sticks with which to beat him. I felt, at the moment, like rushing out in the midst of them; but considering that the old man would be whipped the more for having aided a fugitive slave, and that, perhaps, in the *melée*[20] he might be killed outright, I disobeyed this impulse. They tied him to a tree, and began to whip

20. Fight (French).

him. My own flesh crept at every blow, and I seem to hear the old man's piteous cries even now. They laid thirty-nine lashes on his bare back, and were going to repeat that number, when one of the company besought his comrades to desist. 'You'll kill the d——d old scoundrel! You've already whipt a dollar's worth out of him, even if he stole it!' 'O yes,' said another, 'let him down. He'll never tell us another lie, I'll warrant ye!' With this, one of the company untied the old man, and bid him go about his business.

"The old man left, but the company remained as much as an hour, scouring the woods. Round and round they went, turning up the underbrush, and peering about like so many bloodhounds. Two or three times they came within six feet of where I lay. I tell you I held my stick with a firmer grasp than I did in coming up to your house to-night. I expected to level one of them at least. Fortunately, however, I eluded their pursuit, and they left me alone in the woods.

"My last dollar was now gone, and you may well suppose I felt the loss of it; but the thought of being once again free to pursue my journey, prevented that depression which a sense of destitution causes; so swinging my little bundle on my back, I caught a glimpse of the *Great Bear* (which ever points the way to my beloved star,) and I started again on my journey.[21] What I lost in money I made up at a hen-roost that same night, upon which I fortunately came."

"But you did'nt eat your food raw? How did you cook it?" said Mrs. Listwell.

"O no, Madam," said Madison, turning to his little bundle;—"I had the means of cooking." Here he took out of his bundle an old-fashioned tinder-box, and taking up a piece of a file, which he brought with him, he struck it with a heavy flint, and brought out at least a dozen sparks at once. "I have had this old box," said he,

21. The constellation Ursa Major, the Great Bear, contains the group of stars known as the Big Dipper. An imaginary line running from the cup of the Big Dipper points to the North Star.

"more than five years. It is the *only* property saved from the fire in the dismal swamp. It has done me good service. It has given me the means of broiling many a chicken!"

It seemed quite a relief to Mrs. Listwell to know that Madison had, at least, lived upon cooked food. Women have a perfect horror of eating uncooked food.

By this time thoughts of what was best to be done about getting Madison to Canada, began to trouble Mr. Listwell; for the laws of Ohio were very stringent against any one who should aid, or who were found aiding a slave to escape through that State.[22] A citizen, for the simple act of taking a fugitive slave in his carriage, had just been stripped of all his property, and thrown penniless upon the world. Notwithstanding this, Mr. Listwell was determined to see Madison safely on his way to Canada. "Give yourself no uneasiness," said he to Madison, "for if it cost my farm, I shall see you safely out of the States, and on your way to a land of liberty. Thank God that there is *such* a land so near us! You will spend to-morrow with us, and to-morrow night I will take you in my carriage to the Lake.[23] Once upon that, and you are safe."

"Thank you! thank you," said the fugitive; "I will commit myself to your care."

For the *first* time during *five* years, Madison enjoyed the luxury of resting his limbs on a comfortable bed, and inside a human habitation. Looking at the white sheets, he said to Mr. Listwell, "What, sir! you don't mean that I shall sleep in that bed?"

"Oh yes, oh yes."

After Mr. Listwell left the room, Madison said he really hesitated

22. Upwards of forty thousand runaway slaves escaped to Canadian freedom through Ohio, with the help of antislavery supporters who set up networks of over seven hundred safe houses. Although a "free state," a designation indicating only that its residents could not own slaves, Ohio overall was a dangerous host to the escapees. Bounty hunters crisscrossed the state, and Ohio law rewarded those who turned in or reported runaways.

23. Lake Erie; passage northward across Lake Erie would lead a fugitive slave to safety in Canada.

whether or not he should lie on the floor; for that was *far* more comfortable and inviting than any bed to which he had been used.

We pass over the thoughts and feelings, the hopes and fears, the plans and purposes, that revolved in the mind of Madison during the day that he was secreted at the house of Mr. Listwell. The reader will be content to know that nothing occurred to endanger his liberty, or to excite alarm. Many were the little attentions bestowed upon him in his quiet retreat and hiding-place. In the evening, Mr. Listwell, after treating Madison to a new suit of winter clothes, and replenishing his exhausted purse with five dollars, all in silver, brought out his two-horse wagon, well provided with buffaloes, and silently started off with him to Cleveland.[24] They arrived there without interruption, a few minutes before sunrise the next morning. Fortunately the steamer Admiral lay at the wharf, and was to start for Canada at nine o'clock.[25] Here the last anticipated danger was surmounted. It was feared that just at this point the hunters of men might be on the look-out, and, possibly, pounce upon their victim. Mr. Listwell saw the captain of the boat; cautiously sounded him on the matter of carrying liberty-loving passengers, before he introduced his precious charge. This done, Madison was conducted on board. With usual generosity this true subject of the emancipating queen[26] welcomed Madison, and assured him that he should be safely landed in Canada, free of charge. Madison now felt himself no more a piece of merchandise, but a passenger, and, like any other passenger, going about his business, carrying with him what belonged to him, and nothing which rightfully belonged to anybody else.

Wrapped in his new winter suit, snug and comfortable, a pocket

24. On the southern shore of Lake Erie.

25. Perhaps a reference to the steamer *Admiral*, which was operated on Lake Erie by the Canadian shipowner Donald Bethune (1802–1869). The ship broke down in 1851.

26. An allusion to Queen Victoria (1819–1901) and the antislavery actions taken by the British government during the early to mid-nineteenth century.

full of silver, safe from his pursuers, embarked for a free country, Madison gave every sign of sincere gratitude, and bade his kind benefactor farewell, with such a grip of the hand as bespoke a heart full of honest manliness, and a soul that knew how to appreciate kindness. It need scarcely be said that Mr. Listwell was deeply moved by the gratitude and friendship he had excited in a nature so noble as that of the fugitive. He went to his home that day with a joy and gratification which knew no bounds. He had done something "to deliver the spoiled out of the hands of the spoiler,"[27] he had given bread to the hungry, and clothes to the naked;[28] he had befriended a man to whom the laws of his country forbade all friendship, —and in proportion to the odds against his righteous deed, was the delightful satisfaction that gladdened his heart. On reaching home, he exclaimed, *"He is safe,—he is safe,—he is safe,"*—and the cup of his joy was shared by his excellent lady. The following letter was received from Madison a few days after:

"WINDSOR, CANADA WEST, DEC. 16, 1840.

My dear Friend,—for such you truly are:—

Madison is out of the woods at last; I nestle in the mane of the British lion, protected by his mighty paw from the talons and the beak of the American eagle.[29] I AM FREE, and breathe an atmosphere too pure for *slaves*, slave-hunters, or slave-holders. My heart is full. As many thanks to you, sir, and to your kind lady, as there are pebbles on the shores of Lake Erie; and may the blessing of God rest upon you both. You will never be forgotten by your profoundly grateful friend,

MADISON WASHINGTON."

27. God declares in Jeremiah 21:12: "Execute judgment in the morning, and deliver him that is spoiled out of the hand of the oppressor."

28. Ezekiel 18:7; Matthew 25:36.

29. By the eighteenth century, the lion had become a symbol of Great Britain; the eagle similarly came to serve as a symbol of U.S. collective identity.

Part III.

—His head was with his heart,
And that was far away!

Childe Harold.[30]

JUST upon the edge of the great road from Petersburg, Virginia, to Richmond,[31] and only about fifteen miles from the latter place, there stands a somewhat ancient and famous public tavern, quite notorious in its better days, as being the grand resort for most of the leading gamblers, horse-racers, cock-fighters, and slave-traders from all the country round about. This old rookery, the nucleus of all sorts of birds, mostly those of ill omen, has, like everything else peculiar to Virginia, lost much of its ancient consequence and splendor; yet it keeps up some appearance of gaiety and high life, and is still frequented, even by respectable travellers, who are unacquainted with its past history and present condition.[32] Its fine old portico looks well at a distance, and gives the building an air of grandeur. A nearer view, however, does little to sustain this pretension. The house is large, and its style imposing, but time and dissipation, unfailing in their results, have made ineffaceable marks upon it, and it must, in the common course of events, soon be numbered with the things that were. The gloomy mantle of ruin is, already, out-spread to envelop it, and its remains, even but now remind one of a human skull, after the flesh has mingled with the earth. Old hats and rags fill the places in the upper windows once occupied by large panes of glass, and the moulding boards along the roofing have dropped off from their places, leaving holes and crevices in the rented wall for bats

30. From canto 4, stanza 141, of Byron's *Childe Harold's Pilgrimage*.

31. The Manchester & Petersburg Turnpike, also known as the Richmond-Petersburg Turnpike.

32. Douglass draws on accounts of the Half Way House, one of the earliest taverns in Chesterfield County, Virginia.

and swallows to build their nests in. The platform of the portico, which fronts the highway is a rickety affair, its planks are loose, and in some places entirely gone, leaving effective man-traps in their stead for nocturnal ramblers. The wooden pillars, which once supported it, but which now hang as encumbrances, are all rotten, and tremble with the touch. A part of the stable, a fine old structure in its day, which has given comfortable shelter to hundreds of the noblest steeds of "the Old Dominion" at once, was blown down many years ago, and never has been, and probably never will be, rebuilt. The doors of the barn are in wretched condition; they will shut with a little human strength to help their worn out hinges, but not otherwise. The side of the great building seen from the road is much discolored in sundry places by slops poured from the upper windows, rendering it unsightly and offensive in other respects. Three or four great dogs, looking as dull and gloomy as the mansion itself, lie stretched out along the door-sills under the portico; and double the number of loafers, some of them completely rum-ripe, and others ripening, dispose themselves like so many sentinels about the front of the house. These latter understand the science of scraping acquaintance to perfection. They know every-body, and almost every-body knows them. Of course, as their title implies, they have no regular employment. They are (to use an expressive phrase) *hangers on*, or still better, they are what sailors would denominate *holders-on to the slack,*[33] *in every-body's mess, and in no-body's watch*. They are, however, as good as the newspaper for the events of the day, and they sell their knowledge almost as cheap. Money they seldom have; yet they always have capital the most reliable. They make their way with a succeeding traveller by intelligence gained from a preceding one. All the great names of Virginia they know by heart, and have seen their owners often. The history of the house is folded in their lips, and they rattle off stories in connection with it, equal

33. Nautical term for the part of a rope or sail that hangs loose.

to the guides at Dryburgh Abbey.[34] He must be a shrewd man, and well skilled in the art of evasion, who gets out of the hands of these fellows without being at the expense of a treat.

It was at this old tavern, while on a second visit to the State of Virginia in 1841, that Mr. Listwell, unacquainted with the fame of the place, turned aside, about sunset, to pass the night. Riding up to the house, he had scarcely dismounted, when one of the half dozen bar-room fraternity met and addressed him in a manner exceedingly bland and accommodating.

"Fine evening, sir."

"Very fine," said Mr. Listwell. "This is a tavern, I believe?"

"O yes, sir, yes; although you may think it looks a little the worse for wear, it was once as good a house as any in Virginy. I make no doubt if ye spend the night here, you'll think it a good house yet; for there aint a more accommodating man in the country than you'll find the landlord."

Listwell. "The most I want is a good bed for myself, and a full manger for my horse. If I get these, I shall be quite satisfied."

Loafer. "Well, I alloys like to hear a gentleman talk for his horse; and just becase the horse can't talk for itself. A man that don't care about his beast, and don't look arter it when he's travelling, aint much in my eye anyhow. Now, sir, I likes a horse, and I'll guarantee your horse will be taken good care on here. That old stable, for all you see it looks so shabby now, once sheltered the great *Eclipse*, when he run here agin *Batchelor* and *Jumping Jemmy*.[35] Them was fast horses, but he beat 'em both."

34. Scottish monastery founded in the twelfth century and the burial place of Sir Walter Scott (1771–1832). In 1846, Douglass, who had taken his surname from a character in one of Scott's romances, visited the region near the abbey during an abolitionist speaking tour.

35. Possibly refers to the great New York race horse known as "American Eclipse" (1814–1847), which defeated its southern rival, named Henry, in a famous race of 1822 held in Washington, D.C. Two other less famous horses, named Bachelor and Jumping Jimmy, raced mile heats in the District of Columbia region in the 1810s.

Listwell. "Indeed."

Loafer. "Well, I rather reckon you've travelled a right smart distance to-day, from the look of your horse?"

Listwell. "Forty miles only."

Loafer. "Well! I'll be darned if that aint a pretty good *only*. Mister, that beast of yours is a singed cat, I warrant you. I never see'd a creature like that that was'nt good on the road. You've come about forty miles, then?"

Listwell. "Yes, yes, and a pretty good pace at that."

Loafer. "You're somewhat in a hurry, then, I make no doubt? I reckon I could guess if I would, what you're going to Richmond for? It would'nt be much of a guess either; for it's rumored hereabouts, that there's to be the greatest sale of niggers at Richmond to-morrow that has taken place there in a long time; and I'll be bound you're a going there to have a hand in it."

Listwell. "Why, you must think, then, that there's money to be made at that business?"

Loafer. "Well, 'pon my honor, sir, I never made any that way myself; but it stands to reason that it's a money making business; for almost all other business in Virginia is dropped to engage in this. One thing is sartain, I never see'd a nigger-buyer yet that had'nt a plenty of money, and he was'nt as free with it as water. I has known one on 'em to treat as high as twenty times in a night; and, ginerally speaking, they's men of edication, and knows all about the government. The fact is, sir, I alloys like to hear 'em talk, bekase I alloys can learn something from them."

Listwell. "What may I call your name, sir?"

Loafer. "Well, now, they calls me Wilkes. I'm known all around by the gentlemen that comes here. They all knows old Wilkes."

Listwell. "Well, Wilkes, you seem to be acquainted here, and I see you have a strong liking for a horse. Be so good as to speak a kind word for mine to the hostler to-night, and you'll not lose anything by it."

Loafer. "Well, sir, I see you don't say much, but you've got an insight into things. It's alloys wise to get the good will of them that's acquainted about a tavern; for a man don't know when he goes into a house what may happen, or how much he may need a friend." Here the loafer gave Mr. Listwell a significant grin, which expressed a sort of triumphant pleasure at having, as he supposed, by his tact succeeded in placing so fine appearing a gentleman under obligations to him.

The pleasure, however, was mutual; for there was something so insinuating in the glance of this loquacious customer, that Mr. Listwell was very glad to get quit of him, and to do so more successfully, he ordered his supper to be brought to him in his private room, private to the eye, but not to the ear. This room was directly over the bar, and the plastering being off, nothing but pine boards and naked laths separated him from the disagreeable company below,—he could easily hear what was said in the bar-room, and was rather glad of the advantage it afforded, for, as you shall see, it furnished him important hints as to the manner and deportment he should assume during his stay at that tavern.

Mr. Listwell says he had got into his room but a few moments, when he heard the officious Wilkes below, in a tone of disappointment, exclaim, "Whar's that gentleman?" Wilkes was evidently expecting to meet with his friend at the bar-room, on his return, and had no doubt of his doing the handsome thing. "He has gone to his room," answered the landlord, "and has ordered his supper to be brought to him."

Here some one shouted out, "Who is he, Wilkes? Where's he going?"

"Well, now, I'll be hanged if I know; but I'm willing to make any man a bet of this old hat agin a five dollar bill, that that gent is as full of money as a dog is of fleas. He's going down to Richmond to buy niggers, I make no doubt. He's no fool, I warrant ye."

"Well, he acts d——d strange," said another, "anyhow. I likes to see a man, when he comes up to a tavern, to come straight into the bar-room, and show that he's a man among men. Nobody was going to bite him."

"Now, I don't blame him a bit for not coming in here. That man knows his business, and means to take care on his money," answered Wilkes.

"Wilkes, you're a fool. You only say that, becase you hope to get a few coppers out on him."

"You only measure my corn by your half-bushel, I won't say that you're only mad becase I got the chance of speaking to him first."

"O Wilkes! you're known here. You'll praise up any body that will give you a copper; besides, 'tis my opinion that that fellow who took his long slab-sides up stairs, for all the world just like a half-scared woman, afraid to look honest men in the face, is a *Northerner*, and as mean as dish-water."

"Now what will you bet of that," said Wilkes.

The speaker said, "I make no bets with you, 'kase you can get that fellow up stairs there to say anything."

"Well," said Wilkes, "I am willing to bet any man in the company that *that* gentleman is a *nigger*-buyer. He did'nt tell me so right down, but I reckon I knows enough about men to give a pretty clean guess as to what they are arter."

The dispute as to *who* Mr. Listwell was, what his business, where he was going, etc., was kept up with much animation for some time, and more than once threatened a serious disturbance of the peace. Wilkes had his friends as well as his opponents. After this sharp debate, the company amused themselves by drinking whiskey, and telling stories. The latter consisting of quarrels, fights, *rencontres*,[36] and duels, in which distinguished persons of that neighborhood, and frequenters of that house, had been actors. Some of these stories were frightful enough, and were told, too, with a relish which bespoke the pleasure of the parties with the horrid scenes they portrayed. It would not be proper here to give the reader any idea of the vulgarity and dark profanity which rolled, as "a sweet morsel,"[37]

36. Encounters (French).
37. Job 20:12.

under these corrupt tongues. A more brutal set of creatures, perhaps, never congregated.

Disgusted, and a little alarmed withal, Mr. Listwell, who was not accustomed to such entertainment, at length retired, but not to sleep. He was *too* much wrought upon by what he had heard to rest quietly, and what snatches of sleep he got, were interrupted by dreams which were anything than pleasant. At eleven o'clock, there seemed to be several hundreds of persons crowding into the house. A loud and confused clamour, cursing and cracking of whips, and the noise of chains startled him from his bed; for a moment he would have given the half of his farm in Ohio to have been at home. This uproar was kept up with undulating course, till near morning. There was loud laughing,—loud singing,—loud cursing,—and yet there seemed to be weeping and mourning in the midst of all. Mr. Listwell said he had heard enough during the forepart of the night to convince him that a buyer of men and women stood the best chance of being respected. And he, therefore, thought it best to say nothing which might undo the favorable opinion that had been formed of him in the bar-room by at least one of the fraternity that swarmed about it. While he would not avow himself a purchaser of slaves, he deemed it not prudent to disavow it. He felt that he might, properly, refuse to cast such a pearl before parties which, to him, were worse than swine.[38] To reveal himself, and to impart a knowledge of his real character and sentiments would, to say the least, be imparting intelligence with the certainty of seeing it and himself both abused. Mr. Listwell confesses, that this reasoning did not altogether satisfy his conscience, for, hating slavery as he did, and regarding it to be the immediate duty of every man to cry out against it, "without compromise and without concealment,"[39] it was

38. In Matthew 7:6, Jesus advises his disciples: "Give not that which is holy unto the dogs, neither cast ye your pearls before swine, lest they trample them under their feet."

39. The motto of the New York City–based abolitionist newspaper the *National Anti-Slavery Standard*.

hard for him to admit to himself the possibility of circumstances wherein a man might, properly, hold his tongue on the subject. Having as little of the spirit of a martyr as Erasmus,[40] he concluded, like the latter, that it was wiser to trust the mercy of God for his soul, than the humanity of slave-traders for his body. Bodily fear, not conscientious scruples, prevailed.

In this spirit he rose early in the morning, manifesting no surprise at what he had heard during the night. His quondam[41] friend was soon at his elbow, boring him with all sorts of questions. All, however, directed to find out his character, business, residence, purposes, and destination. With the most perfect appearance of good nature and carelessness, Mr. Listwell evaded these meddlesome inquiries, and turned conversation to general topics, leaving himself and all that specially pertained to him, out of discussion. Disengaging himself from their troublesome companionship, he made his way towards an old bowling-alley, which was connected with the house, and which, like all the rest, was in very bad repair.

On reaching the alley Mr. Listwell saw, for the first time in his life, a slave-gang on their way to market. A sad sight truly. Here were one hundred and thirty human beings,—children of a common Creator—guilty of no crime—men and women, with hearts, minds, and deathless spirits, chained and fettered, and bound for the market, in a christian country,—in a country boasting of its liberty, independence, and high civilization! Humanity converted into merchandise, and linked in iron bands, with no regard to decency or humanity! All sizes, ages, and sexes, mothers, fathers, daughters, brothers, sisters,—all huddled together, on their way to market to be sold and separated from home, and from each other *forever*. And all to fill the pockets of men too lazy to work for an honest living,

40. Most likely an allusion to the Dutch priest and biblical scholar Desiderius Erasmus (1466–1536), who cautiously tried to avoid antagonizing either Catholic or Protestant authorities in the heated theological controversies of the early years of the Reformation.

41. Former (Latin).

and who gain their fortune by plundering the helpless, and trafficking in the souls and sinews of men. As he gazed upon this revolting and heart-rending scene, our informant said he almost doubted the existence of a God of justice! And he stood wondering that the earth did not open and swallow up such wickedness.

In the midst of these reflections, and while running his eye up and down the fettered ranks, he met the glance of one whose face he thought he had seen before. To be resolved, he moved towards the spot. It was MADISON WASHINGTON! Here was a scene for the pencil! Had Mr. Listwell been confronted by one risen from the dead, he could not have been more appalled. He was completely stunned. A thunderbolt could not have struck him more dumb. He stood, for a few moments, as motionless as one petrified; collecting himself, he at length exclaimed, "*Madison! is that you*?"

The noble fugitive, but little less astonished than himself, answered cheerily, "O yes, sir, they've got me again."

Thoughtless of consequences for the moment, Mr. Listwell ran up to his old friend, placing his hands upon his shoulders, and looked him in the face! Speechless they stood gazing at each other as if to be doubly resolved that there was no mistake about the matter, till Madison motioned his friend away, intimating a fear lest the keepers should find him there, and suspect him of tampering with the slaves.

"They will soon be out to look after us. You can come when they go to breakfast, and I will tell you all."

Pleased with this arrangement, Mr. Listwell passed out of the alley; but only just in time to save himself, for, while near the door, he observed three men making their way to the alley. The thought occurred to him to await their arrival, as the best means of diverting the ever ready suspicions of the guilty.

While the scene between Mr. Listwell and his friend Madison was going on, the other slaves stood as mute spectators,—at a loss to know what all this could mean. As he left, he heard the man chained to Madison ask, "Who is that gentleman?"

"He is a friend of mine. I cannot tell you now. Suffice it to say he is a friend. You shall hear more of him before long, but mark me! whatever shall pass between that gentleman and me, in your hearing, I pray you will say nothing about it. We are all chained here together,—ours is a common lot; and that gentleman is not less *your* friend than *mine*." At these words, all mysterious as they were, the unhappy company gave signs of satisfaction and hope. It seems that Madison, by that mesmeric power which is the invariable accompaniment of genius, had already won the confidence of the gang, and was a sort of general-in-chief among them.

By this time the keepers arrived. A horrid trio, well fitted for their demoniacal work. Their uncombed hair came down over foreheads "*villainously low*,"[42] and with eyes, mouths, and noses to match. "Hallo! hallo!" they growled out as they entered. "Are you all there?"

"All here," said Madison.

"Well, well, that's right! your journey will soon be over. You'll be in Richmond by eleven to-day, and then you'll have an easy time on it."

"I say, gal, what in the devil are you crying about?" said one of them. "I'll give you something to cry about, if you don't mind." This was said to a girl, apparently not more than twelve years old, who had been weeping bitterly. She had, probably, left behind her a loving mother, affectionate sisters, brothers, and friends, and her tears were but the natural expression of her sorrow, and the only solace. But the dealers in human flesh have *no* respect for such sorrow. They look upon it as a protest against their cruel injustice, and they are prompt to punish it.

This is a puzzle not easily solved. *How* came he here? what can I do for him? may I not even now be in some way compromised in this affair? were thoughts that troubled Mr. Listwell, and made him eager for the promised opportunity of speaking to Madison.

42. The islander Caliban uses the phrase "foreheads villainous low" in Shakespeare's *The Tempest*, 4.1.248.

The bell now sounded for breakfast, and keepers and drivers, with pistols and bowie-knives gleaming from their belts, hurried in, as if to get the best places. Taking the chance now afforded, Mr. Listwell hastened back to the bowling-alley. Reaching Madison, he said, "Now *do* tell me all about the matter. Do you know me?"

"Oh, yes," said Madison, "I know you well, and shall never forget you nor that cold and dreary night you gave me shelter. I must be short," he continued, "for they'll soon be out again. This, then, is the story in brief. On reaching Canada, and getting over the excitement of making my escape, sir, my thoughts turned to my poor wife, who had well deserved my love by her virtuous fidelity and undying affection for me. I could not bear the thought of leaving her in the cruel jaws of slavery, without making an effort to rescue her. First, I tried to get money to buy her; but oh! the process was *too slow*. I despaired of accomplishing it. She was in all my thoughts by day, and my dreams by night. At times I could almost hear her voice, saying, 'O Madison! Madison! will you then leave me here? can you leave me here to die? No! no! you will come! you will come!' I was wretched. I lost my appetite. I could neither work, eat, nor sleep, till I resolved to hazard my own liberty, to gain that of my wife! But I must be short. Six weeks ago I reached my old master's place. I laid about the neighborhood nearly a week, watching my chance, and, finally, I ventured upon the desperate attempt to reach my poor wife's room by means of a ladder. I reached the window, but the noise in raising it frightened my wife, and she screamed and fainted. I took her in my arms, and was descending the ladder, when the dogs began to bark furiously, and before I could get to the woods the white folks were roused. The cool night air soon restored my wife, and she readily recognized me. We made the best of our way to the woods, but it was now *too* late,—the dogs were after us as though they would have torn us to pieces. It was all over with me now! My old master and his two sons ran out with loaded rifles, and before we were out of gunshot, our ears were assailed with '*Stop*! *stop*! *or be shot down*.' Nevertheless we ran on. Seeing that we gave no heed to their calls, they fired, and my poor wife fell by my side dead, while I received but a slight flesh wound. I now became desperate, and stood my ground, and awaited their attack over her dead body. They rushed upon me, with their rifles in hand. I parried their blows, and fought them 'till I was knocked down and overpowered."

"Oh! it was madness to have returned," said Mr. Listwell.

"Sir, I could not be free with the galling thought that my poor wife was still a slave. With her in slavery, my body, not my spirit, was free. I was taken to the house,—chained to a ring-bolt,—my wounds dressed. I was kept there three days. All the slaves, for miles around, were brought to see me. Many slave-holders came with their slaves, using me as proof of the completeness of their power, and of the impossibility of slaves getting away. I was taunted, jeered at, and berated by them, in a manner that pierced me to the soul. Thank God, I was able to smother my rage, and to bear it all with seeming composure. After my wounds were nearly healed, I was taken to a tree and stripped, and I received sixty lashes on my naked back. A few days after, I was sold to a slave-trader, and placed in this gang for the New Orleans market."[43]

"Do you think your master would sell you to me?"

"O no, sir! I was sold on condition of my being taken South. Their motive is revenge."

"Then, then," said Mr. Listwell, "I fear I can do nothing for you. Put your trust in God, and bear your sad lot with the manly fortitude which becomes a man. I shall see you at Richmond, but don't recognize me." Saying this, Mr. Listwell handed Madison ten dollars; said a few words to the other slaves; received their hearty "God bless you," and made his way to the house.

Fearful of exciting suspicion by too long delay, our friend went to the breakfast table, with the air of one who half reproved the greediness of those who rushed in at the sound of the bell. A cup

43. As a principal port, New Orleans played a major role during the antebellum era in the Atlantic slave trade.

of coffee was all that he could manage. His feelings were too bitter and excited, and his heart was too full with the fate of poor Madison (whom he loved as well as admired) to relish his breakfast; and although he sat long after the company had left the table, he really did little more than change the position of his knife and fork. The strangeness of meeting again one whom he had met on two several occasions before, under extraordinary circumstances, was well calculated to suggest the idea that a supernatural power, a wakeful providence, or an inexorable fate, had linked their destiny together; and that no efforts of his could disentangle him from the mysterious web of circumstances which enfolded him.

On leaving the table, Mr. Listwell nerved himself up and walked firmly into the bar-room. He was at once greeted again by that talkative chatter-box, Mr. Wilkes.

"Them's a likely set of niggers in the alley there," said Wilkes.

"Yes, they're fine looking fellows, one of them I should like to purchase, and for him I would be willing to give a handsome sum."

Turning to one of his comrades, and with a grin of victory, Wilkes said, "Aha, Bill, did you hear that? I told you I know'd that gentleman wanted to buy niggers, and would bid as high as any purchaser in the market."

"Come, come," said Listwell, "don't be too loud in your praise, you are old enough to know that prices rise when purchasers are plenty."

"That's a fact," said Wilkes, "I see you knows the ropes—and there's not a man in old Virginy whom I'd rather help to make a good bargain than you, sir."

Mr. Listwell here threw a dollar at Wilkes, (which the latter caught with a dexterous hand,) saying, "Take that for your kind good will."

Wilkes held up the dollar to his right eye, with a grin of victory, and turned to the morose grumbler in the corner who had questioned the liberality of a man of whom he knew nothing.

Mr. Listwell now stood as well with the company as any other occupant of the bar-room.

We pass over the hurry and bustle, the brutal vociferations of the slave-drivers in getting their unhappy gang in motion for Richmond; and we need not narrate every application of the lash to those who faltered in the journey. Mr. Listwell followed the train at a long distance, with a sad heart; and on reaching Richmond, left his horse at a hotel, and made his way to the wharf in the direction of which he saw the slave-coffle driven. He was just in time to see the whole company embark for New Orleans. The thought struck him that, while mixing with the multitude, he might do his friend Madison one last service, and he stept into a hardware store and purchased three strong *files*. These he took with him, and standing near the small boat, which lay in waiting to bear the company by parcels to the side of the brig that lay in the stream, he managed, as Madison passed him, to slip the files into his pocket, and at once darted back among the crowd.

All the company now on board, the imperious voice of the captain sounded, and instantly a dozen hardy seamen were in the rigging, hurrying aloft to unfurl the broad canvas of our Baltimore built American Slaver.[44] The sailors hung about the ropes, like so many black cats, now in the round-tops, now in the cross-trees, now on the yard-arms; all was bluster and activity. Soon the broad fore topsail, the royal and top gallant sail were spread to the breeze. Round went the heavy windlass, clank, clank went the fall-bit,—the anchors weighed,—jibs, mainsails, and topsails hauled to the wind, and the long, low, black slaver, with her cargo of human flesh, careened and moved forward to the sea.[45]

Mr. Listwell stood on the shore, and watched the slaver till the last speck of her upper sails faded from sight, and announced the

44. Since colonial times, Baltimore had been a major shipbuilding city, and by the 1840s its shipyards were producing the majority of the vessels used in the slave trade. In the 1830s, while still a slave, Douglass himself worked in Baltimore's Fells Point shipyards.

45. Douglass, who worked in shipyards in Baltimore and New Bedford, accurately employs nautical terminology to describe the sails on a large square-rigged sailing vessel.

limit of human vision. "Farewell! farewell! brave and true man! God grant that brighter skies may smile upon your future than have yet looked down upon your thorny pathway."

Saying this to himself, our friend lost no time in completing his business, and in making his way homewards, gladly shaking off from his feet the dust of Old Virginia.

Part IV.

Oh, where's the slave so lowly
Condemn'd to chains unholy,
Who could he burst
His bonds at first
Would pine beneath them slowly?

Moore.[46]

———Know ye not
Who would be free, *themselves* must strike the blow.

Childe Harold.[47]

WHAT a world of inconsistency, as well as of wickedness, is suggested by the smooth and gliding phrase, AMERICAN SLAVE TRADE; and how strange and perverse is that moral sentiment which loathes, execrates, and brands as piracy and as deserving of death the carrying away into captivity men, women, and children from the *African coast*; but which is neither shocked nor disturbed by a similar traffic, carried on with the same motives and purposes, and characterized by even *more* odious peculiarities on the coast of our MODEL REPUBLIC. We execrate and hang the wretch guilty of this

46. From "Where Is the Slave" (1848), by the Irish poet Thomas Moore (1779–1852).

47. From canto 2, stanza 76, of Byron's *Childe Harold's Pilgrimage*.

crime on the coast of Guinea,[48] while we respect and applaud the guilty participators in this murderous business on the enlightened shores of the Chesapeake. The inconsistency is so flagrant and glaring, that it would seem to cast a doubt on the doctrine of the innate moral sense of mankind.

Just two months after the sailing of the Virginia slave brig, which the reader has seen move off to sea so proudly with her human cargo for the New Orleans market, there chanced to meet, in the Marine Coffee-house at Richmond, a company of *ocean birds*,[49] when the following conversation, which throws some light on the subsequent history, not only of Madison Washington, but of the hundred and thirty human beings with whom we last saw him chained.

"I say, shipmate, you had rather rough weather on your late passage to Orleans?" said Jack Williams, a regular old salt, tauntingly, to a trim, compact, manly looking person, who proved to be the first mate of the slave brig in question.[50]

"Foul play, as well as foul weather," replied the firmly knit personage, evidently but little inclined to enter upon a subject which terminated so ingloriously to the captain and officers of the American slaver.

"Well, betwixt you and me," said Williams, "that whole affair on board of the *Creole* was miserably and disgracefully managed. Those black rascals got the upper hand of ye altogether; and, in my opinion, the whole disaster was the result of ignorance of the real character of *darkies* in general.[51] With half a dozen *resolute* white men, (I say it not boastingly,) I could have had the rascals in

48. Name generally used in the nineteenth century to refer to the entire west coast of Africa.

49. Sailors.

50. The actual first mate of the *Creole* was Zephaniah Gifford, who was wounded in the revolt but survived. Williams seems drawn in part on the slave trader and overseer William H. Merritt; see "Protest of the Officers and Crew of the American Brig Creole" and Deposition of William H. Merritt in part 2 of this volume.

51. Derogatory term for a person of African ancestry. It was first used in the eighteenth century to refer to the alleged ability of slaves to go undetected in the dark of night.

irons in ten minutes, not because I'm so strong, but I know how to manage 'em. With my back against the *caboose*,[52] I could, myself, have flogged a dozen of them; and had I been on board, by every monster of the deep, every black devil of 'em all would have had his neck stretched from the yard-arm. Ye made a mistake in yer manner of fighting 'em. All that is needed in dealing with a set of rebellious *darkies*, is to show that yer not afraid of 'em. For my own part, I would not honor a dozen niggers by pointing a gun at one on 'em,—a good stout whip, or a stiff rope's end, is better than all the guns at Old Point[53] to quell a *nigger* insurrection. Why, sir, to take a gun to a *nigger* is the best way you can select to tell him you are afraid of him, and the best way of inviting his attack."

This speech made quite a sensation among the company, and a part of them indicated solicitude for the answer which might be made to it. Our first mate replied, "Mr. Williams, all that you've now said sounds very well *here* on shore, where, perhaps, you have studied negro character. I do not profess to understand the subject as well as yourself; but it strikes me, you apply the same rule in dissimilar cases. It is quite easy to talk of flogging niggers here on land, where you have the sympathy of the community, and the whole physical force of the government, State and national, at your command; and where, if a negro shall lift his hand against a white man, the whole community, with one accord, are ready to unite in shooting him down. I say, in such circumstances, it's easy to talk of flogging negroes and of negro cowardice; but, sir, I deny that the negro is, naturally, a coward, or that your theory of managing slaves will stand the test of *salt* water. It may do very well for an overseer, a contemptible hireling, to take advantage of fears already in existence, and which his presence has no power to inspire; to swagger about whip in hand, and discourse on the timidity and cowardice of negroes; for they have a smooth sea and a fair wind. It is one

52. Nautical term for a ship's galley.

53. Probably refers to Fortress Monroe, located at Old Point Comfort on the Virginia shore of Chesapeake Bay.

thing to manage a company of slaves on a Virginia plantation, and quite another thing to quell an insurrection on the lonely billows of the Atlantic, where every breeze speaks of courage and liberty. For the negro to act cowardly on shore, may be to act wisely; and I've some doubts whether *you*, Mr. Williams, would find it very convenient were you a slave in Algiers, to raise your hand against the bayonets of a whole government."

"By George, shipmate," said Williams, "you're coming rather *too* near. Either I've fallen very low in your estimation, or your notions of negro courage have got up a button-hole too high. Now I more than ever wish I'd been on board of that luckless craft. I'd have given ye practical evidence of the truth of my theory. I don't doubt there's some difference in being at sea. But a nigger's a nigger, on sea or land; and is a coward, find him where you will; a drop of blood from one on 'em will skeer a hundred. A knock on the nose, or a kick on the shin, will tame the wildest *'darkey'* you can fetch me. I say again, and will stand by it, I could, with half a dozen good men, put the whole nineteen on 'em in irons, and have carried them safe to New Orleans too.[54] Mind, I don't blame you, but I do say, and every gentleman here will bear me out in it, that the fault was somewhere, or them niggers would never have got off as they have done. For my part I feel ashamed to have the idea go abroad, that a ship load of slaves can't be safely taken from Richmond to New Orleans. I should like, merely to redeem the character of Virginia sailors, to take charge of a ship load on 'em to-morrow."

Williams went on in this strain, occasionally casting an imploring glance at the company for applause for his wit, and sympathy for his contempt of negro courage. He had, evidently, however, waked up the wrong passenger; for besides being in the right, his opponent carried that in his eye which marked him a man not to be trifled with.

"Well, sir," said the sturdy mate, "you can select your own method for distinguishing yourself;—the path of ambition in this direction

54. Here Douglass followed the historical record, which indicated that nineteen slaves were involved in the uprising.

is quite open to you in Virginia, and I've no doubt that you will be highly appreciated and compensated for all your valiant achievements in that line; but for myself, while I do not profess to be a giant, I have resolved never to set my foot on the deck of a slave ship, either as officer, or common sailor again; I have got enough of it."

"Indeed! indeed!" exclaimed Williams, derisively.

"Yes, *indeed*," echoed the mate; "but don't misunderstand me. It is not the high value that I set upon my life that makes me say what I have said; yet I'm resolved never to endanger my life again in a cause which my conscience does not approve. I dare say *here* what many men *feel*, but *dare not speak*, that this whole slave-trading business is a disgrace and scandal to Old Virginia."

"Hold! hold on! shipmate," said Williams, "I hardly thought you'd have shown your colors so soon,—I'll be hanged if you're not as good an abolitionist as Garrison himself."[55]

The mate now rose from his chair, manifesting some excitement. "What do you mean, sir," said he, in a commanding tone. "*That man does not live who shall offer me an insult with impunity*."

The effect of these words was marked; and the company clustered around. Williams, in an apologetic tone, said, "Shipmate! keep your temper. I mean't no insult. We all know that Tom Grant is no coward, and what I said about your being an abolitionist was simply this: you *might* have put down them black mutineers and murderers, but your conscience held you back."

"In that, too," said Grant, "you were mistaken. I did all that any man with equal strength and presence of mind could have done. The fact is, Mr. Williams, you underrate the courage as well as the

55. The Massachusetts reformer William Lloyd Garrison (1805–79) was so closely identified with the abolitionist movement in the United States that his name became almost synonymous with the cause. He founded and edited the *Liberator* (1831–65), arguably the most influential abolitionist journal. He helped recruit Douglass into the lecturing ranks of the American Anti-Slavery Society, and in 1845 he published Douglass's *Narrative*. The two reformers had a falling-out in the late 1840s, precipitated by Douglass's decision in 1847 to found and edit his own antislavery newspaper.

skill of these negroes, and further, you do not seem to have been correctly informed about the case in hand at all."

"All I know about it is," said Williams, "that on the ninth day after you left Richmond, a dozen or two of the niggers ye had on board, came on deck and took the ship from you;—had her steered into a British port, where, by the by, every wooly head of them went ashore and was free. Now I take this to be a discreditable piece of business, and one demanding explanation."

"There are a great many discreditable things in the world," said Grant. "For a ship to go down under a calm sky is, upon the first flush of it, disgraceful either to sailors or caulkers.[56] But when we learn, that by some mysterious disturbance in nature, the waters parted beneath, and swallowed the ship up, we lose our indignation and disgust in lamentation of the disaster, and in awe of the Power which controls the elements."

"Very true, very true," said Williams, "I should be very glad to have an explanation which would relieve the affair of its present discreditable features. I have desired to see you ever since you got home, and to learn from you a full statement of the facts in the case. To me the whole thing seems unaccountable. I cannot see how a dozen or two of ignorant negroes, not one of whom had ever been to sea before, and all of them were closely ironed between decks, should be able to get their fetters off, rush out of the hatchway in open daylight, kill two white men, the one the captain and the other their master, and then carry the ship into a British port, where every '*darkey*' of them was set free. There must have been great carelessness, or cowardice somewhere!"

The company which had listened in silence during most of this discussion, now became much excited. One said, I agree with Williams; and several said the thing looks black enough. After the temporary tumultuous exclamations had subsided,—

"I see," said Grant, "how you regard this case, and how difficult it

56. Skilled workers who made wooden ships watertight by packing seams with waterproof materials. Douglass trained as a caulker while a teenage slave in Baltimore.

will be for me to render our ship's company blameless in your eyes. Nevertheless, I will state the facts precisely as they came under my own observation. Mr. Williams speaks of 'ignorant negroes,' and, as a general rule, they are ignorant; but had he been on board the *Creole* as I was, he would have seen cause to admit that there are exceptions to this general rule. The leader of the mutiny in question was just as shrewd a fellow as ever I met in my life, and was as well fitted to lead in a dangerous enterprise as any one white man in ten thousand. The name of this man, strange to say, (ominous of greatness,) was MADISON WASHINGTON. In the short time he had been on board, he had secured the confidence of every officer. The negroes fairly worshipped him. His manner and bearing were such, that no one could suspect him of a murderous purpose. The only feeling with which we regarded him was, that he was a powerful, good-disposed negro. He seldom spake to any one, and when he did speak, it was with the utmost propriety. His words were well chosen, and his pronunciation equal to that of any schoolmaster. It was a mystery to us *where* he got his knowledge of language; but as little was said to him, none of us knew the extent of his intelligence and ability till it was too late. It seems he brought three files with him on board, and must have gone to work upon his fetters the first night out; and he must have worked well at that; for on the day of the rising, he got the irons *off eighteen* besides himself.

"The attack began just about twilight in the evening. Apprehending a squall, I had commanded the second mate to order all hands on deck, to take in sail. A few minutes before this I had seen Madison's head above the hatchway, looking out upon the white-capped waves at the leeward. I think I never saw him look more good-natured. I stood just about midship, on the larboard side. The captain was pacing the quarter-deck on the starboard side, in company with Mr. Jameson, the owner of most of the slaves on board.[57] Both were armed. I had just told the men to lay aloft, and was looking to

57. The actual owner of most of the slaves aboard the *Creole* was the Richmond slave trader Thomas McCargo.

see my orders obeyed, when I heard the discharge of a pistol on the starboard side; and turning suddenly around, the very deck seemed covered with fiends from the pit. The nineteen negroes were all on deck, with their broken fetters in their hands, rushing in all directions. I put my hand quickly in my pocket to draw out my jack-knife; but before I could draw it, I was knocked senseless to the deck. When I came to myself, (which I did in a few minutes, I suppose, for it was yet quite light,) there was not a white man on deck. The sailors were all aloft in the rigging, and dared not come down. Captain Clarke and Mr. Jameson lay stretched on the quarter-deck,—both dying,—while Madison himself stood at the helm unhurt.[58]

"I was completely weakened by the loss of blood, and had not recovered from the stunning blow which felled me to the deck; but it was a little too much for me, even in my prostrate condition, to see our good brig commanded by a *black murderer*. So I called out to the men to come down and take the ship, or die in the attempt. Suiting the action to the word, I started aft. You murderous villain, said I, to the imp at the helm, and rushed upon him to deal him a blow, when he pushed me back with his strong, black arm, as though I had been a boy of twelve. I looked around for the men. They were still in the rigging. Not one had come down. I started towards Madison again. The rascal now told me to stand back. 'Sir,' said he, 'your life is in my hands. I could have killed you a dozen times over during this last half hour, and could kill you now. You call me a *black murderer*. I am not a murderer. God is my witness that LIBERTY, not *malice*, is the motive for this night's work. I have done no more to those dead men yonder, than they would have done to me in like circumstances. We have struck for our freedom, and if a true man's heart be in you, you will honor us for the deed. We have done that which you applaud your fathers for doing, and if we are murderers, *so were they*.'

58. The actual captain of the *Creole* was Robert Ensor, who was badly wounded by the slave rebels. The only person to die during the rebellion was John R. Hewell, who was McCargo's hired agent on board ship.

"I felt little disposition to reply to this impudent speech. By heaven, it disarmed me. The fellow loomed up before me. I forgot his blackness in the dignity of his manner, and the eloquence of his speech. It seemed as if the souls of both the great dead (whose names he bore) had entered him. To the sailors in the rigging he said: 'Men! the battle is over,—your captain is dead. I have complete command of this vessel. All resistance to my authority will be in vain. My men have won their liberty, with no other weapons but their own BROKEN FETTERS. We are nineteen in number. We do not thirst for your blood, we demand only our rightful freedom. Do not flatter yourselves that I am ignorant of chart or compass. I know both. We are now only about sixty miles from Nassau.[59] Come down, and do your duty. Land us in Nassau, and not a hair of your heads shall be hurt.'

"I shouted, *Stay where you are, men*,—when a sturdy black fellow ran at me with a handspike, and would have split my head open, but for the interference of Madison, who darted between me and the blow. 'I know what you are up to,' said the latter to me. 'You want to navigate this brig into a slave port, where you would have us all hanged; but you'll miss it; before this brig shall touch a slave-cursed shore while I am on board, I will myself put a match to the magazine, and blow her, and be blown with her, into a thousand fragments. Now I have saved your life twice within these last twenty minutes,—for, when you lay helpless on deck, my men were about to kill you. I held them in check. And if you now (seeing I am your friend and not your enemy) persist in your resistance to my authority, I give you fair warning YOU SHALL DIE.'

"Saying this to me, he cast a glance into the rigging where the terror-stricken sailors were clinging, like so many frightened monkeys, and commanded them to come down, in a tone from which there was no appeal; for four men stood by with muskets in hand, ready at the word of command to shoot them down.

59. Capital of the Bahamas, which was under British control until 1973.

"I now became satisfied that resistance was out of the question; that my best policy was to put the brig into Nassau, and secure the assistance of the American consul at that port. I felt sure that the authorities would enable us to secure the murderers, and bring them to trial.

"By this time the apprehended squall had burst upon us. The wind howled furiously,—the ocean was white with foam, which, on account of the darkness, we could see only by the quick flashes of lightning that darted occasionally from the angry sky. All was alarm and confusion. Hideous cries came up from the slave women. Above the roaring billows a succession of heavy thunder rolled along, swelling the terrific din. Owing to the great darkness, and a sudden shift of the wind, we found ourselves in the trough of the sea. When shipping a heavy sea over the starboard bow, the bodies of the captain and Mr. Jameson were washed overboard. For awhile we had dearer interests to look after than slave property. A more savage thunder-gust never swept the ocean. Our brig rolled and creaked as if every bolt would be started, and every thread of oakum would be pressed out of the seams. To the pumps! to the pumps! I cried, but not a sailor would quit his grasp. Fortunately this squall soon passed over, or we must have been food for sharks.

"During all the storm, Madison stood firmly at the helm,—his keen eye fixed upon the binnacle.[60] He was not indifferent to the dreadful hurricane; yet he met it with the equanimity of an old sailor. He was silent but not agitated. The first words he uttered after the storm had slightly subsided, were characteristic of the man. 'Mr. Mate, you cannot write the bloody laws of slavery on those restless billows. The ocean, if not the land, is free.' I confess, gentlemen, I felt myself in the presence of a superior man; one who, had he been a white man, I would have followed willingly and gladly in any honorable enterprise. Our difference of color was the only ground for difference of action. It was not that his principles were wrong in

60. A case or stand on a ship's deck to house a compass and possibly other nautical instruments.

the abstract; for they are the principles of 1776.[61] But I could not bring myself to recognize their application to one whom I deemed my inferior.

"But to my story. What happened now is soon told. Two hours after the frightful tempest had spent itself, we were plump at the wharf in Nassau. I sent two of our men immediately to our consul with a statement of facts, requesting his interference in our behalf. What he did, or whither he did anything, I don't know; but, by order of the authorities, a company of *black* soldiers came on board, for the purpose, as they said, of protecting the property.[62] These impudent rascals, when I called on them to assist me in keeping the slaves on board, sheltered themselves adroitly under their instructions only to protect property,—and said they did not recognize *persons* as *property*. I told them that by the laws of Virginia and the laws of the United States, the slaves on board were as much property as the barrels of flour in the hold. At this the stupid blockheads showed their *ivory*, rolled up their white eyes in horror, as if the idea of putting men on a footing with merchandise were revolting to their humanity. When these instructions were understood among the negroes, it was impossible for us to keep them on board. They deliberately gathered up their baggage before our eyes, and, against our remonstrances, poured through the gangway,—formed themselves into a procession on the wharf,—bid farewell to all on board, and, uttering the wildest shouts of exultation, they marched, amidst the deafening cheers of a multitude of sympathizing spectators, under the triumphant leadership of their heroic chief and deliverer, MADISON WASHINGTON."

61. Radical political abolitionists such as Douglass and Gerrit Smith believed that the U.S. Constitution had to be interpreted in light of the egalitarian and implicitly antislavery principles of the Declaration of Independence.

62. In historical fact, Governor Francis Cockburn of the Bahamas sent a detachment of twenty black soldiers under a white officer to take control of the *Creole* soon after it arrived in Nassau harbor on 9 November 1841. By 16 April 1842, all the blacks on the *Creole* had been freed by British authorities.

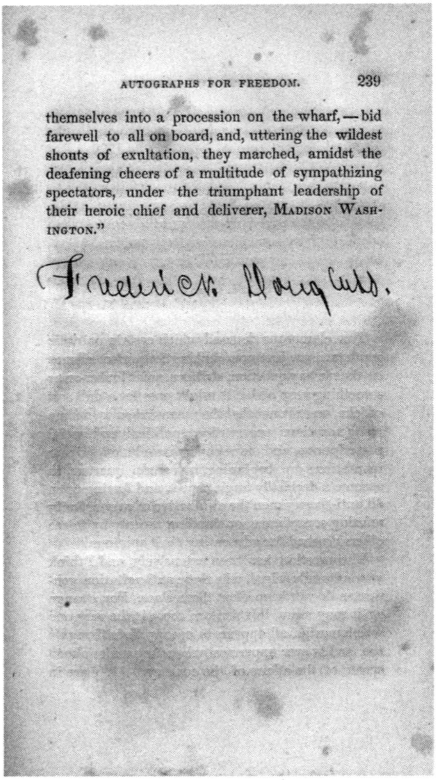

AUTOGRAPHS FOR FREEDOM. 239

themselves into a procession on the wharf, — bid farewell to all on board, and, uttering the wildest shouts of exultation, they marched, amidst the deafening cheers of a multitude of sympathizing spectators, under the triumphant leadership of their heroic chief and deliverer, MADISON WASHINGTON."

Frederick Douglass.

3. *The Heroic Slave*, in *Autographs for Freedom* (1853), final page of the novella with Douglass's signature. All the pieces in *Autographs* were signed by the authors. Collection of John Stauffer.

A Note on the Text

The goal of the Yale University Press edition of Frederick Douglass's *The Heroic Slave* is to provide readers for the first time with a definitive critical text of this historically important work. While a few other editions of Douglass's novella have been reprinted in modern times, none of their texts of *The Heroic Slave* have been guided by the principles of textual editing. Other editions have reproduced an electronic facsimile or have reset the text of one of the work's three earliest printings. Such an "uncritical" preparation of a text overlooks the corruptions of the author's intentions by contemporary copy editors, compositors, or bookbinders. It also ignores any "authoritative" corrections or revisions that Douglass might have instructed for later printings of his work. Instead, our goal for this edition is to recover and reproduce a text that accurately reflects Douglass's intentions for *The Heroic Slave*.

The first step in our work on *The Heroic Slave* was to discover as much as possible about its publication history. Our research uncovered three potentially authoritative texts for the novella: the first edition of *Autographs for Freedom*, published in late December 1852 (copyrighted 1853) by the Boston firm of John P. Jewett; the

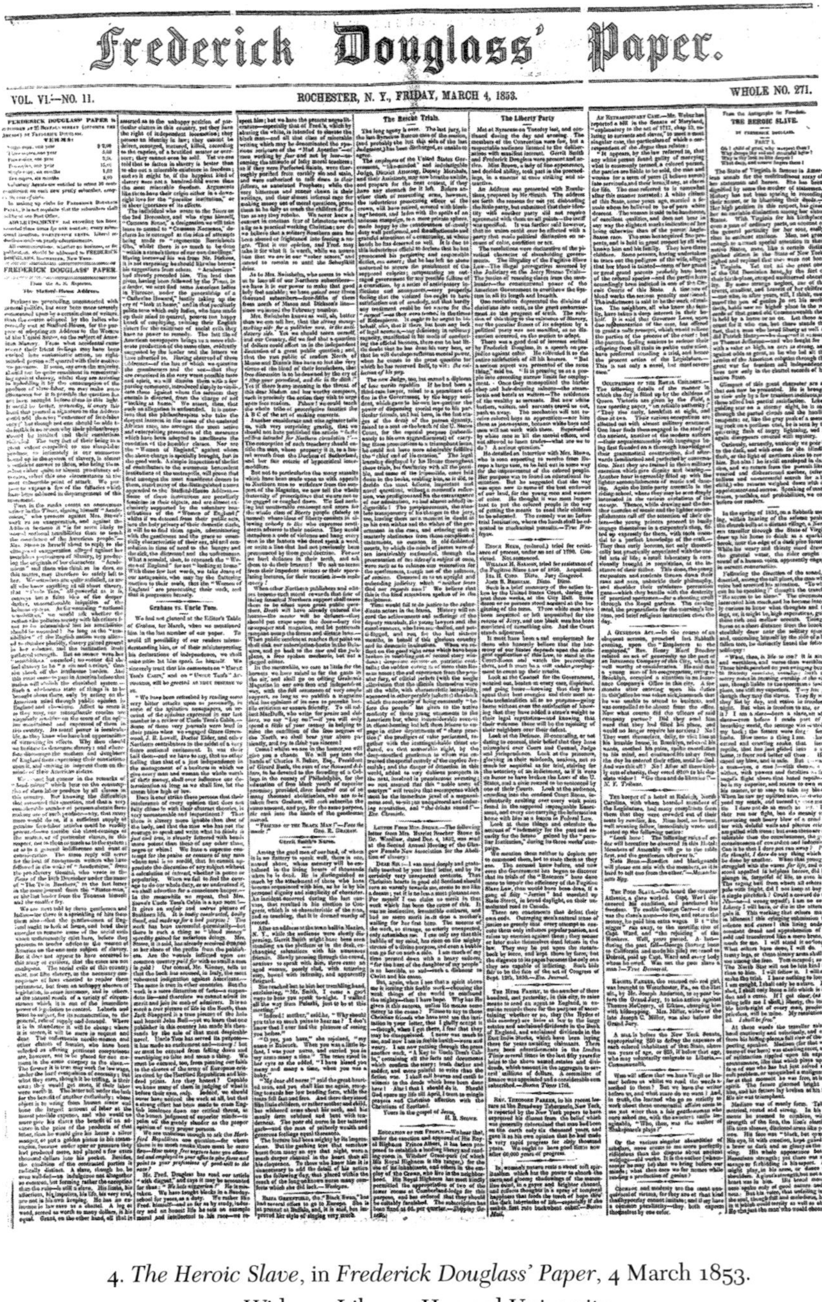

Frederick Douglass' Paper.

VOL. VI.—NO. 11. ROCHESTER, N. Y., FRIDAY, MARCH 4, 1853. WHOLE NO. 271.

4. *The Heroic Slave*, in *Frederick Douglass' Paper*, 4 March 1853.
Widener Library, Harvard University.

second, printed serially in *Frederick Douglass' Paper* on 4, 11, 18, and 25 March 1853; and the third, a British edition of *Autographs for Freedom*, published by the London firm of Low, Son & Company and John Cassell later in the spring of 1853.

Based on our critical reading and the collation of potentially authoritative texts of *The Heroic Slave*, and on an analysis of external evidence, the editors selected the Boston edition of *Autographs for Freedom* as the copy-text to be critically edited. The present text was reproduced as carefully as possible from its original published source, and then checked against the two subsequent versions. The editors strove to preserve the distinctive features, dubbed "accidentals" by textual scholars, of the work that Douglass intended to make available to his readers, so the original spelling, punctuation, capitalization, paragraphing, and other distinctive stylistic usages are reproduced here, although the possibility exists that many such features were introduced by a copy editor or compositor. The editors then compared or collated these three texts and compiled a list of variations in the texts.

Since the editors' goal was to provide the text of *The Heroic Slave* as Douglass intended it for his 1853 readers, we made only twenty-seven alterations, or emendations, to the original Boston-published *Autographs for Freedom* text. Most were intended to correct errors made by the original compositors and were based on intensive study of the subsequent two authoritative texts of the novella. A smaller number of our emendations are what textual editors call "substantives": changes of capitalization, punctuation, or spelling to correct grammatical errors that, the editors believe, Douglass could not have intended, because they produce confusion or provide misinformation. Where possible, Douglass's usage elsewhere in the novella or his other contemporary writings guided such emendations. For a detailed discussion of textual issues in *The Heroic Slave*," see the forthcoming volume *Other Writings* in the Yale University Press Frederick Douglass Papers.

PART 2

Contemporary Responses to the *Creole* Rebellion, 1841–1843

THE *CREOLE* REBELLION OCCURRED on the night of 7 November 1841, approximately two years after the more famous slave rebellion on board the Cuban slaver the *Amistad* and a few months after the U.S. Supreme Court ruled in favor of freeing the *Amistad*'s leader, Joseph Cinqué, and his fellow rebels, who had been imprisoned in Connecticut jailhouses since 1839. The *Creole* rebellion got less attention than the one on the *Amistad* because the rebels escaped to the British Bahamas and thus were not available for newspaper interviews or other forms of publicity. Still, there was considerable interest in the case. The *Creole* was an American slaver, after all, and southerners were disturbed by the specter of black revolt (and the loss of human property), while antislavery northerners saw in both the *Amistad* and the *Creole* rebellions clear indications of blacks' desire for freedom. Because the British refused to return the slaves to slavery, the rebellion exacerbated tensions between Britain and the United States during the time that President John Tyler's secretary of state, Daniel Webster, was negotiating the North American boundary issues central to the Webster-Ashburton Treaty, eventually signed in August 1842. Additionally, the rebellion and its aftermath added to existing tensions among northern and southern politicians about the role that the federal government should play in protecting the rights of slave owners.

This section presents contemporary newspaper, diplomatic, and political responses to the *Creole* rebellion. The emphasis is on those texts that Douglass read or clearly knew about. Douglass followed all aspects of the case. He was an avid reader of William Lloyd Garrison's antislavery newspaper, the *Liberator*, and of African American newspapers; five of the ten selections in this section come from antislavery newspapers, including Garrison's reprinting of the white crew's deposition about the case, known as the "Protest," which first appeared in a New Orleans newspaper. In addition, this section reprints an excerpt from another formal deposition by the white officers and seamen, printed as a U.S. Senate document, and three texts that focus on the diplomatic and political implications of the case, including Daniel Webster's widely disseminated letter about the *Creole* rebellion (which Douglass regularly attacked in his speeches about the uprising). The concluding selection, from Henry Highland Garnet's "Address to the Slaves of the United States," points to the symbolic importance that the *Creole* would come to assume for nineteenth-century African Americans inspired by the histories and legacies of black rebellion against the slave power.

"Another Amistad Case—What Will Grow Out of It?"

News of the 7 November 1841 revolt on the *Creole* initially came from the 8 December 1841 issue of the *New Orleans Advertiser*, which published the lengthy deposition—known as the "Protest"—that white officers and seamen gave to a New Orleans notary shortly after the *Creole* arrived in New Orleans on 2 December 1841. Southern newspapers summarized or reprinted the "Protest" as part of a campaign to compel the British to return the slaves to their owners. Northern antislavery newspapers printed the "Protest" with the very different aim of celebrating the black slaves for their heroic actions. (See the *Liberator's* version below.) Drawing on the "Protest," on 23 December 1845 the *National Anti-Slavery Standard* published an article, "An American Cinquez," that directly linked the *Creole* rebellion to the *Amistad* slave rebellion of 1839, led by Joseph Cinqué. Two days later, the *Colored American*, based in New York City and the leading African American newspaper of the time, published "Another Amistad Case," which also drew on the "Protest." The text here is taken from the 25 December 1841 issue of the *Colored American*.

It appears that on the 27th of Oct., the brig Creole left Richmond, Va.,[1] with 135 slaves, for New Orleans, where they were to be sold—that on the night of the 7th of November, a large number of the slaves arose, killed their owner, or the man who had them in charge, and one other passenger,[2] seri-

1. According to the "Protest," the *Creole* left Richmond on 25 October and Hampton Roads on the 30th. There is confusion in the documents about these dates.

2. John Hewell, the agent for slaveowner Thomas McCargo on board the *Creole*, was the only white killed during the rebellion.

ously wounded the captain and mate, who both fled to the rigging, and finally succeeded in taking full charge of the vessel. The next morning they called the captain and mate down from the rigging, who obeyed; when the mate gave himself up to them, one of the colored men put a pistol to his breast and promised to spare him only on condition that he would take them to an English Island, who promised to do so, and accordingly took the vessel to Nassau, New Providence.[3] Upon arriving at Nassau, nineteen of the slaves were recognized as among the revolters, and were detained in temporary durance by the Governor,[4] who refused, however, to send them to the United States; the remainder of them were set at liberty, as on *English soil slaves cannot breathe*.[5] A vessel being about to embark for Jamaica, with emigrants, many of them took passage in her; the rest are employed at Nassau. Another paper states that four women and one small boy came to New Orleans in the Creole,—very foolish women. One or two of the colored men died from wounds received in the affray on board.[6] It is evident these slaves prepared themselves for the battle before they left Richmond, else whence all their implements of war.

Now here is another Amistad case,[7] a very exciting one too, and more trouble in the camp between this country and England. This country will demand them to be given up, at least the slaveholders will. England will not listen for one moment in the case of the 114, most of whom have gone to Jamaica. They are safe—she never will

3. In the Bahamas, and at the time a colony of Great Britain.

4. Francis Cockburn (1780–1868) served as colonial governor of the Bahamas from 1837 to 1844. It was his decision to imprison Madison Washington and his eighteen fellow conspirators for possible charges of mutiny. In 1842, the rebels were released and granted their freedom after a British admiralty court ruled in their favor.

5. The Slavery Abolition Act of 1833 freed slaves in the British West Indies and nearly all the rest of the British Empire. In his famous ruling on the *Somerset* case of 1772, which affirmed that slavery was not supported by the laws of England, Lord Mansfield declared, "The air of England is too pure for any slave to breathe."

6. Two rebels died during the rebellion: George Grandy (from a head wound) and Adam Carney.

7. The well-known slave rebellion of 1839 on the Spanish slave ship *Amistad*, which had been sailing out of Cuba with slaves taken from West Africa.

at all surrender one of them up. Of the 19 detained as revolters, England may pause a moment, as to whether to give them up or not, she may, and she may not. Our Supreme Court has just given them a precedent in the Africans of the Amistad, she may follow so illustrious an example.[8] But this country has adopted other precedents, in refusing to deliver up her mail robbers, and her murderers, who had taken refuge under our government from Canada.[9] England will never do for us, what we have in like circumstance refused to do for them, especially in the case of men fighting to deliver themselves from chattel slavery. The Southern papers are already in a great rage about this case; we advise then to keep cool, not to be too wrathy, they may be glad yet to back out. John Bull won't be frightened. We advise old Virginia to be careful how she ships her slaves to the South. These Virginia slaves are hard cases.

See another column for later news in this case.[10]

8. The leaders of the *Amistad* rebellion were captured by the U.S. Navy in Long Island, New York, and were held in Connecticut jails while their cases were litigated. In March 1841, the U.S. Supreme Court ruled that the rebels should be freed on the grounds that the international slave trade was illegal.

9. The Webster-Ashburton Treaty of 1842 resolved some of the U.S.-Canadian border questions, including extradition, that had contributed to tensions between the United States and Great Britain in the late 1830s and early 1840s.

10. See the next selection in this volume.

"The Creole Mutiny"

"The Creole Mutiny" appeared in the same issue of the *Colored American* as "Another Amistad Case." This article, too, drew on the New Orleans "Protest," and was more or less a reprint of a piece that had first appeared in the *New York Tribune*. By printing the pieces together in the 25 December 1841 issue of their newspaper, the source of the text below, the editors of the *Colored American* provided their readers with the story of the *Creole* from the time of the rebellion at sea to the immediate aftermath in Nassau.

The New Orleans Advertiser of the 8th[1] contains the Protest of the Officers and crew of the brig Creole against the "winds and waves, and the dangers of the sea generally, but more especially against the insurrection of the nineteen slaves, and the illegal action of the British authorities at Nassau in regard to the remainder of the slaves on board said vessel." The protest recounts all the particulars of the mutiny, which, as we have already given, we shall not repeat. Only nineteen of the slaves had any part in the mutiny; the rest were afraid of them and remained forward of the mainmast.

The occurrences after reaching Nassau have not been so generally published. The officer, Gifford,[2] called upon the Governor of the Bahamas who, at his request, sent a guard of twenty-four negro soldiers on the ship to keep the slaves and cargo on board.

1. 8 December 1841.
2. Zephaniah Gifford was the first mate on the *Creole*.

Capt. Fitzgeralt, who commanded the troops, told the slaves that they were very foolish in not killing all the whites on board.

On the 10th of November, three magistrates came on board and examined all the white persons. The vessel was surrounded by boats filled with men armed with clubs. The nineteen were taken into custody, and the Attorney General[3] said to the others, "My friends, you have been detained a short time on board the Creole for the purpose of ascertaining the individuals who were concerned in this mutiny and murder. They have been identified and will be detained, the rest of you are free and at liberty to go on shore and where you please."

Then addressing the prisoners, he said, "Men, there are nineteen of you who have been identified as having been engaged in the murder of Mr. Hewell, and in an attempt to kill the captain and others. You will be detained and lodged in prison for a time, in order that we may communicate with the English Government, and ascertain whether your trial shall take place here or elsewhere."

Mr. Gifford, the officer in command, protested against allowing the armed boats to come alongside and the slaves to go ashore. The Attorney General, in reply, told him that he had better make no objection, for if he did there might be bloodshed. He then stepped into his boat with one of the magistrates and withdrew into the stream. At a signal from another magistrate on board the Creole, the armed boats came along side and the slaves on board got into them. Three cheers were given and the boats went ashore, where thousands were waiting to receive them. The mutineers were taken ashore in a barge.

On the 15th, the Attorney General wrote to the Captain of the Creole[4] demanding the baggage of the passengers. Gifford, the commanding officer, replied that the slaves being themselves prop-

3. The attorney general of Nassau was G. C. Anderson.

4. Captain Robert Ensor was stabbed during the rebellion, and relinquished command of the *Creole* to Gifford.

erty had no baggage, and that moreover, he could land nothing without a permit from the Custom House and an order from the American Consul[5]—the Attorney got the permit, but not the order, and put an officer on board the Creole who took away such baggage and property as he chose to consider as belonging to the slaves. The master of the Creole made no resistance.

The next day the Captain of the Creole proposed to sell his surplus provisions to pay his expenses. The collector of the Customs refused to allow them to be landed unless the Captain would enter the slaves as passengers. This was refused.

A plan was formed by the American Consul, with Capt. Woodside of the American vessel Louisa, to rescue the Creole from the British officer and take her to Indian Key[6] where was a U.S. vessel of war.

"Accordingly," says the Protest, "on the morning of the 12th of November, Captain Woodside, with his men in a boat, rowed to the Creole. Muskets and cutlasses were obtained from the brig Congress. Every effort had been made, in concert with the Consul, to purchase arms of the dealers at Nassau, but they all refused to sell. The arms were wrapped in the American flag and concealed in the bottom of the boat, as said boat approached the Creole. A negro, who had watched the loading of the boat, followed her, and gave the alarm to the British officer on the Creole. As the boat came up to the Creole, the officer called to them, 'Keep off, or I will fire into you.' His company of twenty-four men were then all standing on deck and drawn up in a line fronting Captain Woodside's boat, and were ready with loaded muskets and fixed bayonets for an engagement. Captain Woodside was forced to withdraw, and the plan was prevented from being executed, the said British officer remaining in command of the Creole. The officers and crew of the Louisa and Congress, and the American Consul were warmly interested in the plan, and everything possible was done for its success."

5. John Bacon.
6. An island in the Florida Keys.

On the day the slaves were liberated, the American Consul requested of the Governor a guard to protect the vessel until he could write to the Florida coast and put her in charge of a United States ship of war. This was refused. He then asked a guard until the crews of the American ships then in port could be collected and put on board the Creole, to take her to New Orleans. This was also refused. A proposition was then finally made to the Governor, that the American seamen then in port and in American vessels should go on board the Creole and be furnished with arms by the Governor to defend the vessel and cargo, (except the nineteen slaves who were to be left behind,) on her voyage to New Orleans. This also the Governor refused. On the 13th the Consul on behalf of the master of the brig Creole and all interested, proposed to the Governor to permit the nineteen mutineers to be sent to the United States on board the Creole for trial; and this too was refused.

Protest of the Officers and Crew of the American Brig Creole,

bound from Richmond to New-Orleans, whose cargo of slaves mutinied on the 7th of Nov. 1841, off the Hole-in-the-Wall, murdered a passenger, wounded the Captain and others, and put into Nassau, N. P., where the authorities confined nineteen of the mutineers, and forcibly liberated nearly all the slaves.

In August 1841, Frederick Douglass became a paid lecturer for William Lloyd Garrison's Massachusetts Anti-Slavery Society, and he would have initially followed reports about the *Creole* rebellion in Garrison's antislavery newspaper, the *Liberator*. In late December, Garrison reprinted the "Protest," which had first appeared in the 8 December 1841 issue of the *New-Orleans Advertiser*. The "Protest"—a deposition offered by five of the white officers and seamen of the *Creole* to a New Orleans notary public—was meant to underscore the barbarity of the black rebels and to make the case for reparations from the British (and for compensation from the ship's insurers). But for antislavery leaders like Garrison and Douglass, what came across most forcefully in the whites' account of the rebellion was the blacks' heroic quest for freedom. In the longer, complete version of the "Protest," the white deponents voice their frustration with the British and discuss their failed efforts, once in Nassau, to regain control of the *Creole*. This opening section, taken from the 31 December 1841 issue of the *Liberator*, offers a dramatic account of the uprising itself and of Madison Washington's role as leader.

By this public instrument of protest be it known that, on the second day of December, eighteen hundred and forty one; before me, William Young Lewis, notary public in and for the city of New-Orleans, duly commissioned and sworn:

Personally came and appeared Zephaniah C. Gifford, acting master of the American brig called the Creole, of Richmond, who declared that the said vessel sailed from the port of Norfolk, in the state of Virginia, on the thirteenth day of October last past, laden with manufactured tobacco in boxes and slaves, then under command of Captain Robert Ensor, bound for the port of New-Orleans, in the State of Louisiana.

That when about 130 miles to the North Northeast of the Hole-in-the-Wall,[1] the slaves, or part thereof on board said vessel, rose on the officers, crew and passengers, killed one passenger, severely wounded the captain, this appearer,[2] and a part of the crew; compelled said appearer, then first mate, to navigate said vessel to Nassau, in the Island of New-Providence, where she arrived, and a portion of the ringleaders of said insurrection were confined in prison, and the remainder of said slaves liberated by the British authorities of said Island: and required me, notary, to make record of the same, intending more at leisure to detail particulars.

And this day again appeared the said acting master, together with Lucius Stevens, acting mate; William Devereux, cook and steward; Henry Speck, John Silvy, Jaques Lecomte, Francis Foxwell, and Blair Curtiss, seamen—all of, and belonging to said vessel, who, being severally sworn according to law, to declare the truth, did depose and say—

That said vessel started as aforesaid, she was tight and strong, well manned, and provided in every respect, and equipped for carrying slaves:

1. At the southern tip of Great Abaco Island in the northern Bahamas.

2. Zephaniah Gifford, first mate, who took command of the *Creole* after Captain Robert Ensor was severely injured. By "appearer," Lewis refers to one of the officers and seamen who appeared before him to offer testimony.

That said vessel left Richmond on the 25th day of October, 1841, with about 102 slaves on board:

That about 90 of said slaves were shipped on board on the 20th of said month, of which 41 were shipped by Robert Lumkin, about 39 by John R. Hewell, 9 by Nathaniel Matthews, and 1 by Wm. Robinson; that from that time, about one of two per day were put on board by John R. Hewell, until about the said 25th day of October, so as to make the whole number of 135 slaves.

The men and women slaves were divided. The men were all placed in the forward hold of the brig, except old Lewis and servant of Mr. Thomas McCargo, who staid in the cabin, as assistant servant, and the women in the hold aft, except six female servants, who were taken in the cabin. Between them was the cargo of the brig, consisting of boxes of tobacco.

The slaves were permitted to go on deck, but the men were not allowed at night to go in the hold aft where the women were.

On the 30th of October, the brig left Hampton Roads for New-Orleans.[3] The slaves were all under the superintendence of William Henry Merritt, a passenger. John R. Hewell had the particular charge of the slaves of Thomas McCargo—Theophilus McCargo being considered too young and inexperienced[4]—and the general charge of the other slaves, all being under the master of the vessel. The slaves were all carefully watched. They were perfectly obedient and quiet, and showed no signs of mutiny and disturbance, until Sunday, the 7th of Nov. about 9 P.M. in lat. 27, 46, N. lon. 75 20 W.

The captain, supposing that they were nearer Abaco than they were, had ordered the brig to be laid to, which was done. A good

3. Based on the chronology in the "Protest," the *Creole* left Norfolk on 13 October and sailed up the James River to Richmond to pick up more slaves. It left Richmond on 25 October and sailed back down the James to Hampton Roads, leaving for New Orleans on the 30th. The U.S. Senate report of 20 January 1842, drawing on depositions from Captain Robert Ensor, First Mate Zephaniah Gifford, and Second Mate Lucius Stevens, confirms the first two dates but states that the *Creole* left Hampton Roads for New Orleans on 27 October.

4. Thomas McCargo had brought along his young son, Theophilus, to teach him the slave-trading business.

breeze was blowing at the time, and the sky was a little hazy, with trade clouds flying.

Mr. Gifford was on watch. He was told by Elijah Morris,[5] one of the slaves of Thomas McCargo, that one of the men had gone aft among the women. Mr. Gifford then called Mr. Merritt, who was in the cabin, and informed him of the fact. Mr. Merritt came up and went to the main hatch, which was the entrance to the after hold, and asked two or three of the slaves who were near, if any of the men were down in that hold, and he was informed that they were. Mr. Merritt then waited until Mr. Gifford procured a match, and then Mr. Merritt went down in the hold and lighted it. Mr. Gifford stood over the hatchway. On striking a light, Merritt found Madison Washington, a very large and strong slave of Thomas McCargo, standing at his back. Merritt said to Madison, 'Is it possible that you are down here? You are the last man on board the brig I expected to find here.' Madison replied, 'Yes, sir, it is me,' and instantly jumped to the hatchway, and got on deck, saying, 'I am going up, I cannot stay here.' He did this in spite of the resistance of Gifford and Merritt, who both tried to keep him back, and laid hold of him for that purpose.

Madison ran forward, and Elijah Morris fired a pistol, the ball of which grazed the back part of Gifford's head. Madison then shouted, 'We have begun, and must go through. Rush, boys, rush aft, and we have them!' and calling to the slaves below, he said—'Come up, every one of you! If you don't lend a hand, I will kill you all, and throw you overboard.'

Gifford now ran to the cabin, and aroused the Captain and others who were asleep, and the passangers, viz:—Theophilus McCargo, Jacob Miller,[6] John R. Hewell; the second mate Lucius Stevens; the

5. Elijah Morris was one of the four leaders of the mutiny, along with Madison Washington, Ben Blacksmith (also known as Ben Johnstone), and D. (or Doctor) Ruffin.

6. Jacob Miller, one of the passengers, is listed as Jacob Leitener (also Lightner and Leidney) in other documents. A Prussian cook, he assisted the steward, William Devereux.

steward Wm. Devereux, a free colored man; and the slave Lewis, belonging to Mr. T. McCargo, acting as assistant steward.[7] The slaves rushed aft, and surrounded the cabin. Merritt, hearing the report of the pistol, blew out his light and came from the hold. In doing this, he was caught by one of the negroes, who cried out, 'Kill him! he is one of them;' and the other slaves immediately rushed upon him. One of them attempted to strike Merritt with a handspike;[8] but missed him, and knocked down the negro who was holding Merritt. Merritt then escaped to the cabin.

Hewell, at this moment, jumped out of his berth, in his drawers, seized a musket, ran to the companion way of the cabin, and after some struggling fired. The negroes instantly wrenched the musket from Hewell's hands. Hewell then seized a handspike, and defended himself from the slaves who pursued him. They thought he had another musket, and retreated a little. He advanced, and they fell upon him with clubs, handspikes and knives. He was knocked down and stabbed in not less than twenty places; but he rose, got away from them, and staggered back to the cabin, exclaiming, 'I am dead—the negroes have killed me!'

It is believed that no more than four or five of the negroes had knives. Ben Blacksmith,[9] had the bowie knife he wrested from the captain, and stabbed Hewell with it. Madison had a jack knife, which appeared to have been taken from Hewell. Morris had a sheath knife, which he had taken from the forecastle, and which belonged to Henry Speck.[10]

Gifford, after arousing the persons in the cabin, ran on deck, and up the main-rigging to the main-top. Merritt tried to get through

7. Lewis McCargo, the slave and servant of Thomas McCargo, also assisted the steward, William Devereux. In this sentence, commas have been corrected from the published account, and semicolons added, to avoid confusion.

8. Metal bar used as a lever.

9. Ben Blacksmith is listed as Ben Johnstone in other documents. He was probably a blacksmith.

10. Henry Speck was one of five sailors on the *Creole*; the others were John Silvy, Jacques LeComte, Francis Foxwell, and Blinn (or Blair) Curtis, who is listed as Blair Blinn in most other documents.

the sky-light of the cabin, but could not, without being discovered. The negroes crowded around the sky-light outside, and the door of the cabin. Merritt then hid himself in one of the berths, and three of the female house servants covered him with blankets, and sat on the edge of the berth, crying and praying. Theophilus McCargo dressed himself on the alarm being given. Hewell, after being wounded, staggered into said McCargo's state-room, where he fell and expired in about half an hour. His body was thrown overboard by order of Madison, Ben Blacksmith and Elijah Morris. McCargo got his two pistols out, and fired one of them at the negroes, then in the cabin; the other missed fire, and McCargo having no ammunition, put his pistols away. After the affray, the sheath-knife of Henry Speck was found in Elijah Morris's possession, and that of Foxwell in the possession of another negro, both covered with blood to the handles.

Jacob Miller, William Devereux and the slave Lewis, on the alarm being given, concealed themselves in one of the state rooms. Elijah Morris called all who were concealed in the cabin to come forward, or they should have instant death. Miller came out first and said—'Here I am, do what you please.' Devereux and Lewis next came out, and begged for their lives. Madison stood at the door, and ordered them to be sent to the hold. Stevens got up on the alarm being given and ran out. Saw Hewell in the affray, and waited in the cabin till Hewell died, and then secreted himself in one of the state rooms, and when they commenced the search for Merritt, made his escape through the cabin. They forced the musket they had reloaded, struck at him with knives and handspikes, and chased him into the rigging. He escaped to the fore-yard.

On the alarm being given, the captain called all hands to get up and fight. Henry Speck, one of the crew, was knocked down with a handspike. The helmsman was a Frenchman.[11] Elijah Morris and Pompey Garrison[12] were going to kill him, when Madison told them

11. Jacques LeComte (also spelled Leconte).

12. One of the nineteen rebels, Pompey Garrison was not considered one of the leaders of the rebellion.

they should not kill him, because he was a Frenchman, and could not speak English; so they spared his life. Blair Curtis, one of the crew, came aft into the cabin and concealed himself in the state room with Stevens, and escaped with him to the fore royal yard.

The captain fought with his bowie knife along-side of Hewell. The captain was engaged in the fight from eight to ten minutes, until the negroes got him down, in the starboard scuppers.[13] He then made his escape to the maintop, being stabbed in several places, and much bruised with blows from sticks of wood found about the brig. After the captain got into the maintop, he fainted from the loss of blood, and Gifford fastened him with the rigging to prevent him from falling, as the vessel was then rolling heavily.

The captain's wife, her child and niece, then came and begged for their lives,[14] and Ben Blacksmith sent them to the hold. Ben then called out for Merritt, and exclaimed that all who had secreted him should be killed. The two female servants then left the berth where Merritt was concealed, and were sent down to the hold by Ben. Jim and Lewis, negroes, belonging to Thomas McCargo, then ran to Theophilus McCargo, who asked Jim if the others were going to kill him. Jim and Lewis exclaimed that 'master, HE should not be killed,' and clung around him, begging Morris and Ben, who were then close with their knives in their hands, not to kill him. They consented, and ordered him to be taken to the hold. Jim and Lewis went voluntarily with Theophilus McCargo to the hold.

After a great deal of search, Merritt was found, and Ben Blacksmith and Elijah dragged him from his berth. They and several others surrounded him with knives, half handspikes, muskets and pistols, raised their weapons to kill him, and made room for him to fall.

On his representing that he had been the mate of a vessel, that he was the only person who could navigate for them, and on Mary, a

13. Openings at deck level to allow water to run off.

14. Captain Robert Ensor had brought along his wife, their fifteen-month-old daughter, and his fifteen-year-old niece.

woman servant belonging to McCargo, urging said Madison Washington to interfere, Madison ordered them to stop and allow Merritt to have a conversation with him. This took place in a state room.

Madison said he wanted to go to Liberia.[15] Merritt represented that they had not water and provisions for that voyage. Ben Blacksmith, D. Ruffin[16] and several of the slaves then said that they wanted to go to the British Islands. They did not want to go any where else but where Mr. Lumpkin's negroes went last year, alluding to the shipwreck of schooner Hermosa on Abaco, and the taking of the slaves on board that vessel, by the English wreckers, to Nassau, in the Island of New-Providence.[17]

Merritt then got his chart and explained to them the route, and read to them the Coast Pilot,[18] and they agreed that if he would navigate them, they would save his life—otherwise death would be his portion. Pompey Garrison had been to New Orleans and knew the route. D. Ruffin and George Portlock[19] knew the letters of the compass. They then set Merritt free, and demanded the time of night, which was half past one o'clock, A.M. by Merritt's watch. The vessel was then put in Merritt's charge.[20]

The nineteen slaves confined at Nassau, are the only slaves who took any part in the affray. All the women appeared to be perfectly ignorant of the plan, and from their conduct, could not have known anything about it. They were crying and praying during the night. None of the male slaves apparently under twenty years took any part in the affray. . . .

15. A country in West Africa that was founded during the 1820s by the American Colonization Society, a white-led organization that hoped to solve the U.S. race problem by shipping blacks to Africa. The Republic of Liberia achieved its independence in 1847.

16. D. Ruffin, one of the leaders of the rebellion, is listed as Doctor Ruffin in other documents.

17. Many of the slaves on board the *Creole* came from Robert Lumpkin's slave pen in Richmond, Virginia, and thus would have known about the wreck of his ship *Hermosa* and the subsequent liberation of the slaves on board.

18. A navigation guide.

19. George Portlock was one of the nineteen rebels.

20. See Merritt's deposition below.

Done and protested at New-Orleans, this 7th day of December, 1841, the protestors herewith signing their respective names with said notary.

[Signed] ZEPHANIAH C. GIFFORD,
HENRY SPECK,
BLAIR CURTISS,
JOHN SILVEY,
FRANCIS FOXWELL.

Mr. Merritt and Mr. Theophilus McCargo have certified on the original of this protest to the truth of the above.

"The Hero Mutineers"

The New Orleans "Protest" was the first of a number of pieces about the *Creole* that Garrison would print in his newspaper. In the 7 January 1842 issue of the *Liberator* (the source of the text below), he published an account of the rebellion that had first appeared, in a slightly different form, in December 1841 issues of the *New York Evangelist* and the *New York Journal of Commerce*.

In publishing the Protest of the officers and crew of the Creole, we have wished to place an important providential event in such a manner before our readers, as to enable them to give it the most thorough consideration. Like the death of Lovejoy[1] and the case of the Amistad captives, it forms a part of that train of high providences by which God is developing to this nation the nature of slavery—its deleterious influence, and the absolute necessity of its abolition. The Protest is from the officers and crew of the Creole, given before a Notary Public, in New-Orleans, and cannot be supposed to represent in too favorable colors the conduct of the mutineers. We hope every reader of the Evangelist will give it a thorough perusal.

We read it with surprise and admiration. Whether we consider the force and presence of mind displayed, the clemency exercised, the unsleeping vigilance maintained, or the sublime reliance on the justice of their cause, as they approached Nassau, we confess that

1. The antislavery journalist Elijah Parish Lovejoy (1802–1837) was killed by a proslavery mob during an assault on his press in Alton, Illinois.

we can think of nothing in the long range of history which gives a nobler impression.

Of the 135 slaves confined in the hold, only 19 appear to have taken any active part in the revolt. Of these 19, four appear to have been the chief agents.[2] Of these, one who wore a name unfit for a slave, but finely expressive for a hero, seems to have been the master spirit—that name was Madison Washington! By the way, we have always thought it a singular, nay, a dangerous practice, to confer such emphatic names upon men in bondage.

It does not appear whether the mutineers had previously digested their plan, or not. If they had, they betrayed remarkable fidelity and efficiency in bringing it to an issue. If not, the leaders, and especially Madison Washington, manifested astonishing presence of mind and decision of character, in his movement. His reply to Merritt, when found in the hold where the women were kept—his escape to the deck, in spite of the united resistance of Merritt and Gifford—his commanding attitude and daring orders, when he stood a freeman on the slaver's deck, and his perfect preparation for the grand alternative of liberty or death, which stood before him, are splendid exemplifications of the true heroic.[3]

His generous leniency towards his prisoners, his oppressors—men who were carrying him and 134 others, from a condition of slavery already intolerable, to one which threatened still more galling chains, is another remarkable feature. He spared the life of the poor Frenchman,[4] because he could not speak English, and the cap-

2. The four leaders of the slave rebellion were Madison Washington, Ben Blacksmith (or Johnstone), Elijah Morris, and D. (or Doctor) Ruffin. The other fifteen mutineers were George Grandy (who died from a head wound received during the mutiny), Richard Butler, Phil Jones, Robert Lumpkin (or Lumpley), Peter Smallwood, Harner Smith, Walter Brown, Adam Carney (who was killed during the mutiny), Horace Beverly, America Addison Tyler, William Jenkins, Pompey Garrison, George Basden, and George Portlock.

3. William H. Merritt, a slave trader on board the *Creole*, was responsible for overseeing the slaves; see his deposition in the next selection below. Zephaniah C. Gifford was the first mate.

4. Jacques LeComte (also spelled Leconte) was the French helmsman.

tain's life, at the entreaty of his wife and children. He dressed the wounds of the poor sailors who had fought against him; he spared the life of Merritt and also of young Theophilus McCargo;[5] and when he had command of the cabin, invited the whites to partake of its refreshments. All his movements show that malice and revenge formed no part of his motives.

Yet this leniency was accompanied with the most vigorous and efficient measures. How nobly he seems, when making Merritt pledge, at the mouth of the musket, at one o'clock at night, to navigate the vessel to New Providence; when commanding the captain and Merritt to have no communication; when placing the sailors on duty at their usual posts, and subjecting them to the same necessary restriction of non-intercourse; when pacing the deck with his three brave associates until morning, with his knife drawn, and his eye upon every spot where the least danger could arise! To heighten the moral grandeur of the scene, remember that he did not know how many of the remaining slaves might side against him; and even feared he should have to quell an insurrection against the new authority. The 19 consulted together, kept their counsels to themselves—and, so far as we can learn, exercised complete self-control over their passions, and maintained uninterrupted harmony of purpose and action.

But nothing in the whole affair appears so sublimely affecting as their conduct on arriving at Nassau. They divested themselves of all their arms, even casting them into the sea, and came before the British authorities defenceless—confiding in the justice of their cause, and in the protection of free and righteous institutions against the claims of their oppressors! Noble men! Here was no sense of guilt, no meanness, no deception. They only wished to say emphatically, what they did; that they only sought to obtain their freedom. This act of theirs is a splendid tribute to the British Government, and is

5. The son of Virginia slave trader Thomas McCargo, who owned many of the slaves on board the *Creole*.

a brighter gem in the diadem of her sovereign, than the victory of any battle field. It was confidence in law, sustained by power, and founded on unquestionable justice. Take it altogether, it was morally magnificent. The liberty which saluted them on landing, by the triumphant shouts of thousands that welcomed them, must have been a glorious reward to these men for their brave and perilous achievement.

In these remarks, our readers will perceive that we have done little more than to translate, in the appropriate language of freedom, the statements of the Protest, written by their enemies. The case before us is important, however, as we suggested at first, on account of its providential relations to the great question of abolition. It differs from that of the Amistad captives in one grand point, viz: that these by law *were* slaves, while those were not.[6] The public at large, and the supreme voice of immutable law, pronounced the Mendians innocent, nay, extolled their conduct. The public is now called upon to decide upon another case, divided from that of the Mendians only by the narrow line of a law, in its nature confessedly unjust, and abominable to every intelligent freeman.

The claim of property in their flesh and bones and souls, asserted by slaveholding law, was not, could not have been binding on the slaves themselves. There are only two grand reasons which render it the duty of men, in any circumstances, to submit to the enforcement of such an ignominious claim on themselves and their offspring. One is the hope of obtaining deliverance by patient waiting, and the other is the impossibility of obtaining it by insurrection. *These two reasons rest over the condition of our Southern slaves at large, and sustain the true abolition doctrine of doing nothing to encourage, but every thing to discourage insurrection.*

But these reasons in the case of the Creole slaves, had vanished. Before *them*, there was a splendid prospect, by valorous resistance,

6. The U.S. Supreme Court decided that the *Amistad* rebels, who were Mende-speaking people from West Africa, could not be considered slaves because of the illegality of the international slave trade.

of immediate and perpetual liberty. Again we repeat it, *the restraining reasons had vanished, and both law and gospel justified their rising.*

Admitting the truth of these positions, (and they will be sustained by the voice of the American public, and of British law,) the institution of slavery will stand out before our people in the most appalling aspect. We do not wish to push the subject too far, at present. But we wish to enquire, whether, if Great Britain refuses to give up these 'murderers,' the American *people* are prepared to enforce the demand against her? We wish to enquire if our readers have reflected on that portion of the Report of the Secretary of the Navy, which points out the danger of our Southern coast in case of war with Great Britain, arising from the existence of slavery?[7] We wish our readers would reflect on these possibilities, and thus discern how great a national risk we run, by the direful bearings of this detestable institution, entrenched in the protection of a system of government, by nature perfectly averse to it.

We suggest these reflections, in order to show the reader the necessity of using every possible means to bring about voluntary emancipation. By all the love we have for the American Union—by all the respect we cherish for the principles of universal law—by all the horror we entertain of war between two such governments as those of Great Britain and the United States, and by the dread with which we regard the spirit of insurrection, as well as by all the immense systems of interests, embossed in the destinies of three millions of slaves, and all the intermingled relations of the church of God, we beseech, as if all these were beseeching, that our readers will universally realize the necessity of the most kind, wise, urgent and immediate exertions, to accomplish their cheerful and voluntary emancipation. We have no time to lose. The voice of Providence speaks sternly against our delay. If we have arguments, let

7. The novelist and playwright James Kirke Paulding (1778–1860) served as secretary of the navy from 1838 to 1841. During that time he submitted an annual report on the state of U.S. naval forces.

us set them all in order; if we have tears, let us bid them flow; if we have eloquence, let us consecrate it to the service; if we have philosophy, let us learn to discern and discriminate on this subject; and if we have religion, let us send up continual prayer before God, that he will overrule all this matter in tender mercy, and bring us to a happy issue of justice, freedom and perpetual union.

Deposition of William H. Merritt

When the *Creole* arrived at the British colony of Nassau, Bahamas, Madison Washington and his fellow rebels were initially jailed by British authorities. But the British refused to return the slaves to the *Creole*'s white officers (and eventually freed Washington and his compatriots), thus setting off a diplomatic incident. To make the case for the return of the slaves, the white officers, sailors, and slave traders told their stories in November 1841 to the New York lawyer and diplomat John F. Bacon (1789–1862), who at the time was U.S. consul in Nassau. From the point of view of Bacon and other U.S officials, the blacks were murderous rebels who should be returned to their white owners, but antislavery people who read the same depositions tended to regard the blacks as resourceful, freedom loving, and compassionate. The depositions became part of the U.S. record of the rebellion, and were presented by President Tyler and Secretary of State Webster to the U.S. Senate on 19 January 1842, and were printed as Senate Document 51, 27th Congress, 2nd session, 1842 (the source of the text below). The deposition of the slave trader William H. Merritt, whose job on the *Creole* was to oversee the slaves, is of particular interest because aspects of his account clearly had an impact on Douglass's conception of Tom Grant in *The Heroic Slave*. Douglass may have read Merritt's full deposition in Senate Document 51; he almost certainly knew the shorter version of Merritt's story given in the New Orleans "Protest."

CONSULATE OF THE UNITED STATES OF AMERICA,
Nassau, Bahamas, November 9, 1841.

Personally appeared before me, John. F. Bacon, consul of the United States of America at Nassau, Bahamas, William H. Merritt, who, being sworn, deposeth and saith: That he was a passenger on board the brig Creole, which sailed from Hampton roads on the 27th October, 1841, bound to New Orleans.[1] That he had no interest in the vessel or cargo, but in consideration of his attending to the slaves during the passage, he was to be charged nothing for his passage. That, on Sunday evening, November 7th, about 9 o'clock, was called by Mr. Gifford, the chief mate[2]; that, on going to the cabin door, Mr. Gifford stated there was a man in the mainhold with the females. Deponent went to the grate of the hatch, where he remained until Mr. Gifford got the lamp and matches; then had the grate taken off; entered the hold, and struck the light, and discovered that the person was Madison Washington, who was head cook of the slaves, and said to him: "Doctor, you are the last person I should expect to find here, and that would disobey the orders of the ship;" to which he only replied, "Yes, sir." He then got out of the hold, deponent trying to prevent him by laying hold of his leg, but having the lamp in one hand, could not hold him. After getting on deck, he ran forward and called for his men to assist him. Deponent blew out the light, and attempted to get to the cabin; but as soon as he got on deck was attacked by one of the slaves, and held by the shoulder, while another came up with a piece of wood, with two or three more following, who said, "That is he, kill him, by God;" which the one that had the piece of wood attempted to do, but hit the one that held deponent, on the head, on which he made his escape and retreated to the cabin; also heard the report of a gun or pistol forward. Does not know whether the mate had previously been to the cabin. Saw the captain go on deck. Saw Mr. Hewell[3] come out of his state-room with a musket, and go to the cabin door, and forbid the slaves from coming down, at the same time trying to prevent them

1. The "Protest," the third document in this section, states that the *Creole* left Hampton Roads on 30 October. This official Senate document probably has the correct date, since it stems from depositions by the ship's captain, Robert Ensor; the first mate Zephaniah Gifford; and the second mate Lucius Stevens.

2. Zephaniah Gifford.

3. John Hewell, who with William Merritt oversaw the slaves on the *Creole*.

with the musket, which had no bayonet on it. The slaves attempted to force their way, and hove a handspike into the cabin, on which, Mr. Hewell fired off the gun to intimidate them, as he thinks there was nothing but powder in it; thinks no one was hurt by the discharge. The slaves then obtained possession of the musket, when Mr. Hewell seized the handspike, and made the same show of defence; on which, one of the slaves said, "He has another gun," and Mr. Hewell replied he had. The slaves then returned from the cabin door, and Mr. Hewell went on deck, but soon returned to the cabin, took hold of the side of the table, and said, "I am stabbed;" on which he sidled away, and fell apparently helpless on the floor. Did not see Mr. Hewell afterward. Deponent then attempted to get out of the skylight, but on account of the noise on deck, and the number of slaves there, desisted, and attempted to conceal himself in one of the after berths, where he was covered over with some bedclothes, and two colored females sitting on him. While there, deponent heard persons come down in the cabin, and some say, "Take it on deck," when some seemed to go on deck. Soon they returned, and the cabin seemed to be full of slaves, searching for persons, and saying, "Come out here, damn you." Heard them say, "Don't hurt the steward—don't hurt Jacob, or Mrs. Ensor."[4] Some one said, "Where is Merritt? bring him out." Those discovered were taken on deck, to wit, Mrs. Ensor, the steward, and Jacob. The women that concealed him then becoming alarmed, left him, and he got under the mattress. Deponent was soon after discovered, hauled out, and menaced with instant death, by a man called Ben Blacksmith,[5] holding a bowie-knife over him, in company with others. Madison Washington, however, interceded for him, and his life was spared, on condition he would navigate the vessel to any port they might require. He supposed, and the slaves seemed to think, also, that the

4. The wife of the captain, Robert Ensor. Jacob Lietner was the ship's Prussian cook. In the "Protest," he is listed as Jacob Miller.

5. Ben Blacksmith is listed as Ben Johnstone elsewhere in the Senate Report and other documents.

captain and mates were all murdered. Their treatment was afterward kind toward deponent, and they desired him to take charge of the vessel. After the slaves had discovered the captain and mates were aloft, they said they should be killed, but deponent persuaded them to save their lives. Gifford was the first that came down, and subsequently the captain was brought down; second mate, also. The captain, his wife, and second mate, were confined in the forehold. The first mate was allowed to do duty, at deponent's solicitation. As contradictory orders were given by the slaves in reference to the destination of the vessel, and in navigating her, he desired that certain persons might be selected for that purpose; on which, Madison Washington, Ben Blacksmith, and Doctor Ruffin, were selected for that purpose.[6] Deponent can identify, by sight, several others besides those named by him, as taking an active part in the murder and mutiny.

WM. H. MERRITT.

Subscribed and sworn to, this 9th November, 1841, before me,

JOHN F. BACON, *U.S. CONSUL.*

6. Madison Washington, Ben Blacksmith (or Ben Johnstone) and Doctor Ruffin (also listed as D. Ruffin) were three of the four leaders of the mutiny. The fourth leader was Elijah Morris.

"Madison Washington: Another Chapter in His History"

In the spring of 1842, stories began to circulate about Madison Washington's whereabouts before the *Creole* rebellion. Articles based on oral accounts appeared in the *Friend of Man*, the *National Anti-Slavery Standard*, and the 10 June 1842 issue of the *Liberator*, the source of the text below (which drew on the earlier pieces). In these articles, Washington is presented as a loyal husband who, after escaping to Canada, chose to return to Virginia in search of his wife. Some recent critics are suspicious of these stories, claiming that the domestic tale may have been invented to make Washington more appealing to a wider audience. But similar stories about Washington were told by three men who claimed to have helped Washington on his way back to Virginia: Hiram Wilson (1803–1864), an abolitionist from New Hampshire who worked with fugitive slaves in Canada; Lindley Murray Moore (1788–1871), a Rochester-based Quaker abolitionist; and Robert Purvis (1810–1898), a prominent black abolitionist of Philadelphia. For Purvis's 1889 account of Washington's return for his wife, see "A Priceless Picture" in part 4.

This name will be remembered as belonging to the leader of the 'Immortal Nineteen,' who fought for and obtained their liberty on board the Creole. Madison was the 'very large and strong slave' found in *the after cabin, who being seized by both the master* and mate, shook them off, and in spite of their endeavors—together with those of a third sailor who stood over the hatchway—forced a passage, and rushing on deck, cried, '*We have begun, and must go through!*'[1]

This scene on the Creole deck was but one chapter in the history of Madison Washington. Nothing could be more absurd than to suppose that this occasion made Madison, and not Madison made the occasion. A new clue to the character of this hero of the Creole has just been furnished us.

About eighteen months since, Madison was in Canada. He there bore this same name. He staid awhile in the family of Hiram Wilson, who describes him, like the 'Creole protestants,' as a very *large* and *strong* slave. Madison had been some time in Canada—long enough to love and rejoice in British liberty. But he loved his wife, who was left a slave in Virginia, still more. At length, Madison resolved on rescuing her from slavery. Although strongly dissuaded by his friends from making the attempt in person, he would not listen, but crossed the line into this State.[2] At Rochester, he fell in with friend Lindley Murray Moore, who collected ten dollars to aid him in his journey towards Virginia. So strong was Madison's determination, that at this time he assured his friends he would have his wife or lose his life.

As he passed along, he was heard from at Utica and in Albany. The next account, he stands a freeman on the deck of the Creole—the master-spirit of the noble nineteen!

We infer, of course, that Madison, in attempting to liberate his wife, was himself re-enslaved. And as it is the custom with slaveholders in the more northern slave States, to send the fugitive when secured by them to the extreme South—lest he escape again—lest he communicate to other slaves the incidents of his day of freedom—as an example that shall strike terror to the breast of his fellows—he is sold to the southern market. So Madison, we suppose, was captured, and as a dangerous slave, sold for New-Orleans, and shipped with his 134 fellow sufferers.

1. The quotations in this selection are from the New Orleans "Protest."
2. New York.

The sequel we all know. Madison Washington is again a freeman under the dominion of Queen Victoria.[3] Long may he remain free! One question, however, we greatly wish to have answered. Is he still without his beloved wife? Remember it was Madison's visit 'aft among the women' that led to the first act of violence on the Creole. Might not his wife have been there among the women?[4] Yes, and this grave Creole matter may prove to have been but a part only of that grand game, in which the highest stake was the liberty of his dear wife. Will not some British abolitionists obtain for us the story from Madison's own lips?

3. In Nassau, Bahamas. Queen Victoria (1819–1901) was monarch of the United Kingdom of Great Britain and Ireland from 1837 to 1901.

4. These are the questions the novelist Pauline E. Hopkins takes up in "A Dash for Liberty" (1901), her fictionalized account of the *Creole* rebellion. The story can be found in part 4 of this volume. In *The Heroic Slave*, Washington's wife is shot and killed as Madison tries to free her; Hopkins imagines her joining the rebellion. There remains no known documentation about whether she joined Washington on the *Creole*.

DANIEL WEBSTER

Letter to Edward Everett

On 29 January 1842, Daniel Webster (1782–1852), secretary of state under President John Tyler (1790–1862), wrote to Edward Everett (1794–1865), the U.S. minister to Great Britain, to elaborate the official position of the United States on the matter of the *Creole*. Webster and Tyler believed that the British had acted illegally in freeing the slaves, whom they regarded as murderers, and thus wanted the British to indemnify the slaves' owners for their loss of property. At the time, Webster was in the midst of the negotiations that would result in the Webster-Ashburton Treaty of 1842, so he was especially concerned about resolving the *Creole* case amicably. When he saw that he would fail in his effort to compel the British to offer compensation, he downplayed the incident so that he could secure the treaty, which helped set the borders between the United States and British North America. Webster and Everett were two of the most notable politicians and orators of the antebellum period, and both were from Massachusetts. Though neither was an enthusiast of slavery, they believed that the South's right to hold slaves was constitutionally guaranteed and central to the survival of the Union. Webster's commitment to the Union would eventually lead him to support the Fugitive Slave Act, part of the Compromise of 1850, which he hoped would forestall a civil war. Webster's letter to Everett first appeared in Senate Documents, 27th Congress, 2nd session (1842), document 137, 2–7, the source of the text below, and was subsequently reprinted in *Niles' National Register* 61 (1842) and other newspapers and journals of the period.

Mr. Webster to Mr. Everett

DEPARTMENT OF STATE, January 29, 1842

I regret to be obliged to acquaint you with a very serious occurrence, which recently took place in a port of one of the Bahama islands.

It appears that the brig "Creole," of Richmond, Virginia, Ensor, master, bound to New Orleans, sailed from Hampton Roads on the 27th of October last, with a cargo of merchandise, principally tobacco, and slaves (about one hundred and thirty-five in number); that on the evening of the 7th of November, some of the slaves rose upon the crew of the vessel, murdered a passenger, named Hewell, who owned some of the negroes, wounded the captain dangerously, and the first mate and two of the crew severely; that the slaves soon obtained complete possession of the brig, which, under their direction, was taken into the port of Nassau, in the island of New Providence, where she arrived on the morning of the 9th of the same month; that at the request of the American consul in that place, the Governor ordered a guard on board, to prevent the escape of the mutineers, and with a view to an investigation of the circumstances of the case; that such investigation was accordingly made by two British magistrates, and that an examination also took place by the consul; that on the report of the magistrates, nineteen of the slaves were imprisoned by the local authorities as having been concerned in the mutiny and murder, and their surrender to the consul, to be sent to the United States for trial for these crimes, was refused, on the ground that the Governor wished first to communicate with the Government in England on the subject; that through the interference of the colonial authorities, and even before the military guard was removed, the greater number of the remaining slaves were liberated, and encouraged to go beyond the power of the master of the vessel, or the American consul, by proceedings which neither of them could control. This is the substance of the case, as stated in two protests, one made at Nassau and one at New Orleans, and the consul's letters, together with sundry depositions taken by him, copies of all which papers are herewith transmitted.

The British Government cannot but see that this case, as presented in these papers, is one calling loudly for redress. The "Creole" was passing from one port of the United States to another, in a voyage perfectly lawful, with merchandise on board, and also with slaves, or persons bound to service, natives of America, and belonging to American citizens, and which are recognised as property by the Constitution of the United States in those States in which slavery exists. In the course of the voyage, some of the slaves rose upon the master and crew, subdued them, murdered one man, and caused the vessel to be carried into Nassau. The vessel was thus taken to a British port, not voluntarily by those who had the lawful authority over her, but forcibly and violently, against the master's will, and with the consent of nobody but the mutineers and murderers; for there is no evidence that these outrages were committed with the concurrence of any of the slaves, except those actually engaged in them. Under these circumstances, it would seem to have been the plain and obvious duty of the authorities at Nassau, the port of a friendly Power, to assist the American consul in putting an end to the captivity of the master and crew, restoring to them the control of the vessel, and enabling them to resume their voyage, and to take the mutineers and murderers to their own country to answer for their crimes before the proper tribunal. One cannot conceive how any other course could justly be adopted, or how the duties imposed by that part of the code regulating the intercourse of friendly states, which is generally called the comity of nations, could otherwise be fulfilled. Here was no violation of British law attempted or intended on the part of the master of the "Creole," nor any infringement of the principles of the law of nations. The vessel was lawfully engaged in passing from port to port in the United States. By violence and crime she was carried, against the master's will, out of her course, and into the port of a friendly Power. All was the result of force. Certainly, ordinary comity and hospitality entitled him to such assistance from the authorities of the place as should enable him to resume and prosecute his voyage, and bring the offenders to justice. But, instead of this, if the facts be as represented in these papers, not only did the authorities give no aid for any such purpose, but they did actually interfere to set free the slaves, and to enable them to disperse themselves beyond the reach of the master of the vessel or their owners. A proceeding like this cannot but cause deep feeling in the United States. It has been my purpose to write you at length upon this subject, in order that you might lay before the Government of her Majesty fully and without reserve, the views entertained upon it by that of the United States, and the grounds on which those views are taken. But the early return of the packet precludes the opportunity of going thus into the case of this despatch; and as Lord Ashburton may shortly be expected here, it may be better to enter fully into it with him, if his powers shall be broad enough to embrace it.[1] Some knowledge of the case will have reached England before his departure, and very probably his Government may have given him instructions. But I request, nevertheless, that you lose no time in calling Lord Aberdeen's[2] attention to it in a general manner, and giving him a narrative of the transaction, such as may be framed from the papers now communicated with a distinct declaration that if the facts turn out as stated, this Government thinks it a clear case for indemnification.

You will see that in his letter of the 7th January, 1837, to Mr. Stevenson, respecting the claim for compensation in the cases of the "Comet," "Encomium," and "Enterprise," Lord Palmerston says that "his Majesty's Government is of opinion that the rule by which these claims should be decided, is, that those claimants must be considered entitled to compensation who were lawfully in possession of

1. The British diplomat and financier Alexander Baring, 1st Baron Ashburton (1774–1848).

2. The British politician and diplomat George Hamilton-Gordon, 4th Earl of Aberdeen (1784–1860), served as foreign secretary (1841–46) and prime minister (1852–55), among other governmental positions.

their slaves within the British territory, and who were disturbed in their legal possession of those slaves by functionaries of the British Government."[3] This admission is broad enough to cover the case of the "Creole," if its circumstances are correctly stated. But it does not extend to what we consider the true doctrine, according to the laws and usages of nations; and, therefore, cannot be acquiesced in as the exactly correct general rule. It appears to this Government that not only is no unfriendly interference by the local authorities to be allowed, but that aid and succor should be extended in these, as in other cases which may arise, affecting the rights and interests of citizens of friendly states.

We know no ground on which it is just to say that these colored people had come within, and were within, British territory, in such sense as that of the laws of England affecting and regulating the conditions of persons could properly act upon them. As has been already said, they were not there voluntarily; no human being belonging to the vessel was within British territory of his own accord, except the mutineers. There being no importation, nor intent of importation, what right had the British authorities to inquire into the cargo of the vessel, or the condition of persons on board? These persons might be slaves for life; they might be slaves for a term of years, under a system of apprenticeship; they might be bound to

3. Lord Palmerston, the British statesman Henry John Temple, 3rd Viscount Palmerston (1784–1865), served as secretary of state of foreign affairs (1830–34, 1835–1841, 1846–51) before becoming prime minister (1855–58, 1859–65). The Virginian Andrew Stevenson (1784–1857), a slave owner, served in Congress (1821–34) and was the American minister to the United Kingdom from 1836 to 1841. Webster refers to cases of U.S. slave ships that had been forced by bad weather or accidents to seek refuge in British territory: 164 slaves were liberated from the *Comet* when it was damaged near the Abaco Islands in the northern Bahamas in 1830; 45 slaves were liberated from the *Encomium* when it suffered similar damages off the Abacos in 1834; and in the most famous case, British authorities liberated 78 slaves from the *Enterprise* in 1835 when it docked in Bermuda because of storms. For the exchange between Stevenson and Palmerston, see *Public Documents Printed by Order of the Senate of the United States: Third Session of the Twenty-Fifth Congress*, 3, document 216, 12–15.These cases were debated until 1855, when an Anglo-American Claims Commission awarded partial compensation to the ships' owners.

service by their own voluntary act; they might be in confinement for crimes committed; they might be prisoners of war; or they might be free. How could the British authorities look into and decide any of these questions? Or, indeed, what duty or power, according to the principles of national intercourse, had they to inquire at all? If, indeed, without unfriendly interference, and notwithstanding the fulfillment of all of their duties of comity and assistance, by these authorities, the master of the vessel could not retain the persons, or prevent their escape, then it would be a different question altogether, whether resort could be had to British tribunals, or the power of the Government in any of its branches, to compel their apprehension and restoration. No one complains that English law shall decide the condition of all persons actually incorporated with [the] British population, unless there be treaty stipulation making other provision for special cases. But in the case of the "Creole" the colored persons were still on board an American vessel, that vessel having been forcibly put out of the course of her voyage by mutiny; the master desiring still to resume it, and calling upon the consul of his Government resident at the place and upon the local authorities to enable him so to do, by freeing him from the imprisonment to which mutiny and murder had subjected him, and furnishing him with such necessary aid and assistance as are usual in ordinary cases of distress at sea. These persons, then, cannot be regarded as being mixed with the British people, or as having changed their character at all, either in regard to country or personal condition. It was no more than just to consider the vessel as still on her voyage, and entitled to the succor due to other cases of distress, whether arising from accident or outrage. And that no other view of the subject can be true is evident from the very awkward position in which the local authorities have placed their Government in respect to the mutineers still held in imprisonment. What is to be done with them? How are they to be punished? The English Government will probably not undertake their trial or punishment; and of what use would it be to send them to the United States, separated from their ship, and at a period so late as that, if they should be sent, before proceedings could be instituted against them, the witnesses might be scattered over half the globe. One of the highest offences known to human law is thus likely to go altogether unpunished.

In the note of Lord Palmerston to Mr. Stevenson, above referred to, his lordship said that, "slavery being now abolished throughout the British empire, there can be no well-founded claim for compensation in respect of slaves who, under any circumstances, may come into the British colonies, any more than there would be with respect to slaves who might be brought into the United Kingdom." I have only to remark upon this, that the Government of the United States sees no ground for any distinction founded on an alteration of British law in the colonics. We do not consider that the question depends at all on the state of British law. It is not that in such cases the active agency of British law is invoked and refused; it is, that unfriendly interference is deprecated, and those good offices and friendly assistances expected which a Government usually affords to citizens of a friendly Power when instances occur of disaster and distress. All that the United States require in those cases, they would expect in the ports of England, as well as in those of her colonies. Surely, the influence of local law cannot affect the relations of nations in any such matter as this. Suppose an American vessel, with slaves lawfully on board, were to be captured by a British cruiser, as belonging to some belligerent, while the United States were at peace; suppose such prize carried into England, and the neutrality of the vessel fully made out in the proceedings in Admiralty, and a restoration consequently decreed—in such case, must not the slaves be restored, exactly in the condition in which they were when the capture was made? Would any one contend that the fact of their having been carried into England by force set them free?

No alteration of her own local laws can either increase or diminish, or any way affect, the duty of the English Government and its colonial authorities in such cases, as such duty exists according to the law, the comity, and the usages of nations. The persons on board the "Creole" could only have been regarded as Americans passing from one part of the United States to another, within the reach of British authority only for the moment, and this only by force and violence. To seek to give either to persons or property thus brought within reach an English character, or to impart to either English privileges, or to subject either to English burdens or liabilities, cannot, in the opinion of the Government of the United States, be justified.

Suppose that by the law of England all blacks were slaves, and incapable of any other condition; if persons of that color, free in the United States, should, in attempting to pass from one port to another in their own country, be thrown by stress of weather within British jurisdiction, and there detained for an hour or a day, would it be reasonable that the British authority should be made to act upon their condition, and to make them slaves! Or suppose that an article of merchandise, opium for instance, should be declared by the laws of the United States to be a nuisance, a poison—a thing in which no property could lawfully exist or be asserted; and suppose that an English ship with such a cargo on board, bound from one English port to another, should be driven by stress of weather, or by mutiny of the crew, into the ports of the United States, would it be just and reasonable that such cargo should receive its character from American law, and be thrown overboard and destroyed by the authorities? It is in vain that any attempt is made to answer these suggestions by appealing to general principles of humanity. This is a point in regard to which nations must be permitted to act upon different view, if they entertain different views, under their actually existing condition, and yet hold commercial intercourse with one another, or not hold any such intercourse at all. It may be added, that all attempts by the Government of one nation to force the influence of its laws on that of another, for any object whatsoever, generally defeat their own purposes, by producing dissatisfaction, resentment, and exasperation. Better is it, far better in all respects, that each nation should be left without interference or annoyance, direct or indirect, to its undoubted right of exercising its own regard to all things belonging to its domestic interests and domestic duties.

There are two general considerations, of the highest practical importance, to which you will, in the proper manner, invite the attention of her Majesty's Government.

The first is, that, as civilization has made progress in the world, the intercourse of nations has become more and more independent of different forms of government and different systems of law or religion. It is not now, as it was in ancient times, that every foreigner is considered as therefore an enemy, and that, as soon as he comes into the country, he may be lawfully treated as a slave; nor is the modern intercourse of states carried on mainly, or at all, for the purpose of imposing, by one nation on another, new forms of civil government, new rules of property, or new modes of domestic regulation. The great communities of the world are regarded as wholly independent, each entitled to maintain its own system of law and Government, while all, in their mutual intercourse, are understood to submit to the established rules and principles governing such intercourse. And the perfecting of this system of communication among nations requires the strictest application of the doctrine of non-intervention of any with the domestic concerns of others.

The other is, that the United States and England, now by far the two greatest commercial nations in the world, touch each other both by sea and land at almost innumerable points, and with systems of general jurisprudence essentially alike, yet differing in the forms of their government and in their laws respecting personal servitude; and that so widely does this last-mentioned difference extend its influence, that without the exercise to the fullest extent of the doctrine of non-interference and mutual abstinence from anything affecting each other's domestic regulations, the peace of the two countries, and therefore the peace of the world, will be always in danger.

The Bahamas (British possessions) push themselves near to the shores of the United States, and thus lie almost directly in the track of that great part of their coasting traffic, which, doubling the cape of Florida, connects the cities of the Atlantic with the ports and harbors on the gulf of Mexico and the great commercial emporium on the Mississippi. The seas in which these British possessions are situated are seas of shallow water, full of reefs and sandbars, subject to violent action of the winds, and to the agitations caused by the gulf stream. They must always, therefore, be of dangerous navigation, and accidents must be expected frequently to occur, such as will cause American vessels to be wrecked on British islands, or compel them to seek shelter in British ports. It is quite essential that the manner in which such vessels, their crews, and cargoes, in whatever such cargoes consist, are to be treated, in these cases of misfortune and distress, should be clearly and fully known.

You are acquainted with the correspondence which took place a few years ago, between the American and English Governments, respecting the cases of the "Enterprise," the "Comet," and the "Encomium." I call your attention to the Journal of the Senate of the United States, containing resolutions unanimously adopted by that body respecting those cases.[4] These resolutions, I believe, have already been brought to the notice of her Majesty's Government, but it may be well that both the resolutions themselves and the debates upon them should be again adverted to. You will find the resolutions, of course, among the documents regularly transmitted to the legation, and the debates in the newspapers with which it has also been supplied from this Department.

You will avail yourself of an early opportunity of communicating to Lord Aberdeen, in the manner which you may deem most expedient, the substance of this despatch; and you will receive further instructions respecting the case of the "Creole," unless it shall become the subject of discussion at Washington.

4. See *Journal of the Senate of the United States of America, Being the First Session of the Twenty-Sixth Congress, Begun and Held at the City of Washington, Dec. 2, 1839* (1840), 13 January 1840, 101–2.

In all your communications with her Majesty's Government, you will seek to impress it with a full conviction of the dangerous importance to the peace of the two countries of occurrences of this kind, and the delicate nature of the questions to which they give rise.

I am, sir, your obedient servant,

DANIEL WEBSTER.

EDWARD EVERETT, Esq., &c., &c.

WILLIAM ELLERY CHANNING

from *The Duty of the Free States, or Remarks Suggested by the Case of the Creole*

Daniel Webster's letter to Edward Everett, widely reprinted, immediately elicited angry responses from a number of antislavery northerners, including William Ellery Channing (1780–1842), the best-known Unitarian minister of his time. An important influence on Ralph Waldo Emerson and others in the Transcendentalist movement, the Boston-based Channing began arguing against slavery during the 1830s, most notably in his *Slavery* (1835). His two-volume *The Duty of the Free States, or Remarks Suggested by the Case of the Creole* (Boston: William Crosby, 1842), the source of the text below, refuted numerous legal aspects of Webster's letter, but the main point that he underscored again and again is that slavery is a creature only of municipal (state or local) law, whereas the natural law of nations—which many defined as "higher law"—decrees that a human being cannot be regarded as property. Channing died less than six months after completing the manuscript of *The Duty of the Free States* in late March 1842.

I respectfully ask your attention, fellow-citizens of the Free States, to a subject of great and pressing importance. The case of the Creole, taken by itself, or separated from the principles which are complicated with it, however it might engage my feelings, would not have moved me to the present address. I am not writing to plead the cause of a hundred or more men, scattered through the West Indies, and claimed as slaves. In a world abounding with so much wrong and wo, we at this distance can spend but a few thoughts on these strangers. I rejoice that they are free; I trust that they will remain so; and with these feelings, I dismiss them from my thoughts. The case of the Creole involves great and vital principles, and as such I now invite to it your serious consideration. . . .

This document[1] I propose to examine, and I shall do so chiefly for two reasons: First, because it maintains morally unsound and pernicious doctrines, and is fitted to deprave the public mind; and secondly, because it tends to commit the free states to the defence and support of slavery. This last point is at this moment of peculiar importance. The free states are gradually and silently coming more and more into connexion with slavery; are unconsciously learning to regard it as a national interest; and are about to pledge their wealth and strength, their bones and muscles and lives, to its defence. Slavery is mingling more and more with the politics of the country, determining more and more the individuals who shall hold office, and the great measures on which the public weal depends. It is time for the free states to wake up to the subject; to weigh it deliberately; to think of it, not casually, when some startling fact forces it up into notice, but with earnest, continued, solemn attention; to inquire into their duties in regard to it; to lay down their principles; to mark out their course; and to resolve on acquitting themselves righteously towards God, towards the South, and towards themselves. The North has never come to this great matter in earnest. We have trifled with it. We have left things to take their course. We have been too much absorbed in pecuniary interests, to watch the bearing of slavery on government. Perhaps we have wanted the spirit, the manliness, to look the subject fully in the face. Accordingly, the slave-power has been allowed to stamp itself on the national policy, and to fortify itself with the national arm. For the pecuniary injury to our prosperity which may be traced to this source, I care little or noth-

1. Webster's letter to Everett of 29 January 1842.

ing. There is a higher view of the case. There is a more vital question to be settled than that of interest, the question of duty; and to this my remarks will be confined. . . .

In regard to the reasonings and doctrines of the document, it is a happy circumstance, that they come within the comprehension of the mass of the people. The case of the Creole is a simple one, which requires no extensive legal study to be understood. A man who has had little connexion with public affairs, is as able to decide on it as the bulk of politicians. The elements of the case are so few, and the principles on which its determination rests, are so obvious, that nothing but a sound moral judgment is necessary to the discussion. Nothing can darken it but legal subtlety. None can easily doubt it, but those who surrender conscience and reason to arbitrary rules.

The question between the American and English governments turns mainly on one point. The English government does not recognize within its bounds any property in man. It maintains, that slavery rests wholly on local municipal legislation; that it is an institution not sustained and enforced by the law of nature, and still more, that it is repugnant to this law; and that of course no man, who enters the territory or is placed under the jurisdiction of England, can be regarded as a slave, but must be treated as free. The law creating slavery, it is maintained, has and can have no force beyond the state which creates it. No other nation can be bound by it. Whatever validity this ordinance, which deprives a man of all his rights, may have within the jurisdiction of the community in which it had its birth, it can have no validity any where else. This is the principle on which the English government founds itself.

This principle is so plain, that it has been established and is acted upon among ourselves, and in the neighboring British provinces. When a slave is brought by his master into Massachusetts, he is pronounced free, on the ground that the law of slavery has no force beyond the state which ordains it, and that the right of every man to liberty is recognized as one of the fundamental laws of the commonwealth. A slave flying from his master to this commonwealth is indeed restored, but not on account of the validity of the legislation of the South on this point, but solely on the ground of a positive provision of the constitution of the United States; and he is delivered, not as a slave, but as a "person held to service by law in another state."[2] We should not think for a moment of restoring a slave flying to us from Cuba or Turkey. We recognize no right of a foreign master on this soil. The moment he brings his slave here, his claim vanishes into air; and this takes place because we recognize freedom as the right of every human being. . . .

I repeat it, for the truth deserves reiteration, that all nations are bound to respect the rights of every human being. This is God's law, as old as the world. No local law can touch it. No ordinance of a particular state, degrading a set of men to chattels, can absolve all nations from the obligation of regarding the injured beings as men, or bind them to send back the injured to their chains. The character of a slave, attached to a man by a local government, is not and cannot be incorporated into his nature. It does not cling to him, go where he will. The scar of slavery on his back does not reach his soul. The arbitrary relation between him and his master cannot suspend the primitive indestructible relation by which God binds him to his kind.

The idea that a particular state may fix, enduringly, this stigma on a human being, and can bind the most just and generous men to respect it, should be rejected with scorn and indignation. It reminds us of those horrible fictions, in which some demon is described as stamping an indelible mark of hell on his helpless victims. It was the horrible peculiarity of the world in the reign of Tiberius,[3] that it had become one vast prison. The unhappy man, on whom the blighting suspicion of the tyrant had fallen, could find no shelter or escape through the whole civilized regions of the globe. Every where his

2. A reference to the Fugitive Slave Act of 1793. A belief among many proslavery people that this act was inadequate led to the adoption of a more forceful fugitive slave law as part of the Compromise of 1850.

3. Tiberius (42 BC–AD 37) was emperor of Rome from AD 14 to 37.

sentence followed him like fate. And can the law of a despot, or of a chamber of despots, extend now the same fearful doom to the ends of the earth? Can a little state at the South spread its web of cruel, wrongful legislation over both continents? Do all communities become spell-bound by a law in a single country creating slavery? Must they become the slave's jailers? Must they be less merciful than the storm which drives off the bondman from the detested shore of servitude and casts him on the soil of freedom? Must even that soil become tainted by an ordinance passed perhaps in another hemisphere? Has oppression this terrible omnipresence? Must the whole earth register the slave-holders' decree? Then the earth is blighted indeed. Then, as some ancient sects taught, it is truly the empire of the Principle of Evil, of the power of Darkness. Then God is dethroned here; for where injustice and oppression are omnipotent, God has no empire.

I have thus stated the great principle on which the English authorities acted in the case of the Creole, and on which all nations are bound to act. Slavery is the creature of a local law, having power not a hand-breadth beyond the jurisdiction of the country which ordains it. Other nations know nothing of it, are bound to pay it no heed. I might add that other nations are bound to tolerate it within the bounds of a particular state, only on the grounds on which they suffer a particular state to establish bloody superstitions, to use the rack in jurisprudence, or to practice other enormities. They might more justifiably put down slavery where it exists, than enforce a foreign slave code within their own bounds. Such is the impregnable principle which we of the free states should recognize and earnestly sustain.

JOSHUA R. GIDDINGS

Resolutions

By March 1842, debate on the *Creole* had heated up in a Congress already divided about the gag rules: the effort by southern leaders of the U.S. House of Representatives to ban debate on antislavery petitions. The Massachusetts congressman John Quincy Adams (1767–1848), the sixth president of the United States (1825–29), led the opposition to the gag rules, and he was joined by Congressman Joshua R. Giddings (1795–1864) of Ohio. When southerners and their northern supporters (known as "doughfaces") failed in their effort to censure Adams, Giddings felt emboldened to address the *Creole* rebellion. With the help of the prominent abolitionist Theodore Dwight Weld (1803–1895), who formulated some of his language, Giddings drew up a series of resolutions offering support for the *Creole* rebels and questioning the legality of slavery beyond the jurisdiction of the slave states. Giddings proposed the resolutions on the House floor on 21 March 1842. Making use of an arcane procedural move, southern leaders refused either to table or to vote on the resolutions, which allowed them to put forth a resolution the very next day to censure Giddings. That censure passed on a vote of 125–60, with the entire Democratic Party and most southern Whigs voting against Giddings. In response, Giddings resigned from the House in protest, only to be reelected by his constituents in a special election on 5 May 1842. Giddings and Adams continued their campaign against the gag rules, which were eventually repealed on 3 December 1844. Giddings's resolutions on the *Creole* rebellion and Virginia congressman John Minor Botts's censure resolution are taken from the *Congressional Globe*, 27th Congress, 2nd session, 21–22 March, 1842.

Mr. GIDDINGS said he had a series of resolutions upon a subject which had called forth some interest in the other end of the Capitol, and in the nation. He desired to lay them before the country, and would call them up for action at the next opportunity.

The resolutions were read as follows:

Resolved, That, prior to the Adoption of the Federal Constitution, each of the several States composing this Union exercised full and exclusive jurisdiction over the subject of slavery within its own territory, and possessed full power to continue or abolish it at pleasure.

Resolved, That by adopting the Constitution, no part of the aforesaid powers were delegated to the Federal Government, but were reserved by and still pertain to each of the several States.

Resolved, That by the 8th section of the 1st article of the Constitution, each of the several States surrendered to the Federal Government all jurisdiction over the subjects of commerce and navigation upon the high seas.

Resolved, That slavery being an abridgment of the natural rights of man, can exist only by force of positive municipal law, and is necessarily confined to the territorial jurisdiction of the power creating it.

Resolved, That when a ship belonging to the citizens of any State of the Union leaves the waters and territory of such State and enters upon the high seas, the persons on board cease to be subject to the slave laws of such State, and therefore are governed in their relations to each other by, and are amenable to, the laws of the United States.

Resolved, That when the brig Creole, on her late passage for New Orleans, left the territorial jurisdiction of Virginia, the slave laws of that State ceased to have jurisdiction over the persons on board such brig, and such persons became amenable only to the laws of the United States.

Resolved, That the persons on board the said ship, in resuming their natural rights of personal liberty, violated no law of the United States, incurred no legal penalty, and are justly liable to no punishment.

Resolved, That all attempts to regain possession of, or to re-enslave said persons, are unauthorized by the Constitution or laws of the United States, and are incompatible with our national honor.

Resolved, That all attempts to exert our national influence in favor of the coastwise slave trade, or to place this nation in the attitude of maintaining a "commerce in human beings," are subversive of the rights and injurious to the feelings and the interests of the free States; are unauthorized by the Constitution and prejudicial to our national character.

Mr. BOTTS . . . then asked leave . . . to offer a resolution— . . .

Whereas the Hon. JOSHUA R. GIDDINGS, the member from the 16th Congressional district of the State of Ohio, has this day presented to the House a series of resolutions touching the most important interests connected with a large portion of the Union, now a subject of negotiation between the United States and Great Britain of the most delicate nature, the result of which may eventually involve those nations, and perhaps the whole civilized world in war:

And whereas it is the duty of every good citizen, and particularly every selected agent and representative of the people to discountenance all efforts to create excitement, dissatisfaction, and division among the people of the United States at such a time, and under such circumstances, which is the only effect to be accomplished by the introduction of sentiments before the legislative body of the country, hostile to the grounds assumed by the high functionary having in charge this important and delicate trust:

And whereas mutiny and murder are therein justified and approved in terms shocking to all sense of law, order, and humanity; therefore

Resolved, That this House holds the conduct of the said member as altogether unwarranted, and unwarrantable, and deserving the severe condemnation of the people of this country, and of this body in particular.

HENRY HIGHLAND GARNET

from "An Address to the Slaves of the United States of America"

On 16 August 1843, at the National Convention of Colored Citizens held at Buffalo, New York, the African American Presbyterian minister Henry Highland Garnet (1815–1882) addressed the approximately seventy delegates in attendance. Rejecting the nonviolent, moral-suasion approach championed by William Lloyd Garrison and his supporters, including Frederick Douglass, Garnet, in "An Address to the Slaves," celebrated slave resistance as an act of patriotism and self-defense, invoking such black freedom fighters as Denmark Vesey, Nat Turner, and Madison Washington. This speech marks the first notable invocation of Washington beyond the newspaper accounts of 1841 and 1842, showing that he had entered the pantheon of black revolutionary heroes. Garnet came under fire from the Garrisonian abolitionists who made up most of the delegates, and after much debate the "Address" failed by one vote in winning the endorsement of the subcommittee charged with formulating the convention's recommendations for future action. Douglass, who was on that committee, voted against Garnet's speech. By the mid-1840s, however, Douglass had moved much closer to Garnet's position, in part because of his shared admiration for the rebels of the *Creole*. In his speeches on Washington of the late 1840s (which are excerpted in the next section), he could be just as vociferous as Garnet in calling for slave resistance. The text below of the closing paragraphs of Garnet's speech is taken from *Walker's Appeal, with a Brief Sketch of His Life. By Henry Highland Garnet. And also Garnet's Address to the Slaves of the United States of America* (New York: J. H. Tobbit, 1848), a reprinting of two major black-revolutionary documents funded by the white abolitionist and revolutionary John Brown.

Fellow-men! patient sufferers! behold your dearest rights crushed to the earth! See your sons murdered, and your wives, mothers, and sisters, doomed to prostitution! In the name of the merciful God! and by all that life is worth, let it no longer be a debatable question, whether it is better to choose LIBERTY or DEATH![1]

In 1822, Denmark Veazie, of South Carolina, formed a plan for the liberation of his fellow men. In the whole history of human efforts to overthrow slavery, a more complicated and tremendous plan was never formed. He was betrayed by the treachery of his own people, and died a martyr to freedom.[2] Many a brave hero fell, but History, faithful to her high trust, will transcribe his name on the same monument with Moses, Hampden, Tell, Bruce, and Wallace, Touissaint L'Ouverture, Lafayette and Washington.[3] That tremendous movement shook the whole empire of slavery. The guilty soul thieves were overwhelmed with fear. It is a matter of fact, that at that time, and in consequence of the threatened revolution, the slave states talked strongly of emancipation. But they blew but one blast of the trumpet of freedom, and then laid it aside. As these men became quiet, the slaveholders ceased to talk about emancipation: and now, behold your condition to-day! Angels sigh over it,

1. The famous credo of Virginia's revolutionary patriot Patrick Henry (1736–1799).

2. In 1822, Denmark Vesey (1767?–1822) allegedly attempted to bring about a slave insurrection in Charleston, South Carolina. He was executed after a house servant revealed the plot.

3. References to revolutionary heroes from antiquity to the nineteenth century. Moses led the Jewish people out of slavery in Egypt; John Hampden (1594–1643) helped lead the Puritan opposition to Charles I during the late 1630s and early 1640s; William Tell was a legendary (perhaps apocryphal) Swiss freedom fighter of the fourteenth century; the Scots Robert Bruce (1274–1329) and William Wallace (1272?–1305) championed popular resistance to England during the thirteenth century; Toussaint-Louverture (1743–1803) was one of the leaders of the late-eighteenth-century Haitian uprising against French colonial control; and the Frenchman the Marquis de Lafayette (1757–1834) and George Washington (1732–1799), the eventual first president of the United States, were celebrated American Revolutionary military leaders.

and humanity has long since exhausted her tears in weeping on your account!

The patriotic Nathaniel Turner[4] followed Denmark Veazie. He was goaded to desperation by wrong and injustice. By Despotism, his name has been recorded on the list of infamy, but future generations will number him among the noble and brave.

Next arose the immortal Joseph Cinque, the hero of the Amistad.[5] He was a native African, and by the help of God he emancipated a whole ship-load of his fellow men on the high seas. And he now sings of liberty on the sunny hills of Africa, and beneath his native palm trees, where he hears the lion roar, and feels himself as free as that king of the forest. Next arose Madison Washington, that bright star of freedom, and took his station in the constellation of freedom. He was a slave on board the brig Creole, of Richmond, bound to New Orleans, that great slave mart, with a hundred and four others. Nineteen struck for liberty or death. But one life was taken, and the whole were emancipated, and the vessel was carried into Nassau, New Providence. Noble men! Those who have fallen in freedom's conflict, their memories will be cherished by the true hearted, and the God-fearing, in all future generations; those who are living, their names are surrounded by a halo of glory.

We do not advise you to attempt a revolution with the sword, because it would be INEXPEDIENT. Your numbers are too small, and moreover the rising spirit of the age, and the spirit of the gospel, are opposed to war and bloodshed. But from this moment cease to labor for tyrants who will not remunerate you. Let every slave throughout the land do this, and the days of slavery are numbered. You cannot be more oppressed than you have been—you cannot

4. Tuner (1800–1831) led a slave rebellion in Southampton County, Virginia, on 22 August 1831 that resulted in the deaths of approximately sixty whites.

5. Joseph Cinqué was one of the leaders of the 1839 slave uprising on the Spanish slave ship *Amistad*. The U.S. Navy seized the ship and mutineers, but in 1841 the U.S. Supreme Court granted the rebels their freedom. Abolitionists helped Cinqué and others return to Africa.

suffer greater cruelties than you have already. Rather DIE FREEMEN, THAN LIVE TO BE SLAVES. Remember that you are THREE MILLIONS.

It is in your power so to torment the God-cursed slaveholders, that they will be glad to let you go free. If the scale was turned, and black men were the masters, and white men the slaves, every destructive agent and element would be employed to lay the oppressor low. Danger and death would hang over their heads day and night. Yes, the tyrants would meet with plagues more terrible than those of Pharaoh. But you are a patient people. You act as though you were made for the special use of these devils. You act as though your daughters were born to pamper the lusts of your masters and overseers. And worse than all, you tamely submit, while your lords tear your wives from your embraces, and defile them before your eyes. In the name of God we ask, are you men? Where is the blood of your fathers? Has it all run out of your veins? Awake, awake; millions of voices are calling you! Your dead fathers speak to you from their graves. Heaven, as with a voice of thunder, calls on you to arise from the dust.

Let your motto be RESISTANCE! RESISTANCE! RESISTANCE!—No oppressed people have ever secured their liberty without resistance. What kind of resistance you had better make, you must decide by the circumstances that surround you, and according to the suggestion of expediency. Brethren, adieu. Trust in the living God. Labor for the peace of the human race, and remember that you are three millions.

PART 3

Douglass on the *Creole* and Black Revolution

DOUGLASS DID NOT SPEAK OR write about the *Creole* rebellion in the early 1840s, or if he did, those comments are no long extant. But beginning in the fall of 1845, when he commenced a nearly two-year antislavery lecture tour in Great Britain and Ireland, Douglass regularly referred to Madison Washington and the *Creole* rebellion in his speeches, praising both the bravery of the *Creole* rebels and the courage of the British in refusing to return the former slaves to their U.S. owners. Douglass's British tour of 1845–47 was motivated by his need to leave the United States after the May 1845 publication of his *Narrative*, for suddenly the celebrated author—who was still legally a slave—was vulnerable to fugitive slave hunters. (Douglass was bought out of slavery in 1846 by his British admirers.) Speaking in Ireland, Scotland, and England, Douglass no doubt identified with Washington as a person who took refuge with the British, and on several occasions he made the connection himself. Increasingly, he expressed his admiration for Washington as a black who was willing to use violence to bring about his and his compatriots' freedom. As a lecturer in William Lloyd Garrison's antislavery organization, Douglass from 1841 to 1845 had generally followed Garrison in advocating moral suasion over violence. But by the late 1840s, he was arguing that violent rebellion could well be an appropriate response to the violence of slavery. In 1851, he publicly broke with Garrison, and in his writings of the 1850s, including *The Heroic Slave*, he celebrated black rebels as belonging in the heroic tradition of the American revolutionaries of 1776 and the Haitian revolutionaries of the 1790s and early 1800s.

The eight selections in part 3 follow Douglass from his first known remarks on the *Creole* rebellion in 1845 to his last, in an 1861 essay applauding the resourceful militancy of William Stillman. Though his famous 1852 speech, "What to the Slave Is the Fourth of July?," does not refer to the *Creole* rebellion, it is included here for its evocation of the American Revolutionary violence that gave birth to a country that was founded on the egalitarian ideals of Jefferson's Declaration of Independence and yet had become a nation of slavery. Douglass drew on these ironies for his novella, published just six months later, about a black man with the American Revolutionary name of Madison Washington.

FREDERICK DOUGLASS

from "American Prejudice against Color"

Douglass's first extant remarks on Madison Washington came at the end of a lecture delivered in Cork, Ireland, on 23 October 1845. Still legally a slave, Douglass had fled the United States out of concern that his new celebrity status as the author of the *Narrative of the Life of Frederick Douglass, An American Slave* (May 1845) would leave him vulnerable to capture by fugitive slave hunters. Embraced as an antislavery speaker in Great Britain, he identified with Washington as a fugitive who had wide support in antislavery circles in Great Britain, along with the tacit support of the British government. Douglass used the occasion of the speech to challenge U.S. whites' antiblack racism and to support slaves' right to resist all forms of tyranny. The speech was reported in the 27 October 1845 issue of the *Cork Examiner*; the excerpt below is taken from *The Frederick Douglass Papers: Series One: Speeches, Debates, and Interviews: Volume 1: 1841–46*, edited by John W. Blassingame et al. (New Haven, Conn.: Yale University Press, 1979), which draws on the *Cork Examiner* printing.

My friends, there are charges brought against coloured men not alone of intellectual inferiority, but of want of affection for each other. I do know that their affections are exceedingly strong. Why, but a short time ago we had a glorious illustration of affection in the heart of a black man—Maddison[1] Washington, he has made some noise in the world by that act of his, it has been made the ground of some

1. This is the spelling adopted by the reporter for the *Cork Examiner*, the source of this text.

diplomacy:—he fled from Virginia for his freedom—he ran from American republican slavery, to monarchical liberty, and preferred the one decidedly to the other—he left his wife and little ones in slavery—he made up his mind to leave them, for he felt that in Virginia he was always subject to be removed from them; he ran off to Canada, he was there for two years, but there in misery; for his wife was perpetually before him, he said within himself—I can't be free while my wife's a slave. He left Canada to make an effort to save his wife and children, he arrived at Troy where he met with Mr. Garrett;[2] a highly intellectual black man, who admonished [him] not to go, it would be perfectly fruitless. He went on however to Virginia where he was immediately taken, put with a gang of slaves on board the brig *Creole*, destined for Southern America. After being out nine days, he could sometimes see the iron-hearted owners contemplating joyfully the amount of money they should gain by reaching the market before it was glutted.

On the 9th day Maddison Washington succeeded in getting off his irons, and reaching his head above the hatchway he seemed inspired with the love of freedom, with the determination to get it or die in the attempt. As he came to the resolution he darted out of the hatchway, seized a handspike, felled the Captain—and found himself with his companions masters of the ship. He saved a sufficient number of the lives of those who governed the ship to reach the British Islands; there they were emancipated. This soon was found out at the other side of the Atlantic and our Congress was thrown into an uproar that *Maddison Washington* had in imitation of *George Washington* gained liberty. They branded him as being a thief, robber and murderer; they insisted on the British Govern-

2. Douglass refers to the Reverend Henry Highland Garnet (1815–1882). Born a slave in Maryland, Garnet escaped slavery with his parents in 1824 and was educated at the African Free School in New York City. One of the founders of the American and Foreign Anti-Slavery Society, he remains best known for his militant speech of 1843, "An Address to the Slaves of the United States of America," which concludes with a peroration to the slaves: "Let your motto be RESISTANCE! RESISTANCE! RESISTANCE!" (See the excerpt from Garnet's "Address" in part 2.)

ment giving him back. The British Lion refused to send the bondsmen back. They did send Lord Ashburton[3] as politely as possible to tell them that they were not to be the mere watchdogs of American slaveowners; and Washington with his 130 brethren are free. We are branded as not loving our brother and race. Why did Maddison Washington leave Canada where he might be free, and run the risk of going to Virginia? It has been said that it is none but those persons who have a mixture of European blood who distinguish themselves. This is not true. I know that the most intellectual and moral colored man that is now in our country is a man in whose veins no European blood courses—'tis the Rev. Mr. Garrett; and there is the Rev. Theodore Wright[4]—people who have no taint of European blood, yet they are as respectable and intelligent, they possess as elegant manners as I see among almost any class of people. Indeed my friends those very Americans are indebted to us for their own liberty at the present time, the first blood that gushed at Lexington, at the battle field of Worcester, and Bunker Hill (applause).[5] General Jackson has to own that he owes his farm on the banks of the Mobile to the strong hand of the Negro. I could read you General Jackson's own account of the services of the blacks to him,[6] and after having done this, the base ingrates enslave us. Mr. Douglas[s] here sat down amidst the warmest applause of the meeting.

3. The British diplomat and financier Alexander Baring, 1st Baron Ashburton (1774–1848).

4. Theodore Sedgwick Wright (1797–1847), who worked with Garnet to help found the American and Foreign Anti-Slavery Society in 1840. Wright and Garnet both served as pastors at Shiloh Presbyterian Church in New York City.

5. Famous battles in Massachusetts during the Revolutionary War. Approximately 5,000 blacks fought on the side of the patriots, most famously Crispus Attucks, who died during the Boston Massacre on 5 August 1770.

6. During the War of 1812, Andrew Jackson (1767–1845), the seventh president of the United States (1829–37), issued a proclamation that was widely hailed by African Americans: praise for the African Americans who helped defend New Orleans in 1814. For many African American leaders, the proclamation legitimated blacks' claims to U.S. citizenship. See William C. Nell's influential *Services of Colored Americans in the Wars of 1776 and 1812* (1851) and *The Colored Patriots of the American Revolution* (1855). (An excerpt from *Colored Patriots* can be found in part 4 below.)

FREDERICK DOUGLASS

from "America's Compromise with Slavery and the Abolitionists' Work"

On 6 April 1846, Douglass lectured at an antislavery meeting at the Secession Church, Abbey Close, in Paisley, Scotland. Among the topics he addressed was the diplomatic controversy between Great Britain and the United States over the *Creole* case. Like Joshua Giddings, William Ellery Channing, and William Jay, he feared that slave interests were driving U.S. politics. The speech was reported in the 11 April 1846 issue of the *Renfrewshire Advertiser*; the selection below, like the previous one, is taken from volume 1 of *The Frederick Douglass Papers*, which draws on the printing in the *Advertiser*.

The Northern States are but the tools of slaveholders; a man belonging to the Free States cannot go into the Southern or Slaveholding States, although the law says he shall enjoy equal rights in all states, he cannot go into these states with the Declaration in one hand and the word of God in the other to declare the rights of all men, but he makes himself liable to be hung at the first lamp post. People talk here of the political rights enjoyed by the Americans, suffrage, &c. I admit that they enjoy the suffrage to a considerable extent. Who are the voters of America? The slaves of slaves. Our history shows the entire power of government to have been under the domination of slavery. It has elected our President, our senators, &c., and one of the first duties of our minister was to negotiate with Britain for the return to bondage of Maddison Washington,[1] who braved the dangers of the deep; who, with one mighty effort, burst asunder the chains of one hundred and thirty-five fellow men, and after much fatigue and many severe struggles, steered them into a British port, and there found shelter under the British lion. Our whole country was thrown into confusion by the fact of him liberating himself and so many of his brethren, and Britain thus aiding them in their emancipation. I can well remember the speeches of Messrs. Clay, Calhoun,[2] Webster, and others, on that occasion. Mr. Clay called attention to a most appalling occurrence on the high seas, and a breach of that law between nation and nation, &c.; but now Maddison Washington and his compeers are treading upon British soil, they have fled from a republican government and have chosen a monarchical, and are basking under the free sun amid the free hills and valleys of a free monarchical country.

1. Daniel Webster's letter to Edward Everett, in part 2 of this volume, charged the U.S. minister to the United Kingdom to negotiate for the return of the *Creole*'s slaves.

2. The Kentucky politician Henry Clay (1777–1852) and the South Carolina politician John C. Calhoun (1782–1850) supported the rights of slave owners and took the side of the *Creole*'s owners; see Senate Documents, 27th Congress, 2nd session (1842), 46–47, 115–16, 203–4.

FREDERICK DOUGLASS

from "American and Scottish Prejudice against the Slave"

During his antislavery travels in Great Britain, Douglass regularly conveyed his admiration for the British for supporting the right of Madison Washington and his fellow slaves to rise up against their oppressors. On 1 May 1846, Douglass took up this theme in a lecture at the Music Hall in Edinburgh before approximately 2,000 people. The speech was reported in the 7 May 1846 issue of the *Edinburgh Caledonian Mercury* and other newspapers in Edinburgh and Glasgow. The excerpt below is taken from volume 1 of *The Frederick Douglass Papers*, which draws on the printing in the *Caledonian Mercury*.

Mr. Douglas[s] was received with much applause. He said, that one of the greatest drawbacks to the progress of the Anti-Slavery cause in the United States was the inveterate prejudices which existed against the coloured population. They were looked on in every place as beasts rather than men; and to be connected in any manner with a slave—or even with a coloured freeman—was considered as humbling and degrading.

Amongst all ranks of society in that country, the poor outcast coloured man was not regarded as possessing a moral or intellectual sensibility, and all considered themselves entitled to insult and outrage his feelings with impunity. Thanks to the labours of the abolitionists, however, that feeling was now broken in upon, and was, to a certain extent, giving way; but the distinction was still so broad as to draw a visible line of demarcation between the two classes. If the coloured man went to the church to worship God, he must occupy a certain place assigned for him; as if the coloured skin was designed to be the mark of an inferior mind, and subject its possessor to the contumely, insult, and disdain of many a white man, with a heart as black as the exterior of the despised negro—(cheers).

Mr. Douglas[s] then alluded to the case of Maddison[1] Washington, an American slave, who with some others escaped from bondage, but was retaken, and put on board the brig *Creole*. They had not been more than seven or eight days at sea when Maddison resolved to make another effort to regain his lost freedom. He communicated to some of his fellow-captives his plan of operations; and in the night following carried them into effect. He got on deck, and seizing a handspike, struck down the captain and mate, secured the crew, and cheered on his associates in the cause of liberty; and in ten minutes was master of the ship—(cheers). The vessel was then taken to a British port (New Providence), and when there the crew applied to the British resident for aid against the mutineers. The Government refused—(cheers)—they refused to take all the men as prisoners; but they gave them this aid—they kept 19 as prisoners, on the ground of mutiny, and gave the remaining 130 their liberty—(loud cheers). They were free men the moment they put their foot on British soil, and their freedom was acknowledged by the judicature of the land—(cheers).

But this was not relished by brother Jonathan[2]—he considered it as a grievous outrage—a national insult; and instructed Mr. Webster, who was then Secretary of State, to demand compensation from the British Government for the injury done; and characterised the noble Maddison Washington as being a murderer, a tyrant, and a mutineer. And all this for the punishment of an act, which, according to all the doctrines "professed" by Americans, ought to

1. This is the spelling adopted by the reporter for the *Edinburgh Caledonian Mercury*, the source of this text.

2. Fictional, folkloric character who personified the U.S. nation.

have been honoured and rewarded—(cheers). It was considered no crime for America, as a nation, to rise up and assert her freedom in the fields of fight; but when the poor African made a stroke for his liberty it was declared to be a crime, and he [was] punished as a villain—what was an outrage on the part of the black man was an honour and a glory to the white; and in the Senate of that country —"the home of the brave and the land of the free"—there were not wanting the Clays, the Prestons,[3] and the Calhouns, to stand up and declare that it was a national insult to set the slaves at liberty, and demand reparation—these men who were at all times ready to weep tears of red hot iron—(cheers and laughter)—for the oppressed. Monarchical nations of Europe—now talked about being ready to go to all lengths in defence of the national honour and present an unbroken front to England's might—(loud cheers). But the British Government, undismayed by the vapouring of the slaveholders, sent Lord Ashburton to tell them—just in a civil way—(laughter)—that they should have no compensation, and that the slaves should not be returned to them—(loud cheers)—thus giving practical effect to the great command—"Break the bonds, and let the oppressed go free"[4]—(great cheering).

3. Like John C. Calhoun, William Campbell Preston (1794–1860), also a senator from South Carolina, was proslavery and angry about the British response to the *Creole* rebellion. At the urging of Calhoun, he demanded more information about what President Tyler was doing to compel the British to return the slaves (Senate Documents 27th Cong., 2nd session [1842], 47, 115–16, 204).

4. Isaiah 58:6.

FREDERICK DOUGLASS

from "Meeting in Faneuil Hall"

On the evening of 30 May 1848, Douglass addressed a meeting of the New England Anti-Slavery Society at Boston's historic Faneuil Hall. His comments were reported in the 9 June 1848 issue of the *Liberator*, the source of the selection below. In his remarks, Douglass spoke about his continued belief, shared by William Lloyd Garrison and other abolitionists associated with the society, that the Constitution was a proslavery document (he would change his mind on that in 1851 when he publicly broke with Garrison). But in the company of a number of white abolitionists who championed moral suasion, Douglass celebrated black revolutionary violence, linking Madison Washington to Nat Turner (1800–1831), whose slave rebellion in Southampton County, Virginia, in August 1831 resulted in the deaths of approximately sixty whites and (in reprisal) over one hundred blacks.

FREDERICK DOUGLASS was warmly cheered on taking the platform. I am glad, said Mr. Douglass, to be once more in Faneuil Hall, and to address those whom I regard as among the enslavers of myself and my brethren. What I have to say may not be very pleasant to those who venerate the Constitution, but, nevertheless, I must say to you that, by the support you give to that instrument, you are the enslavers of my southern brethren and sisters. Now you say, through the Constitution,—'if you, slaves, dare to rise and assert your freedom, we of the North will come down upon you like an avalanche, and crush you to pieces.' We are frequently taunted with *cowardice* for being slaves, and for enduring such indignities and sufferings. The taunt comes with an ill grace from you. You stand eighteen millions strong, united, educated, armed, ready to put us down; we are weak, ignorant, degraded, unarmed, and *three* millions! Under these circumstances, what can we hope to effect? We call upon you to get out of this relation,—to stand away from the slaveholders' side, and give us fair play. Say to the slaveholders—'If you will imbrue your hands in the blood of your brethren, if you will crush and chain your fellow-men, do it at your own risk and peril!' Would you but do this, oh, men of the North, I know there is a spirit among the slaves which would not much longer brook their degradation and their bondage. There are many Madison Washingtons and Nathaniel Turners in the South, who would assert their right to liberty, if you would take your feet from their necks, and your sympathy and aid from their oppressors.

Mr. D. spoke of Nathaniel Turner, a noble, brave and generous soul—patient, disinterested, and fearless of suffering. How was he treated, for endeavoring to gain his own liberty, and that of his enslaved brethren, by the self-same means which the Revolutionary fathers employed? When taken by his enemies, he was stripped naked, and compelled to walk barefooted, some thirty yards, over burning coals, and, when he reached the end, he fell, pierced by a hundred American bullets![1] I say to you, exclaimed Mr. Douglass, get out of this position of body-guard to slavery! Cease from any longer rendering aid and comfort to the tyrant-master!

I know how you will reply to this; you will say that I, and such as I, are not *men*; you look upon us as beneath you; you look upon us as naturally and necessarily degraded. But, nevertheless, we are MEN! (Cheers.) You may pile up statutes against us and our manhood as high as heaven, and still we are not changed thereby. WE ARE MEN. (Immense cheering.) Yes! we are *your* brothers!

1. Turner was tried in a local court and executed by hanging on 11 November 1831. Before the trial, whites killed approximately 120 blacks in retaliation.

FREDERICK DOUGLASS

from "Address at the Great Anti-Colonization Meeting in New York"

On 23–24 April 1849, African American leaders met in New York City to voice their opposition to the American Colonization Society (ACS), an organization established in 1816 by whites who hoped to ship the nation's blacks to Africa. In an effort to achieve their goals, the colonizationists purchased land in Africa and founded the country of Liberia. In 1847, Liberia became an independent nation, but it continued its association with the ACS. During the summer of 1848, Liberia's first president, J. J. Roberts, toured New York City and, with the support of the ACS, tried to entice free blacks to immigrate to his country. Douglass and other abolitionists, black and white, were infuriated by what they regarded as the ACS's racist agenda of trying to create a white America by insisting that Africa was blacks' "natural" home. At the 1849 meeting, Douglass reiterated his opposition to the ACS, arguing for African Americans' rights to citizenship in their native country while warning of the possibility of black violence from the Madison Washingtons of the United States. The minutes of the meeting were published in an article titled "Great Anti-Colonization Meeting in New York," which appeared in the 11 May 1849 issue of Douglass's *North Star*, the source of the excerpt below.

The cry of the slave goes up to heaven, to God, and unless the American people shall break every yoke, and let the oppressed go free, that spirit in man which abhors chains, and will not be restrained by them, will lead those sable arms that have long been engaged in cultivating, beautifying and adorning the South, to spread death and devastation there. (Great applause.) Some men go for the abolition of Slavery by peaceable means. So do I; I am a peace man; but I recognize in the Southern States at this moment, as has been remarked here, a state of war. Sir, I know that I am speaking now, not to this audience alone, for I see reporters here, and I learn that what is spoken here is to be published, and will be read by Colonizationists and perhaps by slaveholders. I want them to know that at least one colored man in the Union, peace man though he is, would greet with joy the glad news should it come here tomorrow, that an insurrection had broken out in the Southern States (Great Applause.) I want them to know that a black man cherishes the sentiment—that one of the fugitive slaves holds it, and that it is not impossible that some other black men (A voice—we are all so here,) may have occasion at some time or other, to put this theory into practice. Sir, I want to alarm the slaveholders, and not to alarm them by mere declamation or by mere bold assertions, but to show them that there is really danger in persisting in the crime of continuing Slavery in this land. I want them to know that there are some Madison Washingtons in this country (Applause.) The American people have been accustomed to regard us as inferior beings. The Colonization Society has told them that we are inferior beings, and that in consequence of our calm and tame submission to the yoke which they have imposed upon us; to their chains, fetters, gags, lashes, whipping-posts, dungeons and blood-hounds, we must be regarded as inferior—that there is no fight in us,—and that is evidence enough to prove that God intended us to retain the position which we now occupy. I want to prevent them from laying this flattering unaction to their souls. There are colored persons who hold other views, who entertain other feelings, with respect to this matter.

As an illustration of the spirit that is in the black man, let me refer to the story of Madison Washington. The treatment of that man by this Government was such as to disgrace it in the eyes of the civilized world. He escaped some years ago from Virginia, and succeeded in reaching Canada, where, nestled in the mane of the British Lion, the American Eagle might scream in vain above him, from his bloody beak and talons he was free. There he could repose in quiet and peace. But he remembered that he had left in bondage a wife, and in the true spirit of a noble minded and noble hearted man, he said; while my wife is a slave I cannot be free. I will leave the shores of Canada, and God being my helper, I will go to Virginia, and snatch my wife from the bloody hands of the oppressor. He went to Virginia, against the entreaties of friends, against the advice of my friend Gurney,[1] whom to name here ought to secure a round of applause. (Loud applause.) He went, contrary to the advice of another—I was going to say, a nobler hero, but I can scarcely recognize a nobler one than Gurney. Robert Purvis[2] was the man: he advised him not to go, and for a time he was inclined to listen to his counsel. He told him it would be of no use for him to go, for that as sure as he went he would only be himself enslaved, and could of course do nothing towards freeing his wife. Under the influence of his counsel he consented not to go; but when he left the house of Purvis, the thoughts of his wife in Slavery came back to his mind to trouble his peace and disturb his slumbers. So he resolved again to take no counsel either on the one hand or the other, but to go back to Virginia and rescue his wife if possible. That was a noble resolve (applause;) and the result was still more noble. On reaching there he was unfortunately arrested and thrown into prison and put under heavy irons. At the appointed time he was brought manacled upon the auctioneer's block, and sold to a New Orleans trader. We see nothing more of Madison Washington, until we see him at the head of a gang of one hundred slaves destined for the Southern market. He, together with the rest of the gang, were driven on board the brig Creole, at Richmond, and placed beneath the hatchway, in irons; the slave-dealer—I sometimes think I see him—walking the deck of that ship freighted with human misery,

1. The British abolitionist and Quaker Joseph John Gurney (1788–1847) spoke against slavery during tours of North America and the West Indies during 1837–40. He may have met Madison Washington in Canada.

2. The African American abolitionist Robert Purvis (1810–1898) resided most of his life in Philadelphia. He used his considerable wealth to support abolitionism and black uplift. He met Madison Washington when Washington was traveling from Canada to Virginia; see Purvis's account of their meeting in "A Priceless Picture," in part 4.

quietly smoking his segar, calmly and coolly calculating the value of human flesh beneath the hatchway. The first day passed away—the second, third, fourth, fifth, sixth and seventh passed, and there was nothing on board to disturb the repose of this iron-hearted monster. He was quietly hoping for a pleasant breeze to waft him to the New Orleans market before it should be glutted with human flesh. On the 8th day it seems that Madison Washington succeeded in getting off one of his irons, for he had been at work all the while. The same day he succeeded in getting the irons off the hands of some seventeen or eighteen others. When the slaveholders came down below they found their human chattels apparently all with their irons on, but they were broken. About twilight on the ninth day, Madison, it seems, reached his head above the hatchway, looked out on the swelling billows of the Atlantic, and feeling the breeze that coursed over its surface, was inspired with the spirit of freedom. He leapt from beneath the hatchway, gave a cry like an eagle to his comrades beneath, saying, *we must go through* (Great Applause.) Suiting the action to the word, in an instant his guilty master was prostrate on the deck, and in a very few minutes Madison Washington, a black man, with woolly head, high cheek bones, protruding lip, distended nostril, and retreating forehead,[3] had the mastery of that ship, and under his direction, that brig was brought safely into the port of Nassau, New Providence (Applause.)

Sir, I thank God that there is some part of his footstool upon which the bloody statutes of Slavery cannot be written. They cannot be written on the proud, towering billows of the Atlantic. The restless waves will not permit those bloody statutes to be recorded there. This part of God's domain is free, and I hope that ere long our own soil will be also free. (Applause.)

3. Here Douglass is mocking the derogatory descriptions of blacks popularized by the era's racial ethnologists. See Douglass's attack on the "science" of ethnology in his *The Claims of the Negro Ethnologically Considered: An Address, Before the Literary Societies of Western Reserve College, at Commencement, July 12, 1854* (Rochester, N.Y., 1854).

FREDERICK DOUGLASS

from "What to the Slave Is the Fourth of July?"

On 5 July 1852, Douglass delivered his famous Fourth of July speech before a racially mixed audience of approximately six hundred people in Rochester, New York. He spoke on 5 July because of a tradition among black and white abolitionists to postpone Fourth of July celebrations as a way of highlighting the nation's failure to live up to the egalitarian ideals of the Declaration of Independence. By year's end, when Douglass had composed *The Heroic Slave*, he had come to conceive of Madison Washington as, in part, a black rebel in the Jeffersonian tradition, but one who was willing to fight for the principles that the slaveholding Jefferson and the nation itself had been willing to abandon. Douglass published the speech as a pamphlet in 1852, and then in 1855 published "Extract from the Oration" (several key pages from the longer work) in the appendix to his second autobiography, *My Bondage and My Freedom* (New York and Auburn: Miller, Orton, and Mulligan, 1855), the source of the text below.

Fellow-Citizens—Pardon me, and allow me to ask, why am I called upon to speak here to-day? What have I, or those I represent, to do with your national independence? Are the great principles of political freedom and of natural justice, embodied in that Declaration of Independence, extended to us? and am I, therefore, called upon to bring our humble offering to the national altar, and to confess the benefits, and express devout gratitude for the blessings, resulting from your independence to us?

Would to God, both for your sakes and ours, that an affirmative answer could be truthfully returned to these questions! Then would my task be light, and my burden easy and delightful. For who is there so cold that a nation's sympathy could not warm him? Who so obdurate and dead to the claims of gratitude, that would not thankfully acknowledge such priceless benefits? Who so stolid and selfish, that would not give his voice to swell the hallelujahs of a nation's jubilee, when the chains of servitude had been torn from his limbs? I am not that man. In a case like that, the dumb might eloquently speak, and the "lame man leap as an hart."[1]

But, such is not the state of the case. I say it with a sad sense of the disparity between us. I am not included within the pale of this glorious anniversary! Your high independence only reveals the immeasurable distance between us. The blessings in which you this day rejoice, are not enjoyed in common. The rich inheritance of justice, liberty, prosperity, and independence, bequeathed by your fathers, is shared by you, not by me. The sunlight that brought life and healing to you, has brought stripes and death to me. This Fourth of July is *yours*, not *mine*. *You* may rejoice, *I* must mourn. To drag a man in fetters into the grand illuminated temple of liberty, and call upon him to join you in joyous anthems, were inhuman mockery and sacrilegious irony. Do you mean, citizens, to mock me, by asking me to speak to-day? If so, there is a parallel to your conduct. And let me warn you that it is dangerous to copy the example of a nation whose crimes, towering up to heaven, were thrown down by the breath of the Almighty, burying that nation in irrecoverable ruin! I can to-day take up the plaintive lament of a peeled and woe-smitten people.

"By the rivers of Babylon, there we sat down. Yea! we wept when we remembered Zion. We hanged our harps upon the willows in the midst thereof. For there, they that carried us away captive, required of us a song; and they who wasted us required of us mirth, saying, Sing us one of the songs of Zion. How can we sing the Lord's song in a strange land? If I forget thee, O Jerusalem, let my right hand

1. Isaiah 35:6; a hart is a male red deer.

forget her cunning. If I do not remember thee, let my tongue cleave to the roof of my mouth."[2]

Fellow-citizens, above your national, tumultuous joy, I hear the mournful wail of millions, whose chains, heavy and grievous yesterday, are to-day rendered more intolerable by the jubilant shouts that reach them. If I do forget, if I do not faithfully remember those bleeding children of sorrow this day, "may my right hand forget her cunning, and may my tongue cleave to the roof of my mouth!" To forget them, to pass lightly over their wrongs, and to chime in with the popular theme, would be treason most scandalous and shocking, and would make me a reproach before God and the world. My subject, then, fellow-citizens, is AMERICAN SLAVERY. I shall see this day and its popular characteristics from the slave's point of view. Standing there, identified with the American bondman, making his wrongs mine, I do not hesitate to declare, with all my soul, that the character and conduct of this nation never looked blacker to me than on this Fourth of July. Whether we turn to the declarations of the past, or to the professions of the present, the conduct of the nation seems equally hideous and revolting. America is false to the past, false to the present, and solemnly binds herself to be false to the future. Standing with God and the crushed and bleeding slave on this occasion, I will, in the name of humanity which is outraged, in the name of liberty which is fettered, in the name of the constitution and the bible, which are disregarded and trampled upon, dare to call in question and to denounce, with all the emphasis I can command, everything that serves to perpetuate slavery—the great sin and shame of America! "I will not equivocate; I will not excuse;"[3] I will use the severest language I can command; and yet not one word shall escape me that any man, whose judgment is not blinded by prejudice, or who is not at heart a slaveholder, shall not confess to be right and just.

2. Psalms 137:1–6.

3. From "To the Public," an editorial by William Lloyd Garrison in the inaugural issue of his antislavery newspaper the *Liberator* (1 January 1831).

But I fancy I hear some one of my audience say, it is just in this circumstance that you and your brother abolitionists fail to make a favorable impression on the public mind. Would you argue more, and denounce less, would you persuade more and rebuke less, your cause would be much more likely to succeed. But, I submit, where all is plain there is nothing to be argued. What point in the anti-slavery creed would you have me argue? On what branch of the subject do the people of this country need light? Must I undertake to prove that the slave is a man? That point is conceded already. Nobody doubts it. The slaveholders themselves acknowledge it in the enactment of laws for their government. They acknowledge it when they punish disobedience on the part of the slave. There are seventy-two crimes in the state of Virginia, which, if committed by a black man, (no matter how ignorant he be,) subject him to the punishment of death; while only two of these same crimes will subject a white man to the like punishment. What is this but the acknowledgement that the slave is a moral, intellectual, and responsible being. The manhood of the slave is conceded. It is admitted in the fact that southern statute books are covered with enactments forbidding, under severe fines and penalties, the teaching of the slave to read or write. When you can point to any such laws, in reference to the beasts of the field, then I may consent to argue the manhood of the slave. When the dogs in your streets, when the fowls of the air, when the cattle on your hills, when the fish of the sea, and the reptiles that crawl, shall be unable to distinguish the slave from a brute, then will I argue with you that the slave is a man!

For the present, it is enough to affirm the equal manhood of the negro race. Is it not astonishing that, while we are plowing, planting, and reaping, using all kinds of mechanical tools, erecting houses, constructing bridges, building ships, working in metals of brass, iron, copper, silver, and gold; that, while we are reading, writing, and cyphering, acting as clerks, merchants, and secretaries, having among us lawyers, doctors, ministers, poets, authors, editors, orators, and teachers; that, while we are engaged in all manner of enterprises common to other men—digging gold in California, capturing the whale in the Pacific, feeding sheep and cattle on the hillside, living, moving, acting, thinking, planning, living in families as husbands, wives, and children, and, above all, confessing and worshiping the christian's God, and looking hopefully for life and immortality beyond the grave—we are called upon to prove that we are men!

Would you have me argue that man is entitled to liberty? that he is the rightful owner of his own body? You have already declared it. Must I argue the wrongfulness of slavery? Is that a question for republicans? Is it to be settled by the rules of logic and argumentation, as a matter beset with great difficulty, involving a doubtful application of the principle of justice, hard to be understood? How should I look to-day in the presence of Americans, dividing and subdividing a discourse, to show that men have a natural right to freedom, speaking of it relatively and positively, negatively and affirmatively? To do so, would be to make myself ridiculous, and to offer an insult to your understanding. There is not a man beneath the canopy of heaven that does not know that slavery is wrong *for him.*

What! am I to argue that it is wrong to make men brutes, to rob them of their liberty, to work them without wages, to keep them ignorant of their relations to their fellow-men, to beat them with sticks, to flay their flesh with the lash, to load their limbs with irons, to hunt them with dogs, to sell them at auction, to sunder their families, to knock out their teeth, to burn their flesh, to starve them into obedience and submission to their masters? Must I argue that a system, thus marked with blood and stained with pollution, is wrong? No; I will not. I have better employment for my time and strength than such arguments would imply.

What, then, remains to be argued? Is it that slavery is not divine; that God did not establish it; that our doctors of divinity are mistaken? There is blasphemy in the thought. That which is inhuman cannot be divine. Who can reason on such a proposition! They that can, may; I cannot. The time for such argument is past.

At a time like this, scorching irony, not convincing argument, is needed. Oh! had I the ability, and could I reach the nation's ear, I would to-day pour out a fiery stream of biting ridicule, blasting reproach, withering sarcasm, and stern rebuke. For it is not light that is needed, but fire; it is not the gentle shower, but thunder. We need the storm, the whirlwind, and the earthquake. The feeling of the nation must be quickened; the conscience of the nation must be roused; the propriety of the nation must be startled; the hypocrisy of the nation must be exposed; and its crimes against God and man must be proclaimed and denounced.

What to the American slave is your Fourth of July? I answer, a day that reveals to him, more than all other days in the year, the gross injustice and cruelty to which he is the constant victim. To him, your celebration is a sham; your boasted liberty, an unholy license; your national greatness, swelling vanity; your sounds of rejoicing are empty and heartless; your denunciations of tyrants, brass-fronted impudence; your shouts of liberty and equality, hollow mockery; your prayers and hymns, your sermons and thanksgivings, with all your religious parade and solemnity, are to him mere bombast, fraud, deception, impiety, and hypocrisy—a thin veil to cover up crimes which would disgrace a nation of savages. There is not a nation on the earth guilty of practices more shocking and bloody, than are the people of these United States, at this very hour.

Go where you may, search where you will, roam through all the monarchies and despotisms of the old world, travel through South America, search out every abuse, and when you have found the last, lay your facts by the side of the every-day practices of this nation, and you will say with me, that, for revolting barbarity and shameless hypocrisy, America reigns without a rival.

FREDERICK DOUGLASS

from "West India Emancipation"

Abolitionists traditionally celebrated the 1 August 1834 emancipation of British West Indian slaves with gatherings that included songs and orations. Douglass gave his speech "West India Emancipation" on 3 August 1857 before approximately one thousand people, predominately African Americans, at an amphitheater in the Ontario County Agricultural Society fairgrounds in Canandaigua, New York. The speech was published shortly thereafter in a pamphlet, *Two Speeches, by Frederick Douglass; One on West India Emancipation, Delivered at Canandaigua, August 4th, and the Other on the Dred Scott Decision, Delivered in New York on the Occasion of the Anniversary of the American Abolition Society, May, 1857* (Rochester, N.Y., 1857), the source of the excerpt below. (The 4 August date in the title is incorrect.) Typically, West Indian emancipation speeches praised British leaders for their enlightened action and called on U.S. leaders to follow their example. But Douglass shifts the emphasis in this speech, crediting the blacks of the West Indies with bringing about their own emancipation through their use of violent resistance. By invoking Madison Washington and other black rebels, Douglass calls on blacks to continue to exert similar pressure in the United States.

Let me give you a word of the philosophy of reform. The whole history of the progress of human liberty shows that all concessions yet made to her august claims, have been born of earnest struggle. The conflict has been exciting, agitating, all-absorbing, and for the time being, putting all other tumults to silence. It must do this or it does nothing. If there is no struggle there is no progress. Those who profess to favor freedom and yet depreciate agitation, are men who want crops without plowing up the ground, they want rain without thunder and lightning. They want the ocean without the awful roar of its many waters.

This struggle may be a moral one, or it may be a physical one, and it may be both moral and physical, but it must be a struggle. Power concedes nothing without a demand. It never did and it never will. Find out just what any people will quietly submit to and you have found out the exact measure of injustice and wrong which will be imposed upon them, and these will continue till they are resisted with either words or blows, or with both. The limits of tyrants are prescribed by the endurance of those whom they oppress. In the light of these ideas, Negroes will be hunted at the North, and held and flogged at the South so long as they submit to those devilish outrages, and make no resistance, either moral or physical. Men may not get all they pay for in this world, but they must certainly pay for all they get. If we ever get free from the oppressions and wrongs heaped upon us, we must pay for their removal. We must do this by labor, by suffering, by sacrifice, and if needs be, by our lives and the lives of others.

Hence, my friends, every mother who, like Margaret Garner, plunges a knife into the bosom of her infant to save it from the hell of our Christian Slavery, should be held and honored as a benefactress.[1] Every fugitive from slavery who like the noble William Thomas at Wilkesbarre, prefers to perish in a river made red by his own blood, to submission to the hell hounds who were hunting and shooting him, should be esteemed as a glorious martyr, worthy to be held in grateful memory by our people.[2] The fugitive Horace, at Mechanicsburgh, Ohio, the other day, who taught the slave catch-

1. Margaret Garner (c. 1833–1861) was a Kentucky slave who fled to Ohio with her family in 1856, and then attempted to kill her four children when she was trapped by fugitive slave hunters. She killed one daughter with a butcher knife. After a trial in Ohio, she was sent back into slavery, and in 1861 she died in a steamship collision. The case helped to inspire Toni Morrison's *Beloved* (1987).

2. The fugitive slave William Thomas was working as a waiter at a hotel in Wilkes-Barre, Pennsylvania, when he was confronted by fugitive slave hunters. Initially, he jumped into the Susquehanna River, declaring that he would rather drown than be remanded into slavery. Aided by Wilkes-Barre citizens, he made his escape.

ers from Kentucky that it was safer to arrest white men than to arrest him, did a most excellent service to our cause.[3] Parker and his noble band of fifteen at Christiana, who defended themselves from the kidnappers with prayers and pistols, are entitled to the honor of making the first successful resistance to the Fugitive Slave Bill.[4] But for that resistance, and the rescue of Jerry, and Shadrack, the man-hunters would have hunted our hills and valleys here with the same freedom with which they now hunt their own dismal swamps.[5]

There was an important lesson in the conduct of that noble Krooman in New York, the other day, who, supposing that the American Christians were about to enslave him, betook himself to the mast head, and with knife in hand, said he would cut his throat before he would be made a slave.[6] Joseph Cinque on the deck of the Amistad, did that which should make his name dear to us.[7] He bore nature's burning protest against slavery. Madison Washington who struck

3. Probably a reference to a fugitive slave named Addison White, who had taken refuge in Mechanicsburg, Ohio. On 21 May 1857, several months before Douglass gave this speech, seven men from Kentucky, including two U.S. deputy marshals, attempted to arrest White, who escaped with the help of a local farmer. The farmer, Udney Hyde, was initially arrested by the marshals but then freed by a local court.

4. The Fugitive Slave Act, which was part of the Compromise of 1850, made it illegal to assist or harbor fugitive slaves. In September 1851, the Maryland slave owner Edward Gorsuch attempted to capture two of his slaves who had taken refuge at the home of William Parker in Christiana, Pennsylvania, which was a predominately black community. Parker, a former slave, along with some of his neighbors, fought back against Gorsuch and the white men who had accompanied him, killing Gorsuch. Parker then took flight to Rochester, where he met Douglass, who helped him on his way to Canada.

5. Douglass refers to two famous fugitive slave cases. On 1 October 1851, in Syracuse, New York, abolitionists freed a runaway slave from Missouri known as Jerry and helped him reach the safety of Canada; and on 15 February 1851, a runaway slave from Virginia known as Shadrach was captured in Boston and then freed by blacks who crowded into the courthouse. Like Jerry, Shadrach successfully made his way to Canada.

6. In a widely reported incident just two weeks before Douglass gave his West Indian emancipation speech, a native African, supposedly of the Krooman tribe, became so fearful that he was going to be remanded into slavery that he climbed the rigging of the ship, stating that he would rather die than become a slave. He was eventually coaxed down. His subsequent history, and reasons for being on the ship in the first place, remains obscure.

7. On Cinqué and the *Amistad*, see "A Priceless Picture," in part 4.

down his oppressor on the deck of the Creole, is more worthy to be remembered than the colored man who shot Pitcaren at Bunker Hill.[8]

My friends, you will observe that I have taken a wide range, and you think it is about time that I should answer the special objection to this celebration. I think so too. This, then, is the truth concerning the inauguration of freedom in the British West Indies. Abolition was the act of the British Government. The motive which led the Government to act, no doubt was mainly a philanthropic one, entitled to our highest admiration and gratitude. The National Religion, the justice, and humanity, cried out in thunderous indignation against the foul abomination, and the government yielded to the storm. Nevertheless a share of the credit of the result falls justly to the slaves themselves. "Though slaves, they were rebellious slaves." They bore themselves well. They did not hug their chains, but according to their opportunities, swelled the general protest against oppression. What Wilberforce[9] was endeavoring to win from the British Senate by his magic eloquence, the Slaves themselves were endeavoring to gain by outbreaks and violence. The combined action of one and the other wrought out the final result. While one showed that slavery was wrong, the other showed that it was dangerous as well as wrong. Mr. Wilberforce, peace man though he was, and a model of piety, availed himself of this element to strengthen his case before the British Parliament, and warned the British government of the danger of continuing slavery in the West Indies. There is no doubt that the fear of the consequences, acting with a sense of the moral evil of slavery led to its abolition. The spirit of freedom was abroad in the Islands. Insurrection for freedom kept

8. Black tradition maintained that the emancipated slave Peter Salem (1750–1816) killed the British major John Pitcairn (1722–1775) at the Battle of Bunker Hill on 17 June 1775. See William C. Nell, *The Colored Patriots of the American Revolution* (Boston, 1855).

9. The British politician and reformer William Wilberforce (1759–1833) had an important role in the public campaigns and debates in Parliament that led to the abolition of slavery in the British Empire.

the planters in a constant state of alarm and trepidation. A standing army was necessary to keep the slaves in their chains. This state of facts could not be without weight in deciding the question of freedom in these countries.

I am aware that the rebellious disposition of the slaves was said to arise out of the discussions which the abolitionists were carrying on at home, and it is not necessary to refute this alleged explanation. All that I contend for is this: that the slaves of the West Indies did fight for their freedom, and that the fact of their discontent was known in England, and that it assisted in bringing about that state of public opinion which finally resulted in their emancipation. And if this be true, the objection is answered.

Again, I am aware that the insurrectionary movements of the slaves were held by many to be prejudicial to their cause. This is said now of such movements at the South. The answer is that abolition followed close on the heels of insurrection in the West Indies, and Virginia was never nearer emancipation than when General Turner[10] kindled the fires of insurrection at Southampton.

Sir, I have now more than filled up the measure of my time. I thank you for the patient attention given to what I have had to say. I have aimed, as I said at the beginning, to express a few thoughts having some relation to the great interests of freedom both in this country and in the British West Indies, and I have said all that I meant to say, and the time will not permit me to say more.

10. Nat Turner.

FREDERICK DOUGLASS

"A Black Hero"

Three months after the outbreak of the Civil War, and at a time when Douglass was urging Lincoln and other northern leaders to conceive of it as a war of emancipation, he learned of the amazing rebellion at sea led almost single-handedly by the twenty-seven-year-old free black William Tillman. Tillman was the steward and cook on the Long Island–based schooner *S. J. Waring*, which was seized on its way to Uruguay by the *Jeff Davis*, a privately owned ship with a crew authorized by the Confederacy to attack northern ships and positions. On the night of 16 July 1861, Tillman killed several of the privateers, gained control of the *S. J. Waring*, and guided it back to New York Harbor, where he was greeted as a hero. Two weeks later, the popular *Harper's Weekly* ran an article about the revolt, including several illustrations of Tillman (see figure 5). For Douglass, Tillman exhibited virtues shared by Madison Washington and other black rebels he admired. Tillman's bravery and military skills led Douglass to redouble his efforts to convince Lincoln to recruit African Americans for the Union army. "A Black Hero" appeared in the August 1861 issue of *Douglass's Monthly*, the source of the text below.

While our Government still refuses to acknowledge the just claims of the negro, and takes all possible pains to assure 'our Southern brethren' that it does not intend to interfere in any way with this kind of property; while the assistance of colored citizens in suppressing the slaveholders' rebellion is peremptorily and insultingly declined; while even Republicans still deny and reject their natural allies and unite with pro-slavery Democrats in recognizing their alleged inferiority—it has happened that one of the most daring and

5. "The Attack on the Second Mate," engraving of William Tillman, *Harper's Weekly*, 3 August 1861. Widener Library, Harvard University.

heroic deeds—one which will be likely to inflict the heaviest blow upon the piratical enterprizes of JEFF. DAVIS[1]—has been struck by an obscure negro. All know the story of this achievement: The schooner 'S.J. Waring,' bound to Montevideo,[2] having on board a valuable cargo, when, scarcely beyond the waters of New York, was captured by the privateer 'Jeff. Davis.' The captain and the mate of the Waring were sent home, and a prize crew, consisting of five men, were put on board of her. Three of the original crew, two seamen and WILLIAM TILLMAN, the colored steward, besides a passenger, were retained. TILLMAN, our hero, very soon ascertained from conversations which he was not intended to hear, that the vessel was to be taken to Charleston, and that he himself was to be sold as a slave. The pirates had chuckled over their last item of their good luck; but, unfortunately for them, they had a man to deal

1. The ship was named after Jefferson Davis (1808–1889), who served as the president of the Confederate States of America from 1861 to 1865.

2. The capital and chief port of Uruguay.

with, one whose brave heart and nerves of steel stood athwart their infernal purposes.

TILLMAN took an early occasion to make known to his fellow prisoners the devilish purpose of the pirates, and declared that they should never succeed in getting him to Charleston alive. Only one of his fellow prisoners, a German named STEDDING, consented to take part in the dangerous task of recapturing the vessel. He watched anxiously for a favorable moment to slay the pirates and gain his freedom. So vigilant, however, were the prize captain and crew, that it was not until they had nearly reached the waters of Charleston, in the very jaws of a fate which he dreaded more than death, that an opportunity offered. They were within fifty miles of Charleston; night and sleep had come down upon them—for even pirates have to sleep. STEDDING, the German, discovered that NOW was the time, and passing the word to TILLMAN, the latter began his fearful work—killing the pirate captain, mate and second mate, and thus making himself master of the ship with no other weapon than a common hatchet, and doing his work so well that the whole was accomplished in seven minutes, including the giving the bodies of the pirates to the sharks. The other two men were secured, but afterwards released on condition that they would help to work the ship back to New York. Here was a grand difficulty, even after the essential had been accomplished, one before which a man less hopeful and brave than TILLMAN would have faltered. Neither himself nor his companions possessed any knowledge of navigation, and they might have fallen upon shores quite as unfriendly as those from which they were escaping, or they might have been overtaken by pirates as savage as those whose bodies they had given to the waves. But, despite of possible shipwreck and death, they managed safely to reach New York, TILLMAN humorously remarking that he came home as captain of the vessel in which he went out as steward.

When we consider all the circumstances of this transaction, we cannot fail to perceive in TILLMAN a degree of personal valor and presence of mind equal to those displayed by the boldest deeds recorded in history. The soldier who marches to the battle field with all inspirations of numbers, music, popular applause, 'the pomp and circumstance of glorious war,'[3] is brave; but he who, like TILLMAN, has no one to share danger with him, in whose surroundings there is nothing to steel his arm or fire his heart, who has to draw from his own bosom the stern confidence required for the performance of the task of man-slaying, is braver. The soldier knows that even in case of defeat there are stronger probabilities in his favor than against him. TILLMAN, on the other side, was almost alone against five, and well knew that if he failed, an excruciating death would be the consequence. He was on the perilous ocean, at the mercy of the winds and waves, with whose powers he was as well acquainted as he was conscious of his inability by skill and knowledge to defy them. How much nerve, moreover, does it not require in a man unaccustomed to bloodshed, a stranger to the sights and scenes of the battle field, to strike thus for liberty! TILLMAN is described as anything but a sanguinary man. His whole conduct in sparing the lives of part of the pirate crew proves that the description of his good-natured and gentle disposition is no exaggeration of his virtues. Love of liberty alone inspired him and supported him, as it had inspired DENMARK VESEY, NATHANIEL TURNER, MADISON WASHINGTON, TOUSSAINT L'OUVERTURE, SHIELDS GREEN, COPELAND,[4] and other negro heroes before him, and he walked to his work of self-deliverance with a step as firm and dauntless as the noblest Roman of them all.[5] Well done

3. Shakespeare, *Othello*, 3.3.355.

4. Douglass had regularly compared Madison Washington to the Haitian revolutionary leader Toussaint-Louverture (1743–1803), the South Carolina conspirator Denmark Vesey (c. 1767–1822), and the Virginia rebel Nathaniel Turner (1800–1831). The former slave Shields Green (c. 1836–1859) and the free black John A. Copeland (1834–1859) participated in John Brown's raid on the federal arsenal at Harpers Ferry and were hanged on 16 December 1859.

5. Shakespeare, *Julius Caesar*, 5.5.68. Antony ironically describes Caesar's assassin Brutus as "the noblest Roman of them all"; Douglass probably was using these words with reference to Caesar himself.

for TILLMAN! The N. Y. *Tribune* well says of him, that the nation is indebted to him for the first vindication of its honor on the sea. When will this nation cease to disparage the negro race? When will they become sensible of the force of this irresistible TILLMAN argument?

PART 4

Narratives of the *Creole* Rebellion, 1855–1901

THIS SECTION PRESENTS SIX narrative accounts of the *Creole* rebellion published after Douglass's 1853 *The Heroic Slave*. Some of the accounts draw on the historical record, some draw on Douglass, and some draw on each other; William Wells Brown's chapters on Madison Washington in his black histories of the 1860s were particularly influential. Genre is important to representations of Washington and the *Creole* rebellion. Whereas Douglass clearly made use of fictional techniques, the writers that follow vary in their approaches. William C. Nell's short sketch of Madison Washington for his 1855 history of black revolutionaries works with the known facts. Samuel Ringgold Ward writes about Washington in his 1855 autobiography, and he too stays close to the historical record. William Wells Brown, however, in his 1863 and 1867 histories of black freedom fighters of the Americas (which focus on African Americans and the Civil War) goes the route of Douglass in using fictional techniques to create a lively historical narrative. Lydia Maria Child draws on Brown, but in her 1865 educational anthology for freedpeople, she uses the rebellion to offer lessons for domestic life. Later in the nineteenth century, Robert Purvis approached the rebellion through the mode of personal reminiscence, providing new information about Washington and himself. Approximately ten years later, Pauline E. Hopkins offered fresh perspectives on Brown's and perhaps Douglass's accounts, using fictional techniques to reimagine the *Creole* rebellion and its gender implications. For Hopkins, who was writing at the turn into the twentieth century, the *Creole* rebellion remained a compelling moment in a usable African American historical past.

WILLIAM C. NELL

"Madison Washington"

The Boston-based African American William Cooper Nell (1816–1874) was a staunch Garrisonian. From 1847 to 1851, he served as assistant editor of Douglass's newspaper the *North Star*, and was its original publisher; but when Douglass broke with Garrison in 1851, Nell resigned from the paper. Like Douglass, Nell believed that African Americans should have all the rights of U.S. citizenship, and to that end he campaigned to integrate Boston's public schools. To support his argument for black citizenship, he turned to history, writing two books that sought to demonstrate blacks' crucial military contributions to the United States: *Services of Colored Americans in the Wars of 1776 and 1812* (Boston: Prentiss & Sawyer, 1851) and *The Colored Patriots of the American Revolution, with Sketches of Several Distinguished Colored Persons: To Which Is Added a Brief Survey of the Condition and Prospects of Colored Americans* (Boston: Robert F. Wallcut, 1855); the latter had an introduction by Harriet Beecher Stowe. The 1851 volume focused on blacks' participation in the wars that helped found and sustain the nation; the 1855 volume, from which this selection is taken, took a more aggressive (and decidedly non-Garrisionian) stance in adding admiring accounts of such black rebels as Denmark Vesey, Nat Turner, David Walker, and Madison Washington.

An American slaver, named the *Creole*, well manned and provided in every respect, and equipped for carrying slaves, sailed from Virginia to New Orleans, on the 30th October, 1841, with a cargo of one hundred and thirty-five slaves. When eight days out, a portion of the slaves, under the direction of one of their number, named MADISON WASHING-

TON, succeeded, after a slight struggle, in gaining command of the vessel. The sagacity, bravery and humanity of this man do honor to his name; and, but for his complexion, would excite universal admiration. Of the twelve white men employed on board the well-manned slaver, only one fell a victim to their atrocious business. This man, after discharging his musket at the negroes, rushed forward with a handspike, which, in the darkness of the evening, they mistook for another musket; he was stabbed with a *bowie knife wrested from the captain*. Two of the sailors were wounded, and their wounds were dressed by the negroes. The captain was also injured, and he was put into the forehold, and his wounds dressed; and his wife, child and niece were unmolested. It does not appear that the blacks committed a single act of robbery, or treated their captives with the slightest unnecessary harshness; and they declared, at the time, that all they had done was for their freedom. The vessel was carried into Nassau, and the British authorities at that place refused to consign the liberated slaves again to bondage, or even to surrender the "mutineers and murderers" to perish on Southern gibbets.

SAMUEL RINGGOLD WARD

"Men and Women of Mark"

The black abolitionist Samuel Ringgold Ward (1817–ca. 1866) began his career as an antislavery lecturer for William Lloyd Garrison but broke with him in 1840 to embrace the religious and political abolitionism of the American and Foreign Anti-Slavery Society. In 1849 and 1850, he debated Douglass on whether the Constitution was a proslavery or antislavery document. Influenced by Garrison, Douglass in these debates argued that the Constitution was a proslavery document, but by 1851 he had adopted Ward's politically pragmatic view that it was antislavery. By the early 1850s, Douglass had also publicly rejected Garrison's insistence on nonviolent moral suasion and found himself more congenial with Ward's position on the value of violent black resistance. In 1851, Ward joined the Syracuse Vigilance Committee and helped free the fugitive slave William "Jerry" McHenry from federal custody. Disillusioned with the United States, he moved to Canada and eventually to Jamaica. Ward's account of Madison Washington and the *Creole* rebellion is taken from the chapter "Resistance to Slave Policy" in his *Autobiography of a Fugitive Negro: His Anti-Slavery Labours in the United States, Canada, & England* (London: John Snow, 1855).

The slaves advertised as having run away, or as having been arrested upon suspicion of being runaways—as any one may see in any Southern newspaper, political or religious—are men and women of mark. "Large frames" are ascribed to them; "intelligent countenances;" "can read a little;" "may pass, or attempt to pass, as a freeman;" "a good mechanic;" "had a bold look;" "above the middle height, very ingenious, may pass for white;" "very intelligent." No one who has seen such advertisements can fail to be struck with them. A mulattress left her master, Mr. Devonport, in Syracuse, in 1839, who "had no traces of African origin": as advertised. Mr. D. said she was worth 2,500 dollars, nearly £500. Such are the slaves who run away, as a rule. I do not deny that some of "inferior lots" come too, but such as those described form the *rule*.

Then, as fugitives, when we recollect what they must undergo in every part of their *exodus*, we can but see them as among the most admirable of any race. The fugitive exercises patience, fortitude, and perseverance, connected with and fed by an ardent and unrestrained and resistless love of liberty, such as cause men to be admired everywhere—that is, *white men everywhere*, but in the United States. The lonely, toiling journey; the endurance of the excitement from constant danger; the hearing of the yell and howl of the bloodhound; the knowledge of close, hot pursuit; the dread of capture, and the determination not to be taken alive—all these, furnaces of trial as they are, purify and ennoble the man who has to pass through them. All these are inseparable from the ordinary incidents in the northward passage of the fugitive: and when he reaches us, he is, first, what the raw material of nature was; and, secondly, what the improving process of flight has made him. Both have fitted him the more highly to appreciate, the more fully to enjoy, and the more wisely to use, that for which he came to us, for which he was willing to endure all things, for which, indeed, he would have yielded life itself—liberty.

Let me illustrate these points by a few facts. A Negro, Madison Washington by name—a name, a pair of names, of which he was well worthy—was a slave in Virginia. He determined to be free. He fled to Canada and became free. There the noble fellow was dissatisfied—so dissatisfied, that he determined to leave free Canada, and return to Virginia: and wherefore? His wife was there, a *slave*. Freedom was too sweet to be enjoyed without her. That she was a slave marred his joys. She must share them, even at the risk of *his* losing them. So in 1841 he went back to Virginia, to the neighbourhood in which his wife lived, lingered about in the woods, and sent word to her of his whereabouts; others were unfortunately informed as well, and he was captured, taken to Washington, and sold to a Negro-trader. One scarcely knows which most to admire—the heroism this man displayed in the freeing of himself, or the noble manliness that risked all for the freedom of his wife. One cannot help thinking that, as his captors led Madison Washington to the slave pen, they must have been smitten with the thought that they were handling a man far superior to themselves. When a load of Negroes had been made up, Madison Washington, with a large number of others—119, I think—was put on board the schooner "Creole," to sail out of the mouth of the Potomac River and southwards to the Gulf of Mexico, up the Mississippi, and to New Orleans, the great slave-buying port of America. But on the night of the 9th of November, 1841, Madison Washington and two others, named respectively Pompey Garrison, and Ben Blacksmith, arose upon the captain and crew, leading all the other slaves after them, and gave the captain the alternative of sailing the vessel into a British port, one of the Bahamas, or of going overboard. The captain, wisely and safely for himself, chose the former; and these three brave blacks, naturally distrusting the forced promise of the Yankee captain, stood sentry over him until he *did* steer the "Creole" into the port of Nassau, island of *New Providence*, touching which they became freemen. The United States Government, through the Honourable Edward Everett, demanded of Lord Palmerston gold to pay for these men.[1] The Court of St. James[2] entertained the demand—not one moment. What lacked these men of being Tells, Mazzinis, and Kossuths,[3] in their way, except white or whitish skins?

1. Ward included this note: "This was during the time when the Honourable Daniel Webster first was Secretary of State. It was the first time the British Government had rejected such a demand, I am sorry to say." See the selection from Webster in part 2 of the volume.

2. The central court of Great Britain and the official residence of the British monarchy.

3. Renowned revolutionaries: William Tell was the legendary Swiss revolutionary of the fourteenth century; Giuseppe Mazzini (1805–1872) fought for Italian unification and was the leader of the Roman Revolution of 1848–49; and the Hungarian nationalist Lajos Kossuth (1802–1894) led the Hungarian revolution of 1848–49.

WILLIAM WELLS BROWN

"Slave Revolt at Sea"

Born into slavery, William Wells Brown (1814–1884) escaped in 1834 and quickly emerged as a black abolitionist leader. Over the years, he also became a man of letters, writing novels, plays, autobiographies, travel narratives, and histories. Among his published works are *Narrative of William W. Brown, A Fugitive Slave* (1847); *Clotel* (1853), generally regarded as the first novel by an African American; *The Escape; or, A Leap for Freedom. A Drama in Five Acts* (1858); and *My Southern Home; or, The South and Its People* (1880). Initially linked with William Lloyd Garrison, who published his *Narrative*, Brown soon went his own way, and during the late 1850s he became involved with the movement encouraging blacks to immigrate to Haiti. But with the coming of the Civil War, he abandoned that cause and argued for blacks' rights to citizenship in the United States. To make his case, he wrote a series of histories showing blacks' contributions to the nation, emphasizing the important role of black soldiers in the Civil War. But he also highlighted blacks' willingness to use violence to gain their freedom, and in both *The Black Man: His Antecedents, His Genius, and His Achievements* (1863) and *The Negro in the American Rebellion: His Heroism and His Fidelity* (Boston: Lee & Shepard, 1867), the source of the text below, he presents portraits of a number of revolutionary blacks. He first wrote about Madison Washington in *The Black Man*, and that chapter influenced Lydia Maria Child's account of the *Creole* rebellion in her 1865 *The Freedmen's Book*. For his 1867 chapter on Washington, Brown added new material, connecting Washington with such black revolutionary heroes as Denmark Vesey and Nat Turner.

The revolt on board of the brig "Creole," on the high seas, by a number of slaves who had been shipped for the Southern market, in the year 1841, created at the time a profound sensation throughout the country. Before entering upon it, however, I will introduce to the reader the hero of the occasion.

Among the great number of fugitive slaves who arrived in Canada towards the close of the year 1840, was one whose tall figure, firm step, and piercing eye attracted at once the attention of all who beheld him. Nature had treated him as a favorite. His expressive countenance painted and reflected every emotion of his soul. There was a fascination in the gaze of his finely cut eyes that no one could withstand. Born of African parentage, with no mixture in his blood, he was one of the handsomest of his race. His dignified, calm, and unaffected features announced at a glance that he was endowed with genius, and created to guide his fellow-men. He called himself Madison Washington, and said that his birthplace was in the "Old Dominion."[1] He might have been twenty-five years; but very few slaves have any correct idea of their age. Madison was not poorly dressed, and had some money at the end of his journey, which showed that he was not from amongst the worst-used slaves of the South. He immediately sought employment at a neighboring farm, where he remained some months. A strong, able-bodied man, and a good worker, and apparently satisfied with his situation, his employer felt that he had a servant who would stay with him a long while. The farmer would occasionally raise a conversation, and try to draw from Madison some account of his former life, but in this he failed; for the fugitive was a man of few words, and kept his own secrets. His leisure hours were spent in learning to read and write; and in this he seemed to take the utmost interest. He appeared to take no interest in the sports and amusements that occupied the attention of others. Six months had not passed ere Madison began

1. Virginia.

to show signs of discontent. In vain his employer tried to discover the cause.

"Do I not pay you enough, and treat you in a becoming manner?" asked Mr. Dickson one day when the fugitive seemed in a very desponding mood.

"Yes, sir," replied Madison.

"Then why do you appear so dissatisfied of late?"

"Well, sir," said the fugitive, "since you have treated me with such kindness, and seem to take so much interest in me, I will tell you the reason why I have changed, and appear to you to be dissatisfied. I was born in slavery, in the State of Virginia. From my earliest recollections I hated slavery, and determined to be free. I have never yet called any man master, though I have been held by three different men who claimed me as their property. The birds in the trees and the wild beasts of the forest made me feel that I, like them, ought to be free. My feelings were all thus centred in the one idea of liberty, of which I thought by day and dreamed by night. I had scarcely reached my twentieth year, when I became acquainted with the angelic being who has since become my wife. It was my intention to have escaped with her before we were married, but circumstances prevented.

"I took her to my bosom as my wife, and then resolved to make the attempt. But, unfortunately, my plans were discovered; and, to save myself from being caught and sold off to the far South, I escaped to the woods, where I remained during many weary months. As I could not bring my wife away, I would not come without her. Another reason for remaining was that I hoped to get up an insurrection of the slaves, and thereby be the means of their liberation. In this, too, I failed. At last it was agreed, between my wife and I, that I should escape to Canada, get employment, save my earnings, and with it purchase her freedom. With the hope of attaining this end, I came into your service. I am now satisfied, that, with the wages I can command here, it will take me not less than five years to obtain by my labor the amount sufficient to purchase the liberty of my dear

Susan. Five years will be too long for me to wait; for she may die, or be sold away, ere I can raise the money. This, sir, makes me feel low spirited; and I have come to the rash determination to return to Virginia for my wife."

The recital of the story had already brought tears to the eyes of the farmer, ere the fugitive had concluded. In vain did Mr. Dickson try to persuade Madison to give up the idea of going back into the very grasp of the tyrant, and risking the loss of his own freedom without securing that of his wife. The heroic man had made up his mind, and nothing could move him. Receiving the amount of wages due him from his employer, Madison turned his face once more towards the South. Supplied with papers purporting to have been made out in Virginia, and certifying to his being a freeman, the fugitive had no difficulty in reaching the neighborhood of his wife. But these "free papers" were only calculated to serve him where he was not known. Madison had also provided himself with files, saws, and other implements, with which to cut his way out of any prison into which he might be cast. These instruments were so small as to be easily concealed in the lining of his clothing; and, armed with them, the fugitive felt sure he should escape again were he ever captured. On his return, Madison met, in the State of Ohio, many of those whom he had seen on his journey to Canada; and all tried to prevail upon him to give up the rash attempt. But to every one he would reply, "Liberty is worth nothing to me while my wife is a slave." When near his former home, and unable to travel in open day without being detected, Madison betook himself to the woods during the day, and travelled by night. At last he arrived at the old farm at night, and hid away in the nearest forest. Here he remained several days, filled with hope and fear, without being able to obtain any information about his wife. One evening, during this suspense, Madison heard the singing of a company of slaves, the sound of which appeared nearer and nearer, until he became convinced that it was a gang going to a corn-shucking; and the fugitive resolved that he would join it, and see if he could get any intelligence of his wife.

In Virginia, as well as in most of the other corn-raising slave-States, there is a custom of having what is termed "a corn-shucking," to which slaves from the neighboring plantations, with the consent of their masters, are invited. At the conclusion of the shucking, a supper is provided by the owner of the corn; and thus, together with the bad whiskey which is freely circulated on such occasions, the slaves are made to feel very happy. Four or five companies of men may be heard in different directions, and at the same time, approaching the place of rendezvous, slaves joining the gangs along the roads as they pass their masters' farms. Madison came out upon the highway; and, as the company came along singing, he fell into the ranks, and joined in the song. Through the darkness of the night he was able to keep from being recognized by the remainder of the company, while he learned from the general conversation the most important news of the day.

Although hungry and thirsty, the fugitive dared not go to the supper-table for fear of recognition. However, before he left the company that night, he gained information enough to satisfy him that his wife was still with her old master; and he hoped to see her, if possible, on the following night. The sun had scarcely set the next evening, ere Madison was wending his way out of the forest, and going towards the home of his loved one, if the slave can be said to have a home. Susan, the object of his affections, was indeed a woman every way worthy of his love. Madison knew well where to find the room usually occupied by his wife, and to that spot he made his way on arriving at the plantation; but, in his zeal and enthusiasm, and his being too confident of success, he committed a blunder which nearly cost him his life. Fearful that if he waited until a late hour, Susan would be asleep, and in awakening her she would in her fright alarm the household, Madison ventured to her room too early in the evening, before the whites in the "great house"[2] had retired. Observed by the overseer, a sufficient number of whites were called

2. The whites' main residence on the plantation.

in, and the fugitive secured ere he could escape with his wife; but the heroic slave did not yield until he with a club had laid three of his assailants upon the ground with his manly blows; and not then until weakened by loss of blood. Madison was at once taken to Richmond, and sold to a slave-trader, then making up a gang of slaves for the New-Orleans market.

The brig "Creole," owned by Johnson & Eperson of Richmond, and commanded by Capt. Enson, lay at the Richmond dock, waiting for her cargo, which usually consisted of tobacco, hemp, flax, and slaves. There were two cabins for the slaves,—one for the men, the other for the women. The men were generally kept in chains while on the voyage; but the women were usually unchained, and allowed to roam at pleasure in their own cabin. On the 27th of October, 1841, "The Creole" sailed from Hampton Roads, bound for New Orleans, with her full load of freight, a hundred and thirty-five slaves, and three passengers, besides the crew. Forty of the slaves were owned by Thomas McCargo, nine belonged to Henry Hewell, and the remainder were held by Johnson & Eperson. Hewell had once been an overseer for McCargo, and on this occasion was acting as his agent.

Among the slaves owned by Johnson & Eperson, was Madison Washington. He was heavily ironed, and chained down to the floor of the cabin occupied by the men, which was in the forward hold. As it was known by Madison's purchasers that he had once escaped, and had been in Canada, they kept a watchful eye over him. The two cabins were separated, so that the men and women had no communication whatever during the passage.

Although rather gloomy at times, Madison on this occasion seemed very cheerful, and his owners thought that he had repented of the experience he had undergone as a runaway, and in the future would prove a more easily-governed chattel. But, from the first hour that he had entered the cabin of "The Creole," Madison had been busily engaged in the selection of men who were to act parts in the great drama. He picked out each one as if by intuition. Every thing was done at night and in the dark, as far as the preparation was concerned. The miniature saws and files were faithfully used when the whites were asleep.

In the other cabin, among the slave-women, was one whose beauty at once attracted attention. Though not tall, she yet had a majestic figure. Her well-moulded shoulders, prominent bust, black hair which hung in ringlets, mild blue eyes, finely-chiselled mouth, with a splendid set of teeth, a turned and well-rounded chin, skin marbled with the animation of life, and veined by blood given to her by her master, she stood as the representative of two races. With only one-eighth of African blood, she was what is called at the South an "octoroon." It was said that her grandfather had served his country in the Revolutionary War, as well as in both Houses of Congress. This was Susan, the wife of Madison. Few slaves, even among the best-used house-servants, had so good an opportunity to gain general information as she.

Accustomed to travel with her mistress, Susan had often been to Richmond, Norfolk, White-Sulphur Springs, and other places of resort for the aristocracy of the Old Dominion. Her language was far more correct than that of most slaves in her position. Susan was as devoted to Madison as she was beautiful and accomplished.

After the arrest of her husband, and his confinement in Richmond jail, it was suspected that Susan had long been in possession of the knowledge of his whereabouts when in Canada, and knew of his being in the neighborhood; and for this crime it was resolved that she should be sold, and sent off to a Southern plantation, where all hope of escape would be at an end. Each was not aware that the other was on board "The Creole;" for Madison and Susan were taken to their respective cabins at different times. On the ninth day out, "The Creole" encountered a rough sea, and most of the slaves were sick, and therefore were not watched with that vigilance that they had been since she first sailed. This was the time for Madison and his accomplices to work, and nobly did they perform their duty. Night came on, the first watch had just been summoned, the wind blowing high, when Madison succeeded in reaching the quarter-deck, followed by eighteen others, all of whom sprang to different parts of the vessel, seizing whatever they could wield as weapons. The crew were nearly all on deck. Capt. Enson and Mr. Merritt, the first mate, were standing together, while Hewell was seated on the companion,[3] smoking a cigar. The appearance of the slaves all at once, and the loud voice and commanding attitude of their leader, so completely surprised the whites, that—

"They spake not a word;
But, like dumb statues or breathless stones,
Stared at each other, and looked deadly pale."[4]

The officers were all armed; but so swift were the motions of Madison that they had nearly lost command of the vessel before they attempted to use them.

Hewell, the greater part of whose life had been spent on the plantation in the capacity of a negro-driver, and who knew that the defiant looks of these men meant something, was the first to start. Drawing his old horse-pistol from under his coat, he fired at one of the blacks, and killed him. The next moment Hewell lay dead upon the deck, for Madison had struck him with a capstan bar.[5] The fight now became general, the white passengers, as well as all the crew, taking part. The battle was Madison's element, and he plunged into it without any care for his own preservation or safety. He was an instrument of enthusiasm, whose value and whose place was in his inspiration. "If the fire of heaven was in my hands, I would throw it at those cowardly whites," said he to his companions, before leaving their cabin. But in this he did not mean revenge, only the possession of his freedom and that of his fellow-slaves. Merritt and Gifford,

3. Companionway (nautical); a stairway leading from one deck to another.
4. Shakespeare, *Richard III*, 3.7.24–26.
5. The wood or metal lever used with the machine (capstan) that hauls in heavy ropes.

the first and second mates of the vessel, both attacked the heroic slave at the same time. Both were stretched out upon the deck with a single blow each, but were merely wounded: they were disabled, and that was all that Madison cared for for the time being. The sailors ran up the rigging for safety, and a moment more he that had worn the fetters an hour before was master of the brig "Creole." His commanding attitude and daring orders, now that he was free, and his perfect preparation for the grand alternative of liberty or death which stood before him, are splendid exemplifications of the true heroic. After his accomplices had covered the slaver's deck, Madison forbade the shedding of more blood, and ordered the sailors to come down, which they did, and with his own hands dressed their wounds. A guard was placed over all except Merritt, who was retained to navigate the vessel. With a musket doubly charged, and pointed at Merritt's breast, the slaves made him swear that he would safely take the brig into a British port. All things now secure, and the white men in chains or under guard, Madison ordered that the fetters should be severed from the limbs of those slaves who still wore them. The next morning "Capt. Washington" (for such was the name he now bore) ordered the cook to provide the best breakfast that the storeroom could furnish, intending to surprise his fellow-slaves, and especially the females, whom he had not yet seen. But little did he think that the woman for whom he had risked his liberty and life would meet him at the breakfast-table. The meeting of the hero and his beautiful and accomplished wife, the tears of joy shed, and the hurrahs that followed from the men, can better be imagined than described. Madison's cup of joy was filled to the brim. He had not only gained his own liberty, and that of one hundred and thirty-four others, but his dear Susan was safe. Only one man, Hewell, had been killed. Capt. Enson, and others who were wounded, soon recovered, and were kindly treated by Madison, and for which they proved ungrateful; for, on the second night, Capt. Enson, Mr. Gifford, and Merritt, took advantage of the absence of Madison from the deck, and attempted to retake the vessel. The slaves, exasperated at this treachery, fell upon the whites with deadly weapons. The captain and his men fled to the cabin, pursued by the blacks. Nothing but the heroism of the negro leader saved the lives of the white men on this occasion; for, as the slaves were rushing into the cabin, Madison threw himself between them and their victims, exclaiming, "Stop! no more blood. My life, that was perilled for your liberty, I will lay down for the protection of these men. They have proved themselves unworthy of life which we granted them; still let us be magnanimous." By the kind heart and noble bearing of Madison, the vile slave-traders were again permitted to go unwhipped of justice. This act of humanity raised the uncouth son of Africa far above his Anglo-Saxon oppressors.

The next morning "The Creole" landed at Nassau, New Providence, where the noble and heroic slaves were warmly greeted by the inhabitants, who at once offered protection, and extended hospitality to them.

But the noble heroism of Madison Washington and his companions found no applause from the Government, then in the hands of the slaveholders. Daniel Webster, then Secretary of State, demanded of the British authorities the surrender of these men, claiming that they were murderers and pirates: the English, however, could not see the point.

Had the "Creole" revolters been white, and committed their noble act of heroism in another land, the people of the United States would have been the first to recognize their claims. The efforts of Denmark Vesey, Nat Turner,[6] and Madison Washington to

6. In 1822 the free black Denmark Vesey (c. 1767–1822) allegedly planned a massive slave rebellion in Charleston, South Carolina, which was discovered by white authorities; Vesey and his accomplices were subsequently put on trial and executed. On 22 August 1831, the slave preacher Nat Turner (1800–1831) led a bloody slave rebellion in Southampton Country, Virginia. Vesey and Turner were regularly invoked as revolutionary heroes by black abolitionists.

strike the chains of slavery from the limbs of their enslaved race will live in history, and will warn all tyrants to beware of the wrath of God and the strong arm of man.

Every iniquity that society allows to subsist for the benefit of the oppressor is a sword with which she herself arms the oppressed. Right is the most dangerous of weapons: woe to him who leaves it to his enemies.

LYDIA MARIA CHILD

"Madison Washington"

Lydia Maria Child (1802–1880) was one of the great literary activists of the nineteenth century. Born in Massachusetts, she began her writing career with the novel *Hobomok: A Tale of Early Times* (1824), which shocked readers for its positive representation of an interracial romance between a white woman and an Indian man. In 1833, she published *An Appeal in Favor of That Class of Americans Called Africans*, which called for immediate emancipation. Over the course of her long career, Child remained committed to antislavery and antiracist reforms. Her short story "The Quadroons" (1842) was an important source for William Wells Brown's *Clotel* (1853), the first novel by an African American, and in 1860 she helped Harriet Jacobs edit *Incidents in the Life of a Slave Girl* (1861). Child wrote "Madison Washington" for *The Freedmen's Book* (Boston: Ticknor and Fields, 1865), which she edited and which is the source of the text below. Among the writers included in Child's anthology were Frederick Douglass, Harriet Beecher Stowe, John Greenleaf Whittier, and Harriet Jacobs. Child also wrote a biographical sketch of Frederick Douglass for the volume.

This man was a slave, born in Virginia. His lot was more tolerable than that of many who are doomed to bondage; but from his early youth he always longed to be free. Nature had in fact made him too intelligent and energetic to be contented in Slavery. Perhaps he would have attempted to escape sooner than he did, had he not become in love with a beautiful octoroon slave named Susan. She was the daughter of her master, and the blood of the white race predominated in several of her ancestors. Her eyes were blue, and her glossy dark hair fell in soft, silky ringlets. Her lover was an unmixed black, and he also was handsome. His features were well formed, and his large dark eyes were very bright and expressive. He had a manly air, his motions were easy and dignified, and altogether he looked like a being that would never consent to wear a chain.

If he had hated Slavery before, he naturally hated it worse after he had married Susan; for a handsome woman, who is a slave, is constantly liable to insult and wrong, from which an enslaved husband has no power to protect her. They laid plans to escape; but unfortunately their intention was discovered before they could carry it into effect. To avoid being sold to the far South, where he could have no hopes of ever rejoining his beloved Susan, he ran to the woods, where he remained concealed several months, suffering much from privation and anxiety. His wife knew where he was, and succeeded in conveying some messages to him, without being detected. She persuaded him not to wait for a chance to take her with him, but to go to Canada and earn money enough to buy her freedom, and then she would go to him.

He travelled only in the night, and by careful management, after a good deal of hardship, he reached the Northern States, and passed into Canada. There he let himself out to work on the farm of a man named Dickson. He was so strong, industrious, intelligent, and well behaved, that the farmer hoped to keep him a long time in his employ. He never mentioned that he was born a slave; for the idea was always hateful to him, and he thought also that circumstances might arise which would render it prudent to keep his own secret. He showed little inclination for conversation, and occupied every leisure moment in learning to read and write. He remained there half a year, without any tidings from his wife; for there are many difficulties in the way of slaves communicating with each other at a distance. He became sad and restless. His employer noticed it, and tried to cheer him up. One day he said to him: "Madison, you seem to be discontented. What have you to complain of? Do you think you are not treated well here? Or are you dissatisfied with the wages I give you?"

"I have no complaint to make of my treatment, sir," replied Madison. "You have been just and kind to me; and since you manifest so much interest in me, I will tell you what it is that makes me so gloomy."

He then related his story, and told how his heart was homesick for his dear Susan. He said she was so handsome that they would ask a high price for her, and he had been calculating that it would take him years to earn enough to buy her; meanwhile, he knew not what might happen to her. There was no law to protect a slave, and he feared all sorts of things; especially, he was afraid they might sell her to the far South, where he could never trace her. So he said he had made up his mind to go back to Virginia and try to bring her away. Mr. Dickson urged him not to attempt it. He reminded him of the dangers he would incur: that he would run a great risk of getting back into Slavery, and that perhaps he himself would be sold to the far South, where he never would be able to communicate with his wife. But Madison replied, "I am well aware of that, sir; but freedom does me no good unless Susan can share it with me."

He accordingly left his safe place of refuge, and started for Virginia. He had free-papers made out, which he thought would protect him till he arrived in the neighborhood where he was known. He also purchased several small files and saws, which he concealed in the lining of his clothes. With these tools he thought he could effect his escape from prison, if he should be taken up on the suspicion of being a runaway slave. Passing through the State of Ohio, he met several who had previously seen him on his way to Canada. They all tried to persuade him not to go back to Virginia; telling him there were nine chances out of ten that he would get caught and carried back into Slavery again. But his answer always was, "Freedom does me no good while my wife is a slave."

When he came to the region where he was known, he hid in

woods and swamps during the day, and travelled only in the night. At last he came in sight of his master's farm, and hid himself in the woods near by. There he remained several days, in a dreadful state of suspense and anxiety. He could not contrive any means to obtain information concerning his wife. He was afraid they might have sold her, for fear she would follow him. He prowled about in the night, in hopes of seeing some old acquaintance, who would tell him whether she was still at the old place; but he saw no one whom he could venture to trust. At last fortune favored him. One evening he heard many voices singing, and he knew by their songs that they were slaves. As they passed up the road, he came out from the woods and joined them. There were so many of them that the addition of one more was not noticed. He found that they were slaves from several plantations, who had permits from their masters to go to a corn-shucking. They were merry, for they were expecting to have a lively time and a comfortable supper. Being a moonless evening, they could not see Madison's face, and he was careful not to let them discover who he was. He went with them to the corn-shucking; and, keeping himself in the shadow all the time, he contrived, in the course of conversation, to find out all he wanted to know. Susan was not sold, and she was living in the same house where he had left her. He was hungry, for he had been several days without food, except such as he could pick up in the woods; but he did not dare to show his face at the supper, where dozens would be sure to recognize him. So he skulked away into the woods again, happy in the consciousness that his Susan was not far off.

He resolved to attempt to see her the next night. He was afraid to tap at her window after all the people in the Great House were abed and asleep; for, as she supposed he was in Canada, he thought she might be frightened and call somebody. He therefore ventured to approach her room in the evening. Unfortunately, the overseer saw him, and called a number of whites, who rushed into the room just as he entered it. He fought hard, and knocked down three of them in his efforts to escape. But they struck at him with their bowie-knives till he was so faint with loss of blood that he could resist no longer. They chained him and carried him to Richmond, where he was placed in the jail. His prospects were now dreary enough. His long-cherished hope of being reunited to his dear wife vanished away in the darkness of despair.

There was a slave-trader in Richmond buying a gang of slaves for the market of New Orleans. Madison Washington was sold to him, and carried on board the brig Creole, owned by Johnson and Eperson, of Richmond, and commanded by Captain Enson. The brig was lying at the dock waiting for her cargo, which consisted of tobacco, hemp, flax, and slaves. There were two separate cabins for the slaves: one for the men and the other for the women. Some of the poor creatures belonged to Johnson and Eperson, some to Thomas McCargo, and some to Henry Hewell. Each had a little private history of separation and sorrow. There was many a bleeding heart there, beside the noble heart that was throbbing in the bosom of Madison Washington. His purchasers saw that he was intelligent, and they knew that he was sold for having escaped to Canada. He was therefore chained to the floor of the cabin and closely watched. He seemed quiet and even cheerful, and they concluded that he was reconciled to his fate. On the contrary, he was never further from such a state of mind. He closely observed the slaves who were in the cabin with him. His discriminating eye soon selected those whom he could trust. To them he whispered that there were more than a hundred slaves on board, and few whites. He had his saws and files still hidden in the lining of his clothes. These were busily used to open their chains, while the captain and crew were asleep. They still continued to wear their chains, and no one suspected that they could slip their hands and feet out at their pleasure.

When the Creole had been nine days out they encountered rough weather. Most of the slaves were sea-sick, and therefore were not watched so closely as usual. On the night of November 7, 1841, the wind was blowing hard. The captain and mate were on deck, and nearly all the crew. Mr. Henry Hewell, one of the owners of the cargo of slaves, who had formerly been a slave-driver on a plantation, was seated on the companion, smoking a cigar. The first watch had just been summoned, when Madison Washington sprang on deck, followed by eighteen other slaves. They seized whatever they could find to use as weapons. Hewell drew a pistol from under his coat, fired at one of the slaves and killed him. Madison Washington struck at him with a capstan-bar, and he fell dead at his feet. The first and second mates both attacked Madison at once. His strong arms threw them upon the deck wounded, but not killed. He fought for freedom, not for revenge; and as soon as they had disarmed the whites and secured them safely, he called out to his accomplices not to shed blood. With his own hands he dressed the wounds of the crew, and told them they had nothing to fear if they would obey his orders. The man who had been a chained slave half an hour before was now master of the vessel, and his grateful companions called him Captain Washington. Being ignorant of navigation, he told Merritt, the first mate, that he should have the freedom of the deck, if he would take an oath to carry the brig faithfully into the nearest port of the British West Indies; and he was afraid to do otherwise.

The next morning Captain Washington ordered the cook to prepare the best breakfast the store-room could furnish, for it was his intention to give all the freed slaves a good meal. The women, who had been greatly frightened by the tumult the night before, were glad enough to come out of their close cabin into the fresh air. And who do you think was among them? Susan, the beautiful young wife of Madison, was there! She had been accused of communicating with her husband in Canada, and being therefore considered a dangerous person, she had been sold to the slave-trader to be carried to the market of New Orleans. Neither of them knew that the other was on board. With a cry of surprise and joy they rushed into each other's arms. The freed slaves threw up their caps and hurrahed again and again, till the sea-gulls wondered at the noise. O, it was a joyful, joyful time! Captain Washington was repaid for all he had suffered. He had gained his own liberty, after having struggled for it in vain for years; he had freed a hundred and thirty-four of his oppressed brethren and sisters; and he had his beloved Susan in his arms, carrying her to a land where the laws would protect their domestic happiness. He felt richer at that moment than any king with a golden crown upon his head.

There had been but two lives lost. One white man was killed in the affray, and he was the slave-driver who shot down one of the slaves. Captain Enson and others who were wounded were kindly cared for by Captain Washington. They proved ungrateful, and tried to regain possession of the vessel and the slaves. The blacks were so exasperated by this attempt, that they wanted to kill all the whites on board. But Captain Washington called out to them: "We have got our liberty, and that is all we have been fighting for. Let no more blood be shed! I have promised to protect these men. They have shown that they are not worthy of it; but let us be magnanimous."

Next morning the Creole arrived at Nassau, in the island of New Providence. Captain Washington and his companions sprang out upon free soil. There he and his beloved Susan are living under the protection of laws which make no distinctions on account of complexion.

ROBERT PURVIS

"A Priceless Picture
History of Sinque, the Hero of the Amistad"

In 1889, the Philadelphia-based African American Robert Purvis (1810–1898), who had played a key role in the antislavery movement, told a reporter from the *Philadelphia Inquirer* the story of his 1841 encounter with Madison Washington. Frederick Douglass had mentioned that encounter in his anticolonization speech of April 1849 (excerpted in this volume). For the first time, Purvis offered an account that directly linked Washington to the *Amistad* rebellion of July 1839. In that rebellion, Africans on board the Cuban slave ship *Amistad* killed a number of their captors, took control of the ship, and guided it to Long Island, New York, where it was seized by the U.S. Navy. The leader of the rebellion, Cinqué (the *Philadelphia Inquirer* adopts an alternative spelling), and some of his compatriots were arrested and held for two years in jails in New Haven, Connecticut, before former president John Quincy Adams (1767–1848) convinced the U.S. Supreme Court to grant the rebels their freedom. Purvis, who was wealthy, was so inspired by the *Amistad* rebellion that he commissioned the New Haven–born artist Nathaniel Jocelyn (1796–1881) to paint a portrait of Cinqué (see figure 6). According to Purvis, the painting arrived at his Philadelphia home on the same day that Washington was passing through on his way from Canada to Virginia. Purvis's story may not be completely historically reliable, but it remains important for offering a strong link between the *Amistad* and *Creole* rebellions. For many African Americans of the nineteenth century, these two rebellions constituted part of a heroic legacy of black resistance to slavery. The article appeared in the 26 December 1889 issue of the *Philadelphia Inquirer*, the source of the text below.

"Do you know that that painting was the cause of freeing several hundred slaves and settling forever the rights of freedom to slaves who sought refuge on British soil?"

Robert Purvis, the old-time Abolitionist, Independent Republican and Reformer, asked this question of an INQUIRER reporter in the sitting room of Mr. Purvis' residence, at the northwest corner of Sixteenth and Mount Vernon streets, yesterday. The painting referred to hangs on the south wall of the room directly above Mr. Purvis' desk. It is the half-length representation of a full-blooded African negro. The right side of the body is nude and the other side is covered by a strip of white cloth. The right hand grasps a heavy spear. The man is powerful and athletic looking, but the face wears an unusually intelligent expression. The forehead is high and broad; the eyes bright and fearless; the chin strong, and the picture gives one the impression of being the faithful likeness of a brave, intrepid leader, with strong arms, iron will and superb intellect.

"The history of that picture has never been fully written," continued Mr. Purvis, "though some events which have since become a part of the history of this country, and of Great Britain, too, might be traced to it. The painting represents 'Sinque, the Hero of the Amistad.' I had it painted almost fifty years ago, by Nathaniel Jocelyn, then a well-known artist, whom I sent to New Haven to obtain sittings from Sinque. Only a few weeks ago I received a letter from a gentleman in New Haven, stating that he had in his possession an engraving copied from the picture by John Sartain,[1] and having just learned that I was the owner of the original painting, he wrote to ask me its history."

1. The London-born artist John Sartain (1808–1897) immigrated to the United States in 1830. He was known for pioneering the development of high-quality engravings called mezzotints.

6. Nathaniel Jocelyn, *Cinque*, 1839. Oil on canvas.
The New Haven Museum.

History of the Painting

Mr. Purvis' visitor expressed himself as anxious to hear the history of the painting, which is only one of many interesting relics in the distinguished Abolitionist's residence.

"Well, it's a long story, but I think an excellent one," began Mr. Purvis. "You have doubtless read of the treaty which was formed in the days of our early struggles in the Anti-Slavery cause, between this country, England and Spain, and, I think, Germany for the suppression of the African slave trade.[2] Poverty-stricken Spain assented to the treaty with great reluctance, as it meant a large reduction in that country's revenue. All of the nations stood by this treaty except Spain, and she surreptitiously carried on the business of supplying Cuba with slaves from the coast of Africa. The prices secured for these slaves were so high that even if only one slave vessel in six escaped capture by the English and other cruisers on the African coast, and succeeded in landing the human cargo in Cuba a large profit would be realized. As the Cubans worked their slaves eighteen or twenty hours a day, and as a slave's life averaged there but seven years, there was always a large demand.

"It was in the year 1840, I think, that one of these vessels succeeded in landing a cargo of slaves in Havana. There were about thirty-five men and three women. They were all bought by two planters, Don Pedro and Montez, who lived on the island of Principe.[3] Montez's body servant was a young slave whom he had captured a year or two before this. The boy was named Antonio, and he had learned to speak Spanish very well. Among these slaves was Sinque, the subject of that painting. He had been captured by a rival tribe of savages in the Mendi country[4] and had been taken to the coast and delivered to the slave traders.

2. In 1817, England and Spain signed a treaty abolishing the slave trade north of the Equator and establishing protocols for searching ships for slaves. The treaty called for the end of the slave trade by June 1820.

3. Located off the northwestern coast of Africa.

4. Western part of Africa now known as Sierra Leone.

Capturing the "Amistad"

"Don Pedro and Montez owned a small vessel named the Amistad, which they used to carry the slaves from Havana to their sugar cane plantations on the Island of Principe. These slaves, including the three women, were placed on board the Amistad. They were put below decks and fettered. When the vessel had been out two days, Sinque, although unable to get his own fetters off, assisted the others and succeeded in freeing them of their chains. They armed themselves with short knives, which were to be used to cut the sugar cane, and, springing on deck, seized the vessel and killed the captain and steward, who made resistance. The crew of three or four men became frightened, sprang overboard and were drowned. Montez resisted, but Sinque cut him slightly across the head, not desiring to kill him, and he finally surrendered. Don Pedro submitted quietly and was not harmed.

"Then Sinque showed his wonderful sagacity and ability. He was ignorant of the rules of navigation, but he determined to take his people back to their African homes. He used Antonio, the body servant of Montez, as an interpreter and through him told Montez that if he wished to escape with his life he would have to navigate the vessel back to African shores. Montez agreed and Sinque watched him night and day, even sleeping by his side, but the Cuban deceived him. He knew how to 'box the compass,' which makes it appear that a vessel is going in a direction exactly opposite to that which is it really bound, and he made for the United States.

"I well recollect a newspaper item that went the rounds of the press at that time, stating that 'a small vessel, moving in a listless way and evidently filled with blacks, had been seen lying off New London, Conn.' This was finally reported to the government, which sent a cruiser, under command of Captain Gedney, to find the suspicious craft.

Sinque's Desperate Resistance

"Meanwhile the limited allowance of bread and provisions on board the Amistad had become exhausted, and Sinque and several companions got into a small boat and rowed ashore to get more supplies. While they were gone Captain Gedney sighted the Amistad and boarded her. Montez immediately demanded his protection and told him how the slaves had seized the vessel. Captain Gedney ordered a file of marines on board and seized the slaves. He awaited the return of Sinque, who, as he approached the Amistad in the row-boat, was confronted with a file of marines with leveled muskets.

"His companions surrendered, but when the marines lowered a boat to take them on board Sinque refused to go, and finally jumped overboard. He swam around until he became exhausted and was then unable to resist, but Captain Gedney said afterward that even in the moment of his surrender Sinque 'sat upon the water like a king.' He was lifted on board and with the captured slaves was taken to New Haven and placed in prison. The Spanish Government demanded their return to Cuba as murderers and as property. Abolitionists throughout the entire country became interested in the case and the demand was resisted. They held that if the slaves had been imported from Africa in violation of the treaty they should not be surrendered to Spain.

"Then began a law suit in the United States District Court of New Haven that interested the whole civilized world. After a year's imprisonment, during which the good people of New Haven, particularly the ladies, became interested in the blacks and taught them to read and speak a little English, and in a few instances even to write it, the case came up. While it was pending President Van Buren[5] meanly ordered a vessel of war on duty off New Haven, with instructions that if the black people were found to have been

5. Martin Van Buren (1782–1862), eighth president of the United States (1837–41).

imported as slaves, they were not to be molested as an appeal would be taken to the Supreme Court, but if the decision be that they were legitimate Spanish property, they were to be put on board the vessel at once and hurried off to Cuba before their case could be taken to the Supreme Court.

Victory for the Africans

"Well, the case was so one-sided that there was no doubt. Many of the slaves were unable to speak English, and it was overwhelmingly shown that they were imported Africans, that the decision of the court was in their favor. The Spanish Minister carried the case to the Supreme Court, and after another year's delay it came up once more. Again the prisoners won by a unanimous decision of this high tribunal. It was about this time that my admiration for this man Sinque's courage led me to send Nathaniel Jocelyn down to New Haven to secure this painting.

"While the case was pending before the Supreme Court ex-President John Quincy Adams, who, although not an Abolitionist, saw the injustice of Spain's demand, volunteered his services to defend these poor Africans. When the decision against Spain was announced the blacks were set free and brought East, where they were cared for by the Abolitionists. I had twenty-two at my house at one time. The men were afterwards sent back to their own country. The three women remained here and they were sent to Oberlin[6] to receive a collegiate education. One of them, named Morgrew, afterwards turned out to be a scholarly, intelligent woman and did excellent work among her people as a missionary. Sinque returned on the vessel with his comrades but did not go back to Africa. He left the ship at Sierra Leone and engaged in the business of selling tobacco. I never heard of him afterwards and don't know whether he is dead or alive.

6. Oberlin College, in Oberlin, Ohio, was a center of abolitionist activity.

Inspired by Sinque's Example

"Now comes the strange part of the story. I was at that time in charge of the work of assisting fugitive slaves to escape. Among the slaves who came into my keeping in this way was a man named Madison Washington. We sent him to Canada, but, to my astonishment, on the day that I received this painting Washington returned and came to my house and asked me to help him secure the release of his wife, who he had left in slavery two years previous. He had opened correspondence with a young white man in the South,[7] whom he trusted implicitly and who had promised to bring his wife from the plantation during the Christmas holidays and deliver her to Washington at a certain spot where they were to meet.

"I showed Washington this painting and he asked me who it represented. I told him the story of Sinque, and he became intensely interested. He drank in every word and greatly admired the hero's courage and intelligence. Well, Washington went South to get his wife, and never came back. How he was betrayed or who it was that betrayed him I never knew until some years later, when I learned that he was captured while escaping with his wife, and put on board a vessel bound from Virginia to New Orleans.

Lord Palmerston's Brave Words

"During the voyage Madison Washington, inspired by the example of Sinque, secured his release, killed the captain, freed the other slaves, numbering about two hundred, and compelled the mate to navigate the vessel into English waters. He landed them at Nassau, English province. At the insistence of the South, this Government demanded from Great Britain the immediate return of these slaves as murderers and as property. The authorities of Nassau refused to

7. Historians have been unable to identify this person or to determine whether such a person existed.

send them back, but detained them by putting them in prison, and referred the matter to the home government.

"Lord Palmerston was then Prime Minister of England,[8] and he settled the question then and forever by replying that 'England knows of no act, even to the taking of life, that can be construed as a crime, when committed in pursuit of the natural and inalienable right of freedom.' The United States recognized the justice of this decision, and never pushed its claim.[9]

"And all this grew out of the inspiration caused by Madison Washington's sight of this little picture.

Exhibited at the Academy

"But that is not all that this painting has accomplished. One more little story and I am done. I had the picture engraved by John Sartain, who had just originated the mezzotint engraving process. Mr. Sartain was much interested in the painting, and he asked that it be sent to the Academy of Fine Arts,[10] of which he and the painter, Mr. Jocelyn, were members.

"The picture was sent, and within the next twenty-four hours I received a letter from Mr. Nagle, of the managers, stating that pictures of that character could not be placed on the walls of the Academy. This offended Mr. Sartain, Mr. Jocelyn and other members who sympathized with them, and they seceded from the Academy. A bitter fight followed between the managers and seceders, which finally resulted in victory for the latter. They returned to the Academy, when the managers finally yielded and placed the picture on

8. Palmerston (1784–1865) served as England's prime minister from 1859 to 1865. In 1839 he was foreign secretary.

9. In fact, the owners of the *Creole*, with the support of the U.S. government, continued to push their claims, and in 1853 an Anglo-American claims commission decided on behalf of the claimants (the owners of slaves on the *Creole*). In 1855 they were awarded $110,330.

10. The Pennsylvania Academy of the Fine Arts is located in Philadelphia.

the walls of that institution. Their principal objection to the painting was that its subject was a hero, and they considered that a black man had no right to be a hero.

"Such is the history of the painting of 'Sinque the Hero of the Amistad,'" concluded Mr. Purvis. "It only cost me two hundred and sixty odd dollars, but I would not part with it now for that many thousands. In fact, it is priceless."

PAULINE E. HOPKINS

"A Dash for Liberty"

Born in Portland, Maine, and raised in Boston, the African American novelist and editor Pauline E. Hopkins (1859–1930) is best known for her four novels published at the turn of the twentieth century: *Contending Forces* (1900), *Hagar's Daughter* (1901), *Winona* (1902), and *Of One Blood* (1902). All except *Contending Forces* were serialized in the *Colored American Magazine*, where she worked as literary editor. In 1901 she began publishing in the magazine a series of sketches that she called "Heroes and Heroines in Black." Her fictionalized account of the *Creole* rebellion, "A Dash for Liberty," appeared in the August 1901 issue of the *Colored American Magazine*, the source of the text below. At the time of its publication, Hopkins gave the story a subtitle, "Founded on an article written by Col. T. W. Higginson, for the Atlantic Monthly, June 1861," but the noted editor of the *Atlantic Monthly* never wrote on Madison Washington. His June 1861 essay was on the black conspirator Denmark Vesey, who allegedly plotted to burn Charleston, South Carolina, to the ground in an effort to liberate the city's black slaves. Perhaps the essay inspired Hopkins to consider Madison Washington in the tradition of Vesey, as William Wells Brown did at the end of his chapter on the *Creole* rebellion in *The Negro in the American Rebellion*. Hopkins admired Douglass and Brown, but it is unclear whether she had read Douglass's *The Heroic Slave* (she seems more familiar with Brown's accounts in *The Black Man* and *The Negro in the American Rebellion*). More than other authors writing on the *Creole*, she presents Washington's wife as actively engaged in the rebellion. Hopkins lost her job at the *Colored American Magazine* in 1904 when Booker T. Washington gained control of the magazine and fired those challenging his accommodationist approach to race relations. Hopkins continued to work in journalism, and in subsequent years cofounded her own publishing house and magazine, both of which were short-lived, while working as a stenographer at the Massachusetts Institute of Technology.

"So, Madison, you are bound to try it?"

"Yes, sir," was the respectful reply.

There was silence between the two men for a space, and Mr. Dickson drove his horse to the end of the furrow he was making and returned slowly to the starting point, and the sombre figure awaiting him.

"Do I not pay you enough, and treat you well?" asked the farmer as he halted.

"Yes, sir."

"Then why not stay here and let well enough alone?"

"Liberty is worth nothing to me while my wife is a slave."

"We will manage to get her to you in a year or two."

The man smiled and sadly shook his head. "A year or two would mean forever, situated as we are, Mr. Dickson. It is hard for you to understand; you white men are all alike where you are called upon to judge a Negro's heart," he continued bitterly. "Imagine yourself in my place; how would you feel? The relentless heel of oppression in the States will have ground my rights as a husband into the dust, and have driven Susan to despair in that time. A white man may take up arms to defend a bit of property; but a black man has no right to his wife, his liberty or his life against his master! This makes me low-spirited, Mr. Dickson, and I have determined to return to Virginia for my wife. My feelings are centred in the idea of liberty," and as he spoke he stretched his arms toward the deep blue of the Canadian sky in a magnificent gesture. Then with a deep-drawn breath that inflated his mighty chest, he repeated the word: "Liberty! I think of it by day and dream of it by night; and I shall only taste it in all its sweetness when Susan shares it with me."

Madison was an unmixed African, of grand physique, and one of the handsomest of his race. His dignified, calm and unaffected bearing marked him as a leader among his fellows. His features bore the stamp of genius. His firm step and piercing eye attracted the attention of all who met him. He had arrived in Canada along with many other fugitives during the year 1840, and being a strong, able-bodied man, and a willing worker, had sought and obtained employment on Mr. Dickson's farm.

After Madison's words, Mr. Dickson stood for some time in meditative silence.

"Madison," he said at length, "there's desperate blood in your veins, and if you get back there and are captured, you'll do desperate deeds."

"Well, put yourself in my place: I shall be there single-handed. I have a wife whom I love, and whom I will protect. I hate slavery, I hate the laws that make my country a nursery for it. Must I be denied the right of aggressive defense against those who would overpower and crush me by superior force?"

"I understand you fully, Madison; it is not your defense but your rashness that I fear. Promise me that you will be discreet, and not begin an attack." Madison hesitated. Such a promise seemed to him like surrendering a part of those individual rights for which he panted. Mr. Dickson waited. Presently the Negro said significantly: "I promise not to be indiscreet."

There were tears in the eyes of the kind-hearted farmer as he pressed Madison's hand.

"God speed and keep you and the wife you love; may she prove worthy."

In a few days, Madison received the wages due him, and armed with tiny saws and files to cut a way to liberty, if captured, turned his face toward the South.

It was late in the fall of 1840 when Madison found himself again at home in the fair Virginia State. The land was blossoming into ripe maturity, and the smiling fields lay waiting for the harvester.

The fugitive, unable to travel in the open day, had hidden himself for three weeks in the shadow of the friendly forest near his old home, filled with hope and fear, unable to obtain any information about the wife he hoped to rescue from slavery. After weary days and nights, he had reached the most perilous part of his mission. Tonight there would be no moon and the clouds threatened a storm; to his listening ears the rising wind bore the sound of laughter and singing. He drew back into the deepest shadow. The words came distinctly to his ears as the singers neared his hiding place.

"All dem purty gals will be dar,
Shuck dat corn before you eat.
Dey will fix it fer us rare,
Shuck dat corn before you eat.
I know dat supper will be big,
Shuck dat corn before you eat.
I think I smell a fine roast pig,
Shuck dat corn before you eat.
Stuff dat coon an' bake him down,
I spec some niggers dar from town.
Shuck dat corn before you eat.
Please cook dat turkey nice an' brown.
By de side of dat turkey I'll be foun,'
Shuck dat corn before you eat."[1]

"Don't talk about dat turkey; he'll be gone before we git dar."

"He's talkin,' ain't he?"

"Las' time I shucked corn, turkey was de toughes' meat I eat fer many a day; you's got to have teef sharp lak a saw to eat it."

"S'pose you ain't got no teef, den what you gwine ter do?"

"Why ef you ain't got no teef you muss gum it!"

"Ha, ha, ha!"

Madison glided in and out among the trees, listening until he was sure that it was a gang going to a corn-shucking, and he resolved to join it, and get, if possible some news of Susan. He came out upon the highway, and as the company reached his hiding place, he fell

1. Lyrics to the call-and-response slave work song "Shuck That Corn Before You Eat."

into the ranks and joined in the singing. The darkness hid his identity from the company while he learned from their conversation the important events of the day.

On they marched by the light of weird, flaring pine knots, singing their merry cadences, in which the noble minor strains habitual to Negro music, sounded the depths of sadness, glancing off in majestic harmony, that touched the very gates of paradise in suppliant prayer.

It was close to midnight; the stars had disappeared and a steady rain was falling when, by a circuitous route, Madison reached the mansion where he had learned that his wife was still living. There were lights in the windows. Mirth at the great house kept company with mirth at the quarters.

The fugitive stole noiselessly under the fragrant magnolia trees and paused, asking himself what he should do next. As he stood there he heard the hoof-beats of the mounted patrol, far in the distance, die into silence. Cautiously he drew near the house and crept around to the rear of the building directly beneath the window of his wife's sleeping closet. He swung himself up and tried it; it yielded to his touch. Softly he raised the sash, and softly he crept into the room. His foot struck against an object and swept it to the floor. It fell with a loud crash. In an instant the door opened. There was a rush of feet, and Madison stood at bay. The house was aroused; lights were brought.

"I knowed 'twas him!" cried the overseer in triumph. "I heern him a-gettin' in the window, but I kept dark till he knocked my gun down; then I grabbed him! I knowed this room'd trap him ef we was patient about it."

Madison shook his captor off and backed against the wall. His grasp tightened on the club in his hand; his nerves were like steel, his eyes flashed fire.

"Don't kill him," shouted Judge Johnson, as the overseer's pistol gleamed in the light. "Five hundred dollars for him alive!"

With a crash, Madison's club descended on the head of the nearest man; again, and yet again, he whirled it around, doing frightful execution each time it fell. Three of the men who had responded to the overseer's cry for help were on the ground, and he himself was sore from many wounds before, weakened by loss of blood, Madison finally succumbed.

The brig "Creole" lay at the Richmond dock taking on her cargo of tobacco, hemp, flax and slaves. The sky was cloudless, and the blue waters rippled but slightly under the faint breeze. There was on board the confusion incident to departure. In the hold and on deck men were hurrying to and fro, busy and excited, making the final preparations for the voyage. The slaves came aboard in two gangs: first the men, chained like cattle, were marched to their quarters in the hold; then came the women to whom more freedom was allowed.

In spite of the blue sky and the bright sunlight that silvered the water the scene was indescribably depressing and sad. The procession of gloomy-faced men and weeping women seemed to be descending into a living grave.

The captain and the first mate were standing together at the head of the gangway as the women stepped aboard. Most were very plain and bore the marks of servitude, a few were neat and attractive in appearances; but one was a woman whose great beauty immediately attracted attention; she was an octoroon.[2] It was a tradition that her grandfather had served in the Revolutionary War, as well as in both Houses of Congress. That was nothing, however, at a time when the blood of the proudest F. F. V.'s[3] was freely mingled with that of the African slaves on their plantations. Who wonders that Virginia has produced great men of color from among the exbondmen, or, that illustrious black men proudly point to Virginia as a birthplace? Posterity rises to the plane that their ancestors bequeath, and

2. One-eighth black; a term used at the time to describe a light-complexioned black.

3. First Families of Virginia.

the most refined, the wealthiest and the most intellectual whites of that proud State have not hesitated to amalgamate with the Negro.

"What a beauty!" exclaimed the captain as the line of women paused a moment opposite him.

"Yes," said the overseer in charge of the gang. "She's as fine a piece of flesh as I have had in trade for many a day."

"What's the price?" demanded the captain.

"Oh, way up. Two or three thousand. She's a lady's maid, well-educated, and can sing and dance. We'll get it in New Orleans. Like to buy?"

"You don't suit my pile,"[4] was the reply, as his eyes followed the retreating form of the handsome octoroon. "Give her a cabin to herself; she ought not to herd with the rest," he continued, turning to the mate.

He turned with a meaning laugh to execute the order.

The "Creole" proceeded slowly on her way towards New Orleans. In the men's cabin, Madison Monroe[5] lay chained to the floor and heavily ironed. But from the first moment on board ship he had been busily engaged in selecting men who could be trusted in the dash for liberty that he was determined to make. The miniature files and saws which he still wore concealed in his clothing were faithfully used in the darkness of night. The man was at peace, although he had caught no glimpse of the dearly loved Susan. When the body suffers greatly, the strain upon the heart becomes less tense, and a welcome calmness had stolen over the prisoner's soul.

On the ninth day out the brig encountered a rough sea, and most of the slaves were sick, and therefore not watched with very great vigilance. This was the time for action, and it was planned that they should rise that night. Night came on; the first watch was summoned;

4. Fortune; funds.

5. During the time that Hopkins was writing the story, she was in fierce disagreement with the black leader Booker T. Washington, whom she distrusted for his conciliatory relations with whites. She may have changed the name of the historical Madison Washington to Madison Monroe in order to excise the name of Washington, though ultimately her reason for making the name change is unclear.

the wind was blowing high. Along the narrow passageway that separated the men's quarters from the women's, a man was creeping.

The octoroon lay upon the floor of her cabin, apparently sleeping, when a shadow darkened the door, and the captain stepped into the room, casting bold glances at the reclining figure. Profound silence reigned. One might have fancied one's self on a deserted vessel, but for the sound of an occasional footstep on the deck above, and the murmur of voices in the opposite hold.

She lay stretched at full length with her head resting upon her arm, a position that displayed to the best advantage the perfect symmetry of her superb figure; the dim light of a lantern played upon the long black ringlets, finely-chiselled mouth and well-rounded chin, upon the marbled skin veined by her master's blood,—representative of two races, to which did she belong?

For a moment the man gazed at her in silence; then casting a glance around him, he dropped upon one knee and kissed the sleeping woman full upon the mouth.

With a shriek the startled sleeper sprang to her feet. The woman's heart stood still with horror; she recognized the intruder as she dashed his face aside with both hands.

"None of that, my beauty," growled the man, as he reeled back with an oath, and then flung himself forward and threw his arm about her slender waist. "Why did you think you had a private cabin, and all the delicacies of the season? Not to behave like a young catamount,[6] I warrant you."

The passion of terror and desperation lent the girl such strength that the man was forced to relax his hold slightly. Quick as a flash, she struck him a stinging blow across the eyes, and as he staggered back, she sprang out of the doorway, making for the deck with the evident intention of going overboard.

"God have mercy!" broke from her lips as she passed the men's cabin, closely followed by the captain.

6. Short-tailed wildcat, such as a lynx.

"Hold on, girl; we'll protect you!" shouted Madison, and he stooped, seized the heavy padlock which fastened the iron ring that encircled his ankle to the iron bar, and stiffening the muscles, wrenched the fastening apart, and hurled it with all his force straight at the captain's head.

His aim was correct. The padlock hit the captain not far from the left temple. The blow stunned him. In a moment Madison was upon him and had seized his weapons, another moment served to handcuff the unconscious man.

"If the fire of Heaven were in my hands, I would throw it at these cowardly whites. Follow me: it is liberty or death!"[7] he shouted as he rushed for the quarter-deck. Eighteen others followed him, all of whom seized whatever they could wield as weapons.

The crew were all on deck; the three passengers were seated on the companion smoking. The appearance of the slaves all at once completely surprised the whites.

So swift were Madison's movements that at first the officers made no attempt to use their weapons; but this was only for an instant. One of the passengers drew his pistol, fired, and killed one of the blacks. The next moment he lay dead upon the deck from a blow with a piece of a capstan bar in Madison's hand. The fight then became general, passengers and crew taking part.

The first and second mates were stretched out upon the deck with a single blow each. The sailors ran up the rigging for safety, and in short time Madison was master of the "Creole."

After his accomplices had covered the slaver's deck, the intrepid leader forbade the shedding of more blood. The sailors came down to the deck, and their wounds were dressed. All the prisoners were heavily ironed and well guarded except the mate, who was to navigate the vessel; with a musket doubly charged pointed at his breast, he was made to swear to take the brig into a British port.

7. An echo of the 1775 revolutionary declaration attributed to the Virginia patriot Patrick Henry (1736–1799).

By one splendid and heroic stroke, the daring Madison had not only gained his own liberty, but that of one hundred and thirty-four others.

The next morning all the slaves who were still fettered, were released, and the cook was ordered to prepare the best breakfast that the stores would permit; this was to be a fête in honor of the success of the revolt and as a surprise to the females, whom the men had not yet seen.

As the women filed into the captain's cabin, where the meal was served, weeping, singing and shouting over their deliverance, the beautiful octoroon with one wild, half-frantic cry of joy sprang towards the gallant leader.

"Madison!"

"My God! Susan! My wife!"

She was locked to his breast; she clung to him convulsively. Unnerved at last by the revulsion to more than relief and ecstacy, she broke into wild sobs, while the astonished company closed around them with loud hurrahs.

Madison's cup of joy was filled to the brim. He clasped her to him in silence, and humbly thanked Heaven for its blessing and mercy.

The next morning the "Creole" landed at Nassau, New Providence, where the slaves were offered protection and hospitality.

Every act of oppression is a weapon for the oppressed. Right is a dangerous instrument; woe to us if our enemy wields it.

PART 5
Criticism

IN 1982, ROBERT B. STEPTO PUBLISHED the first critical study of *The Heroic Slave*. Since then, Douglass's novella has received considerable critical attention. Critics have deepened our appreciation of the novella's aesthetics and explored its racial politics (Douglass's views on black resistance and nationalism in particular). There has also been work on Douglass's use of historical sources, his awareness of the larger diplomatic context surrounding the *Creole* revolt, his interest in interracial friendship, and his interactions with other writers of the time, such as Harriet Beecher Stowe. Critics have debated key aspects of *The Heroic Slave*. Though an admirer of the novella, Richard Yarborough took Douglass to task for his emphasis on black male leadership, while Maggie Montesinos Sale, Celeste-Marie Bernier, and others developed alternative perspectives on gender in the novella. The seven selections in this section, running from Stepto's pioneering essay on Douglass's artful storytelling to Carrie Hyde's consideration of meteorological motifs, provide a sampling of the major work on *The Heroic Slave* published over the last three decades. The selections are excerpted from essays and chapters; by excerpting, we could present the greatest number of critical voices. Bibliographical information is provided for those who would like to read the essays or chapters in their entirety. At the end of the volume, we also provide a selected bibliography of work on *The Heroic Slave* and the *Creole* rebellion.

ROBERT B. STEPTO

from "Storytelling in Early Afro-American Fiction"[1]

The novella is full of craft, especially of the sort which combines artfulness with a certain fabulistic usefulness. Appropriately enough, evidence of Douglass' craft is available in the novella's attention to both theme and character. In Part 1 of "The Heroic Slave," we are told of the "double state" of Virginia and introduced not only to Madison Washington but also to Mr. Listwell, who figures as the model abolitionist in the story. The meticulous development of the Virginia theme and of the portrait of Mr. Listwell, much more than the portrayal of Washington as a hero, is the stuff of useful art-making in Douglass' novella.

The theme of the duality or "doubleness" of Virginia begins in the novella's very first sentence: "The State of Virginia is famous in American annals for the multitudinous array of her statesmen and heroes." The rest of the paragraph continues as follows:

1. From Robert B. Stepto, "Storytelling in Early Afro-American Fiction: Frederick Douglass' 'The Heroic Slave,'" originally appeared in *Georgia Review* 36, No. 2/ (Summer 1982): 355–68; the excerpt is from 360–68. Copyright © 1982 by The University of Georgia/ © 1982 by Robert B. Stepto. Reprinted by permission of Robert B. Stepto and *The Georgia Review*. The footnotes have been renumbered and, unless otherwise indicated, are the author's.

> She has been dignified by some the mother of statesmen. History has not been sparing in recording their names, or in blazoning their deeds. Her high position in this respect, has given her an enviable distinction among her sister States. With Virginia for his birth-place, even a man of ordinary parts, on account of the general partiality for her sons, easily rises to eminent stations. Men, not great enough to attract special attention in their native States, have, like a certain distinguished citizen in the State of New York, sighed and repined that they were not born in Virginia. Yet not all the great ones of the Old Dominion have, by the fact of their birthplace, escaped undeserved obscurity. By some strange neglect, *one* of the truest, manliest, and bravest of her children,—one who, in after years, will, I think, command the pen of genius to set his merits forth—holds now no higher place in the records of that grand old Commonwealth than is held by a horse or an ox. Let those account for it who can, but there stands the fact, that a man who loved liberty as well as did Patrick Henry—who deserved it as much as Thomas Jefferson—and who fought for it with a valor as high, an arm as strong, and against odds as great as he who led all the armies of the American colonies through the great war for freedom and independence, lives now only in the chattel records of his native state.[2]

At least two features here are worthy of note. The paragraph as a whole, but especially its initial sentences, can be seen as significant revoicing of the conventional opening of a slave narrative. Slave narratives usually begin with the phrase "I was born"; this is true of Douglass' 1845 *Narrative* and true also, as James Olney reminds us, of the narratives of Henry Bibb, Henry "Box" Brown, William Wells Brown, John Thompson, Samuel Ringgold Ward, James W. C. Pennington, Austin Steward, James Roberts, and many, many other former slaves.[3] In "The Heroic Slave," however, Douglass trans-

2. Douglass, "The Heroic Slave," in Abraham Chapman, ed., *Steal Away: Stories of the Runaway Slaves* (New York: Praeger, 1971), p. 146. All future page references are to this republication of the novella.

3. James Olney, "'I Was Born': Slave Narratives, Their Status as Autobiography and Literature." An unpublished manuscript. [The essay appears in *Callaloo*, no. 20 (1984): 46–73. Eds.]

forms "I was born" into the broader assertion that in Virginia many heroes have been born. After that, he then works his way to the central point that a certain *one*—an unknown hero who lives now only in the chattel records and not the history books—has been born. Douglass knows the slave narrative convention, partly because he has used it himself; but more to the point, he seems to have an understanding of how to exploit its rhetorical usefulness in terms of proclaiming the existence and identity of an individual without merely employing it verbatim. This is clear evidence, I think, of a first step, albeit a small one, toward the creation of an Afro-American fiction based upon the conventions of the slave narratives. That Douglass himself was quite possibly thinking in these terms while writing is suggested by his persistent reference to the "chattel records" which must, in effect, be transformed by "the pen of genius" so that his hero's merits may be set forth—indeed, set free. If by this Douglass means that his hero's story must be liberated from the realm—the text—of brutal fact, and more, that texts must be created to compete with other texts, then it's safe to say that he brought to the creation of "The Heroic Slave" all the intentions, if not all the skills, of the self-conscious *writer*.

The other key feature of the paragraph pertains more directly to the novella's Virginia theme. I refer here to the small yet delightfully artful riddle which permits a certain ingenious closure of the paragraph. After declaring that his hero loved liberty as much as did Patrick Henry, and deserved it as much as Thomas Jefferson, Douglass refuses to name the third famous son of Virginia with whom his hero is to be compared. He speaks only of "he who led all the armies of the American colonies through the great war for freedom and independence." Of course, as any school boy or girl knows, the mystery man is Washington. And that is the answer—and point—to Douglass' funny-sad joke about the "double state" of Virginia as well: *his* mystery man is also a hero named Washington. Thus, Douglass advances his comparison of heroic statesmen and heroic chattel, and does so quite ingenuously by both naming and *not* naming them in such a way that we are led to discover that statesmen and slaves may share the same name and be heroes and Virginians alike. Rhetoric and meaning conjoin in a very sophisticated way in this passage, thus providing us with an indication of how seriously and ambitiously Douglass will take the task of composing the rest of the novella.

"The Heroic Slave" is divided into four parts, and in each Virginia becomes less and less of a setting (especially of a demographic or even historical sort) and more of a ritual ground—a "charged field" as Victor Turner would say—for symbolic encounters between slaves and abolitionists or Virginians and Virginians. For example, in Part I, the encounter between Mr. Listwell, our soon-to-be abolitionist, and Madison Washington, our soon-to-be fugitive slave, takes place in a magnificent Virginia forest. In accord with many familiar notions regarding the transformational powers of nature in its purest state, both men leave the sylvan glen determined and resolved to become an abolitionist and a free man respectively. Thus, the Virginia forest is established as a very particular space within the figurative geography of the novella, one which will receive further definition as we encounter other spaces which necessarily involve very different rituals for slave and abolitionist alike and one to which we'll return precisely because, as the point of departure, it is the only known point of return.

Part II of "The Heroic Slave" takes place in Ohio. Listwell lives there and has the opportunity to aid an escaping slave who turns out to be none other than Madison Washington. This change in setting from Virginia to Ohio assists in the development of the Virginia theme chiefly because it gives Douglass the opportunity to stress the point that something truly happened to each man in that "sacred" forest, one happy result being that their paths did cross once again in the cause of freedom. As Listwell and Washington converse with each other before Listwell's hearth, and each man tells his story of self-transformation in the forest and what happened thereafter, we are transported back to the forest, however briefly and indirectly. By the end of Part II, it becomes clear in the context of the emerging novella that Ohio, as a free state, is an increasingly symbolic state to be achieved through acts of fellowship initiated however indirectly before. Ohio and that part of Virginia which we know only as "the forest" become separate but one, much as our heroic slave and model abolitionist become separate but one as they talk and truly hear each other.[4]

In Part III, the return to Virginia and the forest is far more direct and in keeping with the brutal realities of life in the antebellum South. Listwell is back in Virginia on business, and so is Washington, who has come surreptitiously in quest of his wife still in slavery. Having portrayed Virginia's heaven—the forest replete with pathways to freedom—Douglass now offers Virginia's hell. As one might imagine, given Douglass' zeal for temperance and the abolition of slavery, hell is a tavern full of drunkards, knaves, and traders of human flesh. Hell's first circle is the yard adjacent to the tavern where slaves on their way to market are "stabled" while the souldriver drinks a dram. Its second circle is the remaining fifteen miles to Richmond where a slave auction awaits. The third circle may be sale to a new Virginia master and a long walk to a new plantation, or it may be a horrific re-encounter with middle passage, in the form of a "cruise" aboard a Baltimore-built slaver bound for New Orleans. If the latter, many other circles of Hell await, for there will be another auction, another sale, another master, another long walk, and perhaps yet another auction.

The point to Part III is that while Washington has returned to Virginia, lost his wife in their escape attempt, and been re-enslaved, Listwell is also there and able to provide the means by which Washington may free himself—*and others*. The suggestion is that it is

4. Listwell's role as host and storylistener in Part II suggests that he may be, at least in this section of the novella, a fictive portrait of abolitionist Joseph Gurney. Douglass himself plants this idea when he remarks in "Slavery, the Slumbering Volcano" that Washington debated with Gurney how advisable it would be to attempt to rescue his wife from slavery. [A selection from that speech, also called "Address at the Great Anti-Colonization Meeting," is included in this volume. Eds.]

quite one thing to aid an escaping slave in Ohio and quite another to assist one in deepest, darkest Virginia. Listwell rises to the occasion and, immediately after the slave auction in Richmond, slips Washington several files for the chains binding him. What Washington and the rest do once on board the *Creole* is, of course, a matter of historical record.

One might think that the fourth and last part of "The Heroic Slave" would be totally devoted to a vivid narration of swashbuckling valor aboard the high seas. This is not the case. The scene is once again Virginia; the time is set some time after the revolt on the *Creole*; the place is a "Marine Coffee-house" in Richmond; and the conversation is quite provocatively between two white Virginia sailors, obviously neither statesmen nor slaves.[5] One of the sailors had shipped on the *Creole*, the other had not. The conversation takes a sharp turn when the latter sailor, Jack Williams, makes it clear that, "For my part I feel ashamed to have the idea go abroad, that a ship load of slaves can't be safely taken from Richmond to New Orleans. I should like, merely to redeem the character of Virginia sailors, to take charge of a ship load of 'em to-morrow" (p. 186). Tom Grant, who had been on the *Creole*, soon replies, "I dare say *here* what many men *feel*, but *dare not speak*, that this whole slave-trading business is a disgrace and scandal to Old Virginia" (pp. 186–87). The conversation goes on, and before it's done, Tom Grant has indeed told the story of the revolt led by Madison Washington.[6] The point

5. Placing the sailors in a "Marine Coffee-house" is possibly both an awkward and a revealing touch. To be sure, such establishments existed, but one cannot help but feel that a tavern would be a more "natural" setting. The braggadocio and general belligerence of Jack Williams, for example, suggest the behavior of a man whose cup contains a headier brew than coffee or tea. Of course, the problem for Douglass was that, given his advocacy of temperance, he could not easily situate Tom Grant, the reformed sailor and a voice of reason, in one of the Devil's haunts. This is quite likely an instance where Douglass' politics and penchant for realism conflicted in a way he had not encountered before he attempted prose fiction.

6. Early in Part IV, Tom Grant is referred to as "our first mate" (p. 185). This suggests that Grant is loosely modeled upon Zephaniah Gifford, the actual first mate of the *Creole*. Gifford gave many depositions on the revolt and hence told Washington's story many times. See Howard Jones, "The Peculiar Institution and National Honor: The Case of the *Creole* Slave Revolt," *Civil War History*, 21 (March 1975), pp. 34 ff.

is, however, that Tom Grant, not the narrator, tells this story, and he does so in such a way that it is clear that he has become a transformed man as a result of living through the episode.

Thus, Douglass ends his novella by creating the dialogue between Virginians about the "state" of Virginia which was effectively prefigured in the novella's first paragraph. The duality or doubleness of Virginia (and indeed of America) first offered as an assertion and then in the form of a riddle now assumes a full-blown literary form. More to the point, perhaps, is the fact that Tom Grant—the sailor who was forced to listen, if you will, to both the speech *and* action of Madison Washington—has become something of an abolitionist (though he bristles at the suggestion) and, most certainly, something of a white Southern storyteller of a tale of black freedom. This particular aspect of Grant's transformation is keeping with what happens to our white Northerner, Mr. Listwell. What we see here, then, is an expression within Douglass' narrative design of the signal idea that freedom for slaves can transform the South and the North and hence the nation.

This brings us to Mr. Listwell, whose creation is possibly *the* polemical and literary achievement of the novella. In many ways, his name is his story and his story his name. He is indeed a "Listwell" in that he *enlists* as an abolitionist and does *well* by the cause—in fact, he does magnificently. He is also a "Listwell" in that he *listens* well; he is, in the context of his relations with Madison Washington and in accord with the aesthetics of storytelling, a model storylistener and hence an agent, in many senses of the term, for the continuing performance of the story he and Washington increasingly share and "tell" together. Of course, Douglass' point is that both features of Listwell's "listing" are connected and, ideally, inextricably bound: one cannot be a good abolitionist without being a good listener, with the reverse often being true as well.

Douglass' elaborate presentation of these ideas begins in Part I of "The Heroic Slave" when Washington apostrophizes in the Virginia forest on his plight as an abject slave and unknowingly is *overheard* by Listwell. At the end of his speech, the storyteller slave vows to gain freedom and the storylistener white Northerner vows to become an abolitionist so that he might aid slaves such as the one he has just overheard. This is storytelling of a sort conducted at a distance. Both storyteller and storylistener are present, and closure of a kind occurs in that both performers resolve to embark on new journeys or careers. But, of course, the teller (slave) doesn't know yet that he has a listener (abolitionist, brother in the cause), and the listener doesn't know yet what role he will play in telling the story that has just begun. In this way, Douglass spins three primary narrative threads: one is the storyteller/slave's journey to freedom; another is the storylistener/abolitionist's journey to service; the third is the resolution or consummation of purposeful human brotherhood between slave and abolitionist, as it may be most particularly achieved through the communal aesthetic of storytelling.

In Part II, the three primary threads reappear in an advanced state. Washington has escaped and is indeed journeying to freedom; Listwell is now a confirmed abolitionist whose references to conversations with other abolitionists suggest that he is actively involved; and Washington and Listwell are indeed in the process of becoming brothers in the struggle, both because they befriend each other on a cold night and because, once settled before Listwell's fire, they engage for long hours in storytelling. Several features of their storytelling are worth remarking upon. One is that Washington, as the storyteller, actually tells two stories about his adventures in the Virginia forest, one about a thwarted escape attempt and the resulting limbo he enters while neither slave nor free, and the other about how he finally breaks out of limbo, reasserting his desire for freedom.[7]

7. These two stories of immersion in and ascent from a kind of limbo are central to the history of Afro-American letters, chiefly because they so conspicuously prefigure the trope of hibernation most accessible to the modern reader in Ralph Ellison's *Invisible Man*, published almost exactly one hundred years later. Madison Washington's cave in the realm between the plantation and the world beyond—"In the dismal swamps I lived, sir, five long years,—a cave for my home during day. I wandered at night with the wolf and the bear,—sustained by the promise that my good Susan would meet me in the pine woods, at least once a week"—anticipates the Invisible Man's hole in the region between black and white Manhattan. Once Washington's

The importance of this feature is that it occasions a repetition of the novella's "primary" forest episode which creates in turn a narrative rhythm which we commonly associate with oral storytelling. While it would be stretching things to say that this is an African residual in the novella, we are on safe ground, however, in suggesting that in creating this particular episode Douglass is drawing deeply on his knowledge of storytelling amongst slaves.

Another pertinent feature is that Listwell, as the storylistener, is both a good listener and, increasingly, a good prompter of Washington's stories. Early on, Listwell says, "But this was five years ago; where have you been since?" Washington replies, "I will try to tell you," and to be sure storytelling ensues. Other examples of this abound. In one notable instance, in response to Washington's explanation as to why he stole food while in flight, Listwell asserts, "And just there you were right. . . . I once had doubts on this point myself, but a conversation with Gerrit Smith, (a man, by the way, that I wish you could see, for he is a devoted friend of your race, and I know he would receive you gladly,) put an end to all my doubts on this point. But do not let me interrupt you" (p. 160). Listwell interrupts, but his is what we might call a good interruption, for he *authenticates* the slave's rationale for stealing instead of questioning it. In this way, Listwell's remarks advance both story *and* cause, which is exactly what he's supposed to do now that he's an abolitionist.[8]

---

wolf and bear become in the mind's eye, brer wolf and brer bear, this particular contour in Afro-American literary history is visible and complete.

8. This brief and seemingly utilitarian passage in the novella becomes remarkable when one realizes that Douglass is also about the task of composing a salute or "praise song" for a new friend in the cause, Gerrit Smith. "The Heroic Slave," we must recall, was Douglass' contribution to an anthology collected for the purposes of raising funds for the newly established *Frederick Douglass' Paper*. The *Paper* was created when Douglass' *North Star* merged with Gerrit Smith's *Liberty Party Paper* and Smith committed himself to subsidizing the new publication. Listwell's praise of Smith in the novella is, in effect, both a tribute and a "thank you note" from Douglass to his new business partner. And it is something else as well: praise for Smith and not, say, Garrison is a clear signal from Douglass that he has broken with the Garrisonian abolitionists and aligned himself with new friends. His praise for Smith took an even grander form when Douglass dedicated *My Bondage and My Freedom*: "To Honor-

Resolution of this episode takes the form of a letter from Washington to Listwell, written in Canada a few short days after both men have told stories into the night. It begins, "My dear Friend,—for such you truly are:— . . . Madison is out of the woods at last. . . ." The language here takes us back to the initial encounter in the Virginia forest between Washington and Listwell,—back to a time when they weren't acquaintances, let alone friends—nor on their respective journeys to freedom and service. In examining the essential differences between Washington's apostrophe to no apparent listener and his warm letter to a dear friend, we are drawn to the fact that in each case, a simple voice cries out, but in the second instance a listener is not only addressed but remembered and hence recreated. The great effect is that a former slave's conventional token of freedom and literacy bound and found in Canada takes on certain indelible storytelling properties.

From this point on in "The Heroic Slave" little more needs to be established between Washington and Listwell, either as fugitive slave and abolitionist or as storyteller and listener, except the all important point that their bond is true and that Listwell will indeed come to Washington's aid in Virginia just as promptly as he did before in the North. In a sense their story is over, but in another respect it isn't: there remains the issue, endemic to both oral and written art, of how their story will live on with full flavor and purpose. On one hand, the story told by Washington and Listwell lives on in a direct, apparent way in the rebellion aboard the *Creole*, the resulting dialogue between the two Virginia sailors who debate the state of their State, and the transformation of one of the sailors,

---

able Gerrit Smith, as a slight token of esteem for his character, admiration for his genius and benevolence, affection for his person, and gratitude for his friendship, and as a small but most sincere acknowledgment of his pre-eminent services in behalf of the rights and liberties of an afflicted, despised and deeply outraged people, by ranking slavery with piracy and murder, and by denying it either a legal or constitutional existence, this volume is respectfully dedicated, by his faithful and firmly attached friend, Frederick Douglass." The doffing of the cap in "The Heroic Slave" became, within two years, a full and reverent bow.

Tom Grant, into a teller of the story. On the other, the story lives on in another way which draws the seemingly distant narrator into the communal bonds of storytelling and the cause.

Late in the novella, in Part III, the narrator employs the phrase "Mr. Listwell says" and soon thereafter refers to Listwell as "our informant." These phrases suggest rather clearly that Listwell has told his shared tale to the narrator and that he has thus been a storyteller as well as a storylistener all along. The other point to be made is, of course, that the narrator has been at some earlier point a good storylistener, meaning in part that he can now tell a slave's tale well because he was willing to *hear* it before making it his own tale to tell. What's remarkable about this narrative strategy is how it serves Douglass' needs both as a novelist and as a black public figure under pressure. Here was a theory of narrative distilled from the relations between tellers and listeners in the black and white worlds Douglass knew best; here was an answer to all who cried, "Frederick, tell your story"—and then couldn't or wouldn't hear him.

WILLIAM L. ANDREWS

from "The Novelization of Voice in Early African American Narrative"[1]

In June 1842 the *Liberator* published what it called "Madison Washington: Another Chapter in His History," in which it brought a few new facts to light about Washington's activities before the *Creole* affair. The *Liberator* cited a message from a Canadian abolitionist, Hiram Wilson, who said Washington had been living in Canada for "some time" while planning a trip to Virginia to rescue his enslaved wife. There was evidence from abolitionists in New York who had given Washington money to defray his expenses on his journey south. But as to what had happened when the black man arrived in Virginia, the *Liberator* could only speculate. It inferred that in the process of trying to free his wife, Washington had been apprehended and "sold for New-Orleans," an explanation that would account for why he was part of the human cargo of the New Orleans–bound *Creole*. But what about the fate of his wife? The *Liberator* remembered from the depositions of a year earlier that the discovery of Washington in the slave women's

1. From William L. Andrews, "The Novelization of Voice in Early African American Narrative," *PMLA* 105, no. 1 (1990): 23–34; the selection is from 28–30. Reprinted by permission of the copyright owner, the Modern Language Association of America. The footnotes have been renumbered and are the author's; the Works Cited list has been condensed so that it includes only the works referred to in this selection.

cabin had led to the first violent acts of the slave revolt. "Might not his wife have been there among the women?" And if so, might not the entire insurrection "prove to have been but part of that great game, in which the highest stake was the liberty of [Washington's] dear wife?" Clearly, a romantic dimension to Washington's story was something the *Liberator* wanted to read into the scanty facts it had amassed about his pre-*Creole* past. This effort by the *Liberator* to infer a romantic plot underlying the *Creole* incidents testifies to the strong desire of American abolitionism for *a* story, if not *the* story, about Washington that would realize him as a powerful symbol of black antislavery heroism.

In speeches during the late 1840s Douglass did his part to keep the memory of Madison Washington alive. But it was not until passage of the Fugitive Slave Law in 1850 that Douglass became sufficiently militant on the justifiability of violence against slaveholders to treat Washington as the epitome of the "heroic slave." Still, Douglass could not write a narrative tribute to Washington without facing the problem that the *Liberator* had posed a decade before: how to make a "history" of the fragmentary information available on Washington. Ten fruitless years had passed since the *Liberator* asked that someone get the facts about Washington in the conventional way, in a narrative "from his own lips." It must have become plain to Douglass that for the example of Washington ever to be exploited in antislavery discourse, someone else would have to do Washington's narrating for him. But in order for there to be any narrating, there would have to be a story of Washington to tell. Without a story that explained and justified the climactic action on the *Creole*, that action would lose much of its power to dictate the terms of its own interpretation. Thus the task of the narrator of *The Heroic Slave* became primarily to make Washington narratable, to empower in and through an authenticating story, in a history, that which Washington truly represented—the revolutionary, not the blindly rampaging, slave.

Douglass's approach to the problem of how to make Washington a part of history was novel. He made the lack of knowledge about

Washington, as opposed to the wealth of historical information about other champions of liberty from Virginia, the gambit of his text. Unlike typical slave narrators, who promised the reader facts based on the most intimate knowledge of their subjects, the narrator of *The Heroic Slave* promises his reader only "marks, traces, possibles, and probabilities" relating to a subject that "is still enveloped in darkness" (474). The identity of the subject of *The Heroic Slave* is not specified in the opening paragraphs of the text. The only biographical fact brought out about the unnamed slave in question is that he is Virginia-born. Like the illustrious Patrick Henry, Thomas Jefferson, and George Washington, all the "great ones of the Old Dominion" whose names and deeds have been emblazoned in "American annals," this unnamed slave was "a man who loved liberty." And yet while "history has not been sparing in recording their names," the slave's name "lives now only in the chattel records of his native State."

There could be no more apt way for the first fictive narrator in African American literature to establish intercourse with his white reading audience. What sort of authority should be granted to your "history," he asks, if it celebrates as heroes of liberty slave owners like Henry and Washington while ignoring a slave who "deserved" and "fought for" his liberty every bit as heroically as these men did? To what sources must we go to find the real "history" of the struggle for freedom in Virginia? As long as freedom-loving slaves exist only in records of chattel, they will be disqualified from their rightful place in "history," the authoritative record of people of consequence. Obviously then, the aim of the narrator of *The Heroic Slave* is first to liberate his slave hero from all the records that chattelize him and then to make him a part of history so that his real significance as a son of Virginia can be recognized.

Since the "chattel records" are necessarily commodified and hence perverse and incomplete, the narrator who would do this service to Virginia history must "command the pen of genius." Instead of simply recording the known, he must penetrate the unknown, the "marks, traces, possibles, and probabilities" left by the fragmentary "chattel records." The narrator of *The Heroic Slave* does not go so far as to say that the "genius" he will employ will be that of the novelist, but one cannot escape this implication, nor does the narrator want the reader to miss it. If, in writing the history of a slave the narrator is compelled to create what might be called a "fiction of factual representation" (White 121), he wants it clear that Virginia's "chattel records" leave him no alternative. To historicize, to *realize* this son of Virginia in history, it is necessary to fictionalize him. The entire narrative enterprise of *The Heroic Slave* rests on the reader's accepting the paradoxical necessity of the fictiveness of Washington's history.

As a storyteller, the narrator of *The Heroic Slave* plays a number of roles after justifying the fictiveness of his work. Because Robert B. Stepto has given close attention to the storytelling dimension of Douglass's text, I do not devote more of my discussion to it here. Suffice it to say that after the introduction to the story, the narrator makes no effort to authenticate any specific contention made about Washington in the rest of the narrative. The narrator offers no means of distinguishing between facts, "possibles," and "probabilities." By structuring the story around speeches that he seems merely to report verbatim to the reader, the narrator gives the narration an appearance of objectivity. As his source for most of the speeches and much of the behavior of Washington, he names a Mr. Listwell, whom he also claims as a personal acquaintance. This disclosure lends to the narration of the first three parts of the text a consistent and plausible point of view. We seem to be reading one of those narratives "told by X [Listwell] to Y [the narrator] apropos of Z [Washington]" that make up "the very fabric of our 'experience'" in the real world (Genette 239).[2] In ways like these, the narrator of *The Heroic Slave* tries to make Washington's story sound objectively told with-

2. In the fourth part of *The Heroic Slave*, where two sailors discuss the events aboard the *Creole*, Listwell does not figure as the source of the narrator's privilege, nor is any other source of privilege offered.

out holding himself accountable for the authenticity of anything in particular said by or about Washington.

In taking these steps to objectify the narrating of *The Heroic Slave*, Douglass finesses the problem of authenticating what that narrating voice actually says. Unlike in the traditional slave narrative, which predicates the narrator's authority on authentication provided by the facts in the text or the testimonials that preface and append the text, in *The Heroic Slave* the authority of the narrator is insisted on from the start by him alone. Indeed, his right to tell his story in his own way, free from the obligation to limit himself only to the few facts available to him, is insisted on before any narrating actually takes place. Herein lies the fundamental importance of *The Heroic Slave* to the evolution of African American narrative from "natural" to "fictive" discourse: priority in *The Heroic Slave* is given to the empowering of a mode of fictive discourse whose authority does not depend on the authentication of what is asserted in that discourse. The authority of fictive discourse in African American narrative depends on a sabotaging of the presumed authoritative plenitude of history as "natural" discourse so that the right of the fictive to supplement (that is, to subvert) "history" can be declared and then exploited.

Works Cited

Douglass, Frederick. "The Heroic Slave." *The Life and Writings of Frederick Douglass*. Ed. Philip S. Foner. Vol. 5. New York: International, 1975. 473–505.

Genette, Gérard. *Narrative Discourse*. Trans. Jane E. Lewin. Ithaca: Cornell UP, 1980.

"Madison Washington: Another Chapter in His History." *Liberator* 10 June 1842: 89.

Stepto, Robert B. "Storytelling in Early Afro-American Fiction: Frederick Douglass' *The Heroic Slave*." *Georgia Review* 36 (1982): 355–68.

White, Hayden. "The Fictions of Factual Representation." *Tropics of Discourse*. Baltimore: Johns Hopkins UP, 1978. 121–34.

RICHARD YARBOROUGH

from "Race, Violence, and Manhood"[1]

Douglass's fascination with self-reliance and heroic male individualism thoroughly shapes his conception of Madison as a leader.[2] Thus, although there were reportedly several key instigators of the *Creole* revolt, Douglass omits mention of all but Washington, thereby highlighting the individual nature of his protagonist's triumph as well as the man's superiority in comparison to his fellow blacks.[3] Furthermore, Douglass's celebration of solitary male heroism leaves little room for women. In his 1845 narrative, critics have noted, he downplays the role played by female slaves in his life. As David Leverenz points out, Douglass's wife, Anna, "seems an afterthought. He introduces her to his readers as a rather startling appendage to his escape and

1. From Richard Yarborough, "Race, Violence, and Manhood: The Masculine Ideal in Frederick Douglass's 'The Heroic Slave,'" in *Frederick Douglass: New Literary and Historical Essays*, ed. Eric J. Sundquist (Cambridge: Cambridge University Press, 1990), 166–88; the excerpt is from 176–88. Copyright © Cambridge University Press 1990. Reprinted with the permission of Cambridge University Press. The footnotes have been renumbered and, unless otherwise indicated, are the author's.

2. Douglass's speech on "Self-Made Men" was one of his most often-delivered presentations. See Waldo Martin, *The Mind of Frederick Douglass* (Chapel Hill: University of North Carolina Press, 1984), 253–78.

3. See Howard Jones, "The Peculiar Institution and National Honor: The Case of the *Creole* Slave Revolt," *Civil War History* 21 (March 1975): 30 n7.

marries her almost in the same breath."[4] At first glance, Douglass's treatment of black women in "The Heroic Slave" would appear to differ considerably from that in his narrative. Not only does Madison allude frequently to his wife, Susan, but it is her support that enables him to hide in the wilderness for five years. In addition, he is recaptured after his successful flight from slavery because he decides to return to Virginia to rescue her. However, not only do we receive no description of Susan whatsoever but, more significantly, she is rendered voiceless in a text marked, as Henry Louis Gates notes, by "a major emphasis on the powers of the human voice," on the potency of speech acts.[5] Finally, Douglass has Susan murdered during her attempt to escape with her husband. Her disappearance from the text at this point simply reinforces Washington's heroic isolation.

One way to appreciate fully the strategies underlying the characterization of Madison Washington in "The Heroic Slave" is to compare the novella not just with Douglass's own comments in his 1849 speech[6] but with three other literary dramatizations of the

4. David Leverenz, *Manhood and the American Renaissance* (Ithaca: Cornell University Press, 1989), 128. Frances Smith Foster suggests that Douglass's withholding information regarding Anna enables him to suppress certain positive aspects of his slave experience (Foster, *Witnessing Slavery: The Development of Ante-bellum Slave Narratives* [Westport, CT: Greenwood, 1979], 113). Also see Donald B. Gibson, "Reconciling Public and Private in Frederick Douglass' *Narrative*," *American Literature* 57 (December 1985): 551.

5. Henry Louis Gates, Jr., *Figures in Black: Words, Signs, and the "Racial" Self* (New York: Oxford University Press, 1987), 107. The closest we get to hearing Susan speak is Madison's explanation that in his extreme concern for her safety after his flight to Canada, he "could almost hear her voice, saying 'O Madison! Madison! will you then leave me here? can you leave me here to die? No! no! you will come! you will come!'" (Douglass, "The Heroic Slave," in *Autographs for Freedom*, ed. Julia Griffiths [Boston: John P. Jewett, 1853], 219).

6. [As Yarborough reports earlier in his essay, in 1849, Douglass declared: "Sir, I want to alarm the slaveholders, and not to alarm them by mere declamation or by mere bold assertions, but to show them that there is really danger in persisting in the crime of continuing Slavery in this land. I want them to know that there are some Madison Washingtons in this land" ("Great Anti-Colonization Meeting in New York," *North Star*, 11 May 1849, 2). A section of the speech is reprinted in this volume. Eds.]

incident—by William Wells Brown in 1863, by Lydia Maria Child in 1866, and by Pauline E. Hopkins in 1901.[7] The most significant ways in which Brown, Child, and Hopkins revise Douglass's rendering of the *Creole* revolt involve the handling of violence in the story, the depiction of Susan, Madison's wife, and the role of whites.[8]

First, Brown, Child, and Hopkins all treat Madison Washington's violence more directly than does Douglass in "The Heroic Slave." In describing Washington's recapture, for example, Brown does not qualify the slave's fierce resistance:

> Observed by the overseer, . . . the fugitive [was] secured ere he could escape with his wife; but the heroic slave did not yield until he with a club had laid three of his assailants upon the ground with his manly blows; and not then until weakened by loss of blood.[9]

In depicting the revolt itself, both Brown and Douglass stress Washington's determination to shed no more blood than is absolutely

7. William Wells Brown, "Madison Washington," in *The Black Man, His Antecedents, His Genius, and His Achievements* (1863; reprint, New York: Arno, 1969), 75–83; Lydia Maria Child, "Madison Washington," in *The Freedmen's Book* (Boston: Ticknor and Fields, 1866), 147–54; and Pauline E. Hopkins, "A Dash for Liberty," *Colored American Magazine* 3 (August 1901): 243–7.

8. Some of the minor distinctions among these four versions are revealing as well. For example, Brown's description of Washington is far more ethnically specific than Douglass's: "Born of African parentage, with no mixture in his blood, he was one of the handsomest of his race" (Brown, "Washington," 75). This emphasis on Washington's African background recalls Brown's treatment of Jerome in the 1864 *Clotelle, A Tale of the Southern States*, published one year after *The Black Man* appeared. It must be noted that there are several instances where Brown, Child, and Hopkins employ remarkably similar phrasing. Brown had appropriated material from Child before, in the first edition of *Clotel* (1853). There is evidence of extensive borrowing here as well—either by Brown from an earlier version of Child's sketch or by Child from Brown's in *The Black Man*, or by both Brown and Child from an earlier text by another writer. . . . Pauline Hopkins was familiar with the work of both Brown (whom she had met personally) and Child, and thus would likely have encountered their versions of the *Creole* revolt. To complicate matters, Hopkins cites neither Brown nor Child as her primary source, but rather an article by Thomas Wentworth Higginson.

9. Brown, "Washington," 80.

necessary. However, Brown differs sharply from Douglass by locating his hero at the very center of the violence:

> Drawing his old horse pistol from under his coat, he [a white "negro-driver"] fired at one of the blacks and killed him. The next moment [he] lay dead upon the deck, for Madison had struck him with a capstan bar. . . . The battle was Madison's element, and he plunged into it without any care for his own preservation or safety. He was an instrument of enthusiasm, whose value and whose place was in his inspiration. "If the fire of heaven was in my hands, I would throw it at these cowardly whites," said he to his companions, before leaving their cabin. But in this he did not mean revenge, only the possession of his freedom and that of his fellow-slaves. Merritt and Gifford, the first and second mates of the vessel, both attacked the heroic slave at the same time. Both were stretched out upon the deck with a single blow each, but were merely wounded; they were disabled, and that was all that Madison cared for for the time being.[10]

Like Douglass in "The Heroic Slave," Brown, Child, and Hopkins all portray Madison Washington as a superman, but their hero is one whose strength, courage, and power find unmistakably violent outlet.

In their treatment of Susan, Madison's wife, Brown, Child, and Hopkins again revise Douglass quite extensively. In contrast to the faceless character we encounter in "The Heroic Slave," William Wells Brown's Susan receives an even more elaborate description than does Washington himself:

> In the other cabin, among the slave women, was one whose beauty at once attracted attention. Though not tall, she yet had a majestic figure. Her well-moulded shoulders, prominent bust, black hair which hung in ringlets, mild blue eyes, finely-chiselled mouth, with a splendid set of teeth, a turned and well-rounded chin, skin

10. Ibid., 83.

> marbled with the animation of life, and veined by blood given to her by her master, she stood as the representative of two races. With only one eighth of African, she was what is called at the south an "octoroon." It was said that her grandfather had served his country in the revolutionary war, as well as in both houses of Congress. This was Susan, the wife of Madison.[11]

Furthermore, Brown arranges for Susan to be among the freed blacks when her husband takes over the *Creole*. Susan's death *before* the revolt in "The Heroic Slave" reflects both Douglass's lack of interest in incorporating a sentimental reunion into his happy ending and his conception of Washington as an isolated male protagonist. In Brown's vision of Washington's successful heroic action, liberation leads to a restoration of the integrity of the domestic circle, the black family unit; in Douglass's, it does not.[12]

Although similar in phrasing to Brown's, Child's depiction of Susan manifests an added concern with the beautiful slave as the embodiment of endangered womanhood. Child describes Susan's peculiar plight this way: "[A] handsome woman, who is a slave, is constantly liable to insult and wrong, from which an enslaved husband has no power to protect her."[13] Hopkins, in turn, both corrects and elaborates on Child's comment not only by showing that Madison Monroe (as she calls her hero) *does*, in fact, save his wife from sexual assault but also by making Susan almost as much the protagonist of the story as Madison. In Hopkins's rendering, most of the drama on board the *Creole* centers not on the revolt but on

11. Ibid., 81. Brown's portrayal of Susan closely resembles the sentimental depiction of his light-skinned heroines in *Clotel*.

12. We find what is perhaps the first suggestion that Madison Washington's wife may have been aboard the *Creole* in "Madison Washington: Another Chapter in His History," *Liberator*, June 10, 1842. In his recent article on "The Heroic Slave," William Andrews quite rightly suggests: "This effort by the *Liberator* to infer a romantic plot underlying the *Creole* incidents testifies to the strong desire of American abolitionism for *a* story, if not *the* story, about Washington that would realize him as a powerful symbol of black antislavery heroism" ("The Novelization of Voice in Early African American Narrative," *PMLA* 105 [January 1990], 28).

13. Child, "Washington," 147.

the white captain's attempted rape of Susan, which coincidentally occurs on the same night that Madison has planned his uprising.[14] Even the syntax of the emotional reunion scene reinforces Hopkins's focus on Susan: "*She* was locked to his breast; *she* clung to him convulsively. Unnerved at last by the revulsion to more than relief and ecstasy, *she* broke into wild sobs, while the astonished company closed around them with loud hurrahs."[15] On the one hand, Hopkins implicitly rejects Douglass's obsession with masculine heroism as she gives Susan not only a voice in the text but also force—the first act of black violent resistance aboard the *Creole* is Susan's striking the white captain when he kisses her in her sleep. On the other hand, by having Madison fortuitously appear and interrupt the assault on Susan like some white knight rushing to the aid of his damsel, Hopkins ultimately falls back on the conventions of the sentimental romance. Hopkins does succeed in reinserting the black female into a field of action dominated, in Douglass's fiction, by the male. However, in claiming for Susan a conventional role generally denied black women, she necessarily endorses the accompanying male paradigm in her depiction of Madison, a paradigm drawn from the same set of gender constructions that provides Douglass with his heroic model.

Finally, of the four versions of the *Creole* incident under consideration here, Douglass's places the greatest emphasis upon the role played by whites in the protagonist's life. Granted, for much of "The Heroic Slave," Madison Washington is the epitome of manly self-reliance. At key points in the text, however, Douglass qualifies the isolated nature of the protagonist's liberatory struggle not by creating ties between Madison and a black community but rather by developing a close relationship between Washington and a white

14. Characteristically, Hopkins provides an extensive discussion of Susan's mixed racial pedigree. For a look at the role of ancestry in her most important fictional work, see Yarborough, Introduction to *Contending Forces*, by Pauline E. Hopkins (1900; reprint, New York: Oxford University Press, 1988), xxvii–xlviii.

15. Hopkins, "Liberty," 247; emphasis added.

northerner named Listwell. As Robert Stepto suggests, Douglass probably modeled Listwell on the abolitionist James Gurney.[16] Yet, Douglass claims in his 1849 speech on the *Creole* incident, another abolitionist, Robert Purvis, also played an important role as Washington's friend and advisor. Douglass's decision to incorporate the white Gurney and not the black Purvis into his story reflects his desire to reach and move white readers. Like George Harris's former employer, Mr. Wilson, in *Uncle Tom's Cabin*, Listwell gives the white audience a figure with whom to identify; as Listwell comes to endorse Washington's behavior—to evolve literally before our eyes into an abolitionist—Douglass hopes that the white reader will too.

In none of the three later versions of the revolt do we encounter a white character who plays the central role that Listwell does in "The Heroic Slave." Brown, Child, and Hopkins all depict a sympathetic white named Dickson, who employs Madison after he first escapes; but there is no great intimacy between the men. Furthermore, whereas Douglass has Listwell slip Washington the files and saws that he subsequently uses to free himself and his fellow slaves on board the *Creole*, Brown, Child, and Hopkins each tells us that Madison obtains these implements on his own, before he returns to Virginia in the ill-fated attempt to free his wife. By having Listwell provide Washington with the means of his escape, Douglass doubtless intends the white audience to see that they should not only sympathize with the slaves' plight but work actively to help them gain their freedom. As a result, however, he implies that even the most self-reliant and gifted black male slave needs white assistance.

In composing "The Heroic Slave," Frederick Douglass could have easily taken a strictly documentary approach. The unadorned story of Madison Washington's exploits certainly contained sufficient drama and courageous action to hold an audience. Moreover, Douglass's

16. Robert B. Stepto, "Storytelling in Early Afro-American Fiction: Frederick Douglass's 'The Heroic Slave,'" *Georgia Review* 36 (Summer 1982): 363 n8.

writing to that point had been primarily journalistic; the novella would have hardly seemed the form with which he would have felt most comfortable. In depicting Washington in fiction, however, Douglass ambitiously set out to do more than demonstrate the slave's determination to be free; he sought to transform his black male protagonist into a heroic exemplar who would both win white converts to the antislavery struggle and firmly establish the reality of black manhood. The route that Douglass chose in order to achieve these goals was to master the codes of Anglo-American bourgeois white masculinity, and his own internalization of the values informing mainstream masculine paradigms made this strategy relatively easy to adopt. In addition, as Robert Stepto observes, the act of fictionalizing this story of successful violent male resistance to slavery offered Douglass the opportunity not only to express his ideological independence from Garrison but also to present a potent alternative to the model of the black male hero as victim promoted so successfully in Stowe's *Uncle Tom's Cabin*.[17] Ultimately, however, Douglass's ambitious agenda was undermined by his intuitive sense that he could challenge white preconceptions regarding race only so far without alienating the audience that he sought to win and by problems inherent in the masculine ideal that he so eagerly endorsed.

Douglass's strategies for appealing to white readers in "The Heroic Slave" were flawed in at least three important ways. The first involves the extent to which his representation of Madison Washington as the embodiment of black manhood inevitably emphasizes the distance between his hero and the average slave. In celebrating this unusually self-aware, courageous, aggressive, conventionally educated, and charismatic figure, Douglass never explains his attractive capacities in terms that would encourage the reader to

17. For a further discussion of what Robert B. Stepto calls the "antislavery textual conversation" between Stowe's *Uncle Tom's Cabin* and Douglass's "The Heroic Slave," see Stepto's "Sharing the Thunder: The Literary Exchanges of Harriet Beecher Stowe, Henry Bibb, and Frederick Douglass," in *New Essays on Uncle Tom's Cabin*, 135–53. Stepto contends that Washington's revolt also appealed to Douglass because it "in some measure revises his *own* story" (Stepto, "Thunder," 359).

extrapolate a general sense of the black potential for heroic action from the extraordinarily endowed Washington. The gap between Douglass's protagonist and less gifted blacks is widened even further by the presence of Listwell. That the one character both emotionally and intellectually closest to Washington is white indicates the extent to which Madison's strengths and capabilities, training, and manner distinguish him from other slaves and thereby weaken his usefulness as a counterargument against claims that most blacks were inferior to whites.

A second problem derives from Douglass's attempt, in William Andrews's words, "to domesticate a violence that easily could have been judged as alien and threatening to everything from Christian morality to the law of the high seas."[18] Employing a common abolitionist gambit, Douglass works to establish a link between Washington's rebellion and the American War of Independence. However, doing so, Andrews contends, precipitates Douglass and other antislavery writers into a troublesome conceptual trap: "Even as they violate the ideals of Uncle Tom's pacifism and declare blacks free from bloodguiltiness for killing their masters, they justify such actions by an appeal to the authorizing mythology of an oppressive culture."[19] That is, the very figures whose patriotic heritage Douglass claims for his hero won their fame by working to establish a social order in which the enslavement of blacks like Madison was a crucial component.

In his careful packaging of Washington's manly heroism, Douglass also chooses not to dramatize a single act of physical violence performed by his protagonist. One might argue that this approach reinforces the statesmanlike quality that Douglass may have been striving to imbue in his portrayal of Washington—after all, how often do depictions (literary and otherwise) of George Washington fully convey the violent nature of his heroism? Ultimately, however, Douglass's caution here strips his fictional slave rebel of much of his

18. William L. Andrews, *To Tell a Free Story: The First Century of Afro-American Autobiography, 1760–1865* (Urbana: University of Illinois Press, 1986), 186.
19. Ibid., 187.

radical, subversive force. As Douglass knew from personal experience, revolution usually entails violence, and black self-assertion in the face of racist attempts at dehumanization often necessitates a direct and forceful assault upon the very structures of social power that provide most whites (especially white males) with a sense of self-worth, security, and potency.

In his public statements regarding the *Creole* revolt both before and after he wrote "The Heroic Slave," Douglass apparently felt little need to undermine the implications of the black militancy that Madison Washington embodied. We have already examined his celebration of Washington's heroism in his 1849 speech.[20] In commenting on West Indian emancipation eight years later, Douglass goes even further:

> Joseph Cinque on the deck of the Amistad, did that which should make his name dear to us. He bore nature's burning protest against slavery. Madison Washington who struck down his oppressor on the deck of the Creole, is more worthy to be remembered than the colored man who shot Pitcairn at Bunker Hill.[21]

Granted, the exhaustion of Douglass's patience with the limited efficacy of moral suasion as an antislavery tactic surely informs this quite remarkable repudiation of the popular appeal to an American patriotic past as a way to validate black slave violence. I would argue, however, that there was something about the mode of fiction itself (and possibly about autobiography as well) that stifled the radical nature of Douglass's anger. The "controlled aggression" that Donald Gibson sees as informing every aspect of Douglass's *Narrative* underlies the depiction of Madison Washington in "The Heroic

20. [See note 6 above. Eds.]

21. Philip S. Foner, *The Life and Writings of Frederick Douglass*. Vol. 2, *Pre-Civil War Decade, 1850–1860* (New York: International, 1950), 438. [Yarborough refers to Douglass's 3 August 1857 speech on West Indian emancipation, an excerpt from which is included in this volume. Eds.]

Slave" as well.[22] The key may lie in what Houston Baker describes as the "task of transmuting an authentic, unwritten self—a self that exists outside the conventional literary discourse structure of a white reading public—into a literary representation." Baker continues: "The simplest, and perhaps the most effective, way of proceeding is for the narrator to represent his 'authentic' self as a figure embodying the public virtues and values esteemed by his intended audience."[23] Baker's argument applies with particular force to "The Heroic Slave," for it appears that the freer rein the form offered Douglass in his depiction of the exemplary black male hero paradoxically also confronted him more directly than possibly ever before with the restrictions imposed by the expectations of the whites to whom he was appealing.

The third weakness in his attempt to use fiction to shape his white reader's attitudes toward slavery is structural in nature. That is, by rendering the *Creole* revolt through the recollections of a white sailor, Douglass cuts us off not just from Washington's heroic violence but from his emotional responses to the dramatic events in which he plays such a crucial part. William Wells Brown's straightforward depiction of Washington's rebellious behavior in his sketch dramatizes by contrast the extent to which Madison's role in "The Heroic Slave" is primarily catalytic, as Douglass emphasizes through shifts in point of view his impact upon the whites around him. Such elaborate formal manipulations result in what Raymond Hedin terms "an emphatically structured fiction," which serves to convey a sense of the writer's control and thus to permit a release of anger in a rational and somewhat unthreatening manner.[24] As one result

22. Gibson, "Public and Private," 563. See also David Leverenz's discussion of the tension between Douglass's "genteel self-control and his aggressiveness" in the 1855 edition of his narrative (Leverenz, *Manhood*, 114).

23. Houston A. Baker, Jr., *The Journey Back: Issues in Black Literature and Criticism* (Chicago: University of Chicago Press, 1980), 39.

24. Raymond Hedin, "The Structuring of Emotion in Black American Fiction," *Novel* 16 (Fall 1982): 37.

of this strategy, at the end of the novella Washington stands not as the embodiment of expressive, forceful self-determination, but as an object of white discourse, a figure whose self-assertive drive to tell his own story—to reclaim, in a sense, his own subjectivity—is ultimately subordinated by Douglass to a secondhand rendition by a white sailor who did not even witness the full range of Washington's heroic action. This decentering of the black voice in "The Heroic Slave" may be the greatest casualty of Douglass's polemical appeal to white sympathies.

Finally, like the majority of nineteenth-century black spokespersons, Douglass was unable or unwilling to call into question the white bourgeois paradigm of manhood itself. Consequently, his celebration of black heroism was subverted from the outset by the racist, sexist, and elitist assumptions upon which the Angle-American male ideal was constructed and that so thoroughly permeated the patriarchal structure of slavery. As Valerie Smith points out, "Within his critique of American cultural practices, then, is an affirmation of its definitions of manhood and power." That is, "Douglass . . . attempts to articulate a radical position using the discourse he shares with those against whom he speaks. What begins as an indictment of mainstream practice actually authenticates one of its fundamental assumptions."[25] It should go without saying that one can scarcely imagine how Douglass might have extricated himself from the conceptual briar patch into which he had fallen, given both the political purposes to which he directed his fiction and the extent to which he sought validation in the most conventional, gender-specific terms for himself in particular and for black men in general from a white society unwilling to acknowledge the complex humanity of blacks in any unqualified way. The dilemma so powerfully rendered in Douglass's attempt to dramatize the Madison Washington story in fiction

25. Valerie Smith, *Self-Discovery and Authority in Afro-American Narrative* (Cambridge, MA: Harvard University Press, 1987), 32–46; Leverenz, *Manhood*, 108–34; and Annette Niemtzow, "The Problematic of Self in Autobiography: The Example of the Slave Narrative," in *The Art of Slave Narrative*, ed. John Sekora and Darwin T. Turner (Macomb: Western Illinois University Press, 1982), 96–109.

is one that has plagued most Afro-American fiction writers—and, indeed, most Afro-American thinkers—over the past century and a half.[26] His failures do not qualify the boldness of his attempt, and one can argue that the short-term benefits of his approach must be taken into account in assessing the overall success of his enterprise. Ultimately, however, Douglass's "The Heroic Slave" may be most valuable insofar as it enables us to understand better the complex internal and external obstacles to a balanced, complex depiction of black men and women in Afro-American fiction. If nothing else, it leaves us wondering whether the tools of the master can ever be used to achieve the complete liberation of the slave.

26. In a forthcoming essay entitled "In the First Place: Making Frederick Douglass and the Afro-American Narrative Tradition," Deborah McDowell examines how the tendency to give Douglass's *Narrative*, with its uncritical inscription of sexist Anglo-American concepts of gender, a central position in constructing the Afro-American literary tradition marginalizes black women's texts. [The essay can be found in *Critical Essays on Frederick Douglass*, ed. William L. Andrews (Boston: Hall, 1991), 192–214. Eds.]

MAGGIE MONTESINOS SALE

from "*The Heroic Slave*"[1]

[Madison] Washington not only leads an entire ship of people to freedom, but justifies without qualification their actions by claiming the "American" notion that the cause of liberty justifies rebellion. This transformation worked to convince Douglass's resisting readers that whatever negative connotations they may have associated with Washington's "blackness" insignificantly compare with his bravery, eloquence, willingness to die for liberty, moral restraint, and rationality. I suggest that the principal factor determining whether or not they heard his implicit call for abolition, and accepted his assertion that "we have done that which you applaud your fathers for doing," depended upon whether or not they found his display of masculinity compelling.[2]

1. From Maggie Montesinos Sale, "*The Heroic Slave* (1853)," in *The Slumbering Volcano: American Slave Ship Revolts and Rebellious Masculinity* (Durham, N.C.: Duke University Press, 1997), 173–97; the selection is from 186–88. Republished by permission of the copyright holder, Duke University Press (www.dukeupress.edu); all rights reserved. The footnotes have been renumbered and, unless other indicated, are the author's.

2. Richard Yarborough was the first to analyze manhood as a central feature of *The Heroic Slave*. His assessment and mine differ on the importance of the *representation* of violence and the effects of Douglass's use of normative masculinity. Also see Wiegman 71–78 on gender in *The Heroic Slave*.

In order to grasp why masculinity was so important, we need to recall that the most obvious, yet the most fundamental feature of the revolutionary republican subject was masculine gender. At the time of the Revolution, this subject did not have an explicit class or racial marking, although material conditions and social, political, and economic practices determined that typically elite men of European descent were authorized by what Locke called "Political Power." Class and slavery were masked by the apparently universal address to "all men," and race had not yet come to play the central ideological role that it would in the nineteenth century. Douglass appropriated a late-eighteenth-century notion of manhood, or republican male virtue, characterized by bravery, eloquence, moral restraint, concern for the common good, and a willingness to die for liberty, and transported it into a different historical context, a different social and political field in which racial difference had become one of the most salient ways of signifying relations of power. Like other political orators and writers of his own time, Douglass chose for his heroic model not nineteenth-century nation-builders like Andrew Jackson or Zachary Taylor, or unionists like Daniel Webster and Henry Clay, but republican revolutionaries. Antebellum political rhetoric instead favored Patrick Henry, Thomas Jefferson, and George Washington. But by connecting their known history with the activities of an enslaved man, the opening paragraph of *The Heroic Slave* challenges the legal, social, and economic strategies of dominant groups that defined the national political community—the inheritors and rightful claimants of the rhetoric of the Revolution—as free, white, and male. This definition denied authorization to slave rebellion, as Douglass points out:

> The state of Virginia is famous in American annals for the multitudinous array of her statesmen and heroes. . . . History has not been sparing in recording their names, or in blazoning their deeds. . . . By some strange neglect, one of the truest, manliest, and bravest of her children . . . a man who loved liberty as well

> as did Patrick Henry,—who deserved it as much as Thomas Jefferson,—and who fought for it with a valor as high, an arm as strong, and against odds as great, as he who led all the armies of the American colonies through the great war for freedom and independence, lives now only in the chattel records of his native State. (25)

In creating this connection, this passage asserts that the revolutionary alliance was inherently contradictory because it did not include enslaved people from the Southern colonies, and it suggests a newly configured alliance.

Rather than a founding father in blackface, Douglass's Madison Washington constituted a new position based on masculine gender, which asserted as more fundamental than racial difference or differences in class or status, gender solidarity among men.[3] From this position, Douglass asserted a new meaning for revolutionary rhetoric, not simply the abolition of U.S. slavery, but the *equivalence* of the struggle of enslaved men with that of the republic's masculine founders. Like other political abolitionists, this meaning recast the Revolution as an arrested struggle for general emancipation. But this interpretation also challenged those paternalistic white abolitionists who recognized slavery as evil and anti-Christian, but who did not imagine slaves or African Americans more generally as equal members of the national community.

This challenge presents the possibility of a new national alliance, based on a common masculinity, one that includes the founders and those slave rebels who have broken their fetters and claimed their freedom.[4] This alliance does not "accurately" portray the founders, in that although many of them were aware of a theoretical contra-

3. See David Leverenz for a different view of the interrelations among gender, class, and status in Douglass's work, principally his first two autobiographies. In my view, Leverenz's class-based notions of manhood are provocative but insufficiently nuanced in terms of race.

4. As I argued in relation to the *Amistad*, this formulation unfortunately limits the inclusionary potential of natural rights theory to those who have already successfully

diction between their fight for their own liberty and their status as slaveholders, most did little during their lifetimes actually either to bring about abolition or to emancipate their own slaves. Rather Douglass's (re)vision centralizes what enslaved people and abolitionists considered most valuable and laudable in the Revolution, and marginalizes those acts of the founders that they considered worthless. This rhetorical strategy reimagines the history of the Revolution in the service of a radical agenda, one that projects not just freedom for British colonists, but equality for enslaved men as the goal of the original fight for liberty.

The Heroic Slave develops this argument by asserting that the Virginia of 1841, now an immoral and deteriorating society, differs dramatically from the Virginia of the founders. At the beginning of part 3, the narrator describes the following scene:

> Just upon the edge of the great road from Petersburg, Virginia, to Richmond, . . . there stands a somewhat ancient and famous public tavern, quite notorious in its better days. . . . Its fine old portico looks well at a distance, and gives the building an air of grandeur. A nearer view, however, does little to sustain this impression. . . . The gloomy mantle of ruin is, already, out-spread to envelop it, and its remains, even but now remind one of a human skull, after the flesh has mingled with the earth. (47)

The "fine old portico" with its "air of grandeur," actually decays at the core, no more than a covering for a fleshless skull. This condition results, one learns several pages later, from a change in the state's economic interest, since "almost all other business in Virginia [has been] dropped to engage in [the slave trade]" (50). By juxtaposing past and present, this image undercuts the authority of those

---

rebelled against unjust oppressors; it reproduces as a rule of inclusion the willingness to die for liberty, thereby marginalizing those whose other concerns, such as the security of their children, may outweigh that of liberty. See chap 2 above ["'The *Amistad* Affair' (1839)," in Sale, *The Slumbering Volcano*, 58–119. Eds.].

present-day sons of Virginia who trade in human flesh, while simultaneously renovating the memory of the revolutionary fathers. This description metaphorically represents the festering contradiction at the heart of the republic, the result of slavery in a supposedly free society.

Although Douglass self-consciously characterizes *The Heroic Slave* as created from "marks, traces, possibles, and probabilities" (25–26)—all that the *Creole* archive provides him with—he also presents the story as more trustworthy than the annals of history because it more accurately mirrors the text's notion of the founders' true ideals. The text describes the tavern's inhabitants, for example, as "hangers-on" and "corrupt tongues" whose stories are not recorded because they only tell "of quarrels, fights, *recontes*, and duels," and are full of "vulgarity and dark profanity" (52). The text's reference to these unrecorded stories asserts simultaneously the irrelevance of the tavern's inhabitants' stories and the greater significance of the one the text tells. Rather than a reason to question the validity of the narrative presented, this self-consciousness indicts dominant systems of record keeping and history making, thereby undermining systems of evaluation that separate Madison Washington from James Madison and George Washington. Taken altogether, the tavern passages and the references to the scarcity of historical data represent Madison Washington as a more rightful heir of the legacy of Old Virginia than those currently in power; the demise of the tavern and its inhabitants makes space for, even calls for, the emergence of a new order.

Works Cited

Douglass, Frederick. *The Heroic Slave*. In *Autographs for Freedom*. Ed. Julia Griffiths. Boston, 1853, 174–239. Rpt. *Three Classic African-American Novels*. Ed. William L. Andrews. New York: Penguin, 1990. 23–69.

Leverenz, David. *Manhood and the American Renaissance*. Ithaca: Cornell University Press, 1989.

Locke, John. *Two Treatises of Government* [1689]. Ed. Peter Laslett. Cambridge: Cambridge University Press, 1967.

Wiegman, Robyn. *American Anatomies: Theorizing Race and Gender*. Durham: Duke University Press, 1995.

Yarborough, Richard. "Race, Violence, and Manhood: The Masculine Ideal in Frederick Douglass's 'The Heroic Slave.'" *Frederick Douglass: New Literary and Historical Essays*. Ed. Eric J. Sundquist. Cambridge: Cambridge University Press, 1990. 166–88.

CELESTE-MARIE BERNIER

from "'Arms like Polished Iron'"[1]

In a self-conscious manner, Douglass's *The Heroic Slave* challenged characteristic abolitionist tendencies towards using the slave's body as the sole marker of authenticity. He offered a critique of white interpretations which positioned the black male slave body as the most accurate measure of individual experience by emphasizing the additional importance of language in representations of black male consciousness. Douglass's structural composition of *The Heroic Slave* demonstrates the complex narrative processes by which he displays and (re)presents the black male body. Overall, he resists its straightforward appropriation as an object for consumption by a white audience by reclaiming the importance of the black male body as symbolic, rhetorical figure. He juxtaposes the physical spectacle of the slave with a superlative performance of black male intellectual prowess in Madison Washington's exemplary command of language.

1. From Celeste-Marie Bernier, "'Arms Like Polished Iron': The Black Slave Body in Narratives of a Slave Ship Revolt," in *Slavery and Abolition: A Journal of Slave and Post-Slave Studies* 23, no. 2 (2002): 89–106; the excerpt is from 94–97. Reprinted by permission of Taylor & Francis Group, LLC (http://www.tandfonline.com). The footnotes have been renumbered and, unless otherwise indicated, are the author's.

While Madison is conventionally feminized in his rhetorical speech, 'I neither run nor fight, but do meanly stand, answering each heavy blow of a cruel master with doleful wails and piteous cries';[2] upon his decision to have '*Liberty* . . . or die in the attempt to gain it,'[3] his stature immediately assumes heroic and exaggeratedly 'masculine' dimensions: hence Douglass's introduction of Washington in sculptured proportions, emblematic of a classical model. Variously characterized throughout *The Heroic Slave* as 'our hero,' the 'strong man' and 'a sort of general-in-chief among them [the slaves],'[4] Douglass's description of Washington reads:

> Madison was of manly form. Tall, symmetrical, round, and strong. . . . His torn sleeves disclosed arms like polished iron. His face was 'black, but comely.' His eye, lit with emotion, kept guard under a brow as dark and as glossy as the raven's wing. His whole appearance betokened Herculean strength; yet there was nothing savage or forbidding in his aspect. . . . His broad mouth and nose spoke only of good nature and kindness. But his voice, that unfailing index of the soul, though full and melodious, had that in it which could terrify as well as charm.[5]

Douglass's references to Hercules confirm Washington's statuesque and monumental significance, while his evocation of 'the raven's wing' communicates racial difference. Douglass's physical representations of the archetypal black male heroic figure in his written material on the *Creole* revolt resist conventions of minstrelsy. His emphasis upon black physical prowess, 'arms like polished iron,' is qualified by a preoccupation with rhetorical persuasion, as contained within Washington's 'full and melodious' voice, which undermines associations of black slave heroism with 'savagery.' Furthermore, Doug-

2. F. Douglass, *The Heroic Slave*, in J. Griffiths (ed.), *Autographs for Freedom* (Boston, MA: John P. Jewett, 1853), p. 177. All subsequent quotations are referenced by the abbreviation *HS*.

3. Ibid., p. 178.

4. Ibid., pp. 178, 180 and 217 respectively.

5. Ibid., p. 179.

lass's construction of the male slave figure contains conventionally feminized motifs. For example, such references as 'A child might play in his arms'[6] introduce maternal considerations in *The Heroic Slave*'s depiction of the black male slave model, which complicate any strict definitions of Douglass's narrative design as prescriptively masculine.

Douglass's descriptions of Washington throughout *The Heroic Slave* are in direct contrast to those provided in his speeches, including for example his earlier address, 'Slavery, the Slumbering Volcano' (1849). Given before a black audience in New York to protest against the American Colonization Society, this speech considers Washington's heroism along diametrically opposed lines: 'Suiting the action to the word . . . in a very few minutes Madison Washington, a black man, with woolly head, high cheekbones, protruding lip, distended nostril, and retreating forehead, had the mastery of that ship.'[7] Upon first reading, it would appear that Douglass subscribes to the conventional markers for black representation provided by racist discourse and minstrelsy caricature: 'woolly head' and 'protruding lip.' However, he ultimately subverts white racist stereotypes as they are used positively in order to situate the black male body within an explicitly separatist framework. His use of an exaggerated, unambiguous and highly stylized form draws attention to debates surrounding Douglass's manipulation of theatricality, minstrelsy and varied positioning of audience. In contrast to *The Heroic Slave*, in which he seeks to convince a white readership of black equal manhood by ignoring racial difference, in his oratorical material Douglass celebrates the black male body even as represented by racist discourse, in order to produce generic black role models for a black audience. Indeed, the key phrase, 'suiting

6. Ibid., p. 179.

7. See Douglass, 'Slavery, the Slumbering Volcano: An Address Delivered in New York, on April 23, 1849,' in J. W. Blassingame (ed.), *The Frederick Douglass Papers* (New Haven, CT: Yale University Press, 1979–92), Vol. 2, p. 155. [An excerpt from the speech is included in this volume under the title "Address at the Great Anti-Colonization Meeting in New York." Eds.]

the action to the word,' confirms Douglass's explicit connection between moral suasion and political activism, while it articulates his recognition of the necessity for practical efforts by his black audience to secure emancipation.

Douglass's incorporation of the black female slave figure into *The Heroic Slave* is a source of much ambiguity and accounts for much of the critical controversy surrounding this text.[8] His explanation of Washington's return to the South to rescue his wife from slavery borrows heavily from contemporary speculation in the abolitionist press. Both *The Liberator*'s 'Madison Washington: Another Chapter in His History' (1842) and the *National Anti-Slavery Standard*'s similarly titled 'Madison Washington' (1842) focused upon the unnamed figure of Washington's wife as stimulus to black male rebellion. The first argued that 'This grave Creole matter may prove to have been but a part only of that grand game, in which the highest stake was the liberty of his dear wife,' while the second summarized the public consequences of domestic relationships: 'We would give much to learn whether she was on board the Creole. It would be curious indeed, if this little sub-plot of domestic love should set in motion a great game of nations, with England and the United States for actors.'[9] This interest in the possible existence of Washington's wife not only encourages sensationalism by adding romance to an already adventurous tale but also confirms abolitionist preoccupations with domesticity and their interests in convincing a white au-

8. For an analysis of representations of Susan Washington in this text, see, for example, the following essays: R. Yarborough, 'Race, Violence, and Manhood: The Masculine Ideal in Frederick Douglass's "The Heroic Slave"' in E. J. Sundquist (ed.), *Frederick Douglass: New Literary and Historical Essays* (New York: Cambridge University Press, 1990), M. M. Sale, 'Critiques from Within: Antebellum Projects of Resistance,' *American Literature*, 64.4 (December 1992), pp. 695–719; R. Wiegman, *American Anatomies: Theorizing Race and Gender* (Durham, NC: Duke University Press, 1995); P. G. Foreman, 'Sentimental Abolition in Douglass's Decade: Revision, Erotic Conversion, and the Politics of Witnessing in "The Heroic Slave" and *My Bondage and My Freedom*,' in H. B. Wonham (ed.), *Criticism and the Color Line: Desegregating American Literary Studies* (New Brunswick, NJ: Rutgers University Press, 1996.

9. 'Madison Washington,' *National Anti-Slavery Standard*, 28 April 1842.

dience concerning the sanctity of the black domestic unit and the extent of its violation by slavery.

Thus, Douglass extends the evident preoccupation in the abolitionist press with writing Washington's wife into the historical record by naming her into being in *The Heroic Slave* as Susan Washington. He characterizes her in passive terms: as the black hero's 'Poor thing!,' 'my good angel' and 'my poor wife, whom I knew might be trusted with my secrets even on the scaffold.'[10] The fact of Douglass's authorship confirms the significance of this text for documenting black male narrative strategies for representing the black female body. Thus, Washington's account to the white abolitionist Listwell of his failed rescue attempt betrays Douglass's ideological emphasis:

> My wife . . . screamed and fainted . . . the white folks were roused. . . . It was all over with me now! . . . Seeing that we gave no heed to their calls, they fired, and my poor wife fell by my side dead, while I received but a slight flesh wound. I now became desperate, and stood my ground, and awaited their attack over her dead body.[11]

The preferred critical interpretation of this moment argues for the invincibility of the black male body, set against the vulnerability of the black female slave.[12] However, it is possible to argue in support of the different view that Susan Washington's body facilitates Madison's physical liberation in this text. *The Heroic Slave* offers a clear discrepancy between Susan as Madison's property, 'my poor wife,' and authorial interest in the symbolic importance of the black female slave's body, 'her dead body.' Douglass questions and extends the available conventions within which black male and female slave bodies are presented and defined.

10. *HS*, pp. 180, 192, and 190 respectively.

11. Ibid., pp. 219–20.

12. For example, see R. Yarborough, 'Race, Violence, and Manhood,' p. 176, and R. Wiegman, *American Anatomies*, p. 76.

IVY G. WILSON

from "Transnationalism, Frederick Douglass, and 'The Heroic Slave'"[1]

One of the ironies, or tragedies, of "The Heroic Slave" is that while Douglass wants to impress on his readers the intrinsic eligibility of African Americans for citizenship, the protagonist can find refuge only in another country. This irony makes the work an eerie precursor to James Baldwin. Yet for Douglass to appeal to his audience, he must privilege 1776 and the Declaration of Independence as constitutive elements of American nationalism. He therefore has both Tom Grant and Washington position the events aboard the *Creole* as similar to those that inspired the American Revolution. Despite Grant's earlier admission that Washington and company were motivated by the "principles of 1776" (163), Washington, while laying no less a claim to the national narrative, is more conscious that the cultural apparatus that shapes the narrative is usually regulated by those in possession of political authority.

1. From Ivy G. Wilson, "On Native Ground: Transnationalism, Frederick Douglass, and "'The Heroic Slave,'" *PMLA* 121, no. 2 (2006): 453–68; the selection is from 461–67. Reprinted by permission of the copyright owner, the Modern Language Association of America. The footnotes have been renumbered and are the author's; the Works Cited list has been condensed so that it includes only the works referred to in this selection.

> God is my witness that LIBERTY, not *malice*, is the motive for this night's work. I have done no more to those dead men yonder than they would have done to me in like circumstances. We have struck for our freedom, and if a true man's heart be in you, you will honor us for the deed. We have done that which you applaud your fathers for doing, and if we are murderers, *so were they*. (161)

Douglass knew that the underlying impulses of both 1776 and the Declaration of Independence were global. A year earlier in his Fourth of July speech, he admitted that while he drew "encouragement from the Declaration of Independence," his spirit was also "cheered by the obvious tendencies of the age" (128). Hence, one of the tasks of "The Heroic Slave" is to make manifest and ubiquitous what the Declaration says is self-evident. Philosophically, he may feel that all people are born equal or that they all possess the same right to "life, liberty, and the pursuit of happiness," but he recognizes that such ontological presuppositions must be politically guaranteed. As author, he uses contrast to underscore his position: what is only property in the United States is recognized as a person in British Canada. What should be self-evident in America is truly self-evident in the British Commonwealth.

Notwithstanding his frequent appeals to the Declaration of Independence throughout "The Heroic Slave," ultimately Douglass is not convinced of its proper implementation in the United States and must instead depend on the laws of another nation. The closing scene of part 4, in which Grant details the events aboard the *Creole* when they land at Nassau, illustrates that one's rights must be legally inscribed by a nation. At the marine coffeehouse in Richmond, Grant informs a company of sailors that after a storm on the high seas, Washington leaned toward him and stated, "Mr. mate, you cannot write the bloody laws of slavery on those restless billows. The ocean, if not the land, is free" (162–63). The debate between state law versus natural law is articulated in a conversation between

Grant and Jack Williams. Williams maintains that the events aboard the *Creole* were the result of mismanagement by the white crew. Grant's retort discloses the violent apparatuses that support the institution of slavery:

> It is quite easy to talk of flogging niggers here on land, where you have the sympathy of the community, and the whole physical force of the government, State and national, at your command. . . . It is one thing to manage a company of slaves on the plantation, and quite another to quell an insurrection on the lonely billows of the Atlantic, where every breeze speaks of courage and liberty. (158)

Every breeze of the Atlantic may have spoken of "courage and liberty," but the ocean turns out to be no more free than Virginian soil, since the freedom of Washington and his company is not secured until they are within the pale of the British empire.

Although oceans are the liminal spaces among nations and seem to have no state jurisdiction, they are far from neutral territories.[2] Grant and the rest of the crew of the *Creole* are operating not under maritime logic but under the laws of Virginia and the United States. The *Creole* is a floating, self-contained microcosm of the nation carrying with it the nation's political and legal mandates. Grant assumes that, on reaching Nassau, he can find recourse with the American consul at port. He is disappointed to hear that "they did not recognize *persons* as *property*." His chagrin is exacerbated by his belief that the laws of the United States—specifically, the Fugitive Slave Law—should be enforceable in other nations: "I told them that by the laws of Virginia and the laws of the United States, the slaves on board were as much property as the barrels of flour

2. As Jameson writes, "For the sea is . . . a place of work and the very element by which an imperial capitalism . . . slowly realizes its sometimes violent, sometimes silent and corrosive, penetration of the outlying precapitalist zones of the globe" (*Political Unconscious* 210).

in the hold" (163). Douglass embellishes the irony here by having a company of black soldiers arrive at the port to protect the ship's property. That a company of black soldiers, presumably armed, represent the state accentuates the contrast he has established between the United States and its professed ideals. But if the Bahamas are an idealized territory and Nassau, a place where blacks are freed, is a more perfect state than the United States, why does "The Heroic Slave" not close with the pragmatic idea that the Bahamas should be the destination of every black American? If your inalienable rights are withheld in the United States, why not move to where they are protected? What is it, finally, that compels Douglass to champion Washington as a distinctly American hero and to retain faith that the spirit of one founding document, the Declaration of Independence, will ultimately refashion the other, the Constitution?

Douglass depicts Tom Grant in such a manner as to recall the earlier conversion of Listwell. Whereas Listwell was captivated by Washington's rhetorical eloquence, Grant is captivated by Washington's display of physical restraint. Whereas Listwell pledged to remain true to the abolitionist crusade, Grant promises to abandon the business of slavery. Through Listwell, Douglass is able to envisage an idealized, converted white American who acts on his moral beliefs irrespective of legal codes. Douglass does not imbue Grant with a similar sense of moral indignation concerning slavery; instead, Grant is persuaded by Washington's overwhelming presence. Throughout "The Heroic Slave" the size and strength of the protagonist are detailed but rarely exposed in action, as though to figure a violent black masculinity only to contain it by the man's higher, cerebral nature. Despite Washington's physical presence, Douglass mitigates the violence aboard the *Creole* by refusing to describe it. Instead, he underscores Washington's benevolence.[3] He was surely attempting to preempt accusations of wanton black violence. His audiences may have wanted slavery expelled, but only the most fer-

3. Yarborough's essay on Douglass is seminal here, although my focus is different.

vent abolitionists advocated violent insurrection. Grant's conversion is less a result of Washington's sympathy than a result of Washington's oratorical skill:

> I felt little disposition to reply to this impudent speech. By heaven, it disarmed me. The fellow loomed up before me. I forgot his blackness in the dignity of his manner, and the eloquence of his speech. It seemed as if the souls of both the great dead (whose names he bore) had entered him. (161)

Although Grant submits that he "forgot" Washington's blackness, the black man's speaking ability did not convince him of racial equality, as it did Listwell. Once again Douglass emphasizes the power of speech. Grant confesses that Washington's words "disarmed" him. Although conceded in a figurative sense, the disarming here parallels the earlier physical disarming of the crew. They are held captive by Washington physically and orally—equally. In Virginia, Grant subsequently announces to the men seated about him, "I dare say *here* what many men *feel*, but *dare not speak*, that this whole slave-trading business is a disgrace and scandal to Old Virginia" (159). Douglass's maneuver at this moment is subtle. Instead of having the narrator or even Washington condemn Virginia's participation in slavery, Douglass uses the recently converted Grant for such a statement.

Both Grant and Williams contest the legacy of Virginia. Astonished that the insurrection succeeded, Williams is equally concerned that the reputation of Virginian sailors will be tarnished: "For my part I feel ashamed to have the idea go *abroad*, that a ship load of slaves can't be safely taken from Richmond to New Orleans. I should like, merely to redeem the character of Virginia sailors, to take charge of a ship load on 'em to-morrow" (158; emphasis mine). His frustration reveals how his disappointment regarding the disruption of the dominant racial hierarchy and his allegiance to Virginia are utterly enmeshed, and it reveals how one's regional affinities can supersede one's national affiliation. The tête-à-tête between Grant and Williams exposes more than two men vying to identify the true character of Virginia. That Listwell is a resident of Ohio—one of the free states—presumably accounts for his swift conversion, but, with Grant, Douglass offers the conversion of a man who not only had roots in the gateway to the South but was fully entangled in the business of slavery. With Grant's disavowal of slavery Douglass implies that had the founding fathers atoned for their sin of owning slaves, they could have reemerged as rehabilitated Tom Grants. Imperfect and belated as his conversion is, Grant arrives as the son to redeem the fathers.

If Grant is furnished to redeem the founding fathers, that redemption occurs in the text only when the black body acts as a forfeiture that reifies the boundaries of the United States as a site of white hegemony. Although increasingly characterized as an American, from his adoption of certain speech cadences to being recognized (in the sense that Fanon theorizes recognition) by Listwell and Grant, Washington ultimately is displaced from the United States. This displacement is as much textual as it is actual. Although he never assumes the position of narrator in "The Heroic Slave," the number of lines dedicated to his words is markedly reduced in part 4. Instead, the concluding section features the conversation between Grant and Williams. Though his articulations in and of themselves are resonant, Washington speaks only four times here, and his voice is heard through and by the mouth of Grant. The effect created in this last section is the removal of the black physical presence from the United States. Only Grant and Williams are left, preoccupied with the project of national history.

"The Heroic Slave" is an imperfect allegory, not because it fails to locate Washington as a particular register in the literary precincts of the American historical romance but because it can only nominally approximate the issue of colonial and postcolonial anxiety. Its function as historical romance seemingly undercuts its potential as a postcolonial text, as when Grant superimposes questions of French imperialism onto the question of slavery in the United States: "For the negro to act cowardly on shore, may be to act wisely; and I've some doubts whether *you*, Mr. Williams, would find it very convenient were you a slave in Algiers, to raise your hand against the bayonets of a whole government" (158). The final image of the text, of the cohort not returning to the United States but remaining in Nassau, overwhelmingly conveys much of the postcolonial condition of being without a home, of being an exile. "The Heroic Slave" ends not with a depiction of the United States as a "trans-national America," as Randolph Bourne would later call it, but with a displaced cadre of transnational blacks whose affiliations and affinities are determined less by their reference to the United States than by their relationship to other blacks in the diaspora—a sentiment that Douglass himself earlier announced when he wrote to William Lloyd Garrison, "[A]s to nation, I belong to none" (17).

Works Cited

Andrews, William L., ed. *The Oxford Frederick Douglass Reader*. New York: Oxford UP, 1996.

Bourne, Randolph. "Trans-national America." *Atlantic Monthly* July 1916: 86–97.

Douglass, Frederick. "The Heroic Slave." 1853. Andrews, *Reader* 132–63.

———. "To William Lloyd Garrison." 1 Sept. 1846. Foner 17–20.

———. "What to the Slave Is the Fourth of July? An Address Delivered in Rochester, New York, on 5 July 1852." Andrews, *Reader* 109–30.

Fanon, Frantz. *Black Skin, White Masks*. New York: Grove, 1967.

Foner, Philip, ed. *Frederick Douglass: Selected Speeches and Writings*. New York: Hall, 1999.

Jameson, Fredric. *The Political Unconscious: Narrative as a Socially Symbolic Act*. Ithaca: Cornell UP, 1981.

Yarborough, Richard. "Race, Violence, and Manhood: The Masculine Ideal in Frederick Douglass's 'The Heroic Slave.'" *Frederick Douglass: New Literary and Historical Essays*. Ed. Eric J. Sundquist. New York: Cambridge UP, 1990. 166–83.

CARRIE HYDE

from "The Climates of Liberty"[1]

Strangely, we know more about Listwell's thoughts and desires than about Madison [Washington's]; the closest we come to an understanding of Madison's interior life is through the already externalized—and performative—expression it assumes in his speech.[2] The fact that the aptly named Listwell (who listens well, as several critics note)[3] forms his initial impression of Madison on the basis of voice alone—"that unfailing index of the soul"—suggests just how much their often lauded interracial friend-

1. From Carrie Hyde, "The Climates of Liberty: Natural Rights in the *Creole* Case and 'The Heroic Slave,'" *American Literature* 85, no. 3 (September 2013): 475–504; the excerpt is from 487–94. Republished by permission of the copyright holder, Duke University Press (www.dukeupress.edu); all rights reserved. The footnotes have been renumbered and in some cases reframed by the author. Our thanks to Carrie Hyde for her help in adapting the selection for our volume.

2. Frederick Douglass, "The Heroic Slave," in *Autographs for Freedom*, Michigan Historical Reprint Series (1853; rpt. Ann Arbor: Scholarly Publishing Office, 2005), 179–80. Hereafter cited parenthetically as HS.

3. Listwell, as [Robert] Stepto was the first to point out, "is indeed a 'Listwell' in that he *enlists* as an abolitionist and does *well* by the cause—in fact he does magnificently. He is also a 'Listwell' in that he *listens* well" ("Storytelling in Early Afro-American Fiction: Frederick Douglass' 'The Heroic Slave,'" *The Georgia Review* 36.2 [1982]: 365).

ship depends on disembodiment and spectatorship (HS, 179).[4] When Listwell finally catches "a full view of the unsuspecting speaker," his now increased perception remains one-sided (HS, 178). "As our traveler gazed upon him, he almost trembled at the thought of his dangerous intrusion. Still he could not quit the place. He had long *desired to sound the mysterious depths of the thoughts and feelings of a slave*. He was not, therefore, disposed to allow so providential an opportunity to pass unimproved" (HS, 179, emphasis mine). Here, what might otherwise have been an assumed good—an opportunity to communicate the feelings and humanity of a slave to white abolitionist readers—is given a notably sinister connotation in the depiction of Listwell's overeager and almost eroticized surveillance of the "unsuspecting speaker."

If, as some critics have suggested, Douglass's fragmentary depiction of his protagonist is conditioned in part by the limited historical sources on Madison Washington,[5] this indirection also eschews the type of ostensibly benevolent spectatorship (exemplified by Listwell) that permeates abolitionism. By making, "the lack of knowledge about Washington" the gambit of his text (as William Andrews observes),[6] Douglass turns the fact of historiographical obscurity into an occasion for questioning the model of agency that underwrites biographical narratives of history. Of course, this is not

4. Marianne Noble, for example, reads this gesture more affirmatively, arguing that "The Heroic Slave" "rejects the visual/corporeal model of persuasion . . . and promotes instead a complex idea of sympathy grounded in listening" ("Sympathetic Listening in Frederick Douglass's 'The Heroic Slave' and *My Bondage and My Freedom*," *Studies in American Fiction* 34.1 [2006]: 59).

5. Both Maggie Sale and Paul Jones read Douglass's prefatory remarks as acknowledging his limited archive. Maggie Sale, "To Make the Past Useful: Frederick Douglass' Politics of Solidarity," *Arizona Quarterly: A Journal of American Literature, Culture, and Theory* 51.3 (1995): 25–60, esp. 47; Paul Christian Jones, "Copying What the Master Had Written: Frederick Douglass's 'The Heroic Slave' and the Southern Historical Romance," *Southern Quarterly: A Journal of the Arts in the South* 38.4 (2000): 5.

6. William L. Andrews, "The Novelization of Voice in Early African American Narrative," PMLA 105.1 (1990), 23–34, esp. 29.

to suggest that Madison Washington's evocative name did not help abolitionists situate the *Creole* insurrection firmly within the tradition of the American Revolution, for it did. As the *New York Evangelist* commented, Madison "wore a name unfit for a slave but finely expressive for a hero."[7] Still, without relinquishing either the heroic stature of Madison's actions or the rhetorically powerful link to the Revolution, the novella insistently displaces biographical (or at least character-bound) expectations with unstable natural metaphors.

Douglass forswears the possibility of fathoming Madison's character before the novella proper has even begun.

> Curiously, earnestly, anxiously we peer into the dark, and wish even for the blinding flash, or the light of northern skies to reveal him. But alas! he is still enveloped in darkness, and we return from the pursuit like a wearied and disheartened mother, (after a tedious and unsuccessful search for a lost child,) who returns weighed down with disappointment and sorrow. Speaking of marks, traces, possibles, and probabilities, we come before our readers. (HS, 175–76)

With Madison's interior motivations insistently undisclosed, the narrative uses metaphors of natural phenomena to contextualize actions that (without the causal explanation of intentions) appear not only inscrutable but also erratic. Though glimpsed only in fits and starts—"through the parted clouds and howling tempests . . . the quivering flash of angry lightening" (HS, 175)—what we know most emphatically about Madison derives from the organizing correspondences between his character and nature. "The Heroic Slave," in this way, refrains from the type of exceptionalist individualism that its title leads us to expect—instead establishing Madison's moral character by elaborating its basic comparability with the natural world.

The proliferation of natural imagery in "The Heroic Slave" shapes more than the presentation of Madison's character. Natural phe-

7. "The Hero-Mutineers," *New York Evangelist*, December 25, 1841, 206.

nomena (clouds, conflagrations, and storms) also provide the logic and impetus for the novella's highly episodic structure. Although Madison first attempts to escape just weeks after his forest soliloquy, "a season of clouds and rain set in, wholly preventing me from seeing the North Star, which I had trusted as my guide, not dreaming that clouds might *intervene* between us" (HS, 189, emphasis mine). This "circumstance," Madison explains, "was fatal to my project, for in losing my star, I lost my way; so when I supposed I was far towards the North, and had almost gained my freedom, I discovered myself at the very point from which I had started" (HS, 189–90). Nature, here, is a practical obstacle to freedom rather than a metaphor for its inevitability. The passage, however, does not belie the novella's use of natural imagery as a figure for natural rights. Instead, it underscores, as Peter Meyers argues in another context, that Douglass's imagination of natural law as "self-executing" "did not betray a naive or willful idealism . . . More painfully than most, he was mindful that the dynamism of nature and history brought reversals for ill as for good."[8] Douglass's attention to the erratic character of natural phenomena in "The Heroic Slave" has a similar effect—suggesting that despite its rhetorical and political force, the discourse of natural law does not have the same empirical self-evidence as the physical laws that govern nature. Douglass, however, does more than emplot the prerogatives of natural law; he takes the very restlessness of nature as a model for liberty and reform.

Restless Liberties

The plot of "The Heroic Slave" does not develop as a consequence of Madison's individual agency, but through the sporadic shifts of weather, which structure and contain the virtual world of the novella. Although a "season of clouds" frustrates Madison's initial at-

8. Peter C. Meyers, *Frederick Douglass: Race and the Rebirth of American Liberalism* (Lawrence: University Press of Kansas, 2007), 15.

tempt to reach the North, he is later forced back on his journey by a wildfire that drives him out of his hiding place in the neighboring swamps.

> The whole world seemed on fire, and it appeared to me that the day of judgment had come; that the burning bowels of the earth had burst forth, and the end of all things was at hand. . . . The very heavens seemed to rain down fire through the towering trees; it was by the merest chance that I escaped the devouring element. Running before it, and stopping occasionally to take breath, I looked back to behold its frightful ravages, and to drink in its savage magnificence. It was awful, thrilling, solemn, beyond compare. When aided by the fitful wind, the merciless tempest of fire swept on, sparkling, creaking, cracking, curling, roaring, out-doing in its dreadful splendor a thousand thunderstorms at once. . . . It was this grand conflagration that drove me hither; *I ran alike from fire and from slavery* (HS, 193–94, emphasis mine).

Employing the rhetoric of millennialism, Douglass presents the fire as a divine "judgment" against slavery, which returns Madison on his journey for freedom. Admittedly, the depiction of Madison as all but bereft of agency generates tensions in a text that tacitly invokes heroism as a condition for political legitimacy. However, by depicting nature as the principle agent, Douglass is able to suggest that the opposition to slavery is more fundamental than the actions of any one individual or group.

This insistent downplaying of human agency is most dramatic in the representation of the revolt onboard the *Creole*. The force of the insurrectionists is diminished, on a formal level, by the fact that the revolt is narrated only retrospectively, and narrated, moreover, by a sailor who was unconscious during the event in question. The details of the revolt emerge in the course of a dialogue between two white sailors in a Richmond coffeehouse. Jack Williams, "a regular old salt" "tauntingly" addresses the "first mate" of the *Creole*: "I say, shipmate, you had rather rough weather on your late passage to Orleans?" (HS, 226). The fictional mate, named Tom Grant, replies "Foul play, as well as foul weather" (HS, 226). Williams speaks of bad weather during the insurrection, but it is worth noting that the premise of the squall is one of the fictional elements of Douglass's portrayal. The weather during the revolt was, in fact, unremarkable—there was, to quote the Congressional report, "a fresh breeze, and the sky [was] a little hazy, with trade-clouds flying."[9] Douglass invented the squall, but this fictionalization also responded to the diplomatic history of the revolt—and to [Daniel] Webster's imagined "stress[es] of weather," in particular.[10] We know that Douglass was familiar with Webster's letters, because he refers to them explicitly in two of his speeches.[11] The squall, then, can be seen as a rewriting of Webster, which strategically reappropriates natural metaphors as a figure for natural rights.

In a spirit not unlike Webster's, the "old salt" Williams insists that the real cause of that "whole affair" could not possibly rest solely with the slaves. The "whole disaster," Williams declares, "was the result of ignorance of the real character of *darkies* in general. . . . All that is needed in dealing with a set of rebellious *darkies*, is to show that yer not afraid of 'em" (HS, 226–27). Had the sailors lost control of the ship as a result of the weather alone, Williams continues to

9. Senate Document 51: Message from the President . . . January 20, 1842, 27th Congress, 2nd Session, 37.

10. Webster analogizes the revolt to the ungovernable effects of the "weather" in order to deemphasize the agency of the insurrectionists. See Senate Document 1: Message from the President. . . . December 7, 1842, 27th Congress, 3rd Session, 121.

11. Douglass refers to Webster's role in (and characterization of) the diplomatic dispute in his earlier speeches on the *Creole*. In "Slavery the Slumbering Volcano," Douglass mentions Webster's earlier letter to Edward Everett, as well as Ashburton's role in the dispute. For other allusions to the controversy, see, "American and Scottish Prejudice Against the Slave: An Address Delivered in Edinburgh, Scotland, on 1 May 1846" and "America's Compromise with Slavery," *The Frederick Douglass Papers: Series One: Speeches, Debates and Interviews*, ed. John W. Blassingame, 5 volumes (New Haven: Yale University Press, 1979–92): 2:157–8; 1:245; 1:211. [Earlier in the essay, Hyde discusses the role of Secretary of State Daniel Webster in the diplomatic exchanges between U.S. and British government officials. Webster demanded that the British return the slaves to the U.S. slave traders who claimed them as their property; the British refused to honor his request. Eds.]

suggest, that at least would have "relieve[d] the affair of its present discreditable features" (HS, 231). Acts of nature, as Grant remarks, are seen as unavoidable, and thus more legitimate. "For a ship to go down under a calm sky is, upon the first flush of it, disgraceful either to sailors or caulkers. But when we learn, that by some mysterious disturbance in nature, the waters parted beneath, and swallowed the ship up, we lose our indignation and disgust in lamentation of the disaster, and in awe of the Power which controls the elements" (HS, 231). By establishing a parallel between "foul play" and "foul weather," the premise of the squall allows Douglass to maintain the agency of the slaves, while also suggesting that the revolt (and the resulting emancipation of the slaves) was prompted by an underlying "disturbance in nature."[12]

The retrospective narration of the revolt distances the reader from its drama and urgency, but this remove facilitates Douglass's effort to present Madison's heroism in the more authoritative terms of relative disinterestedness. Tom Grant—who discerns Madison to be "a superior man" but is unwilling to concede that the "principles of 1776" apply to men he deems inferior on the basis of "color" (HS, 238)—is pivotal to the ideological authority of "The Heroic Slave" for this very reason.[13] Offering an intermediary between Listwell's avowed (if still fairly anemic)[14] abolitionism and Williams's blatant bigotry, Grant models a form of conciliatory identification with Madison.[15] The fact that the presentation of Madison's heroism is never free from white mediation in the novella—whether in Grant's

12. As Krista Walter notes, Grant's counterfactual example of ships foundering as a result of natural forces indicates that he can "plainly see the hand of Providence" in the revolt ("Trappings of Nationalism in Frederick Douglass's *The Heroic Slave*," *African American Review* 34.2 [2000]: 240).

13. For an alternate reading of the political significance of the narrative's dependence on white voice, see Ivy G. Wilson, "On Native Ground: Transnationalism, Frederick Douglass, and 'The Heroic Slave,'" *PMLA* 121.2 (2006): 461.

14. The fact that Listwell allows himself to be mistaken as a slaveholder while in the South (in order to avoid disagreeable disputations with the locals) is one of several passages that emphasize his self-interested complacency (HS, 214).

15. As Walter notes, Grant functions as a "figure for the reluctant reader" ("Trappings," 239).

reluctant admission of respect, or in the (fabricated) fact that Listwell provides Madison with the files that he uses to free himself and the other slaves (HS, 223; 235)[16]—has often been regarded as the novella's failure fully to imagine black self-determination.[17] However, the decision to narrate the revolt not only retrospectively, but also dialogically, does not thereby reproduce the ideologically compromised assumptions of the novella's white characters. Instead, the narrative's reliance on figures of mediation tacitly identifies public perception (not the capacity of slaves) as the principal obstacle to emancipation. Douglass's suggestive naming of Grant, which has gone unremarked in scholarship, echoes this emphasis—suggesting that rights (even when conceptualized as natural) still require social and legal recognition.

Despite the fact that both of the venues in which "The Heroic Slave" initially appeared—an antislavery gift book and Douglass's newspaper—were likely to attract readers who already self-identified as abolitionists, the text self-consciously addresses itself to the unconverted reader. The conversation between Grant and Williams provides a formal mechanism for defamiliarizing commonplace stereotypes about the innate servility of slaves. Grant responds to Williams's imputation that the sailors could have prevented the revolt through better management by arguing that the outward submission is strategic and conditioned by context.

> I deny that the negro is, naturally, a coward, or that your theory of managing slaves will stand the test of *salt* water. . . . It is one thing to manage a company of slaves on a Virginia plantation, and quite another thing to quell an insurrection on the lonely billows of the Atlantic, where every breeze speaks of courage and liberty.

16. Before the actual revolt in 1841, the slaves on the *Creole*, in fact, were neither chained nor fettered.

17. The problem, as William Andrews phrases it, is the text's "rhetorical dependence on white precedents for the sanctioning of acts of black violence"; see *To Tell a Free Story: The First Century of Afro-American Autobiography, 1760–1865* (Urbana: University of Illinois Press, 1988), 187.

> For the negro to act cowardly on shore, may be to act wisely; and I've some doubts whether *you*, Mr. Williams, would find it very convenient were you a slave in Algiers, to raise your hand against the bayonets of a whole government (HS, 228).

By contrasting the state of Virginia with the open ocean, Grant intimates that slavery, far from natural, can be maintained only in the artificial environs of a plantation. For this reason, as Grant's alternate scenario of Algerian enslavement dramatizes, slavery can as easily claim white auditors as it does the subjects of their curiosity.

The more general perspectival distance from the insurrectionists helps enforce the objective tone of these pointed remarks, but it becomes more problematic in the representation of the revolt itself. As if to take its formal aesthetic of mediation and opacity to a comic extreme, at the beginning of the revolt, Grant, our only eyewitness, is "knocked senseless to the deck" (HS, 234). When he regains consciousness after an uncertain interval, the violent struggle and subsequent reversal of power have already occurred. Grant explains, "When I came to myself, (which I did in a few minutes, I *suppose*, for it was yet quite light,) there was not a white man on deck. The sailors were all aloft in the rigging, and dared not come down. Captain Clarke and Mr. Jameson lay stretched on the quarter-deck,—both dying,—while Madison himself stood at the helm unhurt" (HS, 234, emphasis mine).

Critics tend to suggest that Douglass uses the premise of Grant's unconsciousness to minimize the scene of violence and so facilitate the idealization of Madison as a hero,[18] but violence, it is worth

18. Maggie Sale, for example, argues that "Douglass disarms gendered, racialist discourses that would figure Washington as a 'black murderer' or raging savage." However, the evasion of violence has led many critics to suggest that the tale is too conciliatory in its address. Richard Yarborough observes that Douglass "strips his fictional slave rebel of much of his radical, subversive force," while Ivy Wilson argues that by narrating the revolt indirectly through a white sailor the story reproduces the authenticating logic of the white abolitionist preface. Without ignoring these tensions, I would like to suggest that this indirection is not a symptomatic omission confined to the depiction of insurrectionary violence, but something that Douglass

stressing, is not absent so much as displaced onto the portentous figure of the squall.

> By this time the apprehended squall had burst upon us. The wind howled furiously,—the ocean was white with foam, which, on account of the darkness, we could see only by the quick flashes of lightning that darted occasionally from the angry sky. All was alarm and confusion. Hideous cries came up from the slave women. Above the roaring billows a succession of heavy thunder rolled along, swelling the terrific din. Owing to the great darkness, and a sudden shift of the wind, we found ourselves in the trough of the sea. When shipping a heavy sea over the starboard bow, the bodies of the captain and Mr. Jameson were washed overboard. . . . A more savage thunder-gust never swept the ocean. (HS, 236–37)

Recalling the constellation of natural metaphors that organizes the elliptical presentation of Madison in the preface—"howling tempests," "the menacing rock on a perilous coast" and "angry lightning" (HS, 175)—Douglass uses the squall to both express and contain the uncomfortable violence of the revolt. With their precise physical condition undisclosed, and with causality eclipsed in the passive voice, we are thus told that "the bodies of the captain and Mr. Jameson *were washed overboard*." Admittedly less gory than the official account of the insurrection (which includes a knife fight and a shooting), the squall, nonetheless, is not only sublime, but "furious," "terrific," "hideous." "The Heroic Slave," in this respect, does not repress the violence of the insurrection so much as reconfigure its underlying cause. Douglass presents the revolt as an effect of nature—more fundamental, if also more fitful, than the actions of an individual agent.

---

insists on self-consciously throughout "The Heroic Slave"—and which significantly informs his conception of the project of liberty. Sale, "To Make the Past Useful," 51–2; Yarborough, "Race, Violence, and Manhood: The Masculine Ideal in Frederick Douglass's 'The Heroic Slave,'" in *Frederick Douglass: New Literary and Historical Essays*, ed. Eric J. Sundquist (New York: Cambridge University Press, 1990, 166–88, esp. 181; Wilson, "On Native Ground," 461.

Evoking a long tradition of representing national turmoil through the figure of the ship of state tossed to and fro at sea, Douglass uses the ocean as a symbolic counterpoint to extant national law. This is particularly emphatic in the passage that appears to have served as the prototype for Madison Washington's often quoted proclamation in "The Heroic Slave" that "you cannot write the bloody laws of slavery on those restless billows. The ocean, if not the land, is free" (HS, 237).[19] In his 1849 speech—whose title, "Slavery, the Slumbering Volcano," itself imagines emancipation as an imminent natural force—Douglass uses the "restless waves" of the ocean as a rhetorical directive for reform:

> Sir, I thank God that there is some part of his footstool upon which the bloody statutes of Slavery cannot be written. They cannot be written on the proud, towering billows of the Atlantic. The restless waves will not permit those bloody statutes to be recorded there; those foaming billows forbid it; old ocean gnawing with its hungry surges upon our rockbound coast preaches a lesson to American soil: 'You may bind chains upon the limbs of your people if you will; you may place the yoke upon them if you will; you may brand them with irons; you may write out your statutes and preserve them in the archives of the nation if you will; but the moment they mount the surface of our unsteady waves, those statutes are obliterated, and the slave stands redeemed, disenthralled.' This part of God's domain then is free, and I hope that ere long our own soil will also be free.[20]

Douglass conceptualizes the ocean as an explicitly denationalizing force. The Atlantic is not only outside of the nation proper; it erodes

19. Douglass's characterization of the "restless[ness]" of the ocean echoes one of the most compelling passages in William Ellery Channing's book-length consideration of the implications of the *Creole* revolt. "The sea is the exclusive property of no nation . . . No state can write its laws on that restless surface." William E. Channing, *The Duty of the Free States, or Remarks Suggested by the Case of the Creole* (Boston: William Crosby & Company, 1842), 28.

20. *Douglass Papers*, 2:158.

the coasts that give it form. The analogy between the soil and the laws is significant in this respect. For in underscoring the link between territoriality and positive law, Douglass presents the ocean as a model for an essentially anarchic freedom. Freedom here, as is so often the case, is an expressly negative concept, imagined alternately as baptism and destruction.

The Atlantic—as the personification of natural law—didactically "preaches a lesson to American soil," but it remains an episodic force, unsteady and transient. Drawing together the archetypal liberal tropes of the state of nature and the founding scene of revolution, Douglass represents the ocean as a political tabula rasa that is both a precondition for constructing political ideals and, if they are not fulfilled, for periodically dissolving and reforming individual communities. Thus, as much as Douglass might idealize the ocean as an extra-national utopian space (which if not "nowhere" is still foremost not the nation),[21] his ultimate objective is not properly transnational or cosmopolitan, as several recent critics have suggested.[22] Instead, Douglass prescriptively uses the universalizing rhetoric of natural law as a model for national reform.

21. As Carl Schmidt suggests in his discussion of the utopian character of the oceanic order, implicit in More's *Utopia* (1516) "and in the profound and productive formulation of the word *Utopia*, was the possibility of an enormous destruction of all orientations based on the old *nomos* of the earth. . . . Utopia did not mean any simple and general nowhere (or erewhon), but a U-*topos*, which, by comparison even with its negation, A-*topos*, has a stronger negation in relation to *topos*." Carl Schmidt, *The Nomos of the Earth in the International Law of the Jus Publicum Europaeum*, Trans. G. L. Ulmen (New York: Telos Press Publishing, 2006), 178.

22. As William Boelhower notes, the *Creole* case and its depiction in "The Heroic Slave" have "become a flashpoint for tracing Atlantic-world trajectories" ("The Rise of the New Atlantic Studies Matrix," *American Literary History* 20, no. 1 [2007], 83–101, esp. 97). See also Ivy G. Wilson, "On Native Ground: Transnationalism, Frederick Douglass, and 'The Heroic Slave,'" *PMLA* 121, no. 2 (2006): 453–68. There also has been a surge of interest in the Atlantic contours of Douglass's career more generally—especially his lectures abroad and his post as U.S. consul in Haiti. The recent *Cambridge Companion to Frederick Douglass*, for example, includes two pieces on the topic (see Ifeoma C. K. Nwankwo, "Douglass's Black Atlantic: The Caribbean," and Paul Giles, "Douglass's Black Atlantic: Britain, Europe, Egypt," in *The Cambridge Companion to Frederick Douglass*, ed. Maurice Lee [New York: Cambridge Univ. Press. 2009]: 146–59 and 132–45.)

Chronology of Frederick Douglass, Madison Washington, and Resistance to Slavery

1492 Christopher Columbus reaches the Bahamas.

1619 Dutch traders bring African slaves to Jamestown, Virginia.

1634 Maryland first settled by English colonists.

1647 British settlement of the Bahamas begins.

1688 Quakers and Mennonites in Germantown, Pennsylvania, circulate first known antislavery petition, partly in response to the fear of insurrection and acknowledgment that slavery represents a state of war.

1712 New York City slaves revolt by setting fire to a building and attacking whites who try to put out the fire. The rebellion is crushed.

1723 First slave laws introduced in the Bahamas.

1739 Stono Rebellion near Charleston, South Carolina, in which 60–100 slaves march toward Spanish Florida, which had offered freedom to Carolinian slaves, carrying a flag and demanding liberty. The rebellion is crushed.

1741 New York City slaves purportedly collaborate with poor whites in a plot to burn the city. After a series of fires, a grand jury claims to have uncovered the plot. The alleged conspirators are tried and executed.

1772 The Lord Chief Justice Mansfield in the *Somerset* case rules that slaves are free as soon as they arrive in England.

1773 Massachusetts blacks petition the legislature for relief against their oppression.

1774 Philadelphia meeting of the Society of Friends adopts rules prohibiting Quakers from buying or selling slaves.
First Continental Congress convenes in Philadelphia.

1775 Battles of Lexington and Concord, Massachusetts, in April, widely considered the beginning of the Revolutionary War.
Lord Dunmore, royal governor of Virginia, issues proclamation of freedom to slaves who desert Patriot masters and serve in the king's army.

1776 Second Continental Congress forbids the importation of slaves into the thirteen colonies.
Congress deletes from the Declaration of Independence a clause accusing the king of bringing African slaves into the thirteen colonies.

1777 Vermont ratifies the first constitution in history outlawing slavery; it adopts gradual emancipation.

1780 Pennsylvania adopts a gradual emancipation law.
Massachusetts Bill of Rights ratified, declaring that "all men are born free and equal," prompting lawsuits by slaves against their masters, which led to the end of slavery in the state in 1783.

1784 Connecticut and Rhode Island enact gradual abolition laws.
Pennsylvania Abolition Society founded.

1785 New York Manumission Society founded.

1786 The British abolitionist Thomas Clarkson publishes *An Essay on the Slavery and Commerce of the Human Species*.

1787 Britain sends poor (free) blacks and emancipated slaves to Sierra Leone to establish a settlement near present-day Freetown.
Society for the Abolition of the Slave Trade founded in Britain.
The U.S. Constitution drafted; slavery's legal status is left ambiguous.
The Northwest Ordinance prohibits slavery in the territories north of the Ohio River and east of the Mississippi.

1791 Black insurgents in Saint-Domingue (modern Haiti) rebel against their French colonial overlords. Ten years later, under Toussaint L'Ouverture, they created the New World's first black republic.

1793 New Jersey Abolition Society is founded.
Congress passes a fugitive slave law to facilitate the capture of runaway slaves.
Eli Whitney invents the cotton gin, enabling the cultivation of short-staple cotton throughout much of the South.

1794 Connecticut adopts immediate emancipation law.

1799 New York State adopts gradual emancipation law.

1804 New Jersey adopts gradual emancipation law.

1806 Virginia requires all manumitted slaves to leave the state within one year of their manumission.
Abolition of the Slave Trade Act abolishes slave trading in the British Empire.
Royal Navy begins patrolling the African coast to suppress the slave trade.

1808 United States bans further importation of slaves from Africa.

1811 Louisiana slaves 40 miles north of New Orleans revolt, and 100–500 slave rebels march downriver toward New Orleans. Federal troops are called out and the rebellion is crushed.

1816 American Colonization Society founded to promote the colonization of free blacks in Africa.

1817 In Philadelphia, 3,000 blacks protest the American Colonization Society.
Amasa Delano, former commander of the brig *Perseverance,* publishes *Narrative of Voyages and Travels in the Northern and Southern Hemispheres*, which includes an account of the 1805 slave mutiny on the Spanish ship *Tyral*, under the command of Benito Cereno.

1818 Douglass is born Frederick Augustus Washington Bailey sometime in February at Aaron Anthony's Holme Hill Farm, Talbot County, Maryland.

1820 American Colonization Society sends free blacks to Africa to establish a settlement.

1821 Missouri enters the Union as a slave state after bitter controversy. As a compromise measure (adopted in 1820), slavery is prohibited in unorganized Louisiana Purchase territories north of 36°30' latitude.

1822 Denmark Vesey's apparent plot for a slave insurrection in South Carolina is exposed and thwarted.

1826 Douglass sent to live with Hugh Auld's family in Baltimore.
David Walker founds the Massachusetts General Colored Association.

1827 Samuel Cornish and John Brown Russwurm publish *Freedom's Journal*, the first black newspaper, which calls for immediate emancipation; the newspaper lasts two years.
Slavery abolished in New York State.

1829 David Walker publishes militant abolitionist pamphlet, *Appeal to the Coloured Citizens of the World*, in Boston and surreptitiously distributes copies to southern blacks.

1830 First black national convention, held in Philadelphia.

1831 William Lloyd Garrison begins publication in Boston of the *Liberator*, which endorses the immediate emancipation of all American slaves.
Nat Turner leads bloody slave uprising in Southampton County, Virginia, prompting the Virginia legislature to consider gradual emancipation in the state.
Less than three months after Nat Turner's rebellion, Jamaica slaves set fire to hilltops and then burn sugar estates throughout the colony in a "Baptist War," but do not molest a single planter.
Douglass undergoes religious conversion, purchases a copy of *The Columbian Orator*, and learns about the abolition movement after seeing a speech by John Quincy Adams reprinted in the *Baltimore American*.

1832 South Carolina state convention nullifies federal tariff duties, which increase the cost of cotton production. President Jackson sends reinforcements to federal forts in Charleston harbor and threatens to send federal troops and execute the state's political leaders. The state repeals nullification, and a congressional compromise measure reduces federal tariff duties.

1833 American Anti-Slavery Society launched in Philadelphia.

Douglass is sent back to Talbot County to live with his new owner, Thomas Auld, son-in-law of the deceased Aaron Anthony.

1834 On 1 August, the Slavery Abolition Act of 1833 takes effect, freeing 800,000 slaves in the British West Indies and most slaves throughout the British Empire. African Americans begin holding annual First of August celebrations.
Douglass spends the year as a field hand hired out to Talbot County "slave breaker" Edward Covey.

1836 After an unsuccessful escape attempt, Douglass is returned to Hugh Auld in Baltimore.
Congress implements the "gag rule," a procedure that tables antislavery petitions and restricts debate on slavery.
New York Committee of Vigilance founded to help fugitive slaves.

1837 The Illinois abolitionist Elijah Lovejoy is murdered in Alton while defending his printing press against a mob.
Financial panic causes a dramatic decrease in northern land values and a six-year depression.

1838 On 3 September, Douglass departs Baltimore and escapes to the North. He marries the free black Anna Murray in New York City on 15 September, and the couple settles in New Bedford, Massachusetts.

1839 African slaves on board the schooner *Amistad* successfully revolt; legal proceedings in New Haven, Connecticut, win freedom for the rebels the following year.
Douglass begins speaking at black antislavery meetings in New Bedford. His first child, Rosetta, is born.
Madison Washington escapes slavery in Virginia around this time and successfully reaches the Dawn Settlement of fugitive slaves near Amherstburg, Canada.
Theodore Dwight Weld publishes *American Slavery As It Is: Testimony of a Thousand Witnesses*, a compilation of facts about American slavery drawn chiefly from southern sources.

1840 Political abolitionists break off from the American Anti-

Slavery Society, which calls government corrupt and the Constitution proslavery, and forms the Liberty Party, the nation's first abolitionist party.

Frederick Douglass's second child, Lewis, is born.

1841 Douglass is hired as a traveling lecturer by Garrisonian abolitionists.

Madison Washington leaves Canada and returns to Virginia in an unsuccessful attempt to liberate his wife and children. In November, he leads the rebellion of slaves aboard the schooner *Creole* and reaches shelter at Nassau in the Bahamas.

1842 In March, British authorities in Nassau free Madison Washington and the *Creole* rebels. Details of Washington's subsequent life are uncertain.

The Webster-Ashburton Treaty is signed in August. Among its provisions are a commitment by the United States to end the slave trade on the high seas and one by Great Britain to halt its navy's "officious interference" with American vessels.

Frederick Douglass's third child, Frederick, is born.

1843 A white mob attacks Frederick Douglass at Pendleton, Indiana, during a lecture tour, and breaks his hand; he continues the tour.

At the black national convention in Buffalo, New York, Henry Highland Garnet calls on slaves to adopt violent resistance.

1844 Congressional gag rule formally repealed after sustained protests by John Quincy Adams, Joshua Giddings, and antislavery northerners.

Frederick Douglass' fourth child, Charles Remond, is born; he is named after a black abolitionist.

1845 Texas admitted to the Union as a slave state.

Douglass publishes his first autobiography, *Narrative of the Life of Frederick Douglass, an American Slave*. In danger of being recaptured as a runaway slave, he departs in August to work for twenty-one months in Great Britain as an abolitionist lecturer. Soon after his arrival, he gives the first of a number of lectures celebrating Madison Washington and the *Creole* rebels.

1846 British abolitionists negotiate the purchase and manumission of Douglass from Hugh Auld.
United States declares war against Mexico over a Texas border dispute.

1847 From his new home in Rochester, New York, Douglass publishes the *North Star*, an independent abolitionist weekly.
He meets John Brown, whom he says "is in sympathy a black man, and as deeply interested in our cause as though his own soul had been pierced with the iron of slavery."

1848 Douglass attends the Seneca Falls Women's Rights Convention on 19–20 July and gives an eloquent speech defending a resolution for women's suffrage. The resolution is approved.
The Free-Soil Party is formed by a coalition of antislavery Whigs, Democrats, and some Liberty Party members.
The Liberty Party changes its name to the National Liberty Party, though it is still commonly referred to as the Liberty Party. The name change reflects its radical platform of universal emancipation and equal rights for all men and women. Gerrit Smith is the party's presidential candidate.
Treaty of Guadalupe Hidalgo ends the Mexican War. The United States acquires the present-day states of California, New Mexico, Nevada, Utah, and most of Arizona and Colorado.
The Wilmot Proviso prohibits slavery in newly acquired territories from Mexico, sparking explosive debates over the spread of slavery. The bill fails in the Senate.
France abolishes slavery in its West Indian colonies.

1849 The British reformer Julia Griffiths joins the staff of Douglass's newspaper as its unofficial business manager. Despite widely circulated rumors of an inappropriate personal relationship with Douglass, she assists him until returning home in 1855.

1850 Congress passes compromise measures in hopes of preventing civil war over slavery. The Compromise of 1850 includes the admission of California as a free state; the abolition of the slave trade (but not slavery) in Washington, D.C.; and a draconian fugitive slave law that denies suspects the right to a trial or judicial hearing and allows police to forcibly deputize citizens to hunt down alleged fugitives.

1851 Douglass revamps his newspaper into *Frederick Douglass' Paper*, an organ of the National Liberty Party; Gerrit Smith, wealthy leader of the National Liberty Party, provides financial support to the paper.

The captured fugitive slave Shadrach Minkins is rescued from the Boston courthouse by antislavery supporters. The rescue receives national coverage.

The fugitive Thomas Sims is arrested in Boston and sent back to Savannah, Georgia, despite efforts to rescue him. His case is a cause célèbre for antislavery Northerners.

1852 Harriet Beecher Stowe publishes *Uncle Tom's Cabin*, which sells 300,000 copies in its first year.

Douglass publishes positive reviews of Stowe's novel and plans a trip to Nassau, possibly to interview Madison Washington.

The black nationalist Martin R. Delany publishes *Condition, Elevation, Emigration and Destiny of the Colored People of the United States*.

1853 Douglass publishes his novella, *The Heroic Slave*, in *Autographs for Freedom*, edited by Griffiths, and in his newspaper.

William Wells Brown publishes *Clotel; or the President's Daughter*, regarded by many as the first African American novel.

Solomon Northup, a free, middle-class New York State black man, publishes *Twelve Years A Slave*, his narrative of being kidnapped in 1841 and sent to Louisiana as a slave for twelve years before being rescued.

An Anglo-American claims commission assesses the *Creole* case and rules that southern claimants are entitled to compensation for the loss of their property. In 1855, U.S. claimants receive $110,330 from Britain.

1854 President Pierce's administration attempts to annex Cuba.

The Kansas-Nebraska Act repeals the Missouri Compromise and opens northern territories to slavery, resulting in the dissolution of the Whig Party, the rise of the Republican Party, and immigration to Kansas Territory by proslavery and antislavery settlers.

Attempts made in Boston to rescue the captured fugitive slave Anthony Burns, but President Pierce sends federal troops to Boston to uphold the law. Burns is sent back to slavery in Virginia, but abolitionists raise over $1,000, purchase his freedom, and send him to Oberlin College.

1855 Douglass's publishes his second autobiography, *My Bondage and My Freedom*.

Herman Melville publishes *Benito Cereno*, a historical novella of the 1805 *Tyral* slave mutiny, drawn from Amasa Delano's 1817 *Narrative*.

Walt Whitman publishes *Leaves of Grass*.

The National Liberty Party changes its name to the Radical Abolition Party. A party convention considers but rejects Douglass as candidate for secretary of state for New York.

1856 Guerrilla warfare erupts in the Kansas Territory as proslavery and antislavery settlers battle each other at Blackjack, Lawrence, and other locations.

Massachusetts senator Charles Sumner delivers "Crime against Kansas" speech in Congress, calling slavery barbarous, and is brutally beaten and almost killed on the Senate floor by the South Carolina representative Preston Books.

John C. Frémont, the first Republican Party presidential candidate, wins a majority of northern votes but is defeated by the Democratic candidate James Buchanan.

Douglass is proposed as the vice presidential candidate on a Radical Abolition Party ticket with Gerrit Smith as president. He loses the nomination after members point out that both Smith and Douglass reside in New York State.

1857 In *Dred Scott v. Sandford*, the U.S. Supreme Court declares unconstitutional any attempt to prohibit the spread of slavery into federal territories, thus rendering unconstitutional the central platform of the Republican Party. The *Dred Scott* decision also denies citizenship rights to blacks and opens the way for southern masters to bring their slaves into any free state.

1859 John Brown and a band of 21 blacks and whites raid the federal arsenal at Harpers Ferry, Virginia, as part of a scheme to end slavery. He and all but 5 fellow raiders are captured and executed.

Douglass flees first to Canada and then Great Britain for safety because of his close connections with John Brown. Douglass is not able to return home until April 1860.

1860 Lincoln elected by a plurality, the first antislavery president since John Quincy Adams's 1824 election. In response, southern states begin secession movement.

1861 The Civil War begins in April following a Confederate attack on Fort Sumter, in Charleston Harbor.

In May, General Benjamin Butler admits slaves into his camp at Fort Monroe, Virginia, declares them "contraband of war," and hires them as laborers rather than sending them back into the Confederacy.

In response to thousands of slaves flocking to Union lines, Congress in August passes the First Confiscation Act, authorizing the Union army to confiscate slaves of rebel masters.

Invoking Madison Washington, Douglass celebrates the free black William Tillman, who single-handedly gained control of a ship pirated by Confederate privateers and brought it back to Long Island.

1863 Emancipation Proclamation issued.

William Wells Brown includes a chapter on Madison Washington and the *Creole* rebels in *The Black Man: His Antecedents, His Genius, and His Achievements*.

After recruiting black troops for the Union army, Douglass has the first of three private interviews with President Lincoln.

1865 The Civil War ends; Lincoln is assassinated. The Thirteenth Amendment, abolishing slavery, is ratified.

Henry Highland Garnet preaches a sermon in U.S. House

of Representatives after the House passes the Thirteenth Amendment; he is the first black to preach in Congress.

1866 Congress approves the Civil Rights Act, which grants citizenship and legal protections to African Americans.

Assassination attempt on Frederick Douglass while giving a speech in Baltimore. Douglass is unharmed, the assassin flees, and no one is arrested.

1868 Ratification of the Fourteenth Amendment, granting citizenship and equal protection under the law to all individuals born or naturalized in the United States.

1870 Ratification of the Fifteenth Amendment, guaranteeing African American men the right to vote.

Douglass relocates to Washington, D.C., and begins editing the *New National Era*, which calls for black civil rights as well as other reforms.

1874 Appointed president of the Freedman's Savings Bank in March, Douglass has to close the institution as insolvent in July.

1877 The Compromise of 1877, which helps decide the presidential election in favor of Rutherford B. Hayes, results in the withdrawal of federal troops from the South. With the loss of federal protection, African Americans suffer a precipitous loss of civil rights and become subject to new Jim Crow laws and a wave of violence.

Douglass appointed U.S. marshal of the District of Columbia by President Hayes, becoming the first black to receive a federal appointment requiring Senate approval.

1881 President James A. Garfield appoints Douglass recorder of deeds for the District of Columbia. Douglass publishes his third autobiography, *Life and Times of Frederick Douglass*.

1882 Anna Murray Douglass dies in August.

1883 The U.S. Supreme Court invalidates the 1875 Civil Rights Act, which had declared unconstitutional segregation in all public establishments except schools.

1884 Douglass's marriage in January to a younger, white woman, Helen Pitts, causes a public controversy.

1889 Douglass accepts appointment as U.S. minister resident and consul general to Haiti.

The black abolitionist Robert Purvis reminisces about Madison Washington in the *Philadelphia Inquirer*.

1891 Douglass resigns Haitian post after clashes with Benjamin Harrison's administration over attempted annexation of a Haitian port to operate as an American naval base.

1892 Douglass serves as commissioner of the Haitian pavilion at the World's Columbian Exposition in Chicago; publishes revised and expanded edition of *Life and Times of Frederick Douglass*.

1895 Douglass dies at his Cedar Hill home in Washington, D.C., on 20 February after attending a women's rights convention.

1896 The U.S. Supreme Court decision in *Plessy v. Ferguson* upholds the constitutionality of "separate but equal" rules mandating racial segregation.

1901 Pauline Hopkins publishes "A Dash for Liberty," a story about Madison Washington and the *Creole* rebels, in the *Colored American Magazine*. In 1900, she published a biographical sketch of Frederick Douglass in the same journal.

Selected Bibliography

Works marked with an asterisk are excerpted in this volume.

*Andrews, William L. "The Novelization of Voice in Early African American Narrative." *PMLA* 105, no. 1 (1990): 23–34.

Beavers, Herman. "The Blind Leading the Blind: The Racial Gaze as Plot Dilemma in 'Benito Cereno' and 'The Heroic Slave.'" In *Criticism and the Color Line: Desegregating American Literary Studies*, edited by Henry B. Wonham, 205–29. New Brunswick, N.J.: Rutgers University Press, 1996.

*Bernier, Celeste-Marie. "'Arms Like Polished Iron': The Black Slave Body in Narratives of a Slave Ship Revolt." *Slavery and Abolition* 23, no. 2 (2002): 91–106.

———. *Characters of Blood: Black Heroism in the Transatlantic Imagination*. Charlottesville: University of Virginia Press, 2012.

———. "A Comparative Exploration of Narrative Ambiguities in Frederick Douglass's Two Versions of *The Heroic Slave* (1853, 1863?)." *Slavery and Abolition* 22, no. 2 (2001): 69–86.

———. "From Fugitive Slave to Fugitive Abolitionist: The Oratory of Frederick Douglass and the Emerging Heroic Slave Tradition." *Atlantic Studies* 3, no. 2 (2006): 201–24.

Cover, Robert M. *Justice Accused: Antislavery and the Judicial Process*. New Haven, Conn.: Yale University Press, 1975.

Finkenbine, Roy E. "The Symbolism of Slave Mutiny: Black Abolitionist Responses to the *Amistad* and *Creole* Incidents." In *Rebellion, Repression, Reinvention: Mutiny in Comparative Perspective*, edited by Jane Hathaway, 233–52. Westport, Conn.: Praeger, 2001.

Foreman, P. Gabriel. "Sentimental Abolition in Douglass's Decade: Revision, Erotic Conversion, and the Politics of Witnessing in 'The Heroic Slave' and *My Bondage and My Freedom*." In *Criticism and the Color Line: Desegregating American Literary Studies*, edited by Henry B. Wonham, 191–204. New Brunswick, N.J.: Rutgers University Press, 1996.

Goldner, Ellen J. "Allegories of Exposure: *The Heroic Slave* and the Heroic Agonistics of Frederick Douglass." In *Racing and (E)racing Language: Living with the Color of Our Words*, edited by Ellen J. Goldner and Safiya Henderson-Holmes, 31–55. Syracuse, N.Y.: Syracuse University Press, 2001.

Hamilton, Cynthia S. "Models of Agency: Frederick Douglass and 'The Heroic Slave.'" *Proceedings of the American Antiquarian Society* 114, no. 1 (2005): 87–136.

Harrold, Stanley. "Romanticizing Slave Revolt: Madison Washington, the *Creole* Mutiny, and Abolitionist Celebration of Violent Means." In *Antislavery Violence: Sectional, Racial, and Cultural Conflict in Antebellum America*, edited by John R. McKivigan and Stanley Harrold, 89–107. Knoxville: University of Tennessee Press, 1999.

Hedin, Raymond. "Probable Readers, Possible Stories: The Limits of Nineteenth-Century Black Narrative." In *Readers in History: Nineteenth-Century American Literature and the Contexts of Response*, edited by James L. Machor, 180–205. Baltimore: Johns Hopkins University Press, 1993.

Hendrick, George, and Willene Hendrick. *The Creole Mutiny: A Tale of Revolt Aboard a Slave Ship*. Chicago: Dee, 2003.

Hole, Jeffrey. "Enforcement on a Grand Scale: Fugitive Intelligence and the Literary Tactics of Douglass and Melville." *American Literature* 85, no. 2 (2013): 217–46.

*Hyde, Carrie. "The Climates of Liberty: Natural Rights in the *Creole* Case and 'The Heroic Slave.'" *American Literature* 85, no. 3 (2013): 475–504.

Jervey, Edward D., and C. Harold Huber. "The *Creole* Affair." *Journal of Negro History* 65, no. 3 (1980): 196–211.

Johnson, Walter. "White Lies: Human Property and Domestic Slavery aboard the Slave Ship *Creole*." *Atlantic Studies* 5, no. 2 (2008): 237–63.

Jones, Howard. "The Peculiar Institution and National Honor: The Case of the *Creole* Slave Revolt." *Civil War History* 21, no. 1 (1975): 28–50.

———. *To the Webster-Ashburton Treaty: A Study in Anglo-American Relations, 1783–1842*. Chapel Hill: University of North Carolina Press, 1977.

Jones, Paul C. "Copying What the Master Had Written: Frederick Douglass's 'The Heroic Slave' and the Southern Historical Romance." *Southern Quarterly* 38, no. 4 (2000): 78–92.

Levecq, Christine. *Slavery and Sentiment: The Politics of Feeling in Black Atlantic Antislavery Writing, 1770–1850*. Durham: University of New Hampshire Press, 2008.

Levine, Robert S. *Martin Delany, Frederick Douglass, and the Politics of Representative Identity*. Chapel Hill: University of North Carolina Press, 1997.

Lock, Helen. "The Paradox of Slave Mutiny in Herman Melville, Charles Johnson, and Frederick Douglass." *College Literature* 30, no. 4 (2003): 54–70.

McKivigan, John R. "The Frederick Douglass–Gerrit Smith Friendship and Political Abolitionism in the 1850s." In *Frederick Douglass: New Literary and Historical Essays*, edited by Eric J. Sundquist, 205–32. Cambridge: Cambridge University Press, 1990.

Miller, Keith D., and Kevin Quashie. "Slavery Mutiny as Argument, Argument as Fiction, Fiction as America: The Case of Frederick Douglass's *The Heroic Slave*." *Southern Communication Journal* 63, no. 3 (1998): 199–207.

Miller, William Lee. *Arguing about Slavery: The Great Battle in the United States Congress*. New York: Knopf, 1996.

Newman, Lance. "Free Soil and the Abolitionist Forests of Frederick Douglass's 'The Heroic Slave.'" *American Literature* 81, no. 1 (2009): 127–52.

Noble, Marianne. "Sympathetic Listening in Frederick Douglass's 'The Heroic Slave' and *My Bondage and My Freedom*." *Studies in American Fiction* 34, no. 1 (2006): 53–69.

Oakes, James. *Freedom National: The Destruction of Slavery in the United States, 1861–1865*. New York: Norton, 2013.

Reynolds, Larry J. *Righteous Violence: Revolution, Slavery, and the American Renaissance*. Athens: University of Georgia Press, 2011.

*Sale, Maggie Montesinos. *The Slumbering Volcano: American Slave Ship Revolts and the Production of Rebellious Masculinity*. Durham, N.C.: Duke University Press, 1997.

Stauffer, John. *The Black Hearts of Men: Radical Abolitionists and the Transformation of Race*. Cambridge, Mass.: Harvard University Press, 2002.

———. "Interracial Friendship and the Aesthetics of Freedom." In *Frederick Douglass and Herman Melville: Essays in Relation*, edited by Robert S. Levine and Samuel Otter, 134–58. Chapel Hill: University of North Carolina Press, 2008.

Stepto. Robert B. "Sharing the Thunder: The Literary Exchanges of Harriet Beecher Stowe, Henry Bibb, and Frederick Douglass." In *New Essays on Uncle Tom's Cabin*, edited by Eric J. Sundquist, 135–53. Cambridge: Cambridge University Press, 1986.

*———. "Storytelling in Early Afro-American Fiction: Frederick Douglass' 'The Heroic Slave.'" *Georgia Review* 36, no. 2 (1982): 355–68.

Sundquist, Eric J. *To Wake the Nations: Race in the Making of American Literature*. Cambridge, Mass.: Harvard University Press, 1993.

Sweeney, Fionnghuala. "Visual Culture and Fictive Technique in Frederick Douglass's *The Heroic Slave*." *Slavery and Abolition* 33, no. 2 (2012): 305–20.

Takaki, Ronald T. "Not Afraid to Die: Frederick Douglass and Violence." In *Violence in the Black Imagination: Essays and Documents*, 17–33. New York: Oxford University Press, 1993.

Troutman, Phillip. "Grapevine in the Slave Market: African American Geopolitical Literacy and the 1841 *Creole* Revolt." In *The Chattel Principle: Internal Slave Trades in the Americas*, edited by Walter Johnson, 203–33. New Haven, Conn.: Yale University Press, 2004.

Walter, Krista. "Trappings of Nationalism in Frederick Douglass's *The Heroic Slave*." *African American Review* 34, no. 2 (2000): 233–47.

Weinauer, Ellen. "Writing Revolt in the Wake of Nat Turner: Frederick Douglass and the Construction of Black Domesticity in 'The Heroic Slave.'" *Studies in American Fiction* 33, no. 2 (2005): 193–202.

Wiegman, Robyn. *American Anatomies: Theorizing Race and Gender*. Durham, N.C.: Duke University Press, 1995.

*Wilson, Ivy G. "On Native Ground: Transnationalism, Frederick Douglass, and 'The Heroic Slave.'" *PMLA* 121, no. 2 (2006): 453–68.

*Yarborough, Richard. "Race, Violence, and Manhood: The Masculine Ideal in Frederick Douglass's 'The Heroic Slave.'" In *Frederick Douglass: New Literary and Historical Essays*, edited by Eric J. Sundquist, 166–88. Cambridge: Cambridge University Press, 1990.

First published nearly a decade prior to the Civil War, *The Heroic Slave* is the only fictional work by abolitionist, orator, author, and social reformer Frederick Douglass, himself a former slave. It is inspired by the true story of Madison Washington, who, along with eighteen others, took control of the slave ship *Creole* in November 1841 and sailed it to Nassau in the British colony of the Bahamas, where they could live free. This new critical edition, ideal for classroom use, includes the full text of Douglass's fictional recounting of one of the most successful slave revolts in American history, as well as an interpretive introduction; excerpts from Douglass's speeches and editorials; short selections by other writers on the *Creole* rebellion; and recent criticism on the novella.

"This critical edition of Douglass's one work of fiction, so richly edited by three scholars who know the author extremely well, is a brilliant illumination of the worlds of Madison Washington, fugitive slave resistance, violence, and antislavery storytelling. It brings to light a major piece of Douglass's versatile writing, within its literary and historical contexts as never before."—DAVID W. BLIGHT, Yale University

"In this scrupulously edited volume, containing an authoritative version of Douglass's novella, a superb introduction, a wealth of relevant nineteenth-century documents, and essential critical statements, *The Heroic Slave* finally receives the publication it deserves."—SAMUEL OTTER, University of California, Berkeley

"*The Heroic Slave: A Cultural and Critical Edition* is simply excellent. This well-conceived, well-executed edition reveals aspects of Douglass that are often forgotten. Some of the historical documents included will be new even to specialists."—MAURICE LEE, Boston University

FREDERICK DOUGLASS (1818–1895) was an American social reformer, orator, author, and statesman. ROBERT S. LEVINE is Distinguished University Professor of English at the University of Maryland. JOHN STAUFFER is chair of the History of American Civilization and professor of English and of African and African American Studies at Harvard University. JOHN R. McKIVIGAN is Mary O'Brien Gibson Professor of History at Indiana University-Purdue University, Indianapolis.

Cover illustration: Engraving of Frederick Douglass from the 1854 *Autographs for Freedom*, based on a photo of 1843 (detail). Yale Collection of American Literature, Beinecke Rare Book and Manuscript Library.

Yale UNIVERSITY PRESS
New Haven and London

yalebooks.com
yalebooks.co.uk

ISBN 978-0-300-18462-4